A Right Honorable Soldier

Secret Soldier Vol. 2

Jane Hadley

A Right Honorable Soldier

This is a work of fiction. The story, all names, characters, and incidents portrayed in this work, while inspired by the historical record, are entirely fictitious.

Content Notice: Crossdressing and light gender dysphoria. Period-typical terminology/pronouns. Moral and ethical debate over slavery by White characters. Reference to period-typical sexism and racism. Discussion and logistics of privies, menstruation, prophylactics, and abortifacients. Accidental outing of gender identity. Depictions of battle.

To anyone who's ever been told you're too much.
(You're not.)
(You're exactly the right amount.)

Author's Note

A Right Honorable Soldier takes place in Minnesota in 1861, at the start of the US Civil War. The next year, the US-Dakota War ravages southern Minnesota, including New Ulm. The systemic dispossession of the Dakota and Ojibwe in Minnesota is not at the center of this story, but it is part of the characters' context. However, the characters are limited by their perspectives and privileges. As European settler colonists, both of the main characters take for granted the land they stand on and they haven't given much thought as to where it came from or what it cost.

The US-Dakota War is a wound that still hasn't healed in Minnesota. Many Dakota people still live on reservations in Nebraska and South Dakota to this day. Their exile is still on the books as legal state statute, and their treaties are still abrogated. It's a violent and horrific event and the way we tell its story still hurts. It's far past time the US-Dakota War narrative centered on Dakota voices, and therefore, it's not a part of this Euro-centric story. However, I want to ensure readers understand that this story takes place on stolen land and I encourage you to watch the Dakota 38 documentary to learn more.

Furthermore, slavery plays a dominant role in the war our main characters participate in as soldiers. Abolition and a great deal of political rhetoric drives our main characters. However, they are both white and free and their perspectives are limited by those privileges. The literary world doesn't need anymore privileged white ladies making tragic romances out of what they imagine it might be like to be a person of color (hear that, Harriet Beecher Stowe?). I invite you to seek out stories written by Black and Indigenous authors. I can highly recommend historical romances by Alyssa Cole and Beverly Jenkins to start.

Your obt. srvt,
Mrs. Jane Hadley

Krueger
Robinson
Hower
Schaefer
Smith
Osborn
Webster
Williamson

PROLOGUE

St. Anthony, Minnesota
Sunday, July 14, 1861

"Truly I cannot fathom what is the point of forcing a commitment to three years service."

For Mrs. Greenleaf's boarders, Sunday dinner was once again going to be a political lecture served by Mr. Richard Ellis, newly appointed law clerk to the mayor of St. Anthony and notorious pedant. Cate Ellis, his reluctant wedded wife, sat to his left at the table and kicked herself for mentioning the news item in the first place. Well, actually she'd done more than mention—she'd exclaimed, really rather woefully, that the Second Regiment was almost full now that Company H had mustered in. It was both flummoxing and distressing to have to sit idly by and watch as the regiment recruited at such a slow pace. When she'd first seen the call, only two months after her wedding to Richard, she'd thought it would fill in a matter of days, just as the First Regiment had. She supposed three years was a much bigger commitment than the three months called for in April, but Cate Ellis, apparently unlike the men of Minnesota, had no compunction about the idea of signing away three years of her life to Lincoln, especially if it could provide three years away from her dear husband. Trouble was, women weren't wanted.

"Three years?" Richard continued. "What will all of the farms do without their workforce for three years? How will the shops maintain their business? How will trade continue? For all the urgency this war requires, and to be very clear, I am in no way for allowing the rebels to simply leave and create their own little country, but I can't help but wonder what could compel the top brass to arrive on such an outrageous request."

Richard's thoughts were greeted with silence. One of the boarders, middle-aged painter Mr. Hailey, rhythmically shoveled roast chicken into his mouth, content to let Richard sit to his left, which just happened to be the ear he was deaf in. Mr. Vawter had done his best to feign ignorance of the English language in Richard's presence, pretending he was French Canadian when all of the boarders knew full well the bank clerk was from Indiana. It was Mr. Plemer, however, who drew Cate's eyes. The mill clerk in his mid-twenties was certainly not a chore to look at, but of more interest, he had the shortest rope for Richard's nonsense and could be relied upon to resist the convoluted and uninformed arguments Richard loved to practice on his captive audience.

"Perhaps," Mr. Plemer muttered, "it could be due to the fact that eleven states have decided to start their own country formed on the cornerstone of enslaving human beings?"

Oh, perfectly put. Cate couldn't have said it better herself. She gripped the edge of the table and looked eagerly toward her husband in hopes of seeing him chastened.

No such luck, unfortunately. Mr. Plemer's aside had either not been heard or went simply unacknowledged, because Richard charged forth. "I can't imagine this war will go on for more than a matter of months. When the Southern states see that we will not stand for a dissolution of the Union, they will quit blustering and compromise, as they have done for the past fifty years. That is, of course, the beauty of a republic."

Cate wrinkled her nose and tried to pretend she had any sort of appetite for her dinner. Richard had no idea what sort of threat the country faced. It could be the end of the nation, and the death of justice for millions of enslaved people across the South. Cate couldn't think of one reason a fellow should hesitate to enlist, with so much on the line and such moral imperatives to fight for. She'd known Richard for nearly a year now, and she'd done her very best to expose him to a multitude of abolitionist books and newspapers. When she first met him, she thought his many opinions would make him a worthy partner in political discourse. By now she had learned that Richard had no interest in deliberation with anyone, much less his wife. He was only interested in the sound of his own voice.

"Perhaps what is needed is a few more states to join the Union as slave states," Richard pondered, thinking aloud. "If those places voted for slavery of their own self determination, then surely the South would feel less threatened."

Cate swallowed around a tightness in her throat and looked desperately toward Mr. Plemer. He would not stand for such ignorant Free Soiler talk. He was friends with W.D. Babbitt, for goodness sake. Mr. Plemer met her gaze with a frown, like he felt sorry for her. As well he should. She'd shackled herself to a man who had made it clear by this point that he would never share her staunch views on abolition. Not that there had been a line of other abolitionist gentlemen willing to offer, but still. Richard left much to be desired.

Sometimes Cate liked to spend the long tedious dinners imagining what life might have been like if she'd married Mr. Plemer instead. He was fairly handsome in a pink-cheeked way and dressed quite appealingly in dashing frock coats and colorful, sloppily-tied cravats (although his breath left much to be desired). He had a short temper and enjoyed debating politics when he'd had a bit to drink, which would be good fun if Richard didn't interrupt Cate every time she made an attempt to respond. But apparently even Mr. Plemer had learned that the best way to quickly end Richard's abhorrent political lectures was to not engage.

It seemed Cate would be the only one left in the service to righteousness this evening.

"The South is not so easily placated," she said sharply, annoyed she was left to do this in the first place. What was the point of politically engaged men if they weren't going to speak up in defense of justice? Was it not their job to exercise the rights of citizenship denied to women on their behalf? "Their secession declarations made it very clear that the election of Lincoln is considered an act of aggression on the institution of slavery. They have rallied widespread support for their white supremacist revolution."

Richard gave a long sigh. Actually, so did a couple of the other boarders. Mrs. Greenleaf, seated at the opposite end of the table from Richard, actually put her head into her hand.

"My beloved, have you been reading those conspiracy rags again?"

Cate scowled and glanced at Mr. Plemer again. He gave her a minute shake of his head. Why? Why the hell did everyone want her to just give up?

"No," Cate groused, slumping back into her chair. "Just the Pioneer and Democrat."

Richard raised his brow at her. "All of the papers these days are just sensational headlines trying to draw you in to take your pennies. I hope you will exercise more discerning judgment in the future."

Cate rolled her eyes. She didn't care who saw it, she didn't care if she appeared petulant and childish. She could not stand to pretend she cared what this highfalutin horse's ass had to say.

Mrs. Greenleaf seized upon the brief pause by standing abruptly. "Mrs. Ellis, could I trouble you for some help with dessert?"

Cate scowled at her, unabashedly, then glanced at Mr. Plemer, then Richard, then Mr. Plemer again. Deal with him, she thought at him. Deal with him because apparently, I am not permitted to.

"Of course," she bit out and pushed her chair out from behind her with a clatter as she stood. Then she stalked down the line of the table and followed Mrs. Greenleaf into the kitchen.

———

Cate had one surefire way of getting Richard to shut up. And that was getting him to screw her.

It wasn't awful. It wasn't even really bad. Certainly, it would be better with a less self-absorbed partner, both because he'd be more appealing and because he would surely be more interested in mutual pleasure, but the act in itself was quite nice. Cate enjoyed feeling stretched and full, delighted in how her sex swelled with arousal for this rude, indulgent act. She had to admit that she was pleased to have an aspect of wifery that she enjoyed. It was a blessing, in its way, and a relief.

Cate had a running reel of things she thought about during copulation with her husband. She squeezed her eyes closed and entertained fantasies that she was married to other men, like Mr. Plemer or Richard's new employer, the mayor of St. Anthony. They didn't give her a second glance in real life, as well they wouldn't because the nicest word anyone could come up with to describe Cate's looks was "handsome." Men didn't want a handsome woman. That was a word they used to describe horses or hogs. So Cate was quite sure there was nothing wrong with fantasizing about other men while her husband fucked her, because there was no chance that anything would come of it.

Her favorite fantasy was one where Mr. Plemer caught her up in some part of the boarding house—the kitchen would be quite fun—and got into heated debate with her about how abhorrent her husband was. He'd implore her to do more to improve him, then turn it around to assert how she was wasted on Richard as a helpmeet, and finally, angrily assert that he would please her better. And then he would prove it. Against the wall, or perhaps over the work table.

These thoughts made Cate's toes curl and her breath short. Sometimes, she'd squeeze her sex around Richard's prick, which felt remarkably good. Richard's equipment was the very epitome of the word prick; it was long and slender just like him, and by this point in their marriage, it pierced her in a lovely way that didn't hurt at all. Of course, sometimes there was discomfort if he did it unceremoniously, but Richard usually liked to kiss on her first and that helped her body ready itself for him (as long as he didn't talk).

Cate kept her eyes squeezed shut, and as Richard's voice began to grunt and sigh, she wondered what types of sounds Mr. Plemer would make. Whether he'd be quiet or noisy, what kinds of faces he would make. Would he say obscene things? She tried a quiet sound herself as Richard rocked her against the mattress. She couldn't be too active or eager or she'd offend Richard's sensibilities. She'd tried to get him on his back once, to ride him, and he'd nearly gone apoplectic at the display of assertion. Apparently, he was not interested in her initiative in any facet of their marriage.

Richard did not seem averse to her sound, so Cate tried another one, one she voiced as she thrust back on his prick and pulled up on her groin muscles to really feel him slide inside her. Richard gave a short, choked shout and gripped the bedstead as he bucked faster. God, yes, that was it. It was working. She could feel the edges of a climax sneaking toward her. She held her hips at the angle, ground down as she reached for the sensation, quick, before he—

Before he shuddered over her with a choked sob, and she felt wet heat swell inside her and start to slip out along with his softening prick.

She hated this part. Well, hated it and loved it. It felt good, and Cate was grateful she'd never have to admit how much she liked the evidence of pleasure, something she'd earned and made her feel desired. But every time he did that, she ran the risk of getting with child. Bearing Richard's progeny, contrary to the advice of many other women including both Mrs. Greenleaf and Cate's stepmother, would be the final nail in the coffin of Cate's life. Once there was a child, she could never leave.

Richard collapsed at her side with a satisfied sigh, rolled over, and was snoring within minutes. Cate waited, carefully trying not to move too much, until she was sure he was sleeping. Then, she slipped out of the bed and crept across the creaky floorboards to the dresser, where the ewer and basin were. She could feel the wet slide of seed dripping down her leg as she dug deep in her drawer for the alum and water solution she'd acquired at the discreet pharmacy across the river.

She performed her ablutions quickly and quietly. It was not an elegant or comfortable ritual, but so far it had done the job of keeping her monthly courses regular. Cate knew she gambled a lot on the efficacy of this process, but she felt hopeful that between the sponge soaked in the liquid she'd inserted before Richard came to bed and the washing with it afterward, she would manage to keep herself safe.

"What are you doing?"

Cate froze with the basin awkwardly between her legs, her nightrail hitched up to her waist. It was dark in the room, but the Great Comet still lit up the night sky, and her rear end was probably glowing in the dim light that came through the window. "Just washing up. Sorry to wake you."

"You didn't," Richard replied, the thickness of his voice belying him. "Why are you washing?"

Cate gritted her teeth and hastily finished what she was doing (caught or not, she wasn't going to leave the job half-done and end up with a fat baby come springtime). "Because I like to be clean before I sleep."

"Is there something unclean about what I just did?"

"No," Cate said with a roll of her eyes she was certain would go undetected in the dark room. "It was just dripping down my leg, and I needed to clean it up." Perhaps if she pushed him into discomfort, he'd leave her the hell alone.

She was fairly certain it worked given the long silence that followed. Then, the bedclothes rustled, and Richard walked over to her, ghostly in his own nightgown. Cate awkwardly replaced the basin on the dresser and dropped her nightrail to preserve her modesty. Her breath caught in her throat as he picked up the alum and water solution and inspected the unlabeled bottle.

"What's this for?"

"Soap."

Richard unstopped the bottle and took a sniff. He looked up at her sharply, and she felt his eyes bore into her as he said, quite mildly, "Is this why you haven't conceived a child yet?"

Cate couldn't think of anything to say. She was still and quiet, and she knew that her lack of response said as much as it would if she'd audaciously agreed with him, but she couldn't bring herself to say she wanted a baby when that couldn't be further from the truth.

Richard made a frustrated noise. "Cate. I understand you are spirited—it's something that drew me to you when we first met—but you cannot behave this way. The purpose of marriage is to have a family. If you did not want to have a family, why entertain and accept my suit in the first place?" He sounded exasperated, hurt even. Like he really thought she'd had a choice, and chosen him.

Cate should apologize. It would be the quickest way out of this, the quickest way to get him back to sleep. After all, her body was no business of his, regardless of whether or not he thought it was. Lying to him was a means to keep him at an appropriate distance, but she couldn't find the words to speak. Something had her by the throat, and she gripped her fists tight to keep her hands from trembling.

"I think we can both agree I tolerate a great deal from you," Richard continued. She wasn't sure what sort of story he was telling himself to explain her silence, but it did not appear to be a favorable one. "There are a lot of men who would take a much harsher tack. But I love you, Cate. I do. I'm not sure what I can do to convince you of it, but it's true nonetheless. And I want to have a family with you."

Cate's eyes pricked with tears. What a horrid thing to say, after all that he'd done to contort her into the shape of the woman he desired her to be. And yet, she also felt ashamed. Indeed, to her, he was nothing more than an obstacle to contend with. She'd cast him as the villain of all the oppressions she'd experienced throughout her life, but he'd truly done nothing more than to love her the best way he knew how.

"I think you owe me that much, at least," Richard finished with a shake of his head.

Cate couldn't help but choke a little on her inhale. At some point, she'd crossed her arms over her body and gripped her elbows. Richard went to the open window and unstoppered the bottle of alum and water solution, pouring it out into the yard below.

"Are you just going to stand there? Don't you have anything to say for yourself?"

"I ... I'm sorry," Cate managed, the words sour and metallic on her tongue.

"And...?"

"And what?"

Richard threw his hands up. "And what? And what? Maybe, 'and I want to have a family with you, too.' Or even just 'I love you.' Truly, do you detest me that much? I thought you wanted a life with me, but I can see now that all you wanted was out from under your father's thumb."

Oh, God. He was right. He was right about everything. She detested him. She couldn't be his wife. She couldn't have his children. Without her precautions, even sex would be fraught, a mildly pleasurable stop on the slow demise of her personhood. She didn't know what the hell she wanted, but she damn well knew it wasn't this. That had been clear for months.

Cate squeezed herself tighter and searched the room with her eyes, looking anywhere except at Richard. "It's late," she said at length. "We're both tired. Let's talk about this in the morning."

Richard scowled at her as he crossed to the bed and flung the counterpane down. "I'm not being absurd. I shan't be made to feel like I am the one who is behaving irrationally."

"Of course not," she murmured automatically. Dear God. She was already becoming a shade of a woman, held together by duties and other people's notions of who she was supposed to be.

"Get in the bed, you exasperating woman," Richard snapped as he laid down and pulled the blankets over his head.

"I just need to visit the privy," Cate murmured as she shuffled out of the room. She couldn't do it. She couldn't get into bed with him. If he wanted to escort her, if his trust was that eroded, then fine. But she would not under any circumstances give him another opportunity to touch her.

Richard didn't follow her. It was warm outside, the Great Comet illuminating the yard with an eerie dark light. It was a reminder that they lived in extraordinary times. Even the celestial bodies were exhibiting warning signs that the world was amiss. A great flood or pestilence was probably next if they didn't pay heed. There was no room in the world for subjugation, for injustice, for silence. Cate stood in the yard in her nightrail and wished for a moment that the comet would just fall from the sky and end her. What good could she do anyway, stuck in the body of a wife and mother? The world couldn't wait while she taught her sons how to make change when they became adults. She couldn't wait for that.

It was no one's fault but her own. Or it was everyone else's fault, and she was just fool enough to have listened to them. If she'd listened to herself, done what she'd known was right, she would never have married Richard in the first place. She would have gone on, taking care of her father and his family, exercising what little freedom that had afforded her.

No. None of it was right. She could not blame herself for taking a gamble on Richard.

Perhaps the trouble was that she had not gambled high enough stakes. She looked up at the comet again and allowed herself, for just a moment, to dream bigger. More than a marriage, more than the boarding house, beyond men or jobs or spinsterhood. And looking up into the night sky, Cate experienced clarity, for the first time in over a year. Perhaps the first time in her adult life.

She knew what she had to do. She'd always known. She just could never have believed it possible, until now when she had nothing left to lose.

———

I

Chicago, Illinois
Wednesday, October 16, 1861

THREE MONTHS LATER, CATE stood in the exact same place where Abraham Lincoln had been nominated for president at the 1860 Republican National Convention, wearing her uniform of Union blue. Shed of skirts and long hair and her husband's name, she was a foot soldier for justice called Charley Smith. She had absolutely no regrets.

Except for the fact that the Wigwam, the temporary building where the entire Second Minnesota Regiment was quartered for the night, had no privies.

They'd marched out of St. Paul with people waving flags and cheering only two days prior. Then, the steamship puffed them down the Mississippi to La Crosse and from there, an uncomfortable, densely-packed train ride landed them in the city of Chicago. Now they were in the finest temporary meeting hall plaster could make, and there was nowhere for her to relieve herself at all, much less to do it privately.

"Where the hell do they expect a thousand men to do their business after a long train ride in a place like this?" she raged, as the rest of her squad stood uncomfortably. Cate was notorious amongst her squad for her short temper, which was accepted with begrudging good humor because young men, unlike women of any age, were assumed to be passionate and volatile as a matter of course.

"I'm sure there's one nearby," Henry Schaefer suggested placatingly in his soft German accent.

Cate turned an annoyed brow at him, not because she was upset by the prospect of a privy nearby, but because she hated that his first urge was to try and placate her. Henry was the only one in the squad who knew Cate's secret, and had done a spectacularly poor job of discovering it, too. He'd watched her for weeks and concluded that she was a *spy*, for Chrissakes, before it even occurred to him that she was a woman. It was only after cornering her and threatening to reveal her clandestine treason that she exchanged her actual secret for his silence. It was a silence that had rapidly grown into something much more pleasurable, especially when the Third Regiment mustered and the Second had been relegated to small, two-person tents while they finished their basic training.

Henry placed his hand discreetly on her shoulder in a stark reminder that it had been three whole days since they'd had the liberty to touch one another. It was jarring enough that she shrugged him off tersely, though whether it was because she didn't want anyone to catch him being too familiar or because she missed him terribly, she could not say.

Jacob Robinson, another member of their squad, snorted. "And I'm sure that whatever poor Chicagoans who usually frequent that privy will be delighted to find a thousand men's worth of waste suddenly stewing in their pit."

"It occurs to me that perhaps the men leading this outfit did not consider that the eight hundred men they needed to find shelter for might also need to relieve themselves at some point," Tom Webster added, his mutton chops hovering somewhere between amusement and sarcastic disdain.

Cate found none of this amusing in the slightest. At that moment, Sergeant Ned Osborn approached, and she turned her full ire on him. "Sir, are you aware that in this entire massive place, there are no facilities for our certain convenience?"

Osborn sighed as he joined them. "Yes, I'm aware, and I'm afraid to report that it's actually rather more inconvenient than that. We are under strict orders to remain within the building until we are marched out again under arms."

The entire squad squawked with outrage. Cate's mouth flapped with a thousand angry expletives and counted herself lucky that none of them managed to get out.

"Whose orders?!" Webster snapped and everyone looked sharply at him, having never seen the normally easygoing father in a temper before. Especially not directed at his childhood friend.

"Command, I expect," Osborn said with a shrug, relatively nonplussed. It seemed that unlike the rest of them, he'd had previous experience with Webster's temper and found its intimidation wanting. "I understand that previous regiments housed here got into some trouble conducting themselves poorly in saloons and other ... uh, disreputable places ... It looks as though we are the unfortunate bearers of their legacy."

Corporal Elias Hower threw up his hands and shook his head as he walked off.

"Where's he going?" asked John Williamson, his youthful eyes wide and curious and completely unaware of how redundant his question was, given they were not allowed to leave the building. If Cate had to guess, she'd expect Hower, a man with a superior manner and a penchant for gossip, was singularly determined to get all the information Osborn lacked. She shook her head and crossed her arms, leveling a firm stare at Osborn.

"Sir, this is unacceptable," she asserted. "We are soldiers of these United States, having just given up hearth and home to fight for this union. We are not cattle to be herded into a pen where we trod among our own filth."

"I hear you," Osborn sighed. "I will do what I can with the Captain."

Osborn walked off, mustache at a slight droop. Cate shook her head again.

"This is what happens," she declared to the remaining six members of her squad, "when the general promotes his friends to Command."

The boys settled on the packed dirt floor as many other squads had done across the vast chamber, and Wilbur Krüger inevitably pulled some playing cards out of his pocket to pass the time. They looked like shabby calling cards in his huge hands. Cate remained standing, trying to keep her anger stoked as they waited for some word from Command about their situation. The longer she waited, the more her anger ebbed, pushed aside by a larger and more present fear.

She'd been dealing with her monthly blood for days now, pinning her sanitary napkins into her uniform trousers carefully and then disposing of them because she had nowhere to clean or store them. She could only hope she'd have a chance to acquire materials for the next month on stops along the way to the front. She'd done all manner of mad things to acquire the ones she was now having to dispose of, including stealing clean diapers off a laundry line. The news that there would be no sanctuary for her to change out her soiled napkin here in Chicago was, to say the least, unwelcome.

Cate deepened her frown. What fool's college chum had designed these uniforms to have light blue trousers? Surely the blood and muck from battle would show most terribly. The fact that the color would also not hide her own secrets was beside the point.

A little while later, Osborn returned with a hopeful expression. Cate perked immediately to attention and the others got to their feet, holding their cards aside.

"The Colonel has allowed for us to march out under arms, company by company, to give us some exercise and attend to … various needs."

"When?" Cate asked at once, talking over several other of the squad's half-formed questions.

"After supper," Osborn replied with a measured nod. Cate scowled. She felt a nudge at her shoulder and turned her scowl on Schaefer.

"That's good news," Henry murmured optimistically. Cate screwed her mouth closed. She wanted to take her anger out on him, but she also didn't want him to know why she was so worked up.

"What are they going to do to prevent a foolish mistake like this from happening again, Ned?" Webster asked Osborn curtly. Williamson looked at Webster with startled eyes for calling his superior officer by his Christian name.

"I'm not privy to that information," Osborn said and frowned as Williamson barked a laugh at the unfortunate and unintended pun.

"It's scarcely better," Cate hissed aside to Henry loud enough only for him to hear.

"Well, no impropriety intended, but can't you hold it for an hour or two more?" Henry whispered in incredulous reply.

"No, because I cannot physically hold my menses, *Henry*," Cate snarled under her breath and immediately regretted it. It would not do at *all* for the man whose thighs made her mouth water to know the extent to which her stupid body was making her soldier existence summarily miserable. To her credit, Henry looked about as mortified as she felt. Her eyes darted to the side to determine if anyone had heard her, but it appeared the rest of the squad was still embroiled in interrogating their sergeant. Her temper was making her stupid. She took a deep breath in.

"When's supper then?" Krüger asked. The big German required several buckets full of soldier's stew a day to sustain himself.

"Ah, in this we are in luck. You are all to get lined up for rations presently," Osborn said, apparently relieved to deliver some good news. "I'm not sure how they want us to stand in ranks, but the space is large enough that it should be fairly self-explanatory."

It was not self-explanatory, and the captains fumbled and clashed amongst themselves to resolve the ranks in an orderly fashion. Finally, Colonel Van Cleve intervened and directed them all to their own place. The quartermaster then walked amongst them and distributed rations.

Cate blinked down the line as she saw Squad Six given a rasher of pork, a paltry spoonful of beans, and coffee. Robinson, Hower, and Schaefer craned around her to get a look too.

"It's pork and beans," Hower reported. A chorus of grumbles amongst their own squad, as well as the Hastings and St. Cloud boys, resounded.

"We're not even in the field yet!" Robinson lamented. "We're in the middle of a metropolis. Is there seriously no better rations to be found here?"

Osborn sighed and held out his tin plate and cup patiently, trying to be a model for his squad. Cate opted to stare daggers at the quartermaster as she begrudgingly held her plate and cup ready for her ration. As Webster accepted his, he hissed, "This is outrageous."

"It almost makes me wish we were back at the Fort eating that awful stew again," Henry said, frowning at his portion.

"Well, get used to it, boys," Osborn said somewhat sarcastically. "There will be more where this comes from for your haversacks in the morning."

The squad grumbled as Captain Noah commanded them all at ease, and they regrouped near the far wall to eat and complain. Despite their grumblings, they made quick work of the ration and were soon wiping their plates as best they could to store in their haversacks. In short order, the Captain rounded up Company K and moved them through the School of the Soldier until they were ready to march under arms to relieve themselves. Cate thought she might develop a headache from the frequency she felt compelled to roll her eyes.

They marched out of the building, an elaborate contradiction in architectural grandeur and temporary building materials. The streets bustled with horses, carriages, and pedestrians, and they soon had a throng of passersby turned spectators as they paraded into the street, stopping traffic.

"Come one, come all," Elias Hower intoned, only loud enough for those in his squad to hear. "See the great Minnesota Second Infantry Volunteers, on parade to the privy!"

"Hower," Osborn warned.

"I hope the Captain knows where we're going, lest we spend the next thirty minutes marching circles around the city," Webster grumbled.

Cate agreed. She also hoped, so hard it hurt, that wherever they were bound would have some semblance of privacy. She was terrified of what might happen if any comrades were to discover her not only with her trousers down, but otherwise soiled as only a woman could be. Captain Noah and Lieutenant Thomas led the troops in formation round Market Street, following the stinking Chicago River round toward where it drained into Lake Michigan. As they marched, the Captain discreetly dismissed squads one at a time to detach and slip off to relieve themselves.

When the Captain directed Squad Seven to detach, Osborn led them between two large shipping warehouses towering on the edge of the river. The area had been so developed that the river had no discernable bank left, brick meeting dock and dock meeting river as though the city were built up directly out of the foul, churning water. Built on a platform of dock was a privy shack, presumably with holes open directly into the river, and it was no wonder why the river water was so disgusting as it flowed sluggishly toward bright blue Lake Michigan.

Cate hung back as the others opened the privy door and looked in at a row of four holes in a bench seat. The fellows entered, while Krüger and Webster took the liberty of unbuttoning their trousers and emptying their bladders directly off the dock, in full view of the sailors floating by on big-sailed boats. Cate dithered. Osborn came out, followed by Williamson and Robinson. Hower was still in there as Henry walked toward the door, glancing over his shoulder at her. She grimaced. This was not the kind of intimacy she wanted with any man. If her secret wasn't held in the balance, Henry would be the last person she would want to relieve herself in front of. She dithered some more.

Osborn gave her an impatient look as Krüger and Webster gathered back together with Williamson and Robinson. She tripped forward toward the privy door. Hower emerged. Just Henry was in there now. She wondered how slowly she could walk toward the privy before she would attract undue attention.

"Hey, Smith," snorted Hower. "You scared you're gonna fall in?"

Williamson honked a laugh. "After the sinks at the Fort, this one is easy breezy. At least here you won't have too far to fall." The sinks at Fort Snelling had been propped up on a scaffold at the top of a cliff. Waste fell nearly a hundred feet before it was swept away by the Mississippi River.

"Yes well, at least at the Fort, there was a good chance that the fall would put you out of your misery before you fell into an army's worth of human waste," Cate retorted and stepped resolutely to the door of the privy, swinging the door in. As she entered, she nearly ran into Henry.

"Huh, fancy meeting you here," he said, his voice playful and quiet enough that only she could hear him.

"Do not. Get out," she commanded, shoving past him and ducking her face, which was beet red by this point she was so embarrassed and terrified. He shut his mouth and raised his eyebrows as he hustled out the door that she slammed behind him.

She was relieved to find a long nail bent to fashion a hook that she promptly threaded through its loop to hold the door shut. She took a deep breath in to steady herself, then immediately regretted it, gagging on the stinking air. In spite of the stench, she wondered if she might manage to disappear here and never show her face among humans again.

———

II

Pittsburgh, Pennsylvania
Friday, October 18, 1861

HENRY SCHAEFER REGARDED THE food before him with eyes as wide as saucers. A large vase of flowers adorned long tables arranged in rows in the Duquesne Grays' Hall. Throughout the room, the Minnesota Second Infantry Regiment was being served by young, patriotic ladies of Pittsburgh in their finest dresses. Between the tables buckling under the weight of sweetbreads and roast goose and aspics of all varieties, and the lovely ladies sweetly offering refreshment, the men were beside themselves with delight. Except for Charley Smith, of course. Charley sat beside him and only managed to look extremely sullen.

To be fair to her, she'd been through somewhat of an ordeal since their departure for the front. Every step of the way, from the boat to the train to the Wigwam to the train again, had been utterly devoid of privacy. She took it in irate stride, and luckily the others didn't seem to assume anything amiss other than that Smith was rather overly modest for someone who swore so much.

Henry was feeling the pressure too, but for entirely different and admittedly selfish reasons. He'd also become accustomed to privacy, and with loutish comrades trundling around everywhere he looked, he'd scarcely had a chance to exchange significant glances with Charley, much less anything close to physical touch. And he missed it. He missed her.

Unfortunately, with the constant barrage of people, Charley had unilaterally locked herself up inside of her prickly Smith persona and become utterly insufferable.

"Smith, are you gonna eat that?" Williamson asked, his eyes covetously on the flank of roast goose left on Smith's plate.

"Yes," Smith retorted from under her petulant brow. Henry tried to hold back a sigh of annoyance as he tried to get a piece of aspic to stay on his fork. The flavor of the peas and gravy suspended in gelatin was rich and delicious, although the texture was still very much an aspic.

"Excuse me, miss," Elias said ingratiatingly over his shoulder. The young woman in question slowed and smiled widely at them all in turn. Her hair was dark and sleek, parted at the center and wound demurely at the nape of her neck. Henry wondered if Charley had set her hair in such a way before cutting it, although with her curls it certainly would not have laid so straight. "Could I trouble you for some more roast goose?"

The girl looked at Hower with doe eyes, like one might regard a stray dog or some other pitiful creature that one longed to care for.

"I'll see what I can do," she replied, her voice light and reedy and wonderfully effeminate. It reminded Henry of how Charley had sounded in the brewer's warehouse last week, voice light and reedy and gasping for more. He squirmed in his seat, trying to hide his little secret smile as he nudged Charley's knee with his own under the table. To his chagrin, she flinched away from him. It was woefully unfair that after a week of consistent carnal satisfaction, Henry should be left in the same condition he'd been in for years prior, but also markedly less capable of bearing it. He supposed it was more difficult when he knew what he was missing.

"I wonder if there will be dancing after dinner," Jacob asked with a grin, watching the girl depart with an appreciative gaze.

"I should think you were too busy missing your wife to worry about that," Smith drawled.

Jacob glared at him and rolled his eyes. "I'm married, I'm not dead. Besides, after that dreary night in Chicago, we deserve a little bit of fun."

Henry added his voice to the murmur of agreement before they fell into a companionable silence, each too focused on shoveling the excellent fare into his mouth to say much more.

A few moments later, the girl returned. "Here we are, fellows," she said, brandishing a plate of cut slices of roast goose. In a conspiratorial tone, she added, "It's the last, so shh—don't tell."

Hower slid a slice onto his own plate and then gestured for Williamson to take some as well. "Our deepest gratitude, Miss … um … ?"

The girl smiled. "Miss Loy, at your service. And you all are?"

"A pleasure to meet you, Miss Loy. I'm Corporal Hower," Elias said with a grin. Henry tried not to raise an eyebrow at how thick he was laying it on. "And this is my squad. Privates Williamson, Webster, Robinson, Krüger, Smith, and Schaefer. And Sergeant Osborn."

"How do you do," Miss Loy said, nodding at each one in turn.

"Say, Miss Loy, are you aware if there are any further festivities after the meal?"

"Oh, yes," Miss Loy replied eagerly. "They will clear the tables, and there's a small quartet that will play, and we'll have a lovely set of dances before you all march back to your quarters."

This news brought a murmur of excitement around the table.

"I'm so happy to hear that," Elias replied with a grin. "May I save a place on your dance card, Miss Loy?"

The girl flushed attractively. "I should be delighted, Corporal."

Henry felt uncomfortable. Miss Loy was charming, and he wasn't the only one in the squad who'd noticed. But there was something to be desired in her sweet, smooth countenance. Perhaps she lacked the dark smolder that Charley wielded without even thinking. It was too bad Henry couldn't save a place on his card to dance with Charley, because if she even bothered to dance, she'd be competing with him for the hands of the lovely loyal ladies of Pittsburgh.

Henry snuck a glance at Smith beside him. The soldier had her hand in her dark curls, hunched over her plate seemingly under some duress. Henry leaned over and hissed, "Anything wrong?"

Henry almost missed her whispered response under the clatter of cutlery and the din of affable conversation. "I don't know how to lead."

Lead? Henry was puzzled a moment before he realized she was referring to dancing.

"Well, I could show you how," Henry offered quietly, his eyes darting around the far corners of the room wondering what other chambers might lead off from the main hall. He could show her how to lead and pull her close and perhaps, if they could find enough privacy for a dance lesson, they might find enough for...

"Don't be absurd," she hissed. "I'd rather pretend to be too fatigued for the entire evening than have everyone see you teach me how to waltz."

"Well, what about the set dances?" Henry suggested. "Those don't require a lead, per se. You just have to make sure you put out the correct hand."

Smith glowered but didn't reply.

"Say," Henry said louder, addressing Miss Loy. "What sort of dances might we expect this evening?"

———

The dancing was lovely. Cate knew this intellectually as she watched from the benches lining the walls. All the boys cut a smart figure in their uniforms while the loyal ladies of Pittsburgh were resplendent in their best wool and silk, their hoops flouncing about like puffs of dandelion fluff in a late spring breeze. There were many lovely young girls, and Henry was an eager partner, doing his best to engage a young lady for every single dance despite a considerable amount of competition. He led his partner with as much grace as possible given that they were dancing a polka, and it was basically just turning and hopping.

Cate spent the duration of the dance watching him while she flipped self-pityingly through memories in her mind; of him squatting during drill to pick up a charge he'd dropped; of his thighs bare while shuffling into his uniform; of his lips ghosting against her skin; of him straining against her as she pulled him off. She should have taken him up on his "dance lesson." Surely there must be a private place somewhere in this enormous market house. She missed his touch. And she hated that he was passing it out so liberally to every adorable little chit who batted her eyelashes at him.

When the polka concluded, Cate sighed and tried to look as unapproachable as possible. Her strategy thus far had been inexcusable rudeness, but her capacity for it was wearing thin. She had no idea what it was—she was doing everything she could to look sullen and surly, but it seemed the younger girls of the group didn't find that very off-putting, because she kept getting giggling teenage girls trying to get her to strike up a conversation with them.

This break in the music was no different, it appeared. Miss Loy, escorted by Hower off the dance floor, attached herself to another girl with fine, white-blonde hair in a blue print wool, and walked straight toward Cate.

"Good evening, Private Smith was it?" Miss Loy said. Cate nodded churlishly as she begrudgingly stood. She wasn't a complete boor to remain seated when approached by a lady. "I'd like to introduce you to my friend and neighbor, Miss Kincaid."

"How do you do," Cate said, taking the girl's hand and receiving a charming giggle. Miss Kincaid was short, a full half foot shorter than Cate, and she wouldn't put her any older than sixteen. Behind her, Cate caught a glimpse of Henry returning from the dance floor with his partner, a round-featured brunette whose silhouette bore some impressive proportions. Cate decided much of it was hip and bust padding in spite of the lively bouncing polka having previously suggested otherwise.

"Miss Loy," Henry greeted with a smile after leaving his previous partner with her companions. "I believe I have you for the next dance?"

"Oh, yes, La Tempête!" Miss Loy replied with a grin. She had lovely teeth. She and Henry would make a whole family of children with perfectly straight, clean teeth. Cate took a perverse pleasure in the proportion of misery that thought delivered.

"I love La Tempête!" Miss Kincaid pouted, her eyes darting sidelong at Cate. "But I sadly am not engaged for this one."

Miss Loy, Miss Kincaid, and Henry all looked at Cate. Cate blinked. "I, uh, I don't think I've ever danced La Tempête before. What is it?"

Miss Loy's eyes narrowed slightly, but her smile stayed strong. "It's a wonderful set dance! It couldn't be simpler, it's really only two figures repeated with different couples. It's such a delight. Oh, Adaline, we must find you a partner so we can be in a set together."

Cate's ears perked at that. Set dances were social dances, where partners danced in sets of usually four or even eight people. Partners were exchanged and returned in simple steps, the idea being to get folks interacting with as many others as possible. It was an excellent way to get all the gossip efficiently. If this were a multi-couple set dance, Cate would dance largely with Miss Kincaid, but she would also dance with Miss Loy and, depending on the set dance, the other gentleman too.

As the two girls made a show of looking around the room for a partner for Miss Kincaid, Cate caught Henry's eye and held it.

"Say, Miss Kincaid," she said, only tearing her eyes away from Henry to look at the girl after she'd turned. "Would you be so kind as to allow me to have this dance?"

Miss Kincaid grinned, and Miss Loy smiled with great satisfaction.

"Why, yes, Private Smith, I would be delighted," Miss Kincaid said, setting her gloved hand in Cate's. Cate gave Miss Kincaid a small half-smile, then glanced up at Henry again. He was watching her carefully, his eyes slightly narrowed, but she couldn't tell quite what he was thinking. It thrilled her.

On the dance floor, they arranged themselves across from one another, one couple facing the other. Two other couples joined them—one was an officer and a matron, the other pair led by Robinson, grinning and looking flushed enough that

Cate suspected some spirits were being passed around under the table.

"Sidle down, Schaef," Robinson insisted, taking up the place across from Miss Kincaid and shoving Henry and Miss Loy down such that Cate was now kitty-corner from him. Apparently Robinson had little interest in being across from the matron, which really shouldn't have gotten under Cate's skin, but it did. As she glared at him, Miss Loy took the liberty of explaining the dance to the group.

"Each figure will start with greeting your opposite," she said, gesturing between the couples facing each other. "Then we'll chassez and exchange places with the couple to our right or left."

Just then, the quartet of instrumentalists struck up the beginning bars of the dance. Miss Loy opened her mouth wordlessly for a moment and then flapped her left hand. "Don't worry, you'll pick it up easily."

Cate grimaced and took Miss Kincaid's gloved hand in hers.

"Leave everything to me, Private Smith," her dance partner said assuringly. "I'll guide you."

Miss Kincaid's eyelashes fluttered, doing nothing for the state of Cate's grimace. Henry snorted back a laugh and did his best to smooth it over with a gentlemanly nod to Miss Loy as they stepped forward and back with the rhythm of the music, honoring the person opposite them with a nod. The matron to Cate's left was older, her braided and looped hair streaked with gray, but her smile was demure and her silk plaid dress fine. It took Cate a moment to realize that her partner was none other than Captain Noah. Cate blinked and tried to focus on what was to be done.

"We pass in front," Miss Kincaid murmured, and she and Cate chassezed to the left in front of Captain Noah and his partner. "Then return behind."

Cate did so. Then they greeted their opposite again. Cate's opposite was Robinson's partner, a young woman with a mouth that curled either in pleasure or disdain (she wasn't quite sure which).

"Right-hand star," Henry directed then, and the music moved so fast, Cate would have missed it if Henry hadn't reached out and snatched her hand in his. The ladies grasped hands over top of Henry and Cate's, and they circled.

She wished it was just that she'd been surprised, but the feel of his hand in hers after the better part of the last week spent unable to touch one another, even in the most trivial of ways, sent a tingle of sensation up her arm. Neither of them had gloves, and the sensation of his calluses were warm and smooth and dry. Cate couldn't help but lock eyes with him.

"Now left," he said and turned abruptly, offering her his left hand this time. Cate scrambled to turn and offer him her left hand, quite off beat by this point. She glanced over at Miss Kincaid, who was turning demure circles with Robinson. Apparently this dance was one that ensured one danced scarcely at all with one's partner.

"Circle four," Henry instructed, and the four in the center grasped hands and spun like a wheel. Cate held his gaze opposite her—she was dependent on his instructions was all—and a small smile quirked at the corners of his mouth. When they returned to their places, Miss Kincaid's hand was waiting for Cate's, and she said, "Now greet your opposite and pass through. There, see, couldn't be easier!"

Cate's feet were already carrying her through the steps as she acknowledged an annoying desire to stay in this set, so that she might grasp hands with Henry once again. She looked at him over her shoulder as she fell into the figure from the top, greeting her opposite rather poorly, looking as she was away from her. Henry was looking back at her too. When he caught her eye, he grinned. Cate swallowed hard. What the hell was she doing? She wrestled her mind to focus on the dance.

The sets proceeded down the line, the couples who made it to the end of their line waiting when needed, then retreating back up to the head of the line to continue the form. It was such a simple dance that after a few rounds, it scarcely took any concentration to repeat the movements.

Cate made a point to grip the hands of the other soldiers in each set firmly, setting her opposite hand at her back in a most gentlemanly fashion. Several of the girls she greeted as her opposite delivered her coy smiles, which was utterly flummoxing. While largely passing unnoticed or willfully ignored as a woman, she seemed to make not only a passable young man, but an appealing one. It was baffling.

Once the initial discomfiture of that realization had settled, Cate began to wonder what would happen if she engaged with this female notice. In the next set, she caught the eye of her opposite, a girl scarcely twenty, with chestnut brown curls rolled and pinned behind her ears. She held the girl's gaze from under her brows, and the girl responded with a slow smile. This was outrageous. Surely, Cate did not make an attractive boy. How could feminine plainness translate to male allure?

The song went on, repeating through the figure set after set, until she and Miss Kincaid ended up at one end of the line and began to proceed back down it in the opposite direction. Cate grew increasingly bold with her newfound boyish charm, adding a sly grin to her arsenal and even taking the liberty of glancing one girl up and down, which earned her a soft oh of parted lips. While not precisely her taste, she did find herself enjoying the attention.

Such was her line of thought when she reached out kitty-corner for the right-hand star and looked up to find she grasped Henry's hand again. His head was tilted to the side, and he looked at her with incredulous amusement. Cate regarded him with wide eyes and lips pressed together, trying hard not to laugh. His hand was warm and solid in hers and this time, she was right on beat with the music as they turned and grasped left hands, spinning opposite. She'd been so caught up playing with flirtatious glances that she found herself applying the expression on Henry without thinking. She could see his Adam's apple bob in his throat as he swallowed, and she smiled impishly.

The figure went all too fast, and before she knew it, they had passed through again, on to the next set of couples. It wasn't long after that—perhaps a figure or two more—before the quartet concluded the song with a tag ending, and Cate was bowing to Miss Kincaid.

Her dance partner regarded Cate with a self-satisfied grin. "See, didn't I tell you? So easy, and so much fun!"

Cate looked at the floor sheepishly. "I suppose."

"Now, there's still at least three dances left before we must see you off. Please don't disappoint the ladies of Pittsburgh by sitting the rest of the night out." Miss Kincaid's blue eyes lingered on Cate's for a moment longer than seemed polite. Cate blushed—not because she resented the attention but because she realized she had absolutely no idea what to do with it now that the dance music had ended, and she was forced to make polite conversation. Luckily, Henry approached just then with Miss Loy.

"Private Smith, I had no idea you were such an accomplished dancer," Miss Loy gushed.

"Indeed, Smith," Henry added, his scarcely contained amusement a little too thick to be entirely sincere. "Why haven't you told me you're a first rate stepper?"

Cate shook her head and rolled her eyes, hiding behind her usual mask of disdain. "Don't be absurd—Miss Loy said it herself, La Tempête couldn't be easier."

"And yet I just had my friend Lottie asking me to make an introduction to you," Miss Loy replied with a significant expression. "She's looking for a partner for the Scot's Reel, and you apparently caught her eye."

Cate blanched. The Scot's Reel was markedly more difficult, and she hadn't been at a dance where it had been done since the last time she'd been in Pennsylvania nearly a decade ago. As a girl.

"I'm terribly sorry to your friend, Miss Loy, but I'm afraid I don't know that one either," Cate demurred, glancing reproachfully at Henry, who was being entirely useless and chortling away under his breath.

"Well, I'm quite sure Lottie—or Miss Price, as you will soon know her—would be more than happy to teach you the steps," Miss Loy replied, then exchanged glances with Miss Kincaid. They both giggled, and Cate was forcibly reminded how simultaneously endearing and terrifying a group of girls giggling could be. The two of them tugged Cate's hand off toward the center of the ballroom. Cate looked imploring over her shoulder at Henry, but he just doubled over laughing.

Miss Price, as it turned out, was the young lady Cate had delivered an appraising and (she hoped) appreciative once-over during La Tempête. This would teach her to play games with the hearts of girls. If she could have got away with it, she would have hid her face in her hands, but as it were, she was forced to face Miss Price, deliver a gracious introduction with flaming cheeks, and accept that to all appearances, she seemed nothing more than a bashful boy with great interest in this particular girl. It didn't help that Henry had seemingly rounded up Robinson and Hower to observe and snicker as Cate led Miss Price onto the dance floor, trying desperately to remember the steps well enough to execute them to speed.

She joined a circle of four couples and put her hand out to Miss Price absently. Miss Price laughed, smiling through puzzled brows as she sweetly turned Cate's hand over, setting her fingertips on Cate's palm. Cate flushed again, mortified that she'd offered her hand in the lady's position as a matter of habit. Just then, the fiddle struck up a lively tune and the group of them were all bouncing on tiptoe, their feet shuffling sevens-and-threes in a circle. Cate could scarcely keep her feet under her as they moved back and forth and then turned straight into a ladies' right-hand star, the gents on the outside in open position. Cate knew only enough about this dance to make it mortifyingly confusing to dance the male position. The couples turned as one, bringing the gents in to circle a left-hand star. Cate scarcely had taken her opposite's hand before the group broke into a grand chain. She felt a rather visceral understanding of why it was called a reel.

Cate was winded at the end of the dance, escorting Miss Price back to where they had met, handing her to her next partner and glaring daggers at Henry, Robinson, and Hower, who stood a little ways off snickering like they had scarcely made it out of primary school.

"I didn't see any of you attempting the Scot's Reel so don't even start," Cate snapped at them as she approached. That only caused them all to bust out in full guffaws. She held herself back from flashing a rude gesture at them.

"Smith—that was—" Hower gasped, unable to form two words together for laughing.

"Masterful, truly!" Robinson exclaimed, his full grin displaying all of his teeth. "Did you see him, Elias? Two left feet the whole way through, but Miss Price was still batting her eyelashes at him all the way off the dance floor."

Henry snorted loudly. Cate tipped her head back, imploring the ceiling to grant her patience.

"What's so funny?" Williamson. Of course. The other fellows ignored him.

"Well, this was truly first rate," Hower said, wiping tears from his eyes, "but I have a lady to lead in our final song of the evening."

"Oh, which is it again?" Williamson asked, and Henry snatched his dance card from his pocket to check.

"Soldier's Joy," he confirmed.

"A fitting tribute, and I haven't even got a partner for it!" Robinson exclaimed woefully.

Couples made their way to the dance floor as the opening melody rang out from the fiddle. There were at least twice as many gents as ladies and given that the dance was titled Soldier's Joy, it was evident that Robinson wasn't the only one who felt left out. From the opposite side of the dance floor, some of the Hastings boys leaped out and partnered with one another, to the great amusement of the dancers on the floor. They joined the line, over-gesticulating to honor their opposite and their partner, kicking up their heels in exaggerated steps.

Williamson laughed aloud, and Robinson grinned.

"I'm not missing my Soldier's Joy just because there aren't any ladies left to dance with!" he exclaimed and snatched Williamson's hand, dragging him out to the dance floor laughing and protesting.

Cate's eyes flicked over to Henry, and his mischievous grin provoked her head to follow warily.

"Don't even—" she began, but he'd already snatched her hand, hauling her to the dance floor and assuming the other side of Williamson and Robinson's set.

The music was quick and lively, reminiscent of "The Sailor's Hornpipe" or other such tunes celebrating the jolly life of a man in service to his country. Henry kicked his heels high and let out a shout, leaping about as he dashed headlong into the ladies' chain as Cate tried her damndest not to fall over laughing. Their hands fell naturally together and despite being in the man's position in the set, Cate's fingers rested upon his palm like they belonged there.

When they passed through, he made a show of swinging his elbows in a dreadful imitation of a jig, and they weren't even through the figure twice before Cate fell into the steps with him, grinning in spite of herself and stomping her feet in time.

———

III

Pittsburgh, Pennsylvania
Friday, October 18, 1861

"WE MUST STOP MEETING like this." Charley's voice floated playfully out of the darkness.

Henry huffed a laugh that was permeated with nervous anticipation. "What, in a shed?"

"That too." Her hand clutched his collar and yanked him into the ramshackle shed they'd found around the corner from the market house they quartered in. It had been surprisingly simple to slip out of one of the many doors as the regiment settled into the large hall to sleep. From there, it was a quick stride down an alley until they found the solitary shed behind a hotel.

The shed was small, housing all matter of sundry tools needed to maintain the small courtyard and stables where guests of the neighboring hotel could put up their horses during their stay. The clapboards were so old and withered that the full moon shone brightly between them, illuminating the cobwebby interior in shades of blue-gray. It smelled like compost, an earthy combination of decaying weeds and horse manure. God, what Henry would give for a room in that hotel. Preferably one with a bed.

Charley kicked the door shut and pushed him up against it, her hands running down from his collar over his chest, pushing into his unbuttoned sack coat and making his voice hum with pleasure.

"You like my chest," he murmured redundantly. "Quite possibly more than I like yours, which is no small feat." His hands roamed in emphasis.

"Every man should learn gymnasticks," she replied with fervor, her teeth nipping at his jaw. "The loyal ladies of Pittsburgh agree. In a room where the ladies were outnumbered four to one, you still managed to have a full dance card."

Henry pulled her chest flush against his and exhaled a sigh of relief he hadn't realized he'd been holding in. He thrilled in the trap her body made of him against the door. "You could have too if you tried."

Charley snorted, and he realized the derisive response delivered self-deprecatingly annoyed him more than when it was aimed at him. He seized her head on either side of her face and pulled her in for a searing kiss.

Hell, how he'd missed this. The heat, the wet, the play of soft lips and intrusive tongues and nipping teeth. The way she sucked his lower lip between her teeth, hard enough for him to feel her ardor but not enough to hurt. The heat of her, the firm weight of her pressing into him, the scent of her crowding out any of the more unpleasant aromas of the shed. It felt like a homecoming. It hadn't been more than a week since they'd kissed like this, but it felt like an eternity to live without something so simple and so necessary.

"That was curious, wasn't it?" she said as he whined at the loss of her mouth against his.

"What?"

"The ladies wanting to dance with me. I thought to myself, how does womanly plainess translate to appealing maleness?"

Henry blinked at her. "Are you joking?"

She jerked her chin down in a way he knew to be defensive. Oh boy.

"I know there were only a few ladies who seemed like they wanted to dance with me," she said in a Smithier tone than he'd have liked, "and I know a dance doesn't mean much in the grand scheme of things, but I can assure you I know what it feels like to be a wallflower and—"

"You were *magnificent*," Henry breathed more vehemently than he intended. "I'm confused by the assumption that you would be anything less than."

Charley shook her head and rolled her eyes. "Ugh, not this again."

"Yes, this again," he replied combatively. "I'll keep saying it until you get it into your head. You're not plain. You're ... enigmatic, and this evening was just proof that I'm not the only one who sees it. Those ladies saw someone who is striking and elegant—" Charley snorted. Henry lifted her chin with his fingertips and looked hard into her eyes. "—and dark and broody. You're beguiling. If I could have, I would have been right there with them vying for a place on your card."

Charley regarded him suspiciously from under her brows. "Would you, though? There were so many lovely girls—"

"*Yes*," Henry seized her shoulders in emphasis. "It made me *crazy* to see them receive your singular attention. My dance card was full because I like to dance, and I'm not afraid to ask. But if I could have my way, I would have rather spent the whole night with you."

Charley huffed a weak little laugh. "Thus, the shed."

Henry's hands skimmed down her arms and held her at the waist. "I'd have you in that hotel if I didn't think it would get us court-martialed."

Charley hummed with pleasure, and it made Henry remember her whispering desperately how she wished he could fuck her when he'd last made her come. "What I would give for a real bed..."

She kissed him again, a coaxing kiss full of desire and need and no small measure of mischief. She was distracting him from continuing to expound upon the full measure of his devotion. If he hadn't been so hard, he might have more stubbornly declared himself. It was appalling how committed she was to this belief that she was forgettable when it was so plain to him that she was goddamned *everything* worth wanting.

He let himself fall into sensation—her mouth on his, his hands pulling her in by the rear, her fingers yanking his shirttails out of his waistband to snake her hands underneath. Breath lingering warm on his cheek. The slip of her waist and the breadth of her shoulders under his palms. Her dark curls a tangle under his fingertips. The relentless press of her yielding cunt against his cock, made vague under layers of fabric, making her whispered words about fucking replay like some sort of siren song in his head. He wanted it so bad it made his balls ache, but he had no idea how to bring it up, so he settled for a breathless murmur, "How do you want me?"

Charley swore, her voice rough and raw. Her fingers clutched into the sides of his trousers as she ducked her head down and buried it in his neck with a frustrated groan. "I don't know how you expect me to answer that question," she whined.

"Very directly, I hope," he replied. "You had an easy enough time saying what you didn't want that time in the tent."

"That's different."

"How?"

"It was a precaution. To keep myself safe. This question, it's—"

"—What you told Robinson and all the other fellows to ask when they want to please a lady?"

"No—Well, yes, but—I didn't tell them to say *that*."

"What?"

"*'How'*—Listen, Schaefer, for Chrissakes, asking 'what do you like' is a lot different than 'how do you want me,' you wanton little bastard." If there had been anything more than scant moonlight seeping through the cracks in the clapboards, Henry was certain he'd see her cheeks brightly flushed.

"Noted," he conceded and let a moment of silence stretch before he added, "So ... how *do* you want me?"

She looked up at him with a puzzling combination of grim mouth and wide, dark eyes that yearned. Her nostrils flared with her elevated breaths, and the silence stretched again like the endless scream of a braking train.

"Charley," he murmured, touching her cheek softly with his fingertips, "what's wrong? I want to please you. Just tell me."

Her lips parted, softening her expression nearer to the side of want and farther from the grip of control she usually tried to seize it with.

"I ..." she said stiltedly. "God, Henry, you're killing me."

"Why?" he breathed.

"You damn well know why," she swore, seizing his collar in her hands. "Because I want you to fuck me more than I've ever wanted anything, and it's the only thing I can't have."

Henry licked his lips as his cock preened at her words. If only he could have found the goddamned French letter his father had given him. "There are ways—"

"No," she shook her head, her voice more a whimper than anything. "I can't risk it, I know I can't, but God, I want to and I need—" She took a shaking breath. "I want you to sit me up on that barrel over there, and fuck me with your fingers so hard I forget how much I want your cock inside me."

He was distantly grateful that the moonlight hid their flush because his flamed all the way down his neck and chest. Christ. If he'd known what kind of answer his question would bring ... well, he would definitely still have asked it. But *Christ.*

He seized her by her thighs, wrapping them around his waist, and carried her the few steps to the barrel in question. He pulled her trousers roughly to her knees and settled between them as he slicked his fingers in between her folds, sinking the tip of one finger into silky softness.

He kissed her neck, behind her ear, along her jaw, as he added another finger, then a third. She was so wet for him that three stretched smoothly inside her. She squeezed tight around him, and his cock screamed for attention, but he'd asked her how *she'd* wanted *him*. This was her desire. And when he'd fucked her well enough with his fingers to slake her lust, then he'd reap his reward. He was going to damn well earn this.

~

Goddamn Henry Schaefer and his fucking hands. Cate was draped boneless over the barrel, her head tossed back against the clapboard wall. Henry braced over her on one hand, the other lingering between her legs. His expression was singularly focused.

"Can you feel that?" she whispered breathlessly.

Henry looked up at her, brow furrowed.

"Here," she squeezed her thighs around his hand. "Can you feel my heartbeat?"

His exhale shook. He nodded, then leaned in and captured her lips with his. She'd yanked his trousers open at one point to feel his stiff piece in her hands as he made her fall apart, and now his cock jutted into her thigh, smearing moisture toward the place she most wanted him to sink it into. She bit his lip, harder than she meant to.

She was playing with fire. Even sated, she still was desperate for him to fuck her. She could have come fifteen times, and she'd still want it. She'd so enjoyed the feeling of being stretched, of being filled, in her former life. She had clutched her eyes shut and imagined it was enough to hold a marriage together. She'd been wrong, but it didn't make her miss the sensation any less.

She wanted to feel what it would be like, to be stretched and filled by this man for whom she harbored actual affection and mutual respect. It would be different to ride the cock of a man whose companionship she actually enjoyed, rather than squeezing her eyes shut and pretending she was with whichever man had caught the fancy of her escapist imagination that week. A bearded lumberman, the barber at the Winslow hotel, Mr. Plemer—anyone but Richard.

"Henry," she murmured. "How do you want me?"

His soft-focused eyes fixed on her. He blinked. "You're right. That is an unfair question."

"Quid pro quo, Schaefer."

"Oh God, I don't know. Your hands would do nicely."

Her fingers skittered over his velvety shaft. His hand shifted out of her way, sliding out from between her legs and gripping the crease where her thigh met her hip. "I don't want to just do nicely. I want to turn you inside out."

His voice hummed in his throat. "Well, obviously, I'd love to, um, have you as you said, but that's not an option, at least not right now."

"You're adorable." She snorted and gave his prick a firm pull. She loved how it made his face crumple with desire. "'Have.' I'm not convinced you can use that expression when you finger-fucked me on a barrel in an abandoned shed."

He shuddered. As much as it startled him to hear her speak so lewdly, she could feel how hard it made him. Which made her want to say more filthy things.

"What would 'have' entail, pray tell?" she cooed, fisting his cock and spreading the moisture at the tip over the head with her thumb.

"I don't understand what's confusing," he replied absently, his breath hot and shallow in her ear.

"I'm not confused. I just want to hear you say it," she growled. When he didn't reply, her hand stilled. She loosened her grip, so that she just barely skimmed his skin, and he whimpered at the loss of contact. "I said, I want to hear you say it."

"I..." he murmured. He pulled back and looked at her. His face was wrecked, twisted with desire. "I want to..."

Her eyes were fixed on him.

"I want to have you under me. I want to fuck you and spend inside you, and I want to do it in a goddamned bed."

Her breath hitched in her chest. *Yes.* Her hand gripped him again, and she guided him closer. She wasn't thinking clearly. She curled her hips up, used her hand to sweep his cock firmly down between her folds, letting the swollen, blunt head slide over the nub of nerves that made her tremble, pressed it at her entrance. Felt her toes curl.

"Charley..." Henry's voice was thick and uncertain.

"I just finished my monthly," she gasped. "Nothing will happen."

"You—you said we can't..."

"Yes, but..." she whimpered. She squeezed her eyes shut, sparks of white dancing behind her lids. It wasn't right, how her fear and the knowledge that this was reckless sharpened her pleasure to a point. He'd made her come already, but she could feel the intensity building again, boiling up from where his cock pressed lightly at her slick and yielding entrance. She whined in helpless frustration, in wanting, in fear and shame too, in her lack of conviction.

The fact was ... this momentary pleasure could so easily lead to disaster if it resulted in a baby. She'd had resources in St. Anthony—alum and water, a private place to wash in or to insert a sponge soaked in the solution ahead of time. She had none of that here. All she had was the knowledge of when her monthlies were coming, enough trust that Henry would listen to her, and luck. And she'd just finished her monthly, not a day ago. There was no way she could conceive a child if he fucked her now.

"Henry, I am cautious," she said, trying to steady her breath, sound rational and controlled. "But trust me when I tell you that if we were to do it now, there'd be no consequence."

He looked into her eyes, searched for a moment. The pressure on her cunt made it hard to train her expression—she was so wet, it would take only the lightest of pressure from him to breach her—but she did her damndest. His eyes were desire itself.

"Okay," he breathed, "I trust you."

Cate pulled Henry into a kiss. At the same time, she tilted her hips and used her hand to guide his cock in. God, he stretched her so well, sliding ever more smoothly as she worked him in inch by inch, slicking him as she went.

"Henry," she gasped as she let go and his hips took charge. "Oh God, Henry." She pushed her nose into his neck, breathed in his grassy scent, that smell of comfort and desire and *Henry*. Closed her eyes and let herself unravel.

Her legs were around his waist and her thighs already trembled. It was happening fast. She clung to his shoulders for leverage as her hips pushed to meet his with each stroke. The pressure of his groin against hers each time he drove all the way in, spearing her, made incoherent noises erupt from her lips. She had a passing worry that he'd dislike her making too much noise, but then he let out a gravelly moan too, and she abandoned any proprietary restraint she'd been holding on to.

His mouth was against her ear now, forming her chosen name in a desperate hush just for her. His hands gripped her hips, pulled her onto him with each thrust. Her thighs trembled, all her muscles seized and swelled, and she gasped in his ear as she began to come.

"Oh dear god," Henry gasped and he spasmed in her arms. He was coming too. Inside her. The heat of it, the intimacy and the taboo, all pushed her anew and her crisis kept swelling, her voice cracking on the intensity of it. Oh, this was bliss. This was perfect. Everything she wanted and everything she'd dreamed it could be. God, she could do nothing but ride this man for the rest of her days and die happy.

———

IV

Pittsburgh, Pennsylvania
Saturday, October 19, 1861

HENRY UNDERSTOOD NOW WHY Jacob Robinson had been such a dope after his honeymoon. When he woke up on the floor of the Duquesene Gray's hall with the rest of the regiment, it was like the sun shone just a little bit brighter. Charley was tucked under her wool blanket beside him, serene in her sleep. This wasn't anything like a honeymoon trip down the Mississippi in a steamship, replete with a state room and universally acknowledged forbearance for their infatuation by the rest of the passengers, but it felt like something was forming between them, something new and fragile.

When she woke up, her dark eyes fluttered open and focused on him. She smiled, soft and open and sleep-rumpled. Henry locked the sight in his memory, to never forget the way she looked at him when she first woke up. It made him want to whisper sweet nothings in her ear, but the snort of Krüger waking and Jacob yawning snapped his awareness back into the wider world.

"Gut–Good morning," he whispered. God, he was so smitten he forgot to speak English instead of German.

"It is a good morning, isn't it?" she murmured, her voice rough and low, just for him to hear.

"Best I can recall. Best company, at any rate."

Her bow lips twitched at the corners, her eyes crinkling.

"Aren't you two just as snug as a bug."

Henry looked up at Elias Hower, standing above them with hands on his hips. He was smiling, but something about it made Henry feel like it was forced.

"What's got your goat?" Charley asked, her countenance closing as she swung her chin toward Hower.

He shook his head. "Best if it comes from the big bugs."

Henry's eyes widened. "You have news, but you're *not* going to share it? Who are you, and what have you done with my corporal?"

Elias shifted on his heels, glancing at Charley. "I'd rather not be the messenger in this case." He retreated before either of them could further engage him.

Charley shoved herself up to sitting, her brows fully furrowed in Smith fashion. So much for the blissful pocket of intimacy. She rolled her blanket quickly and swung it over her shoulder.

"Where are you going?" Henry couldn't help but ask.

"What kind of question is that?" Smith rebutted, not so much snapping as lobbing with a more benign strain of derision. Henry sighed.

"Never mind."

"Come on, we gotta get in ranks. Better get whatever this bad news is over with." She stood, and Henry followed suit. He bundled his blanket into a roll, tied the corners, and slung it over his shoulder. "Will it be easier to swallow if you know something bad is coming or won't it make much of a difference having fair warning?"

"I reckon it might be worse," Charley admitted, pushing her hair back and affixing her cap. Her hair was getting a bit long, curling over her collar at the back of her neck. Henry wished he could bury his nose in it. "Now I'm imagining all sorts of miserable scenarios."

"Maybe it'll be a relief then?" Henry suggested.

"What'll be a relief?" John Williamson said. He slept quite soundly to Henry's other side, at least he had last night, well enough they could sneak away undetected. Apparently now he'd quite dispensed with his rest at the prospect of fresh news. Henry startled, because he'd been about to wonder aloud whether Charley had anything to worry about, and that would have set Williamson off in a line of questioning that might get both he and Charley in a heap of trouble.

"Hower baited us with bad news," Charley grumbled.

"I heard that. I just wondered if you had any ideas of what it was about," Williamson replied. "I had a letter from home saying the weather's gone frigid and there's Indians stealing chickens and the like. The harvest was bad at Yellow Medicine."

Henry's brow furrowed. It hadn't occurred to him that the news might be of where they'd come from, rather than where they were headed. "Remind me where you're from again?"

"North of Birch Coulee," Williamson replied.

Henry frowned further. That was up in Indian Country, on the tract of land held in reserve for the Sioux.

"I thought you were from Faribault?" Charley clarified.

"Well, I was, on account of that's where I enlisted, but my mother lives near Birch Coulee."

"But that's the Indian Reservation," Henry couldn't help but argue. Williamson didn't look like an Indian, but that didn't mean much when so many men who'd come to Minnesota in the fur trade days made marriages with Indian women.

"Yes," Williamson smiled, unaware—or unwilling—to clarify the question Henry didn't ask. Henry looked to Charley, who shrugged. "I didn't grow up there, of course," Williamson offered.

"Where did you grow up?" Henry's curiosity was fully engaged now.

"St. Paul, mostly. My father's work takes him all over, but I went to school there." He said it like Henry imagined someone might say they went to Harvard, with pride. St. Paul was practically wilderness compared to Boston, but a fellow deserved to be proud he could read and write and such, regardless of where he'd learnt it.

They'd fallen into ranks near the exit of the hall as they carried on their conversation. Sergeant Osborn was calling them to attention, so Henry didn't have the chance to pursue any of the frayed threads Williamson had cast out any further. Williamson wasn't the most perceptive fellow, but he wasn't usually so fragmented. Perhaps because Henry hadn't done much apart from try to avoid him, which now that he was acknowledging it, he felt rather guilty about.

"Who's your father?" Charley hissed toward Williamson, even though they were supposed to be standing at attention. It appeared Henry was not the only one whose curiosity had been piqued.

"Smith—" Osborn scolded under his breath.

"John Williamson," John Williamson replied.

Krüger laughed, which set Henry laughing too, then the whole squad was chuckling such that Osborn had to reprimand them.

Captain Noah stepped forward before the ranks to address them.

"Men," he said, "I've been informed that our orders have been countermanded. Instead of heading to Washington D.C., we will be going downriver to join General Buell's Army of the Ohio. We depart shortly, so any soldiers wanting to send word home had better do it presently."

They were ordered at ease then, and in no time, the din of speculative murmurs rose to a fever pitch.

"Ohio?" Jacob Robinson said. "But they're Union."

"Have Rebels invaded Ohio?" Williamson gasped.

"No," Elias sauntered over. News broken, he appeared now ready to play benevolent oracle again. "They're gathering Union troops in Kentucky, trying to keep them from seceding and ensuring the Rebs can't get supplies through railroad lines or other means."

"We're not going to the front," Charley clarified. She looked thunderous.

"I wouldn't say that," Elias replied. "There's good information placing Rebel troops on the border of Kentucky and Tennessee. A General Jollification or something."

"Zollicoffer," Osborn broke in, eyeing Elias. "And I do have information you don't, sometimes."

"Zollicoffer?" Henry scoffed as he pulled canvas tight on their Sibley tent, Williamson and Robinson pulling from the other side. "And folks say my name is strange..."

Hower rolled his eyes. "He's some sort of dandy merchant or something, got the command because he was friends with the top brass."

Osborn gave the squad a withering look. "I'm not concerned we won't see battle, if that's what you're worried about. There will be plenty to fight for in Kentucky."

Charley's jaw worked and flexed, but she said nothing. Henry shifted from one foot to the other as the reality of the decision curdled around him. No Washington D.C. No reuniting with his brother and the First Minnesota. If only he'd managed to get into the First, he would have had months of battle experience already. That one moment when the captain called for men with their own rifles, the one his brothers had seized and he had not, was making a bungle of his entire dream for enlistment. Now, instead of winning honor and glory, he was fated to dig earthworks and wait. A stretch of three years enlistment unfurling before him in an endless unknown. He'd grown up in Cincinnati—even then, all he knew about Kentucky was that it was the wrong side of the river.

———

The steamboats departed under rainy skies around noon, whisking them southwest on the Ohio River as though their transport to Washington D.C. had been nothing more than a ruse to get them so far from home, they had no choice but to obey. The whole regiment was slumped, more against the disappointment of the new orders than the rain. It was gratifying, though, that the weather matched their moods.

The voyage was cramped and smelly. The weather turned as they passed Marietta the next day, the sun warming the decks and the men in their scratchy wool uniforms. They hadn't had the opportunity to wash properly since they'd left Minnesota over a week ago now, and the musk inside the steamboat cabins was vile. Cate spent much of her time out on deck, watching the water churn under the boat and noting the cities as they floated past. Portsmouth, Maysville, Cincinnati. Henry had been eager to watch the last go by, grumbling that they should have stopped to resupply there instead of Maysville. It wasn't as though Henry would have had the opportunity to show her around his childhood town anyway. The stop they had made was scarcely 20 minutes long.

At night, they slept wedged man to man in the cabins and upon the deck. Fine weather allowed for sleeping out under the stars and sleeping quarters were tight enough that Henry's hand could seek out Cate's under the cover of darkness and nothing would appear amiss. The fellow was positively doting despite the new orders, and sought her company to a fault despite the pervasive surliness she couldn't quite shake. She suspected she'd act just as much of a ninnyhammer as he was, especially after what had transpired in Pittsburgh, if it weren't for the fact that she'd lost her chance to fight on the front lines. Even if she wasn't lamenting her terrible luck, he could offer her little in the way of comfort. It wasn't as though there was any occasion to repeat their Pittsburgh encounter. They had no hope of privacy, at least not until they formed camp again, and the perfect timing they'd had in Pittsburgh would already expire by then. Any reprise performance would compromise Cate in ways she had no intention of risking. So why form a tendre when there was nothing to be done about it?

Regardless of her careful distancing, the boys treated her and Henry as a pair. When they were together, they were teased endlessly about how entirely their regard for one another had changed since mustering in at Fort Snelling. When they were apart, Cate was certain she was being dogged by fellows asking her where Henry was, like she was his keeper or something. Most provoking of all, she always knew. Perhaps that was telling.

The steamers docked in Louisville in the darkest hour early Tuesday morning. Cate had slept fitfully, and was stiff as the deckboards they'd reposed upon the last three nights. They were confined to the boats while Colonel Van Cleve and Captain Bishop of Company A went to Union headquarters to report to General Sherman.

The day was cloudy and foreboding, a sign from the heavens that they had arrived in the infernal regions, damned to perdition. She and Henry stood at the deck rail, watching the dingy river landing with mounting repugnance. Slavery was in evidence everywhere, African men and women carrying loads of goods or scrubbing laundry or laboring, young children currying horses and running messages. Cate knew there must be freedmen among them, but she had no idea how to tell. The chains ran so deep, they need not even be in plain view any longer. White Kentuckians moved through the lurid bustle as though nothing at all were amiss, as though they couldn't even see the chattel around them.

"All I know about Kentucky is that it's full of cowards twice over," she hissed as she clenched her fists around the rail. "They're too fearful to secede, but too selfish to liberate their slaves. I'd rather build a hundred earthworks than defend those yellow-bellied swine."

Cate thought she'd understood what she was enlisting to do. But in the time it took for them to float down the Ohio, she'd become increasingly aware of her naivete. The change in their orders upended her expectations. In place of the glorious battles of the righteous versus the morally corrupt, their purpose in this state was a much muddier moral stand. Protect the loyal slavers from the treasonous ones. Defend the Union. Never mind abolition. Never mind the natural rights of man. The willful ignorance of injustice all around them sat like a heavy stone in her belly.

"I suppose you haven't seen much of this, growing up in the North," Henry said.

"You might suppose, but no. St. Anthony was a bevy of hotels bowing and scraping to the Southern tourist," Cate said. "That is, until Eliza Winston was freed."

"How so?"

"After the court emancipated her, the tourists took off all at once. They were too afraid to bring their slaves into free territory. The hotels had no guests."

"Really? I read about her case in the papers, but I didn't realize it all fell apart so quick."

"Yes. The Winslow House is closed now." Cate felt a grin curl into her dark expression. "Serves them right, if you ask me."

"I'm not arguing."

Everything about the activity below them was business as usual. Cate didn't know what she'd expected, but it wasn't this. Folks, white and black alike, worked hard, moved crates and bundles and other sundry goods along efficiently. As though no war was on, as though nothing had changed. Why continue to labor when the Union had split? Why did they not flee, defect, demand their freedom? Why did they stay here? And all the while, smiling white merchants went about their day as though they weren't engaging in a crime against the barest forms of human morality.

"How?" Cate demanded, desperately grasping for some sign of sense in this godforsaken place. "*How* do they live with themselves?"

"Very easily, by all appearances," Henry replied, leaning over the rail and resting his chin on a fist.

Cate threw her hands up. She couldn't watch this any longer. She stormed off to the other side of the boat, where there was nothing more to see but the dingy water of the Ohio churn reflections of the leaden sky.

———

When the Colonel returned, he ordered the regiment to disembark from the boats. From the docks, they marched in formation to the Louisville and Nashville railroad depot. Up and down the ranks, murmurs echoed speculating where they were headed. Henry couldn't be sure of anything.

"Elias," Henry hissed at the corporal as Charley glared daggers at the townspeople they marched past. "Where are we going?"

Elias pressed his lips together and said, "I'm trying to find out, but it's not clear. I'm getting conflicting stories."

"Right, right, but surely there are some consistencies? Something we can hang our fates upon?" All Henry had heard so far was wild conjecture. Zollicoffer was pressing to the east. Battle was in motion and they marched as reinforcements. Zollicoffer's troops were upon the city and the Second Minnesota had arrived just in time.

"It's something to do with a strategic railroad junction," Elias said, "but it's not clear whether the Rebels have taken it yet. I'm not sure whether we'll be on the defensive or offensive."

"But battle," Henry clarified. Charley's eyes snapped over, her attention caught along with several of the other squadmates.

"Yes, battle by morning, I should think," Elias murmured gravely.

Henry frowned and looked up. The leaden sky had gone seething. Though the day had been mild in temperature, as evening fell, so too did the mercury. There was something in the air, something foreboding, and Henry studied the clouds as though they could tell him what waited for them on the other end of this train journey. He gripped the butt of his gun more tightly as they shuffled onto the train platform at the Louisville and Nashville railroad depot.

Flatcars had already arrived for them, reminiscent of cattle cars or some other less-than-human cargo conveyance. Rough board benches were all that distinguished these. The squad packed themselves in with the Hastings boys, and just as the cars were loaded up and began to move, the dark clouds finished amassing and began pouring down their burden on the backs of the Second Minnesota.

The train moved at a glacial pace. The rain soaked them all, and Charley reached into her knapsack and pulled out her greatcoat. Henry, and many of the others, followed suit. The cars afforded them no cover whatsoever, and the trees lining the tracks made no canopy. Dark fell, and the rain sliced like daggers, not cold enough to freeze, but only just.

"My God, do they not have covered passenger trains in this Godforsaken hellhole?" Charley declared, flipping the cape of her greatcoat over her head. It was sodden by this point and did not appear to help at all.

"Does this train not go any faster?" Elias sputtered wetly, water pouring off the bill of his forage cap after about an hour had passed thusly. "I don't mean to be insubordinate, but with all due respect, we could have marched at this speed by foot."

Osborn sighed. His moustache drooped miserably. "Not on those roads."

Through the darkness, they could make out a small mud river flowing down the road that ran adjacent to this leg of the railroad. The train slowed, as though to torture them further.

"Maybe I'll just hop off and walk," Jacob joked, getting to his feet with a mischievous grin only somewhat sodden with cold, his face was shiny wet.

"Sit. Down." Osborn could call up a commanding timbre, when he wanted to. Jacob sat without another word.

The train slowly trundled at a decreasing speed.

"Are we there?" A murmur of voices began to volley up and down the cars. Henry craned his neck up, even as fellows on other cars stood to get a better look down the line. The rain made it difficult to see more than fifty feet in front of them, no matter the dark of night hewing the trees in on them like some sort of ghoulish sentinels.

The train stopped dead. The rain muffled any other sound. Or at least, Henry thought it did until fellows started standing and murmuring.

Two cars ahead, Captain Noah stood—it must have been him, with his wide-brimmed hat—and bellowed, "Stand down, men. Resume your seats. This is not our destination."

The men obeyed as they'd been trained to do, but the murmuring continued.

"Silence," Osborn demanded. "I said, silence!" He lowered his tone as he managed to command the attention of the squad, and the Hastings boys too. "There is no telling where the enemy may be. Do not give away our position."

That chilled them all. Henry's eyes skittered across the impenetrable blackness as the minutes stretched and they remained stopped. His ears strained for any noise that might indicate a covert enemy nearby.

The train remained stagnant for fifteen minutes—or maybe an hour, it was so difficult to tell and too dark to check a pocket watch. Finally, the grind of wheels on the track made everyone jump, and the cars creaked back into glacial motion.

"What was that about?" Charley whispered. Her eyes were buried under her brow and water dripped off the tip of her nose.

A few minutes later, Elias pointed in answer. "Look." There was a sidetrack arching off to the north, with a lever. "Maybe the lever was stuck."

Charley's jaw clenched and a black look scrunched her nose up under her brows too.

Hour after hour passed, their train moved at scarcely six miles an hour, stopping a while at every side track and occasionally for no apparent reason at all. Henry slept fitfully, his head nodding onto Charley's shoulder for snatches of time before the cars jerked back into motion or he shivered or some tiny sound that his bleary dreams heard as enemy Rebels bearing down on them snapped him back to consciousness.

The train stopped, finally, near a lone two-story station at a junction near 4 o'clock in the morning. Orders to disembark trickled down the miserable line of half-drowned men and they blearily streamed off the cattle cars and into ranks on a field of mud and slop.

Henry looked warily around. His senses were deadened by cold and rain and sleeplessness. He couldn't make out much through the darkness, but there was very little to see. Nothing but field and forest, seemingly deserted.

"I wonder if the Rebs have taken cover over there," Henry murmured, pointing at a treeline south of them.

"I damn well hope so," Smith spat, "because if we just sat through that miserable ride to meet a train engineer, I'm going to scream. I wanna shoot some goddamned traitors."

Their first order upon disembarking was to stack arms. They stood in soft mud until sunrise, supposedly to ensure they kept themselves awake so they might be ready to entertain any party of the enemy who might make an early morning call.

They didn't.

———

V

Lebanon Junction, Kentucky
Tuesday, November 5, 1861

Kentucky was the most miserable place Cate had ever been. Truly, Lebanon Junction could very well be the sixth level of Hell. She repeated this to herself like some sort of prayer as she sank her shovel into the soft mud, cold rain falling lightly on her greatcoat and making her curls stick to her feverish forehead.

To be fair, Kentucky hadn't had much of a chance to prove itself otherwise, given that she'd scarcely spent more than an hour in Louisville before being packed on a flatcar for a remote railroad junction in a rainstorm seemingly designed to torture the human spirit. But Cate felt quite confident that her assessment of the state was sound. Of course, it had nothing to do with the fact that she was miserably sick and hocking snot into her already limp handkerchief. Nor was her impression impacted by the ditches they were digging to keep the muddy water from seeping into their tents at night. No, she was entirely unbiased. This place was objectively wretched.

Cate leant upon her shovel for a moment, wiping rain from her brow with a chill, wet hand. It felt marvelous on her fiery skin. The rest of the squad was digging too, plowing shovels and hoes into the mud and spattering the tent canvas with black flecks. Water ran in a stream down the ditch they dug, swirling mud and sticks and dead leaves as it flowed away from the tent stakes. Cate swallowed against a sore, swollen throat and coughed.

She wasn't the only one who was sick. The weather had been cold and relentlessly wet, the ground soggy and unhealthy to sleep upon. The mornings were laced with wet fog that permeated everything—canvas, wool greatcoat, gaiter shoes—all of it. When they first arrived, their baggage and tents didn't come until the next day for some inexplicable reason, despite having left Louisville at the same time and their own train having traveled at a truly glacial speed. They'd spent the day after that hellish ride bivouacked in the mud until the supplies had arrived.

Once tents had arrived, they'd been ordered to set up camp in regulation style in a field within the angle formed by the main and Lebanon branch tracks. The countryside was largely wooded, broken up by fields here and there, sometimes sliced by a road, stream, or split-rail fence. The tents themselves were perhaps the greatest disappointment yet, as it had not even occurred to Cate that they'd have anything other than wedge tents sleeping two fellows each, like they'd had at Fort Snelling. Instead, they'd been with supplied Sibley tents, tall and conical like an Indian tipi, sleeping a whole squad in each.

She'd spent the trip from Pittsburgh to Kentucky certain no privacy could be had until they camped. She hadn't even considered that any scrap of privacy they could have scraped together would be their last safe harbor. She'd put aside her finer feelings, her longings and wantings and lusts, with the assumption that they'd have a chance at the front in a tent all their own. She'd been dead wrong.

Despite this frustrating setback, Henry's hand-holding had carried on in the Sibley tents these past few weeks and thankfully, no one seemed to notice. In fact, as members of their squad fell like dominoes to the illness that was plaguing their camp and the desolation and mundanity of this cursed place sank into their skin deeper than the damp, looking for a touch of comfort among one's comrades seemed increasingly a matter of course. But even if seeking warmth near one's bunkie was nothing to write home about, there was a good deal more she had been hoping to find in the comfort of Henry's arms and being back to assigned lodgings with the rest of the squad was frustrating to say the least.

Cate's head pounded as she took in a wheezy breath, and she realized belatedly that her shovel was listing. *Damnation*. She stumbled and fell on one knee in the mud, hanging onto her shovel handle for dear life to keep the rest of her from going into the mire too.

"Charley?" A hand touched her shoulder, and she looked up into Henry's concerned face, rain dripping off the end of his nose. "You don't look so good."

"It's nothing, I just got distracted and tripped—" she started, but her voice was hoarse and rough and it irritated her throat, sending her into another fit of coughing. Elias Hower appeared in her field of vision as Henry helped her to her feet with a solid hand.

"I mean, he doesn't look that bad," Hower commented, raising one brow and studying Cate like he suspected her of exaggerating her symptoms. "That ain't nothing compared to Webster a few days ago."

Henry gripped her hand and held her steady. Her fingers felt weak and small inside his. It was infuriating. Osborn materialized behind him.

"Smith, do you need to go to the hospital tent?" Osborn asked, leaning in and looking at each of her eyes in turn.

Cate pulled herself upright, snatching her hand away from Henry to show she could stand on her own. "No, sir," she replied, trying her best to sound like she didn't have a frog in her throat. "I'm just a little under the weather. Nothing a little light exertion can't solve."

Osborn, Hower, and Henry all peered at her skeptically. She pressed her lips together and tried to focus her eyes, but it was hard when she could feel every heartbeat pounding painfully behind them.

"Schaefer, take Smith back to the tent and bring him some coffee," Osborn said finally. "You don't need exertion, Smith, you need rest. Take the remainder of the day and we'll see you bright and early tomorrow."

"Sir, I'm alright, really—"

"Wait, Sir, aren't we on picket tonight?" Hower asked.

"Yes, but we'll just have to go without Smith," Osborn replied. "Get back to your tent, soldier, and that's final."

He walked away before Cate could make any further argument. The corporal glowered querimouniously and went back to swinging his hoe. Cate would have rolled her eyes at him, but it hurt her head, so she abandoned the effort.

Henry took her by her elbow and steered her to their squad's tent. He pulled aside the flap and held it while Cate stepped onto the earthen floor. It was dank and dismal inside the tent, the only light filtering in from the small hole where the solitary telescoping tent pole went out the top of the canvas along with the stovepipe. The only virtue of the Sibley tents was that they were equipped with conical stoves that fitted neatly under the tripod legs of the telescoping tent pole.

"Here, get set up on your gum blanket," Henry said, handing Cate her wool blanket and her knapsack that served as her pillow. "I'll be back with some coffee to warm you up."

"Trust me, Schaefer, being warm isn't the problem," she croaked, wiping her flushed face dry as she sat down heavily. Her hands shivered in defiance of her words and she glowered at them as Henry slung their blankets over her shoulders. Then, he took up the poker and opened the Sibley stove, stirring the coals banked inside.

"Smith!" Williamson popped his head into the tent, followed by his lanky frame. "Heard you weren't feeling well."

Cate shrugged. "Yeah."

"I brought you something to make you feel better," Williamson said. He folded himself up like a long-legged spider next to his own bedroll and dug into his haversack, pulling out his tin cup. He dug a folded handkerchief out of his greatcoat pocket and one by one lifted the corners to reveal some wilted green fronds.

Cate curled her lip.

Henry craned his neck to see. "What's that?"

"It's yarrow. Can you believe it's still green this late in the season? Kentucky, I tell ya." He shook his head as though anything about Kentucky could inspire wonderment. Cate felt like she should have been following, but she didn't know the first thing about plants.

"What's yarrow?" she croaked.

"Medicine," Williamson replied. "It's good for all sorts of stuff. It helps with colds, though it'd be better if we had the flowers instead of just the leaves."

"Yarrow? Never heard of it," Henry said.

Williamson blinked. "Really? Maybe it doesn't grow in Germany." He turned to Cate. "But you grew up here, didn't you? Didn't your mother give you cold remedies when you were sick?"

"I didn't have a mother," Cate said shortly. Williamson looked properly chastened, so she decided not to rub it in, even though sometimes, especially when she was feeling sorry for herself, it felt vindicating to do that. But she still felt like she'd been hit by a train, and at the end of the day, she wasn't about to turn down anything that might help. "I suppose my grandmother sometimes gave me elderberry cordial for a sore throat."

"Yeah, like that," Williamson said with a grin. "Elderberries are good too, but they're out of season. Yarrow should work just fine." He held out the handkerchief to her. Cate looked down at the fronds and stared for a moment.

"What am I supposed to do with it?"

Williamson pressed his lips together, as though he were disappointed in her ignorance but wasn't so rude as to show it. "Brew it into a tea, of course."

"Oh."

"Here—I'll brew it for you, since you're sick," Williamson said, standing. It was kind of him to cover for her ignorance. "I'll be right back."

The tent flap closed behind him, and Cate looked up sluggishly at Henry, who gave her his crooked little half-grin as he seated himself next to her.

"Are you warm enough?" he asked.

"I don't need a nursemaid."

"I know. I don't mind."

"You just want to get out of digging the rest of that ditch."

He snorted and shrugged. "Are you gonna lay down and see if you can't get some sleep?"

"In a minute." Her eyes were drawn to the tiny flames in the stove, licking up the sides of a half-charred log, returned to life after Henry had prodded them. She sniffed loudly and let her breath out of her mouth, as it wouldn't flow at all through her nose.

"I'm not sure what I expected from the front," Henry commented after a few minutes, "but it certainly wasn't this."

Cate's head sagged. "I know what you mean."

Henry leaned back on his hands. "I guess I thought there would be a lot more ... I don't know. Peril? Battle, courage, heroics, glory—you know, all that."

"I suppose that's just what they want you to think so you'll sign up."

"True." His mouth twisted wryly. "I don't suppose we'll be remembered for much if the rest of our service ends up like this."

"The Noble Second, protectors of railroad tracks and diggers of ditches," Cate proclaimed, her mirthless bark of a laugh devolving into a cough.

"The Sodden Guardians of Lebanon Junction," Henry added. The two of them laughed, because what else could one do? It had been two weeks of misery and there was no end in sight. It was perfectly reasonable to imagine they might spend Christmas in this slough, sitting and waiting for General Zollicoffer to stumble upon them for a skirmish. Of course, by then they would all be too sick and miserable to resist. Perhaps this was all part of the Confederate strategy...

"Did you hear the Union took Springfield?" Henry asked, scooting himself nearer to her. Their thighs touched.

Cate shook her head and pressed her leg against his. His touch was reassuring in a bone-deep way that made her wary. "Missouri?"

"Yes. A Hungarian by the name of Zagonyi leading the body-guard for General Fremont went rogue. He charged over two thousand rebels with only a hundred and fifty men. They won and raised the Union flag at the Springfield courthouse."

"See, why couldn't *we* have been sent to Springfield?" Cate lamented and let her head flop onto Henry's shoulder.

"That's what I want to know."

"Maybe then I'd be cutting down rebels instead of coughing up a lung."

"Don't feel too sorry for yourself."

"If I die in this mudheap without ever firing my weapon, disgraced and remembered only as that woman who couldn't even survive a month of army camp, I'll haunt every last one of you for the rest of your days."

"You're not going to die," Henry chided, pulling his arm around her and holding her comfortably against his side. "I'm honestly a little surprised you're being so dramatic. I imagined you would be more stoic after falling ill."

"No. If I am able to act stoic, then the misery I feel would be imagined, blown up out of proportion like an unreasonable ninny. I am no ninny—therefore, I am clearly dying."

Henry shot her a look. "Your logic is astounding." He let out a long sigh. "How long do you think we'll be stuck out here?"

"Until we all go mad and kill each other."

"I don't know, I'd be surprised if we were here much longer. It's not a very hospitable place for setting up winter camp. And what with everyone getting sick, I don't think it can really last that much longer."

Cate shrugged dully. "The odds of us being sent outside of Kentucky are mighty slim. Lebanon Junction, Louisville, or the Cumberland—it's all the same shithole as far as I'm concerned."

When she glanced up at him, she noticed his discontented expression and looked away into the fire. She was ashamed to be regarded by him that way, but not in any mood to be more pleasant.

"Do you think the war will be won quickly?" Henry asked, his voice carrying an attempt at ease that betrayed anxiety beneath.

"After that victory at Springfield, I suppose it might be. But Balls Bluff was a disaster, so perhaps not."

Henry groaned. "My brother was at Ball's Bluff. Apparently the Union's scouting party mistook a line of trees for tents and that's how it all started."

"That is utterly idiotic."

"But with blunders like that, perhaps we'll still have a chance to fight yet."

"I suppose that is one silver lining."

"Perhaps, if Springfield represents the success of the western front and Ball's Bluff the east, then we are under the command of the more intuitive leaders and are more likely to bring victory for the Union."

"That is very optimistic of you, but as you pointed out, the victory in Springfield was due to Major Ziggy-Zaggy taking the fate of the battle into his own hands in contradiction to his orders. So I have yet to see any impressive maneuvers coming from the top brass on any front."

"Nothing gets past you." His tone was deadpan and he lifted a brow at her. "And it's Zagonyi."

"Even at the edge of death, I'm still sharp as a tack."

This earned her a squeeze. She turned her face to press her nose against his chest, drawing in his warmth and his scent and his comfortable firmness.

"...Charley?" Henry's voice had gone down a level, both in volume and timbre.

"Mm?"

"...I've missed you these past few weeks."

"I know..." Cate sighed and kept her face pressed into Henry's chest, lest she dare look him in the eyes and attempt to make rational decisions. "Me too."

She could hear the thump of Henry's heart and how it paced a bit faster upon hearing her words. The shed in Pittsburgh seemed like a hundred years ago. It was a damned shame they'd had no opportunity to repeat it since. Even now, Williamson would be back any moment and shatter the tender longing sensation that rose up from her chest and choked her. She buried her head deeper until it passed.

"When this is all over— " Henry began, his fingers brushing through the drying curls at the nape of her neck. "When the war is won, I mean, what … um … what do you plan to do?"

Cate swallowed hard, and her throat sorely protested. This question felt like a trap, one for which it felt like there was a correct answer but one she had no idea what it was or whether it was even something she could imagine giving.

"I don't know," she said. It was true. Miserably true. She turned her head and shrugged. "Maybe I'll write a memoir."

Henry smiled. "*The Lady Soldier: A Memoir of the Fiercest Woman Since Joan of Arc.*"

"Well, that seems a little overindulgent."

"It'll sell well on the book flyers."

"What'll you do?" Cate couldn't help but watch his face from her vantage resting on his shoulder as she turned the tables on him.

"Hmm," he said, looking thoughtfully at the stove. The pause had barely stretched ten seconds, but Cate found she couldn't bear it.

"I suppose you'll go back to New Ulm," she cut in despite herself.

"Yes, I would want to go back there," he nodded. "See my parents and brothers."

"Maybe you'll become a famous tumbler, running a circuit around theaters across the country."

Henry burst out laughing, doubling over such that Cate was jarred from his shoulder and had to hold onto his bicep to steady herself. "Oh, that's hilarious, no, I'm nowhere near good enough to do anything like that. Besides, Turners aren't tumblers. The point is self-improvement, not to show off."

"How very humble of you," she replied and squeezed his arm appreciatively. He smiled and cast a fond look upon her.

"I suppose … if I survive to see the end of the war—"

"—Oh yes, that pesky contingency—"

"—I imagine I'll probably find a homestead—"

"Near New Ulm?" She knew she was interrupting, but she feared what he might dream of. What he might expect or not expect, both of which terrified her in equal measure.

"Yes, I suppose so. It would be good to be near like-minded people."

"Germans?"

"Freethinkers," he shrugged. "At least Turners. As I'm sure you've noticed from Krüger, not all Germans are cut from the same cloth."

"His cloth seems rather Catholic."

"Very."

Cate sat up and shook her head, smirking. "...I knew you were an Atheist."

Henry groaned. "I'm *not* an Atheist. I don't have any answers. I just want to ask questions."

"I'm sure," Cate replied, nodding with a skeptical brow and a jibing smirk.

"Aren't you too busy wasting away to give me trouble about my religion?"

"Ugh, don't remind me."

"Will you go back to dressing ... as you did before? When this is all over?"

Cate blinked. Her eyes slid over to his, and she said quite astonishedly, "I ... don't know."

Henry tilted his head to one side, but said nothing.

"I ... I suppose it all depends on what my conditions are after the war is done," she said. "If I'm caught and dishonorably discharged, I will likely have to return to my family." Her lip curled. "If I have no means of supporting myself, I'll have no choice."

"To your, uh, husband ...?"

"Richard, yes. My father won't give me safe harbor, I'm certain of that."

"But if you're not caught?"

"Then I will have more choices, I suppose. Continue on as I am now, find work elsewhere." A thought occurred to her and it made her giggle. "Perhaps I'll find myself a nice wife and stead a farm of my own."

Henry's eyes widened. "A *wife*??"

Cate laughed. "What? You know well enough a woman doesn't need a prick to enjoy herself."

"That's not what I meant." His brow was raised but his lips looked tense. "But 'need' is a strong word."

"I suppose so. And if I'm honest, I'd miss the damn things, but if it were a choice between living in secret as a man or having to whore myself, I'd bid the pricks a cheerful farewell and marry a nice young lady in disguise."

Henry was most comically caught between amusement, confusion, petulance, and quite possibly arousal. Cate desperately wished she didn't feel like she'd been forced through a laundry wringer. And also that they weren't in a tent that would be invaded with muddy, stinky comrades at any moment.

"It's odd," she said reflectively, trying to clear her throat rather than cough. "I don't really see myself as a man, doing hard physical labor for the rest of my life. But I can't see myself as a wife and mother either. And given I'm not independently wealthy like Susan Anthony, there doesn't seem to be a third option for me."

"The army suits you well enough."

"If we weren't bogged down here in Pitsville watching train tracks, it would."

Henry's expression was rueful and it puzzled Cate for a moment. It made her want to grip his face and kiss it away, but she didn't want to get him sick. Or herself caught. But she let the desire show in her expression anyway.

Tent canvas rustled and Cate looked down as Henry flinched back from her.

"Yarrow tea," Williamson announced as he climbed into the tent steaming tin cup first. "For the ailing soldier."

"Thanks," Cate croaked as she accepted the cup gingerly by the handle. The cup itself was scalding.

"You might want to let it cool off a bit first," Williamson admitted.

Cate breathed in the steam. She couldn't smell a thing, but the steam felt good on her throat in any case.

"We should let you rest," Henry said, shifting toward the tent flap. Cate pressed her lips together and nodded, feeling his warmth replaced with a bone-chilling draft.

"Thanks, Schaefer," she said. "And thanks, Williamson, for the tea."

"Don't mention it," Williamson replied with a little half-salute. The fellow really had no right to be so cheerful. Henry looked at her over his shoulder as he waited for Williamson to pass through the flap, his lips pinched in uncertainty.

"See you on the picket line," Cate said.

Henry frowned and shook his head. "Not if I can help it."

Cate stared at the tent flap long after he'd disappeared behind it, huddled into her blankets. She was making out pretty well today, all considered, if success was measured in the number of fellows nursing her ill health. Despite being stuck in a tent in a disease-ridden muck-hole in the middle of nowhere Kentucky, she thought it might have been the most she'd ever been looked after while being sick. She wasn't sure whether that reflected poorly on her upbringing or warmly on her comrades. Both, she supposed.

She blew on the edge of her cup and took a sip of the tea. It was bitter, but not wholly unpleasant. It felt good on her swollen throat.

"Hm," she murmured consideringly at the cup. It wasn't any hardship to drink the rest of the tea.

———

VI

Lebanon Junction, Kentucky
Sunday, November 10, 1861

CATE STOOD UNCOMFORTABLY AS men around her bowed their heads and prayed. She bowed her head too, of course, but her eyes remained stubbornly open. Losing one's faith never failed to be surreal. Indeed, it wasn't so long ago that her father had accused her of being a zealot. It had been scarcely five years since she'd fallen in hard with the Philadelphia Friends, though in hindsight she had fallen more *into* them, rather than in *with* them. The West Chester Quakers she'd grown up with had tolerated her better, though she supposed an outspoken grandchild of respectable parishioners wasn't nearly as threatening as an outspoken, unattached young woman on a tirade for woman suffrage and abolition. At any rate, the debacle in Philadelphia had been a lesson in the admonishing, underhanded, and very human nastiness that was and had always been her experience in organized religion. Not even God could help an unpalatable personality like hers.

Cate glanced to her left and caught Henry's eye. He was waiting for the prayer to be done too. He shot her a little quirk of a smile before rolling his eyes. She suppressed a grin and wondered what his Freethinker people were like. Were they as preachy against the gospel as so many were for it? She certainly didn't mind a bout of Biblical moralizing in the name of a good cause, but Henry had seemed to chafe at it when they'd talked about Jane Swisshelm. She imagined Henry's Freethinkers were probably just a bunch of arrogant, middle-aged men sitting around smoking cigars and tutting over how much smarter they were than everyone else. That's all any religion was. Why should anti-religion be any different?

At length, the chaplain's florid postulating on the state of their immortal souls concluded and they were sent off for a bit of leisure and dinner before afternoon drill. The squad was headed to picket duty that evening, so Cate splurged and bought an apple hand pie from an enterprising local at supper. The state of their rations were deplorable. If only she had known it could be this bad, she would have better appreciated the offerings at Fort Snelling. But here at the Junction, all they had available was coffee, a bit of hard tack, and whatever apples they could scavenge, which were few and far between given that most of the fall's crop had been carefully harvested by local farmers and were sold to the soldiers at an outrageous markup. Since they had not been visited by the paymaster yet despite being enlisted for nearly *five months*, Cate had only what remained of the money she'd made from selling her hair, which was dwindling to a mere handful of pennies after months of being nickel and dimed, first by the sutler at the Fort, and now the Janus-faced Kentuckians who both exploited unpaid labor and Union protection.

She was doing her best to ignore her grumbling stomach and the leftover rasp in her chest as she walked with the rest of the squad to picket duty when the sky opened up again, sending down a sheet of drizzling, cold rain.

"Oh no, come on!" Robinson shouted at the sky, his hands up in supplication.

The others hunched into their greatcoats and trudged down the footpath to the river's edge. The rain wasn't terrible by the time they made it to their stations, sheltered as they were among the trees, but the cold and damp had been their relentless companions since they'd arrived in cursed Lebanon Junction. There were only so many weeks one could spend with one's feet wet before one became irrationally grumpy about it.

They took up sentry positions staggered along the perimeter within shouting distance of one another, surveying their length of the riverbank and keeping an eye out for enemy mischief, which would presumably come from the opposite bank where reports put a rebel camp not 10 miles away, rumored to number 40,000 men. Except that they'd seen no evidence that that was even true and hadn't for weeks. Cate suspected that the numbers had been grossly exaggerated through word of mouth. Probably the distance too. Maybe it didn't exist at all. Maybe the entire report had been fabricated by command to motivate the troops to bear with the doldrums of Lebanon Junction.

The entire campaign at Lebanon Junction was to protect the railroad and the bridge that serviced it over the Rolling Fork river, the steep banks of which they were now stationed. Their officers had been singularly creative in the numerous ways they had found to describe how important their position here was, but the reality of it was, Cate was realizing, that they were wasted here. Freezing, wet, underfed and underskilled. As Robinson had most aptly put it, "Nothing to write home about. Nothing to leave home about."

It was miserable. Which was much how she felt as she acquired her position, leaned up against a nearby tree, letting out a long sigh. The sun had set, as far as she could tell through the thick clouds. They were in for a long, cold, wet night.

The pine needles were drier than the oak and cedar leaves that had all but turned to mulch in the wet, so Cate took up under a Virginia pine. She sniffed under her collar. Soggy wool, a familiar musk, but she didn't smell terribly bad. Before she'd gotten ill, she'd chucked her stays into the river in a fit of pique during the wee hours of picket duty. The tight-confines of the garment were a comforting shield for her chest, but they prohibited a standing bath. Which was the only kind of bath they could have in this godforsaken place. So she'd tossed them, and now she could enjoy scrubbing with freezing water under her shirt in the Sibley tent with the rest of the fellows. It was more risk than she'd been willing to take in the barracks, but by this point, no one even looked twice at her. Lots of fellows washed modestly under their shirts—it was too damn cold to strip into their birthday suits anyways.

Getting rid of the stays had been the right call, but she missed them something fierce. It felt so strange to have her shirt moving across her chest as she bent and moved; she was used to fabric being quite affixed. Her skin was better able to breathe, but she felt exposed all of the time, even when the many layers of shirt and waistcoat and sack coat and greatcoat made her more wool than human. That, and her back was sore. Ever since she'd first budded breasts, she'd worn some sort of rigid garment that gave firm support around her waist, back, and chest. Without it, her muscles throbbed with fatigue.

All that was going to become inconsequential in comparison with managing her impending monthly courses in this crowded dungheap. They were due any day. It wasn't uncommon for fellows to go off into the woods to seek a little privacy, and to avoid the stinking soldier sinks the Illinois regiment had left for them. But it felt exposed out in the woods, especially since she was affixing new rags in her trousers and wanted to keep her shirttails clear of the whole thing. Once the blood came, she was going to have a doozy of a time sneaking away to keep clean. At least the light blue trousers were now so streaked with mud, any other stains wouldn't be too obvious.

It didn't bear thinking about why her monthly courses hadn't come yet. They weren't terribly late, and she was sure her illness had interrupted her cycle somehow, but she couldn't help but wonder if her moment of weakness in that Pittsburgh shed was enough to set her on a path of imminent doom. It couldn't possibly, could it? Not after months of managing to avoid a baby when Richard insisted on spending inside her. She'd washed and fretted and used alum rinses and it had worked. There was no way Henry would succeed where Richard had so continuously failed when they'd done it only a day after her courses were through. Was there?

It didn't bear thinking about, one way or the other. Thinking about it sure wouldn't make the blood come. Cate pulled out her boot knife and started scraping away at a branch with it, for want of something to do.

She'd taken to humming "John Brown's Body" under her breath when she heard the soft squish of boots in the wet leaves above the steady beat of raindrops. She looked up sharply and lifted her pointy stick like a rifle. "Who's there?"

"Whoa, Charley, it's me." Henry appeared from behind a tree. "And you're supposed to say 'Halt.'"

The warmth that glowed in her chest didn't bear thinking about either. "Aren't you supposed to be at your position?"

"Yeah, but I can't see anything different than what you and Webster can see, so I thought I'd come downriver for a bit."

Cate tried not to smile. She really did her level best. But sitting in the rain watching the darkness for nothing was slightly less dismal with company, and Henry's company was admittedly the best of the squad. Even with his trousers on. Oh, to hell with it. She grinned.

"What are you making?" Henry asked as he leaned against the tree at Cate's side and bumped their shoulders together.

"A sharp stick," Cate replied, proffering it to Henry. He accepted it and inspected it lightly.

"Fearsome," he drawled. Cate looked up at his crooked smirk and wondered what the rain would taste like if she licked it off his chin. He hadn't shaved in a few days. It would be rough.

Henry offered the stick back to her with an eyebrow raised, and she shook her head, flustered that some of what she was thinking might have been visible on her face. He shrugged and took the stick in his hands, considering it. Then he gripped it in one hand and launched it at a nearby tree like a spear. It ricocheted off the trunk, chips of bark flying as the stick and its shrapnel skittered to the ground.

Cate watched for a long moment before she snorted.

"I can't imagine why," she laughed, "but I thought you were about to reveal some sort of ... of *spear* proficiency."

Henry grinned. "There are some Turners who throw javelins."

"But clearly not you!"

He managed an embarrassed chuckle. "I told you I wasn't any good."

Cate turned, her eyes darting around the woods for a moment as she pulled herself against his chest. She bit her lip and craned toward him, his soft breath on her cheek erasing unsubstantiated fears and doubts.

"Hell," Henry said hoarsely, hands settling on her waist. "Maybe I should take up javelin."

"Why?" Cate asked. "I thought you weren't any good?"

His lips quirked at the corners. His hands pulled at her belt, pressing her full against him. "I just like to hear you laugh."

Cate hummed. Her fingers gripped his coat, and she pressed her lips to his. After weeks of cold, of sickness and damp and misery, the memory of his kiss melding with reality drove a hot wedge of longing into her belly. Any lingering shoulds or better-nots seared away. She couldn't help releasing a little moan of relief, and he pressed his advantage as her lips parted, pulling her in with a hand at her nape.

A crack of underbrush, quiet but distinct, caught her ear, and Cate pushed away hard, just as Williamson sidled into view from the opposite direction that Henry had come from.

"What? No one told me we were partnering up," Williamson said as he approached. Cate froze her face in her sternest expression and forced herself to assume he didn't mean romantically. Of course he didn't. Don't be absurd.

"We're not," she said, sparing a glance at Henry, who was doing an excellent job of looking awkward and guilty while leaning against a tree. He pushed a hand over his mouth as if wiping her kiss away, like Williamson might see the imprint of her mouth left on his. Cate couldn't decide if his fumbling transparency was more irritating or endearing. "Schaefer was just making the rounds and we got to chatting."

Just chatting. Face to face. With their mouths touching.

"Oh, okay." Williamson's eyes darted between them for a moment.

Cate was struck by a fit of inspiration. Surely, Williamson could easily be scared off. Because she was shameless, plain and simple, and she wanted Henry to herself. Now. "Say, since you're here, maybe you can give us your take. Schaefer and I are at an impasse and we could use someone to break it."

Williamson shrugged. "Sure."

Henry glanced at her. Cate smirked.

"The chaplain talked a whole lot this morning about patriotism and loyalty to authority, but I'm wondering to what degree does God wish us to do that? A few weeks ago a General Zaggy..."

"Zagonyi," Henry supplied exasperatedly.

"Yeah, that. He refused to obey orders and took Springfield for the Union. So we were discussing the nature of loyalty..." She flagged for a moment. Henry picked up the thread.

"Right, the nature of loyalty and whether it is more patriotic to follow orders and keep to the plan or to cause chaos just to see some action."

"You're stacking it, Schaefer. The question is whether it is more patriotic to do what you believe is the right thing for the cause or to blindly obey orders."

Williamson blinked. Cate and Henry watched him expectantly.

"I, uh..." Williamson shrugged awkwardly. "I don't know that I'd strictly know any better than the folks in charge."

"The folks in charge are men just like any of us," Cate countered. "We're *all* young and inexperienced. What makes them know any better than us?"

"Some of them *are* older and fought in the Mexican War—" Henry pointed out. The fact that he was playing along—and much more smoothly than Cate anticipated—made her stomach curl with pleasure like a dog on a hearth.

"—But they're still making us sit in mud for weeks on end, for what?" Cate charged on. Williamson shrank somewhat. He'd never been much for debate, which was exactly why this was going to work.

"Well, they've got a lot more information about the lay of the land than we do," Henry cut in. Cate turned to face him.

"We could too if anyone would tell us what's going on," she shot back.

"I'm sure there's no reason we need to worry about it," Williamson begged off. "I'm gonna go check on the Corporal."

Cate nodded absently and continued to barrel on about the dangers of too much authority concentrated at the top. Henry countered her as Williamson shrank back the way he came. When he was well out of sight, Henry seized her by the waist and pressed his mouth against hers. His lips were cold and wet and soft, and Cate went silent and pliant in his embrace. His unshaven chin scraped against hers, and it sparked sensation like flint on steel.

When Henry parted from her, he laughed. "Quick thinking, Smith."

Cate shrugged. "I'm not about to spend the rest of the night speculating with Williamson about whatever's going on at home."

"Yeah. We left for a reason."

"Just write them a letter!"

"I actually think replies aren't coming through. Robinson is losing his mind over how many letters he receives compared to how many he sends, and Webster has been having the same issue too."

"Ugh, Schaefer, stop being so generous and understanding."

"Sorry, I'll try to be more unflinchingly judgmental."

"Thank God."

They kissed for a while against the tree, murmuring about how much they'd missed each other and how stupid the other was, which was absurd but enjoyable nonetheless. Henry was just snaking his hands under Charley's sack coat when she pushed them apart.

"We already almost got caught," Charley apologized. "I don't want to push our luck."

Henry scarcely heard her. "Charley—what you got on underneath here?" He wriggled his hands back under her coat and caressed up and down her back to check.

Charley's lips curled up with mischief. "I've expanded my options."

"What's that supposed to mean?" Henry complained, his fingers splayed across her spine. "You mean to tell me you're bare under your shirt?"

"I've thrown those damned dirty stays in the river, but it's hardly any of your—"

"Oh, I'll make it my business." His hands rounded her ribs and shoved up under her waistcoat, cupping soft, pliant flesh in his palms.

"Stop," she said, and she was breathless and dreamy-eyed, but he obeyed nonetheless. Henry looked down scant inches, his eyes dark and lust-blown, and she wished for what seemed like the millionth time for some goddamned privacy.

"We could go down the bluff to the bank," he whispered. "Out of sight of the picket."

"We'll be missed. Or drowned in the high waters. Or shot as enemies. You know I can't take you quietly."

Henry pressed his forehead against hers and groaned. "You'd do well to work on that."

"I would if I had any chance to practice."

"God, I want you again."

"You have no idea how very much I concur," she whispered in his ear. Her voice was thready, her wanting plain. She pressed her thigh against the growing bulge in his trousers. "You know Osborn will check on us soon. You'd better get back to your post."

Henry inhaled sharply, seizing his self-control back, albeit quite reluctantly. "Fine, yes." But he kissed her hard instead of retreating, with his hand tight around the back of her neck and her hands clutched tight in his jacket.

It was yet another few minutes before he managed to withdraw.

———

The rain came down harder and harder. After a few hours and several quick jaunts back to Henry's post for Osborn's rounds, they ended up sitting together under Cate's tree, whose frail, brown leaves pretended to be enough to shield them from the cold bullets of rain.

"Did you ever read about that speech the Reb Vice President gave earlier this year?" Cate asked, her head resting back on the bark of the tree. They were soaked to the bone. She wouldn't be surprised if they all woke up sick again in the morning.

"Who?"

"The Reb's vice president. It was right before Fort Sumter, so it got blasted from the headlines. He said that the cornerstone of their confederacy is the so-called 'great truth that the Negro is not equal to the white man.' That slavery and subordination to the superior race is his natural state." Cate looked down at the faint glitter of river water rushing beneath the bluff. The rain flashed in sheets in the wind. "They cheered for him so loud, no one could hear him over the din. And I hate them for it. I *hate* them, Henry. I think them less human, for believing that the enslaved are less human. So what does that make me?"

Henry regarded her thoughtfully. "A valkyrie."

She smacked him in the chest, harder than was strictly playful. "Please do go to hell."

"Only if you take me." She glowered, but his eyes were still twinkling in the darkness.

"I mean it," she insisted. "I cannot hate people for hating people. It makes me become what I detest. And yet, here I am, chomping at the bit to shoot them, and I cannot get myself to feel even a little bit bad about it." She buried her face in her knees.

The tree bark scraped as Henry leaned forward, his broad palm resting lightly on her shoulder. "Do you believe there is a force for justice?"

Cate snorted. "No."

"I do. But it's not divine, Charley. It's just all of us, together. Mankind, banded together by a common cause, fighting to make our dreams of justice a reality."

"Heathen." His hand dropped away. She missed it.

"It's not God. It's only us."

"You sure have a way of making folks feel hopeful." She looked over at him. His posture mirrored hers, hunching over his knees to stay warm. "No wonder no one's ever heard of your little Freethinker group."

"What sort of benevolent God would let children be sold from their mothers?" Henry replied quietly. "Let humans mutilate and defile each other? Answer some prayers but not others? That's not benevolence."

Cate held her breath and with it, the fear his words inspired in her chest. You could take the man out of the church, but it was very difficult to take the church out of the man. She assumed it was guilt she felt, but when she tentatively scratched the surface, she found the guilt flowing from the fact that she rather agreed with him. And that was … a bit terrifying. She looked up at him wide-eyed.

"If there is a God," Henry continued, "he doesn't give a damn about us. We're on our own. So yeah, you are a valkyrie. You will choose on the field of battle who will die. You will use your bayonet and your rifle to personally escort those sinners to hell. Because if we don't do it, no one else will."

Cate flinched as she swallowed down his words. The memory of the mobs prowling St. Anthony to restore Eliza Winston to slavery came to her mind. She swallowed thickly against the prickle in her eyes and cleared her throat.

"What is it?" Henry asked.

Cate tried to shrug the emotion out of her voice. "My father's a Free-Soiler. He thinks he's anti-slavery, but he doesn't give a damn about what happens to people, as long as they don't bother him. Remember the freedom suit of Eliza Winston?"

"Of course."

"My father was in the mob searching for her to restore her to her master. He raided our free Black neighbors' house looking for her. Because they'd helped her file her freedom suit."

It had been more than a year since that happened. It seemed forever ago and also just yesterday. She recalled the hard eyes of Emily Grey, standing outside her house in the rain holding her infant son. Toussaint died shortly after that raid. He should never have been forced to stand out in the rain—none of them should have. Perhaps instead of screaming at her father, making everything about her anger with him, Cate could have done some good by sheltering the family in her own home. Perhaps she could have had some real courage, instead of false bravado.

Cate risked looking up at Henry.

"That's horrible," Henry said. "What a hypocrite."

"That's my father," Cate managed on her exhale. God, it was such a relief to be understood. He listened and he cared and she was never going to be able to stop looking at him like she was right at that moment. Like he was some sort of wild thing, something precious and rare. Like if she made too swift a movement, he'd dart away. Evaporate like a mist. Because he couldn't possibly be real.

"Look at us," Cate let out a mirthless chuckle. "We're not debating to get rid of Williamson anymore. We just can't help ourselves, can we?"

Henry shrugged. "It's interesting."

"It's people's lives," Cate groaned. "Who cares what we think, looking in from the outside?"

"The Union Army, I suspect, even if it's just to make sure we're fighting for them."

"I sincerely doubt most soldiers are concerned about the moral implications of their enlistment. Or if they are, they're more worried about whether it's justified to wage war to prevent secession. Most people I've met don't give a damn whether the slaves are freed. If the Winston case was any indication, they actively don't want them to be. At least not if it would hurt their bottom line."

"Do you really think so?"

Cate shrugged helplessly. "I know so. I saw it happen."

"Is that why you ran away?"

Cate frowned and glanced up at Henry. He looked like he was holding his breath, frozen like he was afraid he'd spook her if he moved. She hadn't told him her reasons—not in so many words. He knew a lot already. He knew about Richard and her abolition sentiments and her extradition from the Quakers. But she'd never told him how it all went together.

"No," she admitted. "I wish it was. But no."

Henry waited while she gathered her thoughts. It took a long time. The roar of the river and the hammering of rain drowned out any other sounds and made it hard to think. She had official reasons why she left. She could have easily let him believe the reasons he'd already suggested. But she didn't want to. She found herself sitting on the cold ground, shivering a bit, and longing to tell him the whole truth. Not because she had to, but because she wanted to.

"I ..." she began. "I mean, you know my marriage was bad. I had to get out of that." She could feel his questions screaming silently at her through his gaze. "But that doesn't explain why I had to disguise myself. Or enlist."

She exhaled deeply. "I wanted to help the war effort and complained about that for months. As soon as it started, really. But when I decided to run away, enlistment wasn't ... in the forefront of my mind."

Henry's brows furrowed. He hummed encouragingly, bless him.

"I just ... I didn't want to keep spinning in the same typhoon I'd been trapped in for so long. Even if I left Richard and went farther west or something, I'd still be a woman on her own. A person lacking the proper distinction. The proper *supervision*. Scraping by doing odd jobs. I can't whore. I'm terrified of the prospect and it feels like such an inevitability if I were to try and be on my own with no money and no friends. But if I were a man? I could work lumber or stead a farm or learn the law. Henry, there are so many more choices when I put on trousers."

Cate searched his eyes desperately. She was terrified he was going to be upset by her utter lack of femininity and moral resolve. But he wasn't taken aback. He was nodding. Waiting for her to continue.

"So I just ... pulled a suit of clothes from the laundry and I ran. I sold my hair and my dress and when I walked down the street, people stepped out of my way and ..." She shoved her hands into her hair, knocking her cap askew as she buried her face in her knees. "And it felt so good. It felt right, you know?"

Henry hummed, and Cate dared to peek out at him. He was nodding.

"I still can't imagine you in a dress," he said plainly.

"It wasn't a pretty picture, Schaefer. I was pretty pitiful."

"I don't know about that, because I think you're very—"

"—Don't start." She rolled her eyes. "The Second Regiment gave me the path, the route to escape. What had been a fantasy became a tangible plan. And I realized I could finally do something useful, fight for something I believed in. Or fight against something I detested, more like."

Henry hummed again, this time with the corners of his mouth curling up. "That's a sight better than me. I only enlisted because I wanted to prove to my family I was worth something. And then I didn't even get in on my first try."

"You did eventually, though. And you're better equipped than most of us to do the job and do it well." Cate cast a significant glance on his arms and shoulders that made him look down bashfully.

"And I do believe in abolition and amalgamation. Those causes do drive me, fill me with some fighting spirit. But I'd be a liar if I said I was here for noble reasons. I was trying to prove myself to my father. It's really nothing more complicated than that."

"And he's proud of you."

"He is. But, to be entirely honest, by the time I got that letter, I'd all but forgotten them. I didn't miss them. I still don't. I could have written them for months, but I avoided them." He sighed. "I just needed to get away from them all. Be my own man."

"I'm glad you didn't get into the First Regiment." Cate took a deep breath. "Because, even though you would have seen many battles by now, we would have never met. And I'm … really very glad we did." Cate pointedly looked at the ground. She wasn't sure she could face his feelings if they were anything other than mutual. His hand squeezed her shoulder.

"I'm very glad we met too."

Cate squirmed for a moment, twitching with discomfort under the mantle of mutual affection.

"I mean," she blurted, "if you'd ended up in the First Minnesota, you might have gone off to the front a virgin and ended up dying having never known the pleasures of the flesh." It had sounded funny and disarmingly charming in her head. Her head had been *wrong*.

Henry looked at her as though trying to decide if he was annoyed or amused. "If I had, you would have faced the same fate."

Cate scoffed. "My flesh has known pleasures!"

He peered at her sidelong with incredulity. "At the hand of anyone else, though?"

She thought about his hands, broad and callused and eager to learn how to please her. It was a good thing it was dark, because her face was probably bright red. "Fine. Fair point."

His grin lit up his face, and he leaned into her, grasping her cheek in his palm as he pulled himself closer. His lips dodged hers, pressing kisses to her temple, her other cheek, her ear, the side of her neck. He teased her with teeth and tongue as her breath caught in her throat. She gasped, "What about the others?"

"I'm just kissing," Henry murmured into her neck. Poppycock. He wasn't just kissing. He was seducing. Quite effectively. God, he was a quick study. She thought she'd better stop him, for propriety or something, but his touch was the only thing warm enough to cut through the bitter cold and relentless wet. He pushed his hands over her chest and she arched into his touch, pleasure tightening to firm points. God, she wanted his hands on her bare skin. She wanted him naked. In a damned *bed*. With a proper fire and proper privacy. And time. And *contraception*. She wanted to ride his cock, stretch herself around him, make him shake with pleasure. She was about to tell him all of this, to whisper it hotly in his ear, when the ground shook with an unholy crash. She couldn't help it—she yelped in surprise as Henry sprang wildly to his feet.

"What's that?" he shouted. The rain battered his cheeks as the din continued, a creaking, groaning roar. It was so loud, it was difficult to determine where it was coming from. It felt like it was everywhere. Cate scrambled to her feet, unprepared for how heavy her greatcoat had become with rainwater. She stood in stillness for a moment, trying to overcome the confusion and fear and adrenaline to figure out what was going on. All at once, her mind coalesced.

"The bridge!" she exclaimed, snatching up her rifle. Henry seized his as well, and they waded up the mud-slick footpath toward where Williamson was positioned.

When they found him, Osborn was there too, with Krüger, and Robinson, who was shouting that the Rebs must have launched a cannon at the bridge or something.

"Robinson, calm down," Osborn ordered uselessly, then gave up and turned to Henry and Cate. "It's the water. It's been rising all week and this storm flooded the river too fast."

He stepped toward the bluff and pointed down where the water churned thick with clay and splinters of logs. Logs that had once been the bridge they'd been sent here to protect. Cate blinked against the rainwater dripping into her eyelashes and stared down into the rapids.

"What?" she asked uselessly as Webster and Hower dashed toward them.

"Was it Rebs? What's going on?" Hower exclaimed, holding his rifle at the ready.

"Christ, Corporal, stand down," Osborn said, agitated by the rifle pointed in his general direction. "It was just the river flooding with rainwater."

"What the hell are we doing guarding a bridge that was about to collapse the moment a little rain came!?" Cate heard the bellow and realized belatedly that it was coming from her. "We've been squatting here for weeks, men dropping like flies to illness! Company C's Lieutenant *died* for Christ's sake! For what!?"

She dragged her hands over her face, dashing rainwater away only for it to be replaced in seconds. "Why? All the Rebs had to do was wait for some *fucking rain*?"

Henry stepped to her side and put his hand on her shoulder. She jerked away and whirled toward Osborn, squaring her chest. "What the hell have we been doing, building earthworks and digging ditches? We should have been shoring up that hell-be damned *bridge!*"

The others stared at her pointed finger. Williamson held his own arms and shifted uncomfortably. Robinson still appeared to be reeling from his certitude that it was an attack. Webster's mouth was set grimly as he looked from Cate to Osborn and back again. Instead of rallying their ire, she'd made them all uncomfortable.

Osborn's mustache quivered, but his voice was calm. "I don't know, Smith. We'll have to report back and see what they say."

Cate shook her head. "*They* won't tell us anything."

"You're right," he replied calmly. "They probably won't."

Cate opened her mouth to give him a piece of her mind.

"—Smith," Osborn cut in. "I'm just a Sergeant. I don't know what you want me to say."

Her face tensed, bracing against the fury that wanted to geyser out of her. Fury at the incompetence of this entire outfit. Fury at Kentucky for being such a miserable contradiction. Fury at the long days of drill and mud and damp straw, chipping away at her resolve. Fury of her continued powerlessness, a different flavor certainly than the kind she had always known, but powerlessness nonetheless. And fury at herself for having so little self-control; at her own body for wanting Henry so much, for holding the monthly confirmation of her safety back from her. She'd given up *so much* for this. So damn much. She walked every day with the risk of getting caught, getting court-martialed, getting killed or dying by some horrific disease. And it was all just the same demon by another name.

———

VII

Thursday, November 28, 1861

Henry was bedüdelt. While Smith had a point about Kentucky's relative lack of any redeeming qualities, there was one thing it had in spades: apple jack. And if one were to imbibe in any amount of apple jack, surely a frigid Thanksgiving spent in the summer palace of the Sibley tent was the appropriate occasion. Especially since the feast was naught but their usual stale bread and coffee, with the benevolent addition of a rangy baked chicken and apples.

The squad was arranged around a smoking tallow lantern in a circle, passing a glass bottle obtained from a nearby distillery through thoroughly unapproved means. Shadows danced across the tent walls. What little light there was flickered over their faces, casting the squad in grotesque shadow forms of themselves. Men were increasingly arrested for breaking the camp rules, which was entirely due to those rules being arbitrary and idiotic. In the dank, mud-slick camp, one had to find fun wherever one could.

The evening had unspooled efficient evidence as to who could hold their liquor, as Jacob Robinson, Williamson, and Osborn were now collapsed together singing "Battle Hymn of the Republic" at an unbearable level. They were wrapping up yet another chorus when Williamson went green and scrambled out of the tent to deposit the contents of his stomach in one of the drainage ditches. He wasn't the first of the night either. After so many weeks of salt pork and beans, coffee and hard bread, their stomachs were uneasy with fresh food.

"Hey Leute, let's play Cerevis," Krüger shouted, brandishing his worn deck of cards with one hand. Several of the others grumbled (nearly two months with nothing to do but play euchre with Krüger did that to one), and Henry furrowed his brow and replied, "How do you propose they do that if they don't speak German?"

Krüger laughed and said, "They drink—that's the point, natürlich."

Elias cast a wary sidelong look at Krüger and made a point of engaging Webster in describing his children in excruciating detail, which he was near desperate to do whenever a little alcohol was in his cup. It took scarcely any effort to engage Webster in this topic, especially when he had alcohol in his cup, but the gesture was so obviously self-sacrificing, it was essentially equivalent to giving Krüger the cut direct.

It occurred to Henry that if Osborn weren't so sloshed himself, they would be subjected to quite a lot of trouble, as their post was one considered by the top brass as constantly under potential threat. But the generals weren't at Lebanon Junction, so how would they know that nothing interesting ever happened here? Tempting fate by enjoying a few bottles of apple jack between them was hardly a risk, given they'd spent the better part of two months here doing a whole lot of nothing. Besides, it was Thanksgiving. If they didn't have a feast to pour their gratitude upon, they might as well pay three cheers to Bacchus and make do with what they had.

Henry laughed at Krüger. "Niemand will spielen, mein Freund."

Krüger glowered and rose, moving his bulk awkwardly toward the tent flap. He was larger and took his alcohol with more dignity, but the effect was still evident in the way his feet seemed to slide beneath him.

"Have it your way," Krüger grumbled. "Dich brauche ich nicht mehr."

Elias' eyes followed Krüger and once he was gone, muttered, "Good riddance."

Webster frowned disapprovingly at him, to which Elias justified, "There's only so many times a man can bear being trounced in card games before he learns not to play with that fellow anymore."

"Krüger 'as a gamblin' pro'lem," Williamson said gravely, though his hiccup rather undercut the intended gravity.

Henry's eyes cast to Charley, who sat nearby, frowning into the neck of the rapidly depleting bottle. Her eyes were half-buried beneath her thick, dark brows and her lips were pursed thoughtfully in a way that made Henry lament how long it had been since he'd kissed them.

In the weeks since the bridge collapsed, Charley had changed. He wasn't sure what he'd done or why she pulled away, but it was happening. It was subtle too. Little things, like she'd sit across from him rather than next to him. She'd provide clipped responses instead of engaging in conversation with him. His jokes landed flat. Something was wrong, and Henry couldn't figure it out. He'd cataloged their guard duty in the rain before the bridge collapsed, and he couldn't discover anything he'd done that would deserve such a direct cut from her. Maybe it was how he'd pressed physical advances? But he'd stopped as soon as she'd asked him to. Didn't he? Surely she couldn't resent him for that. And he'd kissed her, just before the bridge had gone down. She'd been so responsive—pliant, even. If she'd resented him for his advances earlier, why welcome him so clearly later? It made no sense. She'd been more open with him than ever before. Told him things they'd never discussed before. What could he have done? Trying to parse it out now, after a good dram of apple jack heated his blood, seemed futile.

"Something in there giving you trouble?" Henry asked, leaning in toward Charley and realizing a little belatedly that he was leering.

Smith winced at his sharp cider breath and passed the bottle to him. "Nope. Just need to breathe some fresh air that won't get me any drunker."

Smith rose and followed Krüger's path from the tent. Henry blinked at the spot she'd disappeared through.

"Are you going to drink that or pass it on?" Elias asked covetously.

Henry shook his head and passed the bottle, then got unsteadily to his feet and went out the flap after Smith.

His hot breath split the crisp wintery air as he stepped out. His neck swiveled, looking for where Smith had headed. The railroad and the Junction Hotel, which were the only permanent structures for miles, rose up to his right while the rows of Sibley tents flowed in front of him and to the left. He caught sight of Smith nimbly picking her way around the drainage ditches they'd dug there, moving between the tents to the far side of the field, where a stand of trees marked the end of the camp. Henry gathered himself, doing his best to stride steadily after Smith.

He caught up near the edge of the camp, where Company I's tents butted up to the treeline and gave way to the well-trod path to the picket line.

"Can I help you?" Smith snapped, whirling around to face him.

Henry stumbled a step back. "I was just—"

"Just what?"

"Wondering where you were off to..."

"Sure," she hissed, glancing aside for observers. "Perhaps you'd be more convincing if you weren't so sottish."

Henry leveled a chagrined look at her, crossing his arms across the buttons of his greatcoat. Smith looked the few inches up at him and scowled, crossing her arms in reflection of him. They glared at each other for a few moments at the edge of the woods. Slowly, Smith's scowl melted to reveal a more exposed expression, one that reminded him that Charley was still there, lurking beneath the prickly exterior. It was too dark to see her properly, but he could have sworn he read fear in her eyes.

"What's going on?" he asked, dropping his arms from his chest and taking a step toward her.

Her lips were pressed into a thin line and her brow furrowed, her dark eyes studying him from under them. Then she looked off behind him, her eyes surveying the tents with the same inscrutability with which she'd searched him.

"None of it will matter, will it?" she whispered. Henry's head jerked in surprise.

"None of what?"

"This!" she exclaimed, sweeping her arms to indicate the camp, the tents glowing from within while the muddy ditches crossing between them sparkled faintly with ice and frost. She shoved her hand through her hair, taking a deep breath, and then replaced her cap. "Keeping a train line open to the Union so we may route supplies to troops so we may maneuver to cut off the Rebels so that we may force them back into our Union so that we may—what? Go on just as we had before?"

"Where is this coming from?"

Charley's lips moved for a moment, piecing words together, then wiped her hands over her face. "Goddammit—it's everything! Rumors going on about how the blockade might abolish slavery without the Union needing to do a damn thing. This government doesn't want to speak up for justice. They want to keep walking that line, taking with both hands as they did for almost a hundred years, never having to take a stand for anything! We saw how well that worked, now didn't we?"

Henry blinked. "Are you telling me you are under such great personal duress because of a rumor?"

She growled at him. "It's not just the rumor. It's this damnable post and this morally-bereft state, and ... and ..."

Charley looked up and her angry brows wavered. Henry stepped forward and curled her cold hands into his.

"I'm just so angry," she whispered, her expression strained. "Everyone gave up so much to be here. I just want to make a *goddamned* difference. Dammit, Henry. What are we doing?"

"You gave up a great deal to be here."

"Not like Robinson. He left his new bride at home. Or Webster, with his wife and children, good Lord. Three years from now they might not even remember him."

"No, you gave up more. Because not only did you leave everything you had behind, you never even got to say goodbye." Henry squeezed her freezing fingers tight. "You stand to lose a great deal more if you're discovered, too. You take on just as much risk as the rest of us, but it's that much more because of who and what you are." Damn, apple jack made him earnest. He was leaning into her, hands joined, and he wanted to close the distance and kiss her, right behind one of Company I's tent raucous with their own elicit whiskey and Thanksgiving revels.

Her eyes skittered away, like it was an effort to hold his gaze. "I don't know if I can keep doing this."

Henry flinched, his hands dropping hers. "What, you mean—"

"Any of it," she agonized. "Maybe the army doesn't suit me so well. Maybe I'm not cut out for this kind of life. Maybe I've been a fool, and I'm dragging my whole life into the mire—and for what? Some half-baked idea of justice and displaced vengeance that will never be realized? Because you're wrong, Henry. There is no force of justice in the world, divine nor man-made. One can work and work and work and never see the fruits of one's labor. Fate doesn't care if you're righteous or wicked—it tests us all the same."

"I ... I don't understand. What's happened?"

"Nothing. That's the problem." She tried to keep her face hard, but it broke. The soft firelight glow of the tents glinted against tears gathering in the corners of her eyes.

"What can I do?" Henry's voice sounded more desperate than he'd like. She spread her hand over her face and grimaced with the effort to hold her expression firm. It hurt to see her like that, sobered him more than the cold ever could.

She took a trembling breath and her mouth pressed into a thin white line. "Just go," she said. "Leave me alone."

"But, Charley, I—"

"That's not my name."

She turned and stalked off down the path to the picket line. Henry stood, stunned, at the edge of the wood, the euphoric bubbling of apple jack in his veins going flat. He couldn't understand what had happened, but the tightness around his chest made him certain that something significant had changed. Something that hurt deeply, that frightened Charley—or whatever her real name was. He hadn't worried much about that before. Perhaps he should have. If he cared for her so deeply, should he not have wanted to know her true Christian name? He may have wasted away any chance he might have had to find out.

VIII

Lebanon, Kentucky
Monday, December 9, 1861

CATE WAS CERTAIN IT would make her feel better to get on the train, to travel across the endless Kentucky countryside to a new post, to get away from that shithole railroad junction. She sat on the hard bench in the train car, surrounded by other soldiers talking and jesting and carousing, waiting for the relief to come. But it didn't.

Night had fallen by the time they boarded and the landscape was nothing more than vague shadows outside of the darkened train. Heavy gray clouds obscured the moon and after several hours, snow began to fall in thick, fat flakes. Henry sat with Robinson on a bench across the way and a few rows forward. Their conversation was lost in the din, but they were pointing out the window at something.

He'd listened to her, for once. They hadn't spoken more than two words in a week and a half. It hurt and she missed him, but it was no more than she deserved. She should never have sought his company in the first place. The weakness she harbored for him was indeed going to be her undoing.

The train chugged eastward, toward the location of their winter camp at Lebanon, Kentucky. The small town had been selected by General Thomas as his headquarters for the Army of the Ohio and a vast force was ordered to winter there on the outskirts of town. They rode on the line for a few hours, departing from Lebanon Junction as soon as the Third Minnesota Regiment had arrived to relieve them. The news of their arrival had been the only thing keeping Cate's head above the murky depths of despondency.

Cate shifted in her seat. As much as getting rid of her stays had convenienced her as far as keeping relatively clean in close quarters, her lower back and shoulders still ached. Her back wasn't used to supporting her weight all on its own. Drilling was especially tiring. Part of her worried that she was showing evidence of the implicit weakness of women, made plain by her body's inability to perform without a support garment, but she'd left herself without an alternative. It had been improving—before this cursed uncomfortable train ride—so she hoped it was a matter of getting accustomed and nothing more.

The train began to slow, and she leaned out her southerly-facing window—no more than an opening in the side of the train—catching sight of a shadowed train depot up ahead. There was a small cluster of brick buildings beyond it, the epitome of a Western train town. The candle-lit windows stood in stark relief against the rolling hills of farmland. There were some higher areas, some shadowed hills and gulches, to the south, but otherwise the landscape held hardly anything with which it might distinguish itself.

Steam poured from the engine and engulfed the station platform as the train ground to a halt. Cate stood from the wooden bench and shouldered her knapsack, falling in among the others. Her stomach clenched in response to the movement, and she couldn't tell if she was hungry, ill, or having some sort of stomach cramp. Probably some combination of all three. She had lost hope that it was a sign of her monthly courses. Those had been late for several weeks now, and she was beginning to resign herself to the idea that ... that something was immediately wrong.

Not a day went by that she didn't regret having Henry in that shed. She felt nauseous often, nursed a near constant headache, and she was always hungry—although subsisting on hardtack and salt pork for eight weeks was not precisely satiating—and of course, the most damning sign of all: her blood had not come. The mere thought was enough to make her feel as though she couldn't breathe. Her moment of weakness in Pittsburgh haunted her. She was entirely out of her field of experience and had no one to turn to for insight or advice. She could only wait and see what other changes came next.

She shook her head, making it pound painfully and draw her out of yet another cycle of speculation. Worrying never accomplished anything. What was done was done. She would cross each bridge when she got to it. Providing none of them collapsed in a flash flood.

Now that they were in a proper town, presumably with a druggist and physician, she might manage to acquire a solution that would prevent her from having to reveal her secret and return in humiliation to St. Anthony to await the judgment of her idiot husband.

The Second shuffled out of the north side of the train to the passenger platform and loitered there for a few minutes as the Colonel spoke with a local man on the street below. Then, they were all herded into the depot itself.

"There isn't time nor light enough for us to pitch camp," Osborn relayed as they all grumbled. It was a tight fit for them all in the depot, though Cate was glad that they were out of the snow falling outside.

Henry made a point to face away from Cate when he curled up under his wool blanket. She laid on her back, studying the shadows in the depot's rough-hewn beams for what felt like hours before she finally dozed off.

The next morning, the Second emerged from the depot to be greeted by a group of gently-dressed townspeople, mostly ladies and a few older gentlemen. The lieutenants ordered the soldiers down the platform to the dirt road alongside the railroad track and had them fall into ranks. Lebanon was the end of the line. It felt odd to gather in rank in front of the train that had no further path forward. North and East of the town, Cate could see the tips of Sibley tents poking up on the horizon.

The Lebanon greeting committee stayed upon the platform and as the last of the Second fell into ranks, the committee gathered at the edge of the platform, as though it were a stage. The Black laborers—likely enslaved, Cate couldn't help but remind herself—heaved crates of supplies from the train cars on the opposite side of the platform, in stark contrast with the idling, well-trimmed white people of the welcoming committee. An older gentleman stepped forward to speak.

"Salutations, Colonel Van Cleve, lieutenants, captains, and soldiers. Welcome to Lebanon! I am your humble servant Mayor Benedict Carlisle, and I know I speak on behalf of all of us loyal Lebanonians when I say you are most welcome in our town."

"Lebanonians," mumbled Robinson to Henry, just ahead and left of Cate. "Say that three times fast."

The mayor went on to expound at length about the virtuousness of their mission, of the appreciation held for the Union and its soldiers by those living in the town, and the graciousness of Southern hospitality as though their state weren't being occupied in response to the threat of secession. It was more of the same tactless claptrap, going on and on about saving the Union and protecting the integrity of the Constitution and states' rights and all of the political nonsense with which the morally corrupt gilded their complicity with slavery. Cate's eyes flicked back to the Black laborers and let her anger simmer. It felt much better to be angry than it did to drown in uncertainty.

"We are delighted to extend to you our hospitality, and please don't hesitate to make yourselves at home here in Lebanon through the duration of your stay."

The ladies descended the steps and greeted the officers who stood at the front of ranks, smiling demurely and murmuring their thanks for their service as they passed. The gentlemen, including the mayor, accompanied Colonel Van Cleve, his Lieutenant Colonel, and Adjutant presumably to headquarters, and the captains ordered the rank and file to march to camp.

Another regiment had already arrived and set themselves up just south of the village. The Second Minnesota began organizing their own camp on a dry hill just east of the existing camp. To the naked eye, it seemed obvious that the population of soldiers already easily outweighed the population of the town, which was the county seat to boot. Strings were staked, and Sibley tents were unloaded from the freight cars as the rising sun emerged fully from behind the distant mountains and melted off the inch or two of snow that had fallen in the night. The grass seemed unperturbed by the frost and sprang back green as their boots tramped it down for the floor of their tents.

They puttered around their campsite for a bit, coordinating where to stake the poles and determining how wide their fire pit could be without scorching their boots. Williamson unfolded the canvas and everyone graciously stood aside for him to hang it from the poles himself. Hower was even so kind as to provide several helpful suggestions as to how he might drape it more effectively. Suffice to say, Williamson was not nearly as amused as the rest of the squad was.

"So big news, fellows. We've been brigaded together with a few other regiments," Hower informed them as the squad staked tent poles and draped canvas. "We'll be with two other brigades to make up the First Division of the Army of the Ohio, which General Buell organized only a few days ago."

For once, Cate was grateful for Hower's penchant for the latest camp canard. At present, it was nice to hear that something seemed organized and that their regiment had not been forgotten at a desolate railroad junction due to poor bookkeeping.

"Is General Buell here as well?" Webster asked.

"No, he's still in Louisville as far as I've heard. General George Thomas is charged with leading the First Division, so he's the one setting up headquarters here. I understand that Zollicoffer and his Rebs are floating around these parts, and Thomas intends to set us off on his tail as soon as Buell gives the orders."

"I'm glad the Rebs are using all their military know-how they stole from West Point to promote their friends," Robinson said sarcastically, rolling his eyes.

"I can't wait to give him his fair share of moral justice," Cate growled, stomping a stake into the ground a little harder than strictly necessary.

"Dare I even ask what that entails?" Webster inquired.

Cate shot him a glare as she patted her bayonet scabbard on her hip.

"I'm going to be right back, fellas," Hower said, his attention drawn away by the new regiment marching into the camp from the train depot. "I'm gonna see what these new boys are all about."

When the tent was finished and rations had been collected from the commissary, Cate sat quietly at the edge of the camp-fire next door with the Hastings boys and the rest of the squad. There was actual bread instead of hardtack. Cate shoveled it into her mouth in huge bites.

"I understand Zollicoffer is entrenched on the Cumberland, building up and waiting for us to strike," said Sam Corbett, one of the privates from Hastings. He had a stick in one hand that he used to absently prod the logs.

"Where did you hear that?" another private, John Martin, asked. "I thought he was headed here, and we're being brigaded to head into a full-on battle within the week?"

Several of the Hastings boys looked at him with a renewed sense of excitement and urgency.

"Quiet, the both of you," Corporal Harris said. "Neither of you are right."

Then, he leaned in close to Corbett and Martin, seated side by side, and said, "Zollicoffer's off in Nashville getting his cock shined by some hired belles, before he sets a'riding this way to meet his fateful end."

"Now that *has* to be a rumor," Williamson put in, stuffing a piece of bread into his mouth that was not only *not* hardtack, but was also only a day or two old.

"Did you know that Nashville has a whole city ward dedi-cated just to whores?" Jim Bates, a third Hastings private, said with a leer. "I'm gunning for an assignment to invade Nashville, myself."

Webster frowned at him, and at Corporal Harris too for good measure, before he stood and went off apace to stand with Osborn. Cate could understand why. The Hastings boys were not the most well-mannered young men, but that was why she liked them. They didn't play games or put on airs. They were simply crass, and it was nice to hear the truth for once instead of placating platitudes that no one meant. Even if they did spend an inordinate amount of time talking about women like commodities to be acquired. At least they were honest about it.

Cate could feel her neck prickling, and she turned around to see Henry standing behind her and a few paces down. She looked away quickly and fixed her eyes on the flame.

"*He!*"

Cate looked up to see a group of men she didn't recognize approaching the campfire. The man at the head of the group was tall and lean with a sheaf of yellow hair, and his voice was thickly accented when he spoke.

"Are you Elias Hower's squad? He said there is a Turner in your—"

"Karl?!"

Cate looked up at Henry, whose mouth had dropped open and started pouring out German. It was strange to hear the words and not know their meaning, but the body language made the situation clear enough. Henry hurried around the campfire, spewing German, while the other man made some sort of excited exclamation and held his arms wide to receive him.

The eager exchange of German went on for a few minutes. The men who had accompanied the stranger were grinning excitedly, clearly understanding. Cate stood slowly as Hower approached.

"Ah, I see the Ninth found us!" he said.

"The Ninth?"

"The Ninth Ohio. They've been brigaded with us. They're from Cincinnati and they're *all* German."

"Cincinnati?" said Robinson. "Isn't that where Schaefer's from?"

Hower grinned. "Yes! I thought that too. Most of these fellows are Turners, apparently."

Cate watched the joyful reunion proceed with little understanding. "Hower—do you suppose he knows that fellow?"

"It would seem he does. I didn't meet him specifically when I was over there, I don't think. Scarcely any of them speak any English."

Henry was grinning ear to ear when he turned and dragged
the man by the wrist over to where their squad stood to one side
of the fire. He continued to natter away in German, so it was
jarring to hear her name, along with their comrades, perfectly
comprehensible couched in the middle.

"*Das sind meine kameraden*, Jacob Robinson, Charles
Smith, *und* Elias Hower—*Kennst du schon*?"

The other man shook his head but grinned widely. His smile
spread crooked on his face and though he was at least a decade

older than Henry, they certainly looked akin. Cate fixed him with scrutiny. Cousins?

Henry finally seemed to notice how confused his squadmates were, because he suddenly looked abashed and said in English, "Sorry, fellas. I forgot you don't speak German." He laughed, like this was understandable. Cate held firmly to her annoyance and did not permit herself any tender feelings about the pink tinge of his cheeks. "This is my uncle, Karl Schaefer—my father's younger brother."

"*Schön, Sie kennenzulernen*," Karl Schaefer said, then followed up in thickly accented English, "Pardon me—my English is not so good."

The man's apologetic smile was disarmingly charming. Cate stared at him while Jacob Robinson shook his hand emphatically. There were more of them—these Turners. Of course there were, she knew that. But a whole regiment full? That seemed ... she felt like she should say problematical, but the idea was growing on her too quickly.

"Are you a Turner too, Sergeant Schaefer?" Cate asked, noticing the stripes on the uncle's shoulder.

"Oh no, we don't want you hearing too much of that, Schaef," Hower piled on. "Don't want you getting uppity."

Cate found herself wishing Henry didn't speak English as well as he did. Karl Schaefer was adorably confused as their squad slung English one on top of the other.

"*Ah no*," Sergeant Schaefer said as Robinson finished shaking his arm off his shoulder. "Just Karl. *Bitte*."

"Oh, yes, are you also a Turner, Sergeant?" Robinson repeated Cate's question.

"*Ja*, yes," the uncle confirmed.

"It sounds like the whole regiment is," Hower said. Henry leveled a surprised look at him, then turned to his uncle and asked something in German. The response made Henry's jaw drop.

"Well, that is wonderful news!" he exclaimed. "But of course the Turners were able to recruit a whole regiment. Why am I surprised?"

"Have you been in the field long, Sergeant?" Webster cut in, rejoining the group with Osborn as the excitement built. He glanced at Henry for translation assistance when it became evident that his uncle didn't understand the question. A moment later, Henry relayed the response.

"They have," he reported. "They've been fighting in West Virginia and have seen a few battles and skirmishes already."

"Why an all-German regiment?" Robinson wondered.

"Can't you see?" Hower replied. "They don't speak English so they run the whole show in German."

Henry frowned. "Well, yes, but it's more than that. I imagine they are operating under German strategy as well." He had a brief exchange with his uncle to confirm. "Yes, and they're led by several German revolution veterans."

"The Germans had a revolution? I thought it was just the French?" Poor Williamson garnered quite a few dirty looks from the Germans who did have a grasp of English. One of the men who had accompanied Sergeant Schaefer stepped forward, a hard look on his angular face.

"We Germans aren't so quick to play fast and loose with the freedoms you Americans take for granted." The man spoke with scarcely an accent, his tone hard enough to silence the group of them. His brow shadowed eyes that cut to each of them as they stood abashed, and then, out of nowhere, his long face slid into a wide grin. "August Kloepfer, at your service."

The squad eyed him warily after that bait and switch. The man's hand hung in the air for a moment before Cate took it and nearly winced at his vice grip. Henry's uncle rolled his eyes and said something dismissive. August replied in quick, curt German, his tone suggesting he didn't pay much mind to rank. The man's eyes were confrontational, his smile easy, his shoulders carried with confidence. He spoke critically but wasn't sullen, cantankerous, or combatant. He carried himself as though everyone should agree with him as a matter of course. Cate tried not to feel desperately jealous.

Henry cleared his throat and grinned at Kloepfer and the other men, as well as his uncle. He spoke German, then quickly translated himself into English, "Well, I can't say how delighted I am that we have been brigaded together."

"Yes, it was such a pleasure to meet you," Webster said graciously, taking a turn at shaking Kloepfer's iron fist. "Which reminds me, who are the rest of your comrades?"

Henry, by way of his uncle, made introductions to the other three men from the Ninth who had come along. All of them were solid, fit men with wide shoulders and square, angular faces. If Cate had known she'd meet a whole brigade of Turners, she might have waited Henry out just to see if she had any better choices. She attempted to amuse herself with the notion, but her heart was not in it. It was all she could do to force herself to even recognize the well-made men on display. Something was definitely wrong with her.

———

IX

Lebanon, Kentucky
Tuesday, December 10, 1861

HENRY COULDN'T BELIEVE IT. What were the odds that half the Turners he'd known in Ohio would be brigaded here with them in this tiny little Kentucky railroad town? After morning drill, he went over to the Ninth's encampment and met up with Karl, who paraded him around to all the old familiar faces from his childhood in Ohio. He saw Friederich Bertsch, his old Turner instructor, who was a lieutenant now, and Martin Bruner, also a lieutenant. Karl Joseph and Gustav Kammerling were captains. Once he wrote to his father of all this, he'd be surprised if he didn't receive news of his father's enlistment as well.

He walked side by side with his uncle, feeling a lightness and a sense of ease he hadn't felt since leaving New Ulm. He was invited to join in warm-ups with a group of Turners set to practice hand-to-hand combat, and his body fell into the routine without a second thought. It was so good to be amongst Germans. He hadn't realized how much he'd missed it until he was back in the midst of them, struggling to remember words and surprising himself with how rusty his German had become after the better part of a year away.

Karl invited him to eat luncheon together and the two of them sat in the unseasonably green grass, digging into fresh rustic bread and brisket with more gusto than Henry had ever done with the actual square meals they'd been provided at Fort Snelling.

"Have you heard much from your parents, then?" Karl asked around a mouthful of bread. God, it was such a relief to be socializing in German with someone other than Krüger. Though they were in the middle of the Ninth's camp, where everyone spoke German and that was the point, it somehow made the conversation feel more private.

Henry shrugged. "Not much. I think Father wants to enlist."

"I'm sure your mother is delighted with the idea."

"Of course not. Who will escort her to Turner Hall?"

Karl gave a snort. "What does she think she is? A debutante in her first year out in Stuttgart? This isn't 1840."

Henry shrugged. Only *he* was allowed to complain about his mother like that. "She's just scared. The Indians have been restless, and she worries."

"Well, if your father has the right of it, they have every right to be. New Ulm is on their treaty land."

"No, a land surveyor found that it wasn't."

"Did he then? And who paid him to say that?"

Henry furrowed his brows and took a bite of his own bread to cover his lack of a retort. The Turners had paid the man, of course. There was no squirming round Karl's implication. His father hadn't been among the first men surveying the town—that had been Frederick Beinhorn and the Chicago Turners. There had been multiple conflicts with the local Indians that had ultimately been put to rest by that official land survey. Even if the treaties did say that New Ulm was outside the bounds of the agreed upon reservation, the Indians certainly weren't aware of that information when they signed. If Henry's experience as a young boy with no English was any indication, the translation work available was shoddy at best, and certainly biased.

"So you've been in touch with my father?"

"Of course."

"Then you probably have more news than I do." Karl leveled a confused brow at him and Henry squirmed uncomfortably. "I, um, I missed out on enlisting in the First and I—"

"Yes, yes, I know," Karl said. "He told me all. Judging by your expression, you know how stupid that was, and you don't need me to lay into any more than your mother already has."

Henry wrinkled his nose and nodded. "So you know that Peter is back home on sick furlough, too, then. That at least has Mother off my trail, for the moment anyway. Do you think Father will enlist?"

"I'm sure he will. He had better do it soon, or he'll age out and they won't want him anymore."

"It's too bad New Ulm can't muster an all-German regiment like the 9th. This is amazing. Like taking home to war with you."

"It is, isn't it?" Karl looked around at the men milling about, their warm, lyrical German bouncing around the campsite. "Wishing you hadn't left Cincinnati, then?"

Henry scoffed. "I was sixteen, I could hardly—"

"Certainly you could have. Sixteen is older than many of us were when we became Forty-Eighters."

Henry shrugged. "You know how my mother is. It would have been more effort than it was worth not to go, and besides, I didn't mind. I was excited to be a part of creating the German utopia on the prairie."

"And yet here you are. Trouble in paradise, then?"

Henry leveled his uncle with a discerning look. "No. I just wanted to make something of myself. To fight for something that matters like you and Father did. To do something with all that time we spent training and discussing what was right. One cannot have a utopia if one is not willing to fight to defend it."

Karl smiled. His skin folded at the corners of his mouth now. Henry had always thought of him as a young man, but he must be approaching forty. Henry was used to seeing him in contrast to his father, whose staid stoicism always made the expressive Karl seem so young by comparison.

"I think that's among the best reasons to enlist. I'm proud of you, nephew."

Henry hated how good it felt to hear those words, even when they weren't based on the whole truth.

"Is my father terribly angry with me? I mean, I had a letter from him before we left Fort Snelling, but it was brief."

"No, I think he's proud too," Karl said. "I had a letter from him when I was in West Virginia, and he'd just learned you weren't with the twins. But I think—even though he was vexed you hadn't told them where you were—he was pleased that you'd gone off on your own. You were always lurking in Peter and Franklin's shadows."

Henry glowered. "Not on purpose…"

Karl raised a brow at him but said nothing.

"So what news from Cincinnati?" Henry asked, changing the subject quickly. "Did you ever end up marrying Marta?"

Karl blinked his blue eyes and then said, "Oh, that's right, Marta. No, she ended up with Theodor Rapp. They've got two girls now, and a third on the way."

Henry's brows furrowed. "Teddy Rapp? Really? Why? What did you do?"

Karl's lips pursed, and he shrugged. "Nothing untoward, I assure you. What about you? Do you have some young thing back in St. Paul, staring at your CDV and writing you letters every day?"

Henry couldn't help but laugh bitterly. "No, nothing like that."

"That sounds like a story."

"No, it's really not." He sighed and looked out at the stretching plain of tents pointing into the cold, winter sky. After weeks of being shut out by Charley, it was a relief to get a taste of home. He hadn't realized how lonely he'd been.

When Henry looked at Karl again, he could see his uncle was making quite a point of not pushing at him. The older man gave a wistful half-smile and said, "Story or not, if you want to talk, I'm happy to listen."

Henry pressed his lips together. He'd spent weeks feeling confused and angry and miserable. No one had noticed, because they'd all been miserable in Lebanon Junction, but it was hard not to have anyone to talk to about it. Romance was already so confusing; it was even more difficult to not be able to bounce his experiences off someone else, to find out if he was being completely ridiculous or if Charley was indeed unbearably aloof.

"There was ... someone..." Henry said reluctantly. "I'm not supposed to talk about it though."

"You're not?" Karl said lightly. "But you're speaking German, surely this doesn't count?"

Henry huffed a wistful half-chuckle and rubbed the back of his neck with one hand. "This person told me not to tell anyone about us."

"What, is she married?" Karl said it jokingly, but the smile fell off his face when he saw Henry's expression. "Oh no, Heinrich."

"I didn't know—not at first."

"But once you found out?"

"I ... certainly didn't end things..."

Karl shook his head. "And now?"

"She's ended it. And I don't know why."

"I should think you know full well why."

"No, she's left him. She's not with him anymore." Henry sounded foolish to his own ears—he couldn't imagine what Karl must think of him. "She and I had a good thing going before we left Fort Snelling—"

"—'We' left Fort Snelling?" Karl leveled him with a paternalistic look. "Don't tell me she's a camp follower?"

Henry's mouth parted, but he didn't say anything. Let Karl fill in the blanks for himself. It was easier than lying.

Karl sighed. "Sorry, I'm not trying to be judgmental. Go on."

Henry swallowed hard. "I don't know. We weren't able to be together once we got to the front. These goddamned Sibley tents—there's just no opportunity to be alone."

"So is that when she ended things?"

"No, it's just when we stopped, um ..."

"I see. Were you careful? When you were 'um'?"

Henry's eyes went wide. "Yes! Of course. I ..." Henry couldn't bring himself to say it aloud so he made a vague gesture that he hoped Karl understood. "She assured me I had done nothing to compromise her." His cheeks were on fire, but he couldn't bring himself to say more. He had done something that could have compromised her. But he'd already violated his promise to her by talking of their relationship to Karl. It wasn't anything he could bring into Karl's confidence.

"Alright. So when did she end things?"

"Around Thanksgiving. We were friendly and then perhaps the week before Thanksgiving, she got prickly—but that wasn't unusual because she's normally like that, so I didn't think there was anything amiss." Henry pushed his hair back and replaced his cap with a sigh. "But when I tried to catch her alone, I could tell there was something wrong. She was scared, I think. And she told me to leave her alone. So I have. And that was two weeks ago. I—I didn't think she meant it when she told me to stay away. She always blew a little hot and cold, which is why I was irritated with her. So I thought I'd make her regret her words, show her that she didn't really want to be alone. I thought she'd come back but ... she didn't. She just looks past me now like I'm not there. It's cruel."

Henry's voice broke on the last word, and he scrubbed his face with his hands. Karl didn't say anything, and Henry filled that silence with shame.

"Heinrich," Karl said, his brows knitted together in concern. "I'm sorry. I ... I remember what that feels like and it's awful. Just torture."

Henry blinked up at him. "Did Marta do that to you?"

Karl shrugged. "It was a long time ago. Suffice to say, you deserve to know why. I wish I had asked. It's torture to sit in uncertainty, going over everything again and again to figure out what you did wrong. If she's still around, you should ask her. Get some closure at the very least."

Henry squeezed his brows together and pressed his lips into a thin line to hide what a damned relief it was to talk to someone and to have them listen.

"Thanks," he said instead.

"*He* Sarg!"

Henry looked up and saw August Kloepfer trotting up to them. He was a solid man with a protuberant chin and a long face like a horse that slid into a lopsided, rather silly smile when he saw Henry.

"Ho, what's this? Our cousin from the prairie?"

Henry stood and began to return the other man's smile, but then Kloepfer turned to Karl and said, "We've got drill now? Or what?"

Karl threw himself back into the grass and sighed. "Yes. We've got to make sure you can still load in nine even though you all did it flawlessly yesterday."

"Got to keep in that fighting shape, am I right?" Kloepfer elbowed Henry in the shoulder and Henry stumbled back, surprised at how hard he'd executed what seemed like a casual friendly gesture.

"I had better get back to my regiment," Henry said, rubbing his shoulder with a disconcerted expression.

"No, you should stay with us," Kloepfer said. "Germans belong with Germans, after all. Besides, those Yankees don't know the first thing about fighting. They haven't seen battle since 1812. Well, except that invasion of Mexico, but hardly anyone fought in that."

Henry laughed. "Tempting but I'm not one to be court-martialed for desertion."

"Ach, these officers. They hardly know their head from their ass. Present company excluded, of course."

Karl climbed to his feet and dusted off his trousers. "I'm not commissioned, so no offense taken."

Henry studied Kloepfer for a moment. He couldn't remember ever meeting him before, though they were of an age. He was tall, gangly, but his shoulders showed he was certainly no stranger to Jahn's gymnasticks treatise. He seemed to have no concern for what he said in front of whom, nor much care for social niceties. He regarded Henry with mischievous eyes.

"Well, little Schaefer, when you're ready to see some action and kill some Rebels, you know who to march with." He winked, then strode off toward their parade ground. Henry looked at Karl for some indication of how to respond, but Karl was still watching him go. Kloepfer seemed like a strange amalgamation of Smith and all the Hastings boys put together.

"Don't mind him," Karl said, rolling his eyes. "He's a blood-thirsty bastard on the field and a damn imp in camp. He can't stand tooling around waiting for something to happen. It makes him manic."

Henry pursed his lips. It seemed to him Karl was unusually tolerant of what other officers might find untenable familiarity and insubordination. But it wasn't any of his business.

He made a plan with Karl to explore the town after supper and bade his uncle goodbye. As he trotted back to the Second's campground for drill, he wondered what he might say to Charley. He'd have to get her alone to even have a conversation, but Karl was right. He deserved to know what was going on. Her interest in him couldn't have been contrived. Something had changed. And he deserved to know what it was.

X

Lebanon, Kentucky
Tuesday, December 10, 1861

CATE PUSHED OPEN THE door and a small brass bell chimed. The pharmacy was small, with tiled floors, tin ceiling panels, and a large counter at the back, under which a glass case displayed small, uniform bottles of tinctures, salves, and all manner of medical aids. Behind the counter stood rows and rows of small, wood drawers, with tiny brass slots for neatly handwritten labels. Also behind the counter was a petite Black woman, perhaps thirty, wearing a kerchief wrapped around her hair and a crisp, print cotton dress and knitted sontag. Her coat sleeves were covered by white cotton oversleeves, protecting the fabric from whatever ingredients the woman was tipping into a massive mortar and pestle. The whole shop smelled of peppermint and camphor.

"Pardon me," Cate murmured, slipping into the shop and letting the door swing shut behind her.

"Oh! I'm sorry, sir, I didn't see you there," the woman said, flapping her hands. Her voice was accented with that Kentucky drawl. "I was just closing up. Let me get someone to help you."

Cate frowned. "Oh, I'm terribly sorry. Please don't trouble yourself, I'm sure I shouldn't bother the pharmacist. I, uh, I've just arrived, and I'm getting the lay of the town is all."

The woman regarded her for a moment and then nodded. "Of course, sir. Well, let me know if you need anything."

Cate nodded and approached the counter, at the opposite end of where the clerk stood. She looked down into the glass case and made like she was reading the labels while her mind raced to figure out how she was going to manage to ask for what she needed.

"So, I suppose the pharmacist has retired for the evening?" she ventured.

The Black woman gave her a sidelong glance before she replied, "No, sir, he's enlisted. We do our best to keep the doors open while he's away."

"We?"

"The Missus. And Miss Blackwell, the schoolteacher, assists us as well."

"The schoolteacher? Part-time pharmacist?"

"Someone has to make ends meet while the men are gone, sir."

Cate nodded. A pharmacy run entirely by women? What luck. "And you are ...?"

"Everyone calls me Belle. Sir."

Cate hesitated. "I, um ... I would hate to presume such familiarity with a professional such as yourself—"

"You can call me Miss Belle, if that suits you better. Miss Merrill is the Mistress' daughter—not me." The woman gave Cate a flat look. "Now what can I help you with, sir?"

It occurred to Cate that enslaved people often bore the names of their enslavers. That the Mistress referenced here was likely an owner of human chattel, that this woman standing before her with tired annoyance was waiting for Cate to catch up. What the hell did a pharmacist need slaves for? What kind of slave stayed and ran their master's business while he was away? That bastard had better not be fighting for the Union, taking with one hand and giving with the other. For the first time, she considered how complicated this life must be for this actual person standing in front of her. Hell, she was ignorant. She'd never even met an enslaved person before today. What kind of abolitionist did that make her? Anger and shame and revulsion roared in her ears, over the droning of terrible, foreboding anxiety.

Cate swallowed her anger and tried to focus on the task at hand. It would take her full attention to navigate this conversation without revealing herself, and she was already sleep-deprived and half-mad with worry.

"I don't suppose," Cate began, then cleared her throat to more clearly mask her voice in male affectation. "I don't suppose you have any services that might be of interest to a girl who is ... um, down on her luck?"

Miss Belle raised a brow. "We might. Who's asking?"

Cate set her teeth. "Her beau."

Miss Belle's dark eyes were inscrutable, and her gaze didn't waver even as she continued to work the mortar in the pestle. "I see. What's her troubles then?"

Cate swallowed hard. "I trust that this conversation will be kept in confidence."

"Ain't no one care about what ol' Merrill's slave has to say about anyone," Miss Belle said, assuming a familiar slave vernacular in a manner that struck Cate as rather facetious. "Besides, all y'all will be off to battle in a few weeks anyway. What's it to me?"

Cate gritted her teeth. She deserved that.

"She's not bled in six weeks," Cate said, watching Miss Belle tentatively from under her brow.

"Ah, that is a stroke of bad luck. Or is it?" Miss Belle left off the mortar and inched down the counter, nearer to Cate. She regarded Cate with a glance of clear-eyed scrutiny as she pulled a box of glass bottles out from under the counter.

"There's no reason that I know of that she'd be in a delicate way," Cate said firmly. It had been the day after her courses stopped. It was impossible. Wasn't it?

"Perhaps she's not telling you something."

Cate glowered out from under her brows. "No, I'm certain."

Miss Belle tilted her head and crossed her arms. Her smooth, high cheeks suggested youth, but her eyes belied a tired hardness. "Hm. Well, what's her name then?"

"Excuse me?"

"Because if it's Mary, she might expect to be visited by an angel any day now. Advent has already begun."

"Very funny." Cate scratched her arm and glanced cagily at the entrance to ensure no one was coming in from off the street.

Considering they'd been told not to leave camp, there sure were a lot of uniformed fellows wandering around.

"What conditions has she been living under?"

"Pardon?"

"Is she a ... camp follower, by any chance? What might she be seeing for food while on the march?"

Cate blinked. Miss Belle's gaze was impossible to read, but Cate felt vulnerable, like she could see through her uniform or something. She cleared her throat uncomfortably and said, "Just rations, ma'am."

"I'm sorry, sir, I'm not privy to what that entails."

"Salt pork. Hardtack. The camp we just came from had bad water so mostly coffee to drink."

"Hm. So she hasn't had any carnal contact—" Cate's eyes snapped to Miss Belle's but she didn't say anything. "And hasn't been eating too well. For how long were you eating like that?"

Cate frowned. "Eight weeks. Maybe a bit more."

"Hm. May I?" Miss Belle reached out and took Cate's hand in hers. She pushed Cate's sleeve up and Cate twitched her hand away.

"Terribly sorry, sir, but may I just check something? I assure you I'm healthy and my hands are clean."

Cate's gut sank at the implication. Shame edged ahead of the other emotions battling fiercely in her chest. "That wasn't what I meant to imply, ma'am, I just—just go ahead."

Miss Belle took hold of Cate's hand again and pushed her sleeve up. With her index finger, she pressed into the soft underside of Cate's arm. Cate grit her teeth hard and hoped she wouldn't say anything about how fine and sparse of hair her arms were for a man.

"Mmm, as I thought."

Cate's gorge rose in her throat. Fear was winning now, like a barreling train.

"Look here," Miss Belle said and pressed her finger into Cate's arm again. A slight depression remained for a moment or two after she removed her finger. "You are terribly under-nourished. Your skin shouldn't keep the shape of my finger at all, especially not at such a young age. If your girl is anything like you, she probably doesn't have the nutrition necessary to have her blood."

Miss Belle's eyes met Cate's and held them. Cate's heart raced. This lady knew. She had to. Cate pressed her lips together and looked down, curling her hand away and pulling her sleeve back down. "Are you sure?"

"I am not. I can only guess. But there is more than one way for a woman to miss her monthly." Miss Belle bit her lip thoughtfully for a moment, then added, "It might be nice to not have it while on the march. Perhaps a silver lining for a woman making her way in a man's war."

Cate looked up at her. She could scarcely hear for the roaring in her ears. Relief was battling for her attention, but fear firmly held the reins. Especially since Miss Belle was increasingly abandoning the pretense of the girl being anyone but Cate. Hell.

"I suspect that now that you're here and eating more substantially, the blood will come on, by and by. Only time will tell," Miss Belle added with a shrug. "Unless you are looking for something to bring on the blood, just to be sure?"

Cate grit her teeth so hard her jaw ached. She was right. It was in many ways very convenient to not have her courses. But her desire to know for certain pounded at her so hard it almost physically hurt. She looked at the drawers along the back wall.

"Yeah, just to be sure."

Miss Belle nodded and swept into the back room for a moment. Cate sagged against the counter, her breathing shallow. She tried not to think about what this woman might do with Cate's secret. There was some sort of patient privacy oath among pharmacists, wasn't there? Surely Miss Belle would adhere to such? There was no immediate benefit to revealing Cate's secret, though keeping it could be lucrative if Cate purchased remedies. Yes. This lady had no reason to reveal her secret. Unless she was an indulgent gossip and liked a salacious story. What on earth did she owe to ignorant white people anyway? *Hell*.

Miss Belle came back out of the back room with a glass bottle and paper packet in hand.

"This is cottonroot, for obstructed menses," Miss Belle said, putting the glass bottle filled with a few fat tablets on the counter. "And—if it is just a matter of poor rations—you might want this."

She set a nondescript paper packet on the counter.

Cate looked from the packet to the pharmacist suspiciously. "What is it?"

Miss Belle lifted her eyebrows and scratched discreetly at the edge of her head kerchief. "A, ehm, French letter."

"A what?"

"Have you not heard of them in camp?"

Cate felt, based on how she was being regarded, that she ought to have. She shook her head hesitantly.

Miss Belle stooped beneath the counter and produced a small flyer which she folded around the paper packet. "All you need to know is there."

She proffered it to Cate. Cate reached out and took it. Curiosity joined the fray.

"If anyone asks, you got it mail-order," Miss Belle said, her tone flat and firm enough that it startled Cate to nod as she slipped the packet in her pocket. She still had no idea what it was, but she felt, if she were not to let folks know where she got it, that it was likely unwise to study the material here.

"Understood, ma'am." Cate then reached and took up the female pills. There were five compressed tablets inside the bottle that she slipped into her other pocket.

"Those might lay you—her out for a day or two," Miss Belle said, smoothly correcting her flub and making it so abundantly clear that Cate's cover was blown, that Cate wondered if she'd done it on purpose. Cate felt sweat bead on her forehead as Miss Belle added, "Don't take more than one in a day and stop as soon as the blood comes."

Cate nodded.

"If *she* needs some rags, or a discreet laundry, I'd recommend the girls on Market, between Main and Mulberry." Miss Belle was doing a bang-up job of making sure Cate knew she was on to her. But why?

"What do I owe you?"

"Seventy-five cents," Miss Belle shrugged, watching carefully to determine if Cate would argue with her. Cate grimaced but produced the sum from her pocket. The money she'd earned from the paymaster at Lebanon Junction wasn't enough to replenish how depleted her funds had become. She was quickly approaching the point that she wouldn't be able to buy new clothes in a pinch, were she caught, and this expense wasn't helping. She couldn't be sure she was paying for the remedies or the pharmacist's discretion or both, but despite the fact that she was loath to part with the money, she couldn't bear the thought of making a fuss about paying an enslaved person for their trade. Not to mention what being short-shrift might do to the woman's discretion regarding Cate's secret. So she slapped a dollar on the counter with a quiet thanks and turned for the door.

"Good luck," Miss Belle called as Cate pulled the shop door open and the bell sounded again. "And if you see any Secesh by the name of Merrill—"

Cate turned in the doorway. "Ma'am, if I see any Secesh, I don't expect I'll have time to take his name before I shoot."

Miss Belle's impassive face scarcely flared a nostril, but it was more of a response than she'd shown thus far. With a slow blink of her dark eyes, she replied, "Good."

XI

Lebanon, Kentucky
Tuesday, December 10, 1861

IT WAS DARK BY the time Henry met up with Karl at the edge of town, just south of Water Street. Roll call had been at half past seven o'clock and while they were not expressly permitted to leave their camps, command had enough on their plates trying to supply a brigade of men that they weren't too concerned with what the men were doing with their leisure time. Besides, Karl'd had a friendly word with Sergeant Osborn, and it seemed no one would pay much mind, given that there were no reports of any Rebs in the area.

As Karl and Henry took to Water Street, it became clear that they weren't the only ones taking advantage of the confusion of a new camp, because the street was swathed in Union blue. A hotel across the street from the Depot seemed to be attracting a good number of them.

"That must be Sterling House," Karl said, pointing. "It's got a fast-moving reputation for billiards and bourbon."

Henry lifted his eyebrows. "I know a few boys who'd be eager for that information."

"Your Corporal's way ahead of you." Karl chuckled and tossed a thumb toward Elias, flanked by Jacob and Sam Corbett from the Hastings squad and talking to the proprietress, who frowned and shook her head, hands on hips. "Looks like he's not getting in, though, poor fellow."

Henry shook his head with a grin and tried to catch his friends' eyes as they passed the hotel. He felt somewhat awkward when they didn't see him but when the proprietress did so, he gave a small half-hearted wave. She sighed and went inside, shutting the door in Elias' face.

"Hm," Karl said. "Sure didn't take them long to find the nearest brothel."

Henry whirled around with a startled expression. "That's a brothel? How do you know that?"

Karl looked like he was trying not to laugh. "Oh, schatzi, the things you will learn here at the Front." He slung an arm over Henry's shoulder. "When a hotel is known for its billiards, bourbon, and three beguiling female keepers, you must conclude that it is the most public of houses."

Henry frowned. He hoped Jacob would realize that before gaining entrance. He couldn't imagine what Mrs. Robinson might say if she knew. He was confident Jacob wouldn't want to know either.

He and Karl continued away from the Depot and the public house, then headed right on Market Street to Main Street. The corner was dominated by another hotel, shops, and a well that stood right in the middle of the thoroughfare, as well as a cistern. The tallest building, declared the Norris House in massive painted letters, was three stories of brick and seemed like a monolith compared to the squat buildings and the vast, empty winter fields surrounding the tiny town.

"Schaefer, what are you doing out here?"

Both Henry and Karl froze, shoulders tensing as they looked eastward up Main Street. Henry had expected to see Captain Noah or perhaps even Colonel Van Cleve, though he wasn't convinced the officer knew his name. (However, he had accidentally loosed friendly fire during an inspection by the St. Anthony mayor, so it wasn't as unlikely as it may have otherwise been.) Instead, he saw a formidable and distantly familiar face bearing down upon them. It took him a moment to place the man. Before he could dredge up the name, he felt his childlike apprehension return as if no time at all had passed since preparing for his last Turner festival in Cincinnati at the age of sixteen. Then, the face slotted itself neatly into his memories.

Friederich Mayer had been an assistant gymnasticks instructor to Herr Bertsch, exacting and scrupulous and immune to mistakes. Henry remembered his brothers admiring Herr Mayer, greeting him especially every time they went to the Turner Hall and asking for tips on the vault. Karl hadn't been any better. In fact, his uncle—being more of an age with Mayer—had been pals with him. Henry remembered seeing them together often in the biergartens after lectures at the Hall. Judging from his lieutenant stripes, Mayer was still doing quite well for himself.

"Schaefer, there was no leave allowing soldiers free rein of our village hosts. Explain yourself." Mayer addressed Karl in German. Henry glanced awkwardly between the two of them—the monolithic officer and his scruffy uncle, whose yellow beard showed the weeks spent in the field with better things to worry about than shaving. He'd expected his uncle to crack an easy smile, clap Mayer on the shoulder, and make his excuses, but Karl glared at his superior officer and folded his arms across his chest.

"There was no order strictly confining us to our camps, sir, so the fellows took their liberty," Karl said, tilting his chin up so he could look down his nose at the taller man.

Mayer's eyes narrowed. Even though his gaze wasn't directed at Henry, he felt his stomach curdle anyway and looked anywhere but at the officer. He hovered awkwardly beside his uncle, shuffling back, hoping to avoid any ricochet reprisal that might come his way by association.

"When no order is explicitly given, presume that the status quo is to stay in camp." Mayer's jaw flexed at the point it met his ear, even as his expression remained stoically commanding. "As a sergeant, you should know this."

Karl might as well have rolled his eyes he was behaving so petulantly. What was wrong with him? Henry had thought these two were friends. He took another step back and began searching the street for an escape from this awkward interaction.

That's when his eyes alighted upon a familiar figure walking down Main Street, shoving something in her pocket. Dark hair, thick brows, lips twisted in the definition of disdain—Henry forgot any obligation he might have felt toward his uncle and muttered a quick "Entschuldigung!" before skidding across the muddy street toward Charley Smith.

She saw him coming. Her eyes rounded and her whole body tensed like a deer preparing to flee, but she didn't. Henry scowled. The confusion and anger that he'd dredged up with Karl at luncheon bubbled in his chest. If she were so cowardly as to run to avoid him, he'd be vindictive enough to pursue her. He squared his shoulders and stepped up onto the boardwalk, muddy footprints squelching on the faded wood boards.

She leveled a forbearing look at him, one intended to convey how long-suffering she was. In spite of this, her stance was askance, still poised to retreat. Henry shook his head.

"You can finally see me, huh?" he asked with a curl of his lip. She rolled her eyes at him.

"Not if you intend to make some sort of scene," she retorted and continued striding down the boardwalk toward Market Street as though he weren't there. It shouldn't have surprised him—this was the same game she'd been playing since Thanksgiving—but something inside him that usually stretched and bent actually snapped, and he snatched her arm and pushed her down a narrow alley between two shops.

"What in the damn hell?!" she exclaimed as she tripped off the boardwalk and down onto the packed dirt between the brick buildings. She didn't fall, but she certainly scrambled for balance as she caught her footing. Henry hopped down from the boardwalk after her, into the dark alleyway, and felt his righteous indignation extinguish as she shrank away from him against the brick wall. He took a deep breath in and held his hands up in front of him. He knitted his brow tightly and parted his lips as he exhaled the breath. She glared at him but straightened, her eyes flicking over him warily.

"What the hell is wrong with you?" she scolded, crossing her arms across her chest. "I could have turned an ankle just there. You can't just jump a man on the street with no warning. Surely your Turner masters must have taught you more manners than that."

"Don't," Henry bit out. "Don't pretend like you haven't been avoiding me since that night at the Junction."

"I'll have you know I've been avoiding everyone, so don't act like you're special."

Henry took a step forward. "That's bunkum."

"No, I've been avoiding *everyone*—I've scarcely spoken five words today—"

"Not that part, the part where I'm not special."

She froze.

Henry took another step forward, closer than was polite. "Don't tell me that I'm no different from any of the others because I know I am. You were too, until you cut things off without any explanation. You can't just pretend like nothing happened and treat me like some dirt on your shoe." His voice and his anger wavered. "You at least owe me an explanation."

Charley's chin tucked down, chastened, but she still glared at him. Then she looked away and that chin trembled a bit as she took a shaky breath.

"I ..." she croaked, then groaned and scrubbed her face with her hands. "I hate this."

Henry frowned. "If you don't want to be my, you know, bunkie, just say so. I'll leave you alone. I'm not some ... villain in a gothic novel. I just want to know why. If there was something I did, if I made some sort of misstep—"

Charley pressed the heels of her hands into her eyes and groaned. "No, that's not it at all. God damn it all ..." When she removed her hands, her eyes were shining in a way that made Henry want to reach out and touch her. He didn't dare. "I thought ... I thought I might be pregnant, and I panicked."

Henry choked and his chest flooded with anxiety. He hadn't ever heard anyone say that word aloud before, much less be implicated in the gravely serious reality of what it meant. "What! I—You—*What?*"

"Shh!" she hissed and yanked him by his collar closer.

"We didn't—" Henry glanced up at the boardwalk and lowered his voice to a hiss. "We didn't do anything that would compromise you. You said—"

"—I know! I was certain it was safe in Pittsburgh. It couldn't have happened at that time, but I haven't had any evidence to the contrary so I panicked." She sighed. "I just saw the pharmacist, actually—"

Henry's mouth dropped open. "How?"

"I pretended I was the beau," she explained flippantly, "and she said that I—"

"A lady pharmacist?"

"Yeah. Just up the block."

Henry blinked in surprise but didn't pursue it.

"Anyway, she said that I was likely malnourished and that's why my courses didn't come. Then she gave me some female pills and a 'French letter' for it, so hopefully that will help."

Henry choked. "She gave you a *what*?"

"A French letter?" Charley blinked up at him. "I assumed it was some sort of fortifying remedy. Have you heard of it? She seemed surprised to find I hadn't."

Henry just stared at her. Charley pursed her lips and her regard compressed with disdain. "Are you going to answer or are you just going to stare at me like a slack-jawed jackass?"

Henry felt his cheeks heat and his mouth flapped. "It's a, uh, contraceptive device."

Even in the dark, he could discern her flush. "Device?"

Henry choked on his reply and shrugged uselessly. Charley rolled her eyes. "Spare me your fainting lady routine. Just say it plain."

He wrinkled his nose in discomfort. "It's a rubber ... thing. It goes on the ... um ..." He gestured vaguely at his groin and grimaced. Charley's eyebrow went up, and he couldn't quite tell if she was annoyed with him or alarmed at the proposition.

"Well, I'll be damned," she said with a sigh. "I was sure she had me figured out, but if she thought I'd have use for a French letter, perhaps she did think me a man after all. Please, don't feel obligated to explain further. I'd hate to give you an apoplexy. I'm sure I'll figure it out."

Henry pressed his lips tightly shut. His imagination was running far away from him, at least ten steps ahead. He had to pull himself together and definitely—*definitely*—not offer to give a demonstration. He'd come here for an explanation. He could not assume that just because she had generally determined a cause for her fears that wasn't being pregnant, she would automatically want to resume their previous dealings. He tried to feel his feet on the ground and get his mind out of her trousers. He'd had a lot of time to think about this. Though he knew he was only a convenience for her, she was nothing of the sort for him. He was drawn to her in ways that felt significant, important. Worth fighting for. He felt ashamed that she had not felt like she could trust him with this, even if it did seem likely that it was a false alarm.

"So ... you think you aren't in a delicate way, after all? Because even if you were, I want you to know I would not forsake you."

Charley blinked at him. "Thank you, I suppose."

"I'm not sure how I could make an honest woman out of you, since you're already married, but I'm sure I could find—"

"Shut up, would you?" She smiled at him. "It's a nice thought anyway."

"Is it?" Henry noticed he was leaning forward. She was like a magnet; he couldn't help but be drawn in. "Which thought, specifically?"

She rolled her eyes. Henry felt his mouth stretch into a lopsided grin. She was speaking to him again. She was not glowering. In fact, her eyes were studying him guilefully, drawing him in until he had to tuck his chin down to maintain eye contact with her.

"Please promise me," he breathed, "that you will tell me next time you panic."

"Who says there's going to be a next time?" She was lying. He knew because she already had her hand curled in his greatcoat.

"You're not a monolith," he continued. "And I'm not as big of a nitwit as you think. I can be relied upon."

Charley's eyes raked over his face, a smile playing at the corners of her lips.

"I—" she started, then wrinkled her nose and shook her head.

"What?"

"Nothing, it's really nothing."

"You can't start saying something with that look on your face and not expect me to want to know."

She pressed her lips together grimly.

"Come on," Henry chided.

"I missed you." Her dark eyelashes brushed against her cheek before she looked up and rolled her eyes. "A lot."

Henry stared at her.

"To hell with it," he muttered as he scooped her up against the wall and smashed his lips to hers. They knocked teeth and it hurt a little, but she immediately grasped his face with both hands and steered him back slightly, claiming his mouth with hers. Breath hovered in tiny puffs of condensation between them, and he thrilled at the sensation of her lips, her tongue, her chin sliding against his. The warmth of her body pressing up into him. The eagerness with which her hands cupped his face, her fingers sliding into his hair and knocking his cap askew. God, he missed this. He missed *her*.

He tried to focus on every minute sensation, cataloging each detail because who knew how long it would be before they could find privacy again? Her thumb behind his ear, her teeth nibbling his lower lip, drinking him in. Goddammit. He pressed his hardening length into her hip, and she replied by hooking her heel behind his knee. She pulled at his hair, his shoulders, his thigh with her foot, and to hell with it *all*. He wedged a hand between their hips and pushed greatcoat and coat out of the way, fumbling with her button fly as she gasped into his mouth.

Footsteps sounded on the boardwalk. Henry's hand was half wedged into her trousers so it wasn't the most opportune position in which to freeze, but instincts didn't always respond to logic. He looked up as a pair of Union boys passed—no one they knew as far as he could tell in the darkness—and felt Charley's warm breath on his cheek as she followed his gaze. The passersby were oblivious to what was happening in the shadows of the alley, chatting and laughing uninterrupted. Henry's heart slammed in his chest. They wouldn't look. They'd keep on walking.

And they did. When the coast was clear, Henry's senses came back to the fingers in his hair and the soft belly rising and falling against his palm. Charley made a short growling noise and pulled him farther into the darkness of the alley. She settled herself in between two stacks of crates, concealing them from both the boardwalk and the courtyard behind the buildings, and drew him in to trap her once again against the wall. Henry nosed his way back to her kiss as she grasped his wrist and pushed his hand deeper into her trousers. His fingertips pushed fabric aside and slid between soft folds of flesh. Her breath hitched.

"Damn but I missed you," she whispered against his lips. He used his other hand to release the last of her trouser buttons, providing himself more room to maneuver as he began to rub her, reveling in her sighs as she arched against the brick wall. Her hands dragged heavily over his chest, slipping inside his greatcoat and over his stomach, clutching at his coat with force before she yanked his trouser buttons free.

"Oh, Charley," he groaned as she took hold of his cock in a firm grip. She hummed her approval and a niggling thought took hold of him, refusing to let him fully focus on the pleasure her palm was pumping. "...Is it alright if I call you that?"

She drew back an inch or two and regarded him with breathless lips. "Yes, of course. I like it when you call me that."

"You do?" He should take her at her word. But he wasn't that clever. "Last time I called you that, you told me not to."

She sighed impatiently. "I was not myself. I like to be called Charley. You're the only one who calls me that."

She grasped his wrist to encourage his fingers again, her own palm working him over as though to remind him that they had better things to do than worry about what to call her. His voice caught in his throat, and he groaned as her thumb swept over the slick head, but he couldn't let it go.

"I want to know your real name, though."

"I bet you do. What makes you think I want to tell you?"

"Please, tell me. I swear I won't tell a soul."

"Haven't you collected enough of my secrets? Oh, yes, that—" she gripped his shoulders tightly and gasped. "Do that again."

"No, I'll never get enough of you—your secrets. I'll call you Charley till the day you die if that's what you want, just tell me what your given name is."

"I like the name you gave me," she whispered in his ear, teeth grazing against the lobe. He shuddered. He was so close. "But if you must know, it was Cate."

"Cate," he gasped. It felt foreign and strange on his tongue. It held a lifetime of secrets he struggled to imagine for her. He could come if he wanted, but he bit his lip and bore down hard to try and hold on longer. He adjusted the angle of his fingers slightly and earned a squeak from her. "Cate."

Her opposite hand seized his chin and he startled, his eyes fluttering open. Her eyes were deep, dark, and hazy, but her words were clear. "I said I like the name you gave me. Call me Charley."

"Charley." He triggered his fingers faster, applied more pressure as her hips rose to meet him. Her breath heaved, and she held his eyes fiercely, pumping him harder.

"God, Charley," he growled, pressing his forehead to hers and gritting his teeth against the edge of his climax.

"Just like that," she sighed. "I want you to say it just like that when you fuck me."

It wasn't fair. It wasn't fair that she could say things like that and send him into oblivion, with only her hand and her filthy mouth. He shuddered against her, pressing his face into the curve of her neck as he tried his damndest not to let her rip a deep, inarticulate groan from his throat.

His shirttails were probably a mess again, and she was gripping his hip with her sticky hand but he couldn't care. He was too drawn in by her breath panting in his ear, her slick folds enveloping his industrious fingers, heartbeat thrumming against his fingerprints. The image she'd conjured of her naked and keening beneath him, begging him to call her name was bright against the backs of his eyelids. He shuddered in another pulse of pleasure. Even if they had to sneak out of camp, find a warehouse or even a privy to hole up in, he would do whatever it took to make that fantasy reality. She had a French letter. That completely changed the stakes.

Charley's hands grappled at him as she gasped for air. Her thighs pulsed around his hand and it pushed his pleasure-hazy mind to redouble his efforts. Her head tipped back against the brick wall, and she veritably climbed his calves, suspending herself between him and the wall even as she trembled with the effort. She jerked and bit his shoulder as she came, and he nuzzled her neck, whispering his name for her in her ear.

"Fuck," she whined as she caught her breath. Then she grabbed his face and kissed him hard. So much for restraint. Good riddance, he thought, and kissed her back with enthusiasm.

———

Cate wondered at the stillness she experienced as she and Henry proceeded back toward camp in the dark. The cacophony of shame and fear and anger that had been clanging around in her head, not just when she was in the pharmacy but for weeks prior, waiting and not knowing and avoiding Henry like he were some horrific reminder of how damned she was, had silenced. Drowned out under a blanket of wonderful relief. It seemed silly, now, this fear that she might have been pregnant. She knew her body, and its rhythms, and she couldn't have been compromised by what they had done in Pittsburgh. She felt certain of that now. It was the rations. She'd felt miserable for so long now that it felt normal, but it wasn't. She was starving all the time. Of course her body didn't have the capacity to conduct her courses. It was operating under emergency conditions.

The cool wind nearly took her cap as she dogged after Henry down Market Street, so she snatched a hand upon her head. The relief she felt toward her reconciliation with Henry was somehow even more palpable than knowing she wasn't pregnant. She let the stamp of Henry's kiss still tingling on her lips and the buzz of anticipation emanating from her pocket, where the French letter was stowed, fill her with an energy she hadn't had in weeks.

Henry looked over his shoulder to make sure she was still following him, and when that little crooked smile twitched his lips, she had to very consciously swallow the desire to yank him into another alleyway. God, she loved his damn clever little mouth. Cate should have been sated, and her muscles were loose and warm with relief, but the French letter was burning a hole in her pocket with promises of satisfaction she could barely even fathom. The exquisite potential stoked the fire in her belly.

As they turned the corner onto Water Street, there was a startling number of Union boys gathered outside of a hotel whose sign declared its name 'Sterling House,' a gas lamp casting shadows on the raucous mass. There had to be near fifty men milling on the street.

"Closing time, fellows!" called a jolly female voice. "Thanks for such a good time and come again soon. May your strength and valor bring the Union to a swift victory!"

The boys all shouted in excitement, fists thrown in the air. As they approached, Cate could see the smiling countenance of a lovely woman, swathed in an elegant fringed mantle and dark hair effortlessly swept into a chignon at the nape of her neck. Henry slowed as they approached the crowd, and Cate spotted a broad man standing quietly like a boulder in the doorway of the hotel.

"My uncle says he heard that place is a brothel," Henry divulged in her ear. Cate blinked at him for a moment before looking upon the smiling proprietress under an entirely different light. She probably should have been scandalized, but she wasn't. Her mind was turning. A hotel—brothel or not—had rooms for rent. They'd just received back pay for the whole summer when the paymaster visited Lebanon Junction. Even after the unexpected costs at the pharmacy, surely between the two of them, they could afford it.

"If you don't have a room paid for, return to your camp," the man bellowed as the woman proceeded back into the hotel. Cate looked up at Henry with a quirked brow, letting him see the heat in her gaze.

"It's a shame we haven't got one," she murmured. His Adam's apple bobbed as he swallowed, jaw flexing, and Cate had to bite the inside of her cheek to remind herself that they were in public.

The men gathered didn't appear to be listening to the man as such, though they were following the directive, because at that moment, three officers on horseback approached.

"Soldiers, ATTENTION!"

The boys all scrambled over themselves to form ranks, but with such a motley crew representing a random selection of any number of companies and squads, it was rather poorly done. Henry and Cate lurked in the back.

"Roll call shall begin in five minutes, and you had better be marked present by your superior officer. Any of those who are not will be court-martialed." The officer delivering this message had a sharp, hatchet face. Cate was fairly certain it was Captain Bishop of Company A. The soldiers shivered on their feet under the scrutiny, but most knew better than to dart off without being dismissed.

"Well, get on then," the officer flanking Bishop barked.

"Soldiers, report to roll call on the double," Bishop commanded, understanding better than his angry Lieutenant how to light a fire under the pleasure-seeking soldiers before them. Cate snatched Henry's hand, and they exchanged barely suppressed amusement as they dashed down the street toward camp.

A ways ahead of them, Henry called out to Sam Corbett. The renegade from Hastings turned on his heel but continued to hop half-backward toward camp.

"Schaefer, we didn't see you in there!"

The boys next to Sam turned, and Cate saw Elias Hower and Jacob Robinson were reeling like they had bricks in their hats.

"Don't tell me you managed to get into one of the rooms upstairs!" Hower exclaimed louder than normal. "'Bout time you found a fine woman to teach you the way around a bed!"

He sniggered, and Henry ducked his chin self-consciously as the boys around them all cheered him. Cate felt her mouth purse in a scowl. Pushing against the unpleasant sensation of jealousy, she leveled her ire on Robinson.

"And what were all of you fine fellows up to in that den of iniquity?" she said loud enough to steal the attention from Henry, raising a critical eyebrow at Robinson. Robinson'd clearly had too much to drink, because he responded with indignant pomp, heading back toward her with his chest puffed out like a pigeon.

"What's it to you, Smith?" Robinson said, the bourbon on his breath a little sour. Cate stepped back, mostly because she didn't want a face full of vomit. He was far enough gone that that felt pretty likely at this point.

"What's it to your wife is the better question—"

"Hey, now," said Hower, "we have to get back to roll call. We don't have time for the two of you to fight over Jacob's wife."

"Who knew Smith was pining after Robinson's girl ?" Sam Corbett chuckled. "Last I heard, you were sticking it in Franklin Steele's wife."

Cate clenched her fists in Corbett's direction, but he just laughed as Henry held her back by her shoulders.

"Charley, give it up. It's not worth it," he hissed in her ear. She took a deep breath and rolled her shoulder out of his hand.

They made it back to camp in time but just barely. Osborn glowered at them but said nothing, reporting them present. Cate sneered at Robinson as they crawled in the tent before lying down on her blanket, the rough ground hard on her shoulder. However, she quite forgot about him when she felt a warm hand on her hip.

She rolled onto her other shoulder and strained to make out Henry's features in the darkness. He didn't say anything, but his hand remained where it was, possessive over the curve of her hip. She snaked her hand down to twine her fingers in his. Even as she thrilled at the warm callus of his skin against hers, she couldn't quell the questions popping unbidden into her mind as she tried to calm her stimulated mind for sleep. What did it mean that they'd resumed their—she didn't even know what to call it—arrangement? What did he expect now that he had the means and the consent to fuck her without consequence? And what would he do after he'd had his fill of her?

None of these questions were particularly appealing to contemplate, much less anything she wished to pose in conversation. So she smothered her uncertainty in carefully curated fresh memories of Henry's hands and mouth and cock. Perhaps if they were careful, they could find their way into a private room.

There were multiple hotels in this railroad town, in spite of its small size. If she could have that, she could strip him of his uniform, touch and taste that exquisite, well-honed body at her leisure.

It occurred to her that if that were the case, he'd likely want to see her too. She was surprised to find that, for the first time in her life, she didn't balk at the prospect. Quite the contrary, in fact. She was rather shocked to find that it excited her.

By the time she drifted off to sleep, she was half-crazed, caught between abject terror that someone would see his hand on her hip and deep, abiding desire to curl up in his arms and damn the consequences.

———

XII

Lebanon, Kentucky
Friday, December 13, 1861

THE FIRE IN THE Sibley stove had gone out, as it usually did by dawn, and Henry was shivering. It was colder than it had been in Lebanon so far, but they'd only been there since Tuesday, so he didn't have much in the way of expectations. Cracking an eye open, he saw Charley's dark curls peeking out from the edge of her wool blanket. Beyond her, Osborn and Webster were tucked up tight together, sharing blankets and warmth quite platonically. Henry peered at them for a moment, his jaw set, before he scooted toward Charley and curved himself around her, tossing the edge of his blanket across her side along with his arm.

She stirred as he embraced her, eyes fluttering before she settled back into his chest with a sigh. When it was cold enough, no one cared about personal space. Most fellows with brothers grew up sharing beds. So why did Henry feel like he was getting away with something?

Henry pressed his nose into Charley's hair and enjoyed the bloom of her singular scent. She was warm and comfortable and pliantly sleepy. Though the shape of her was well obscured by her uniform and greatcoat, Henry couldn't help but try to trace the curve of her hip with his hand.

All week he'd been completely wrapped up in daydreams about Charley. It didn't help that she stood behind him during drill, so her presence was a constant awareness prickling at the back of his neck. He couldn't stop thinking about the Sterling

House and the way Charley had looked at him when she'd wished they had a room there. The top brass had tightened up camp rules considerably since that first chaotic day, setting up a perimeter with guards on duty and requiring passes for soldiers to go into town. Command worked them around the clock at picket duty and drills, and Henry scarcely had a chance to visit the Ninth Ohio, much less entertain the thought of finding somewhere private to pull Charley off to. That didn't mean it wasn't constantly at the top of his mind, though.

A private room, perhaps with a fire and a proper bed, would be a godsend. An absolute miracle. If Henry could manage a safe encounter there, perhaps he'd revisit his conclusions about a benevolent god. It was perhaps his greatest dream at present. The idea of being alone with Charley, to have time with her, perhaps to undress her and enjoy the taste of her skin—it was more than he could bear to contemplate.

Henry shifted his hips. The spiral of his thoughts had got his blood pumping, and it being so close to dawn, he couldn't risk the evidence of his interest being noticed. He tried to put a little space between his erection and the curve of Charley's backside, but she immediately noticed. In fact, Henry wasn't convinced she was asleep at all, because she *rolled* her hips back into his groin.

A flush rushed into Henry's cheeks, but it was half-hearted because the majority of his blood had dropped to his prick. What on earth was she trying to do? Torture him? There was nothing to be done about his current state of arousal in a tent full of other men when Reveille was going to play at any moment. He could only conclude she was prime evil.

He was pressing back into her, his hand slipping inside her greatcoat and sliding over her chest, when Reveille played. Her quiet growl of frustration was somewhat of an understatement. Henry had to struggle to hide his disappointment as she turned away from him and sat up.

Later at breakfast, Henry sat next to Charley cross-legged on the ground, slurping up porridge from his tin plate without a spoon. The rest of the squad, and the Hastings boys too, were all gathered round. They lit up the fire they'd built between their

Sibley tents, for percolating coffee but mostly to stave off the lingering early morning cold.

"I am looking forward to when we can return to the Sterling House," Hower declared, to the exasperated groans of Sergeant Osborn and Webster. Henry paid him little attention. He was too busy keeping an eye on Sam Corbett. He was sitting on the other side of Charley and kept whispering in her ear. She was sniggering at something he'd said, and Henry knew it was petty and jealous, but he was certain it wouldn't be an overreaction to pop the snivelling weasel in the chin.

"Hower, you're going to lose your rank if you sneak off," Osborn said. "And I hope you know that you're making my bid for first sergeant particularly difficult."

"Oh, Sarg, we all make your bid for first sergeant difficult," Robinson laughed. Osborn sighed into his tin cup of coffee.

"I'm telling you, though, the place is really very elegant," Hower insisted. Charley elbowed Henry and rolled her eyes. Henry, relieved she'd turned to him instead of Corbett, laughed.

Krüger laughed too. "It's a bawdy house."

"Yes, but that's not what I went there for," Hower scoffed. Henry shook his head. If that man got a chance, any chance at all, he'd take it. Henry had no doubt about that, given his friend's penchant for dirty novels set in brothels much like the one currently being discussed. "They had barrel whiskey and a pool table. There were tables full of fellows playing cards, and I heard the proprietress, well one of them anyway, is a first-rate euchre player."

Krüger's brow indicated he remained unconvinced. Hower was not at all deterred.

"I keep hearing folks accusing the Sterling House of having a less-than-sterling reputation," Hower grinned at his own wordplay as the other fellows groaned, "but how many of them have seen the place for themselves? I shan't jump to conclusions about the nature of our host village, or any of its amenities."

Corporal Harris of the Hastings Squad burst into laughter.

"What?" Hower sniffed.

"You're a veritable man about town, you are," Harris chuckled. "What are you, sixteen?"

Hower puffed up like a rooster. "I'm twenty-two, thank you very much."

"'Twenty-two, la di da,'" Harris replied as he strolled past Hower toward the parade ground. He flicked the bill of Hower's forage cap as he sauntered off, Hower's face turning a lovely shade of fuschia.

Henry's eyes tracked back to Hower, who had straightened with the affront to his dignity. "We'll see how he likes it," Hower said, "when Osborn gets first sergeant, and I'm promoted to sergeant."

"In the meantime," Sam Corbett sniggered, "you best get yourself to Sterling House. Sergeants don't get the privilege of being so many ants under the boot of the big bugs. They're just important enough to be noticed."

"—But not important enough to do anything of use," Charley muttered under her breath. Henry snorted.

Hower continued to smooth his ruffled feathers.

"Ah, don't get your dander up," Corbett sighed as he got to his feet. "You know we're all riled up to go with you."

Hower cast him a wary glance.

Krüger laughed and clapped him on the back. "I'd give my left arm for fresh euchre players."

"First rate," Hower said, a smile creeping onto his lips. "I'll let you all know when there's a good opportunity to slip away."

Henry looked down at Charley with a grin. Knowing Hower, he'd perfectly organize a group escape into town. Hotel or bawdy house—it didn't make a difference. Both had beds. Henry had his backpay burning a hole in his pocket. And Charley had a French letter burning a hole in hers. She glanced up at him and shook her head, but she was smiling too. God, he hoped Hower would find an opportunity sooner rather than later.

———

The rest of the day was spent drilling, and Cate found that in spite of the change in scenery, the drills did not become any more interesting than they had been in Lebanon Junction, or anywhere else for that matter. In the dearth of information from command, rumors abounded as to the whereabouts of Zollicoffer and his Rebel troops. It didn't help that their wagon train of supplies still hadn't arrived from Lebanon Junction. It would have been one thing if the roads were washed out with rain or snowed over, but the weather had been quite mild. The teamsters had no excuse. Spare moments were filled with speculation and the prevailing rumor was that the teamsters had all either been captured by Secesh or defected. Given how little action they had seen, Cate was beginning to wonder if the latter was indeed more likely.

The wagon trains finally arrived after lunch, and Company K was assigned to help them unload. Cate managed to catch up with them quickly after begging a point of personal privilege in the woods—her monthly had come on strong after she'd choked down the pastille from the pharmacist, thank heavens. It had been a fumble to address it without drawing any undue attention, but gratefully, it was exhausting itself as quickly as it had exhausted her.

As she dashed across the camp grounds, she nearly tripped over two young Black children loitering near the cooking tent.

"'Scuse me," she said as a matter of course, teetering around them so she wouldn't collide.

The elder of the children looked up and started. "Begging your pardon, sir," the child said, eyes on the ground as he skittered out of her reach, yanking his younger counterpart along by the collar.

Cate stilled. It was like one of those strange moments when she was reminded how differently people treated her when she walked the world as a man, but instead, it was a reminder of how differently people treated those of color. A reminder that in this town and in this state, there was a caste system, and regardless of whether Cate agreed with it, she was standing near the top. Complicit by association with her officers, her president, and the Union that prioritized loyalty over righteousness. She wished she had something to give these boys, some peace offering. But she had nothing, so she had to settle for a soft, deprecating laugh.

"Please, I beg your pardon. I was gathering wool and wasn't looking where I was going." Cate gave her best approximation of a disarming smile. Admittedly, she was imitating Henry. "Carry on, and pay me no mind."

Cate walked off before the boys could reply, her chest tight with discomfort. She felt like an imposter, not because she wasn't actually a man, but because she rankled under the fearful deference with which the little boys had reacted to her. She couldn't spare it any mind, however, because the whole squad was already starting to unload the first wagon, and she wasn't yet accounted for.

The whole squad was in relatively good spirits as she caught up, bantering about the artillery demonstration from Kenney's Battery the previous day.

"It is quite a heady thing, I should think, to be aiming a cannon," Robinson pontificated.

"I suppose you would know," Hower quipped. "I'm sure your woman veritably shudders to think—"

"*Corporal*," Osborn warned.

"Aw, Sarg, you're no fun."

"Boys." It was Webster and he looked much too serious for the nature of the current discourse. Cate turned her attention to the older man's grim expression and followed his gaze beyond the wagons. A small group of soldiers flanked a sour-looking man looking rather worse for wear as they escorted him toward the village.

"Is that a Reb?" Robinson squeaked.

"It must be," Osborn murmured. Cate glanced toward Hower to get his read on things, but the corporal had already slipped off, presumably on reconnaissance.

"Do you think they saw any action on their way here?" Robinson asked.

"It would explain why it took so long," Henry replied.

"Hell, if I had known guard duty for the mule train was the way to finally fight, I would have been more eager to volunteer," Cate groused, crossing her arms.

They approached the wagons, their heads swiveling back to watch the prisoner as he was marched across camp while Lieutenant Thomas set them to work unloading crates of rations.

"Say," Robinson said to the teamster, Griffith, climbing from the covered wagon bed as Henry started handing crates down from its bed, "did you all see some action on the way here?"

"Oh, aye," Griffith replied tiredly. He was Scottish or Irish—Cate couldn't tell the difference by ear. "Some of the guards were rustling up forage from a local cabin, and the Secesh was particularly uncooperative."

The whole squad stopped what they were doing and leaned in eagerly.

"The bastard shot off some buckshot and caught Cardwell in the arm. We managed to capture him though."

"Capture him? Were you all not armed yourselves?" Cate had an overly large crate in her arms, but that didn't stop her from leveling the man with eyebrowed skepticism. Surely the teamsters knew how to fire a rifle and were able to defend the supplies they'd been entrusted with for the soldiers.

"I couldn't say," Griffith shrugged.

"Is Cardwell alright?" Osborn asked, shooting a sideways glare toward Cate.

Griffith rolled his eyes. "Aye, he's first rate. They got the buckshot out fine, and he's been complaining loudly, but that just goes to show he's not too bad off."

Cate accepted one of the last crates from Henry so he could hop down from the wagon bed. They followed the squad, each laden with a crate, into the camp proper. They carted the crates to the outdoor kitchen and left the cook to dig through their contents. It was around this time that Hower returned.

"Excellent timing, Hower," Webster said crossly, picking at a splinter his crate had lodged in his palm.

"You'll never guess what happened," Hower declared. "It's an outrage."

"A Secesh shot Cardwell from Company D while procuring forage?" Robinson said serenely.

"Yes, but—"

"And they captured the perpetrator but didn't return fire?" Cate added in.

"Yes, but—" Hower flailed. It was too easy. Cate tried to hide a smile.

"And Cardwell is shot and will carry those scars for the rest of his life?" Webster added gravely, leveling the rest of them with disapproval at the flippancy with which they were treating the situation.

"Yes, *and* Command has put the bastard up in a jail cell, waiting on him hand and foot with rations, while Cardwell gets on with his duties," Hower burst out. Cate felt her belly drop out from underneath her and her back teeth ground together. That certainly got the rest of the squad's attention. They all swarmed Hower.

"Turns out a couple of Cardwell's pals were ready to execute the bastard," he continued, "but the officer in charge stopped them and made them march him back here for some sort of court-martial."

Cate had been reprimanded for her outburst at Lebanon Junction, after the bridge had collapsed. She pressed her lips together and tried her damndest not to articulate how damned pigheaded and shortsighted the asses in charge were to privilege the enemy thus.

"Can we court-martial an enemy?" Williamson asked. "Seems like war would be a pretty tedious business if we court-martialed every enemy soldier."

"I don't know," Osborn replied.

"This prick—Jackson's his name—ambushed and shot one of our boys and the damned incompetents in charge of this outfit might as well give him a goddamned medal." Hower curled his lip in disgust. "I got this all from the fellows from D. They're spitting mad and ready to lynch the bastard if command won't implement justice."

Henry's mouth dropped open and he was not the only one. "Isn't that a bit extreme?"

Cate heard a roaring in her ears. Her throat was tight with the effort of keeping her damned fool mouth shut.

Hower shrugged. "I figure if you're willing to shoot, you need to accept that it may result in you getting shot."

"Yes, but we aren't barbarians, who pay violence with more violence, and execute our enemies *carte blanche*. There are rules and rights we must adhere to," Osborn said. "The fact that it's frustrating is how you know you're doing it right."

Cate threw up her arms. "And look at how far *that's* gotten us. The big bugs care more about this one Secesh's rights than all the slaves we've passed by since coming to Kentucky. They're damned hypocrites. I for one hope they give that Secesh what he deserves."

"What makes you think we know the right of it?" Webster replied. "'Beloved, never avenge yourselves, but leave it to the wrath of God.' I'm certain there is a great deal we don't know. After all, we weren't even there."

Cate leveled him with her nastiest glare.

"The boys in D were there," Hower interrupted before Cate could lay in. "And they seem to have a pretty clear idea of what justice should look like."

"'When justice is done, it is a joy to the righteous but terror to evildoers,'" rumbled Krüger, and his dark tone made the hairs on the back of Cate's neck stand up. This was the kind of righteous moralizing she got caught up in, and it brought her back to the abolitionist sermons she'd attended in Pittsburgh and St. Anthony. Any tool that was sharp was good enough for Cate. So long as it cut away at the institution of slavery and pressed closer to liberation for those in bondage.

The words came back to her lips like a homecoming. "'God considers it just to repay with affliction those who afflict you.'"

"That's enough," Osborn cut in, his voice slicing firm and solid through the mounting tension. "None of us will be participating in vigilante justice. I don't care if it's righteous or not. If any among you are out of line or unaccounted for, you can bet I will be kicking it up the chain of command and asking for a court-martial. You can quote Bible verses at me all day long, but until there is an order to execute the man, we'll have nothing to do with him. *Is that clear?*"

Cate gritted her teeth and stared, fuming, at the Sarg, but said nothing more. Williamson and Robinson looked rather chastened, while Hower and Krüger glared defiantly. Cate disgruntledly noticed Henry looked more relieved than anything. Osborn shook his head and turned on his heel, stalking off toward the kitchen tent.

"You'll all report to the parade ground in five minutes," he threw out over his shoulder. Cate clenched her fingers into a fist until her stubby nails dug into her palms. Hower shook his head in frustration. Webster frowned disapprovingly at the rest of them and made to go after Osborn.

"If war isn't the time for men to mete out lethal justice, when is?" Hower drawled, his arms crossed.

Robinson looked at him incredulously but didn't reply. Henry didn't take the bait either. The boys ducked into the tent to get their kits for drill. Cate stalked over to their stacked arms and snatched her rifle from the pile. Henry approached and took up his rifle too.

"If we don't get to fight some Secesh soon, they can't be surprised if we mutiny," she muttered to him, shaking her head.

"You must admit, there is a big difference between firing on a man in the heat of battle and executing him in cold blood," Henry said quietly.

"I'm struggling to see how the Secesh in question did anything but the latter," she said through gritted teeth. "Just because he didn't succeed and Caldwell walked away doesn't erase the attempt."

Henry looked harrowed as the two of them set off toward the parade ground. "This is why I have no interest in becoming an officer."

"I would tend to agree if I didn't fear the utter fallibility of the men who *are* in charge. We are meant to trust their leadership, but they're not any wiser than we are. For Chrissakes, they were all up late studying the drill manual when we were at Fort Snelling so they could look like they knew what they were talking about the next day."

Henry sighed. "You're not wrong. I'm not sure there is an easy answer."

"Neither am I." She frowned at the pale winter grass, watched her boots hit the cold, packed ground beneath it. "I know it's not noble or wise, but if it were up to me, the world could use significantly fewer slavers. Peace and rational argument have long since proven to make no difference."

"I'd tend to agree. But no one ever said this man owned slaves."

Cate looked up at the sky and implored divine patience. "Fine. Yes. That is true." She let out a frustrated growl as they approached the gathering men falling into rank on the parade ground. "But if I'm facing down a line of Secesh on the battlefield, I'm not going to worry about which of them have slaves and which do not. Fact is, they're all fighting for the *right* to have them, whether they do or not. To own another human being—God, Henry, it's revolting. Do you see these people in this town? There's so many people held in bondage here, and I can't see one damn thing that makes them different that isn't skin deep. The children sing and play. They worship every Sunday. They form communities and families and they love and they lose and how, Henry, *how?* How can someone ignore that they are just as human as the rest of us? How can they look at these children and see them as something to be bought and sold?"

Henry blinked. "I don't know. I truly don't."

Cate looked at him for a long moment, searching for a reflection of the fire she was feeling, burning her up on the inside. Henry only looked weary. He didn't have the same fight in him, somehow. For all he knew the arguments and the reasons and the evidence, he didn't feel the imperative to rip it all to shreds the way she did. In all the relief of their reconciliation, she'd forgotten how lonely it could be, even in this crowded camp. She remembered now.

Cate shook her head and stalked off into the ranks. He let her go, and she hated every moment of it.

———

Drills were so rote by this point that they required no thought. Even when the officers thought they were being clever and mixing up the order of their commands, it required scarcely any attention to comply. Henry spent the entirety of forenoon drills moving his body through the motions as the Company proceeded this way and that, puzzling out the moral conundrum of this morning's argument. The squad was a little less playful than usual but there didn't seem to be any hard feelings. That wasn't the problem. The problem was that he didn't know what to think.

He could see the situation from both sides. The Secesh man had shot a Union soldier and justice needed to be served. But the soldier hadn't died and even if he had, would it be justice to kill another, and a civilian at that? He didn't know. And what Charley had said complicated things even further. Was there really that big of a difference between killing an enemy combatant on the battlefield and killing him on the march? What was the difference between an enemy combatant and an armed civilian? A uniform? A commanding officer?

The point of the chain of command was to rest these decisions and moral gray areas in a hierarchy of structure and order. But when he was faced down with a line of men in gray, would he be able to see enemy combatants? Or would he see other men, just as confused and fearful as himself?

It was a thought that struck him somewhere deep, and he flinched away from it, bringing his focus instead to his weapon and the commands from Captain Noah ringing in his ears. He couldn't scarcely remember what he expected when he'd been so eager to enlist. This certainly wasn't it.

After drill was over, Henry lagged behind, bending to tie his boot as the others hustled to the commissary tent to get their dinner. He had this nagging feeling that there was something he needed to unpick in his mind, that in between all of these moral questions was an answer that would satisfy him, but he couldn't figure out what it was. A part of him was scared to try.

He was ambling back toward the main camp when his uncle Karl caught up with him.

"What's got you looking so pensive?" Karl asked in German, nudging his shoulder.

Henry shook his head and smiled guiltily. "Oh, it's nothing. The boys were all in a fit this morning over a Secesh the teamsters captured." He shrugged.

"Sounds very exciting," Karl said with an indulgent sort of smile.

"Say, you've been on the field a good deal already," Henry said. "What is it like?"

"Hm? How do you mean?"

"I don't know. I don't know what I don't know, you see. We haven't seen battle yet, and I'm just wondering what it's like."

Karl frowned. "Well, it's loud. Smoky. Some think it's exciting while others find it terrifying."

"How do *you* find it?"

Karl scratched his beard and frowned deeper. "It's not as gallant as they'd like to make us think. It's messy and bloody and painful and ... well, I count myself lucky to have made it through in one piece thus far."

"Is it worth it?" Henry was singularly focused.

Karl tilted his head and studied him under a furrowed brow. "Pardon?"

"Is it worth it? Is it worth all the mess and the blood and the pain?"

Karl sighed and looked around. "I don't know. I hope to heaven it is, but I suppose that depends on which side wins, ultimately."

Henry looked at him for a moment and sighed. "Well, you're no help."

Karl laughed. "I never claimed to be. Damn—what a dreary topic. Say, did you get a chance to speak to that young thing you were on the outs with?"

"Huh?"

Karl raised an eyebrow at him. "The one who broke things off after you 'um'...?"

Henry blushed hard and spluttered. He felt Karl settle a hand on his shoulder.

"It's alright, Henry, I know," his uncle said quietly, leaning in. Henry's stomach dropped out from under him. "I saw you go into the alley."

Henry turned sharply to face Karl, his eyes wide and face ashen. Oh shit. Charley was going to murder him. His mind scrambled for an excuse but all that came out was, "Uhhh..."

"Don't panic," Karl murmured and glanced up to make sure no one was near enough to overhear. "It's very normal for fellows in this kind of situation to seek comfort among one another."

Henry's eyes widened. He opened his mouth to protest and choked on his denial. If Karl had seen him go into the alley with Charley, anything Henry might say to protest against his insinuation would reveal her secret. Karl was a good man in many respects, but Henry wasn't about to find out if he was the kind of man who would let a woman go into battle. He couldn't do that to Charley. He shut his mouth with a click of his teeth.

Karl had him by both shoulders now and was looking him squarely in the eye. "I will not say a thing. You can count on me, you know you can. This might surprise you, but I'm glad for you. You were twisted up pretty bad over this fellow the other day, and if you can find some comfort, you should take it. War is a nasty business and there are a lot less honorable ways for a man to cope than what you've found."

Henry experienced a stillness. His nerves stopped jangling, and he breathed easier. It scarcely occurred to him to contradict Karl out of some conceptual defense of his interest in women. Because Charley wasn't a woman, not in the way he knew them in bell-shaped dresses and bonnets adorned with flowers and lace. She moved in a space between, carrying herself as a man but in a body that defied expectation. She was both. She was neither. And in that sense, Karl had Henry pegged completely right. So what would be the point of arguing?

"I, um," Henry said, his voice cracking.

Karl shook his head. "It's alright, Henry. You'd be surprised how common it is."

"Common?"

Karl lifted his eyebrows and nodded significantly. "Very."

It took Henry a moment to catch up with what Karl was implicating. Was this happening? Were men slaking desire with each other? When? Where? They had no privacy in camp at all. The implications made his mind reel, all the way back to the Athaeneum in Cincinnati, and several awkward encounters he'd stumbled into in the changing room after a gymnasticks practice. Now that he thought about it, one of those memories featured Karl and Herr Mayer... If it was possible, Henry blushed harder.

"I'm sorry, I didn't mean to embarrass you," Karl said with a light chuckle. "I just wanted you to know you have an ally if you ever need one. And also, you need to be more careful."

"Careful?"

"About your choice of location, for one thing. Anyone on the boardwalk could have seen you as they walked by, had they deigned to look."

Henry flushed, horrified. Karl let go of his shoulders and gave him a long, paternal look.

"You're lucky it was dark, is all I'm saying," Karl said with raised brows and a shrug. "So be careful. But also, be careful with your heart, Heinrich. This is a bloody war and even in the best of times, fellows aren't terribly dependable. If he's cut you once already, you can expect he can do it again."

Henry exhaled shakily. He could only nod. He didn't trust himself to say anything.

"There, now, buck up," Karl said with a smile, letting Henry's shoulders go. "You'll find your way, you'll see. Now, I've got to get back before battalion drill, but I just wanted to check on you." He paused, then chuckled. "Are you going to be alright or do I need to take you to the hospital tent?"

Henry shook his head furiously, and Karl laughed.

"Very good then—I'll see you around." He smiled and turned on his heel toward his own camp.

"Karl, wait."

Karl turned and tipped his head inquiringly.

"Am I—" Henry started, unsure of how to articulate this feeling bubbling up in his chest. "Am I being a fool?"

Karl closed the distance between them again, lips pressed to a thin line. "How so?"

Henry let out a shaky breath and pushed a hand into his hair. "I mean, for chasing after Smith?"

Karl shrugged. "Probably. But remember this: only *you* know what's best for you. Don't let anyone tell you otherwise. And if I've learned anything from the field of battle thus far, it's that life is too short to have regrets."

Henry nodded slowly. That was for damn sure, and Cardwell from Company D was lucky to count himself as living proof.

Karl gave his goodbyes again and trotted off, but Henry continued standing on the hill for a moment. He was deeply relieved he hadn't blown Charley's secret. He was also somewhat surprised to find he didn't care at all that his uncle assumed he was "finding comfort" with another man. In many ways, it was true. He was much more concerned about keeping Charley's secret. Besides, it seemed like every Greek work he'd ever read was filled with fellows finding love amongst themselves. While it hadn't occurred to him that such a thing might be happening under his nose, he found it didn't surprise him. What was really sticking in his craw was that last comment—"Only you know what's best for you."

No one had ever said that to him before. It made him feel incredibly exposed and alone. How was he supposed to know what was best for him when he couldn't even explain what he had enlisted for? He'd said to Charley he was more interested in asking questions than having answers, but was that what he truly wanted, or was it only what he had?

The bugle sounded, calling them all to battalion drill, and shook Henry from his thoughts.

"Henry! You missed dinner."

He turned and saw Charley coming up the hill toward him. She had her rifle over one shoulder and a heel of bread in the other. She put it in his hands as she approached him, then carried on toward the parade ground effortlessly. Her previous ire seemed to have faded. He stood frozen for a moment, crust crumbs on his fingers. She'd never seemed so ... in focus before. Everything about her—her shiny curls, her dark slash of brows, the bow of her lips—seemed crisp and simultaneously both new and achingly familiar. It felt strangely like a reunion, even though he'd seen her only thirty minutes ago.

"What's got your dander up?" she asked, brow lifted, when she realized he'd failed to fall into step with her.

Henry shook his head and trotted after her. "Nothing. Thanks."

———

XIII

Lebanon, Kentucky
Sunday, December 15, 1861

IT WAS SUNDAY, STRANGELY enough, when Elias Hower seized upon his chance to return to Sterling House. Cate and the rest of the squad had been heading to Sunday service after breakfast when Sam Corbett and the other fellows from Hastings had fallen into step with Hower, murmuring about something or other. Cate lurked as Henry asked what Corbett had said, half-expecting an effort to punish the Secesh, who was still being held prisoner. Hower grinned and told them in a very hushed voice that he was off to revisit the fiery Venus of Lebanon, Miss Sterling herself.

Cate rolled her eyes—Hower's tale of fascinating vice had grown more elaborate all week, and she had concluded that the bulk of it was pure bunk. Nevertheless, a hotel with a busy clientele and rooms for hire was very welcome, a thought which encouraged her to glance in Henry's direction. His eyes flicked to hers, and he seemed to be resisting a flush that began to appear at his collar as he said to Hower, "I should like to see that."

"Why don't you come along?"

"How will we get out of camp without being caught?"

"Corbett's got some pals on guard duty tonight that'll look the other way."

"So will we go after nine o'clock roll call, then?" Cate asked, insinuating herself into the conversation and earning an appraising look from Hower.

"Yes, that's the idea," Hower said slowly, looking between the two of them. "Look—Corbett's heading there with a few fellows from his squad. Don't tell anyone else, alright? The larger the group, the less chance we'll get in and out of camp unseen."

Cate raised her eyebrows, pressing her fingertips to her chest. "You don't have to worry about me. I'm quiet as a churchmouse. It's this Johnny-Come-Lately you've got to worry about." She smacked Henry on the shoulder for effect. He glowered at her but said nothing.

They hatched a scheme with Hower and agreed to meet him outside the tent after lights-out. With Osborn in the hospital tent with a bad cold, it was the perfect time to slip out unnoticed. Then they strode off to the Sunday service, which would have been a nice and peaceful gathering in a copse of woods if it weren't for all the moralizing pouring out of the army chaplain's mouth.

They had a little leeway between dinner and brigade drill (it seemed even the Lord's day was cut short in wartime), so Cate took up their squad's bucket and brought it to the well without spending too much time thinking about why washing was her first priority for leisure. Usually, the boys would slop off in the morning before drills with a wet rag. A miserable excuse for a standing bath. There hadn't been an opportunity for a formal bath for months, but there was water and soap and a furtive semblance of privacy under the cover of long shirttails. Cate brought her bucket, so full it was slopping a bit over the edges as she lumbered along to the Sibley tent and was pleased to find the shelter empty.

She salvaged her sliver of soap from her satchel and shrugged off her coat. She thanked all of her lucky stars that as heavy as her courses had been upon their sudden and furious return, they'd spent themselves quickly and were tenuously concluded. She'd sneaked out of camp and pilfered rags from a laundry in town—she wasn't proud—and between changing rags out and washing and drying in a thicket down a ways from the camp, she'd scarcely been able to keep up with the whole affair. Regardless of the burden of secrecy, though, she found she couldn't mind too much given the knowledge she wasn't compromised. The relief was expansive.

Waistcoat was discarded after her sack coat, then suspenders shrugged down and trousers shucked. She'd tied the flap of the tent shut, but that didn't seem to deter whomever it was that attempted entry as Cate was standing over the bucket in her shirttails.

"Hey, can you wait a goddamned minute?" she barked as soon as she heard whoever it was scrabbling at the ties. She reminded herself that she was covered, that there was nothing suspicious to see through her shirt stooped over as she was. "I'm washing."

"In the middle of the day?" It was Williamson's voice. "I just want to get my canteen."

"Aren't you supposed to have that with you already?" Cate replied with exasperation. Dropping the soap in the bucket, she went to Williamson's little burrow on the opposite side of the tent. "I'll get it for you. Just stay there."

The tent flapped open and the sun shone a triangle on the dirt floor. Cate immediately crossed her arms and stomped her still-booted foot. "Williamson! Come on!"

Williamson scowled in her general direction. "I don't want you digging through my things."

"Oh, what am I gonna find, a goddamned love letter to Abe Lincoln?"

Williamson shot her a dubious look.

"Who's writing love letters to Lincoln?"

Cate whirled around to see Henry's shoulders blocking the light through the flap. She was covered, but she also wasn't at all and it felt entirely different for him to cast eyes on her with her legs bare. Not bad, but definitely worse than if Williamson hadn't been there.

"Smith, sounds like," Williamson said, canteen in hand as he sidled around Henry to exit the tent. "Takes one to know one!"

Henry stepped aside for Williamson to leave. A grin was creeping wide onto his blunt jaw as he cheerfully retied the tent flaps.

"What are you up to in here?" His eyes were assessing.

Cate glowered. "Washing up. I haven't had a chance to dunk my hair in weeks, and I need it to feel like separate strands again." Dear God. What the hell was she saying?

Henry's mouth was turned up but only on one side. "What a judicious idea." He shucked his coat and began unbuttoning his waistcoat too. Cate found it was rather hard to swallow. "Well, what are you waiting for? Unless you want me to go first?"

"No! I hauled this water, I'm using it first."

Cate stood over the bucket again and took up her rag, scrubbing it against the soap bar. She looked up at Henry. He was watching her while he pushed his suspenders off his shoulders, and when he caught her eye, he grinned. Oh God, she desperately hoped they'd find a way to some privacy tonight. Not the kind they had presently, furtive and fleeting at any moment. Real, dedicated time, just the two of them. Preferably in the vicinity of a bed, but Cate wasn't about to be picky. Cate watched audaciously as Henry pushed his trousers down and stepped out of them. God, those thighs. Pale skin flashing where his shirttails curved up over his flanks. Cate's breath was short.

"Come here," she said.

"That would be unwise," he replied with that grin.

"I sincerely doubt that."

"I'm alone with a libertine. I should be surprised if I escape with my innocence." His voice was hushed, for who knew what fools were just outside the canvas, but the way his voice husked softly past his lips made her want to plunder them with her tongue. "Well, what are you waiting for?"

"Huh?" Cate blinked.

Henry nodded to the bucket. "Get on with it. I'm freezing."

Cate remembered she had a soapy rag in her hand. Right. There was no point dithering, but she felt utterly exposed under his gaze. She'd intended to soap herself down under her shirt and then wash her hair, but she couldn't bring herself to push the rag under her shirttails with his playful eyes watching her every move. So she bent and gripped the rim of the bucket, rag still scrunched in her palm, and dunked her head in.

With Henry out of sight, she could seize the soap and scrub suds through her scalp under the pretense that he wasn't watching her, even though he was and she could feel his eyes on the back of her neck like a palm. Like a promise.

She scrubbed her hair and rinsed it thoroughly, a bit hesitant to proceed to the next section. Her curls were getting long, long enough to gather in her palms and ring out a bit, so she did that before straightening.

Henry was closer now. Within reach. Her heart leapt toward him in her chest. His cheeks were flushed, even though it wasn't particularly warm in here and both their legs had goosebumps. Cate's eyes were drawn to the front of his shirttails, where the evidence of his arousal was pitching a tent—

The actual tent flaps burst open.

"Honestly, I can't believe they make us drill on the Lord's day at all," Robinson was saying to Webster as they both tumbled into the tent, then paused when they saw Cate and Henry standing around a bucket in their shirts like a couple of loons.

"What're you up to?" Webster asked in that dubious voice he probably used with his children.

Cate found her arms crossed again, to her relief, and glowered. "Washing. What's it look like?"

Robinson raised a brow.

"I was *trying* to snatch some privacy," she rushed to add, "but Schaefer's such a damn *tag-along*—"

"Come now, it's Sunday," Webster sighed. He'd already dug up his kit and was strapping it on. "Do we have to swear on a Sunday?"

"Sorry, Pops. A *flim flam* tag-along," Cate corrected sourly.

"It's been an age since my hair's had a wash," Henry cut in. "And Smith already fetched the water."

Robinson and Webster exchanged looks.

"True enough," Webster said consideringly. "I admit my scalp's been itching for a wash."

"I'd been meaning to do that too," Robinson agreed. "I washed up this morning, but a good scalp scrub wouldn't be amiss."

Cate let out an exasperated sigh. "Well. By all means. Don't let me, the person who fetched the water and bought the soap and who was *trying* to snatch a little privacy, get in your way."

Robinson very graciously let Henry wash his hair next, and Cate finished washing up in the strange veneer of privacy provided by the rest of the fellows being thoroughly distracted with themselves. As she pulled her trousers back on, she caught Henry's eye while he dried his hair with a spare shirt. He smiled, his expression so tender it made Cate feel exposed. She shook her head.

Sterling House. Tonight. She made a point to make sure, as she strapped her kit on, that the French letter was securely in her pocket.

———

Brigade drill went better than ever, entire regiments maneuvering in support of one another without any major collisions. And dress parade after supper was encouraging as they marched through Lebanon proper in their full uniform. The boys were all trying their best, each thinking that he was the particular object of the many young ladies who were viewing the parade.

It tickled even Cate to see the girls waving their handkerchiefs and giggling to one another, making her want to stand a little taller, march a little more crisply. It distantly occurred to her that she should be among them, giggling at the men rather than marching with them, but after so many months of drilling and disguising herself, the thought felt more foreign than nostalgic. Even her own name had tasted strange on her tongue when she'd whispered it to Henry the other night. Somehow, in the process of playing the part of Charley Smith, she was in many ways becoming him.

Hower took roll himself at nine, in Osborn's absence, and reported them all present to Lieutenant Thomas. When he returned, Cate and Henry were ready, quietly slipping out from the tent and making their way under the shadows of the tall, conical Sibley tents. They picked up Sam Corbett, Jim Bates, and Corporal Harris along the way, and the five of them slipped uneventfully past the guard and down the hill toward town.

The streets of Lebanon were quiet, except for the meeting house between the coal and lumber yards on Mulberry Street. Within, they could hear the strains of soulful Negro singing as the Black community of Lebanon gathered for worship. Cate slowed, straining to see through the window of the meeting house. She wondered for a moment how it was that she had come to be heading for a brothel instead of a church. If this were some serialized novel in Harper's Weekly, this would be the point that she realized she had gone astray. But then Henry grasped her wrist and pulled her along with a secretive grin, and she decided that she would rather her life be a novel sold in a yellow jacket, with a title like *The Ruin of Charley Smith* or something. Or perhaps, she thought with a sly smile, she played the libertine in *The Ruin of Henry Schaefer*. She liked that even better.

The Sterling House was another source of light and din in an otherwise quiet, sleepy village. The door was looked after by that tall, broad-shouldered man they'd see the other night, but it wasn't as crowded, and their group had no trouble gaining entrance. The parlor was warm and close, filled with tobacco smoke and the loud laughter of men. There were a good number of uniformed men, but there were others, too. Locals, in suits fine enough to mark a man with the expendable income to gamble and buy the time of lovely women. Or the bodies of the enslaved. Cate recoiled from them as she passed.

Speaking of the women, there were four of them circulating the room. The brown-haired proprietess Cate remembered held court among a handful of adoring men, only one in uniform, as she dealt cards deftly and sipped from a small china cup.

"There she is," Hower said and grinned stupidly. Cate followed his gaze to the bar, where a red-haired woman pulled bourbon from a barrel in a bottle green evening dress. The corporal strode around tables and headed straight to the bar. Henry and Cate began to follow, but Sam Corbett pulled them back.

"Better leave him to his own foolishness," Corbett said.

"What do you mean?" Cate asked, watching curiously as Hower approached the woman. She was all gentle curves—there was not one feature that could be described as angular, except for perhaps her brows as her eyes alighted on Hower.

"He spent an entire month's pay on her last time, and he didn't even get to visit upstairs," Corbett said with a roll of his eyes.

"What did he spend it on, then?" Henry asked. His eyes were so innocent, and it made Cate strive to suppress the lascivious grin that threatened to overtake her face.

"Rounds of cards, drinks, the pleasure of her company at our table," Corbett shrugged. "Damn waste, if you ask me. There's piles of lovely ladies around these parts. No need to pay for what's offered for free, am I right?"

Jim Bates laughed, showing his large buck teeth. Cate scoffed and took a seat at the round table their group claimed. "When was the last time you were offered a lady's attention for free? Last time I checked, ladies weren't handing out favors to just any ugly bastard trying to steal a kiss."

Corbett glowered and the rest of the boys guffawed.

"Like you should talk, Smith. How old are you again? Eleven? Twelve?"

The cards were dealt as they merrily continued to rib each other.

"The game is poker," Corporal Harris declared.

"Thank god," Henry said. "If I have to play another round of euchre, I might throw up."

"Deal us in." Hower had returned and arranged himself into the only remaining chair, inviting the beautiful woman at his side to take a seat on his knee. "By the way, fellas, this is Miss Lucy."

The boys all gave a cordial "how do you do?" even as they grinned rudely. Miss Lucy was even more lovely up close, her eyes keen and bright, her pink lips quick to smile, and her lovely dress casting a veneer of respectability that her ungloved hands belied. Her bertha sloped to reveal her bare, freckled shoulders, and her copper hair curled from its net and delicately decorated her neck. Cate swallowed hard, and she wasn't sure if it was because she was faced with a beautiful woman or if it was because she felt utterly haggard in comparison. She tossed a furtive glance over at Henry. To her relief, he seemed engrossed with his cards.

"Well, fellas, what are we playing?" Miss Lucy asked, her voice bouncing in that hoosier twang as she leaned forward and studied Elias' cards, grasping his hand in hers. Cate stared at the audacity for a moment before she remembered she was in a brothel, and also that she had taken Henry in hand in an alleyway not a few nights previous and had utterly no legs to stand on when it came to judging propriety.

Harris instructed Miss Lucy and Hower on the game at hand, and the men all proceeded to play just as they would were there not a beautiful woman in their midst. Well, that wasn't precisely true. They ribbed each other harder, preened and peacocked, and after the first hand went to Corbett, they fell over one another to explain poker strategy to Miss Lucy. She was amusingly patient with them, especially considering she was much more likely to be a card sharp than a novice, given her place of employment. A round of ciders was delivered to the table with scarcely a twitch of a finger by Miss Lucy and several more rounds of cards and drinks left them all feeling a little lighter, a little looser, and a little louder.

Cate watched with wonder as Miss Lucy played her comrades off one another, encouraging them all in turn with an easy smile or a soft touch of her fingers to her bare decolletage. While she sat on Hower's knee, she lavished very little attention on him, instead fluffing the rest of them up to a point where—and Cate had no idea how she accomplished this—their group of soldiers seemed to understand their game of poker was somehow a competition for Miss Lucy's attention.

"I raise you all five cents, and I dedicate this hand most sincerely to the Venus of Lebanon," Hower declared, tossing a nickel onto the table and settling his other hand quite familiarly on the waist of Miss Lucy. Cate stared at his hand, tucked in the generous curves that corsets were built to assist. A Venus Miss Lucy most certainly was. She had a large, round bosom and a waist quite narrow in proportion, creamy white skin and soft, rounded shoulders and arms. She had a figure that most women—Cate included—had to contrive with all manner of padding and optical illusion, and Cate hated that she could feel herself blushing at the thought as she folded her hand. She sullenly told herself that the figure she saw was probably artifice, but one glance at Miss Lucy's decolletage as she bent forward to merrily rake in Hower's winnings made it clear that wasn't so.

"Deal me out of this next one," Henry said abruptly, standing. "Nature calls."

He sidled out of his chair, and Cate felt his fingers gently brush against the back of her neck as he passed. Shaken from her inward humiliation, she looked up sharply at his withdrawing figure to see him glance quite significantly at her over his shoulder before he went back into the main hallway.

Cate bit her lip as she took up her next hand. She didn't even look at the cards as everyone anted up. She stared at the wall behind Corbett's head, the wall Henry disappeared behind. He wasn't just visiting the privy. He'd touched her neck, given her that look. That meant something. It had to.

Cate blinked at her cards. She exchanged a two of spades for a Jack of diamonds. Her heart raced in her chest and the smoky air felt close and hot.

"I raise you a penny," Bates said, tossing his penny into the pot. The others anted in turn and when it came round to Cate, it was everything she could do to shrug nonchalantly and say, "I fold. I'm going to try my luck at billiards."

She stood and pocketed the rest of her coins, praying that none of the idiots she'd come with would be so inclined as to join her. Luckily, billiards didn't have anything on Miss Lucy, and the boys carried on as if Cate hadn't said anything at all.

She sidled round the table and headed into the main hallway, nearly running full into Henry as she turned the corner.

"Dammit, Schaefer!" she swore to cover her fluster.

He grinned at her, all lopsided over straight, white teeth, and pulled her into the shadows under the stairs. It wasn't fair, what that smile could do to her. Her heart hammered against her chest as Henry pulled her close.

"There's an open room upstairs," he murmured into her ear, his breath tickling her hair.

"What? How do you know that?" she snapped, because his forwardness was turning her legs into jelly and she very much resented it.

"I sneaked up there and checked."

"Ah, so you weren't in the privy."

"I've come to learn that it is the most convenient excuse." His nose was in her hair, and she felt thankful she'd had the foresight to wash it. "Someone's left the key in the lock, too."

She pulled back and regarded him with a serious stare. She felt a rushing in her ears, like a train was approaching too quickly for her to get out of the way. The French letter felt heavy in her pocket and the noise, the press of the thick, smoky air, the light alcoholic pulse of cider in her belly—all of it pulled inextricably on her will such that it only took her a second to say, "Show me."

Henry flashed his eyebrows and peered around the stairs at the man who tended the front door. It only took a minute or two before a group of men retired from the parlor and the door-man saw them out, allowing Henry and Cate the opportunity to tiptoe quietly up the stairs to the second floor. Cate grasped the back of Henry's jacket and felt the absurd urge to giggle as they climbed the steps to the narrow hallway above.

Henry led the way to a room at the back of the hall, the door on the left, and opened it with a quiet creak. Cate wondered absently what was behind these other doors, whether others were engaging in illicit debauchery with Miss Lucy's sisters or something. She still couldn't quite wrap her head around this hotel being a cover for a brothel. She'd always understood pros-titution to be the lowest a woman could fall, but this place didn't feel evil or tragic or anything like nefarious. It was fun, exciting, and ... free.

Miss Lucy had dominated their table, reduced the lot of her comrades to a dithering pile of idiots, and got them to veritably throw their money at her. She'd had her pick of the lot of them and it was her choice who she chose—if she chose anyone at all. Everyone said that marriage was the purest and most ideal condition for a woman, but in Cate's experience, it had been a great deal more demoralizing than what Miss Lucy appeared to do.

She was still looking over her shoulder, listening absently for any sounds to lay proof as to the true nature of the place, when Henry yanked her into the room.

Cate stumbled in, a thrill turning over her stomach, and took in the small room, sparsely furnished, lit by a dimmed oil lamp on the wall, and wholly dominated by a large bed in its center. This was happening. She bit her lip and turned toward Henry, who was facing the door and turning the key in the lock. She let a smile creep across her lips as she advanced on him and ran her hands lightly down his sides as the bolt clunked into place. Henry hummed, a deep vibration she could feel in her hands, but he didn't turn around. She pressed her body against his back, perhaps a little too forcefully, and tasted his neck as she dragged her hands up his arms, kneading his firm shoulders. He was so warm, and pliant, and he'd chosen her. She'd chosen him. He rested his cheek against the door as she kissed his neck, his lovely blue eyes fluttering closed as she reached under his arms and let her hands explore the planes of his chest.

His sack coat was a problem. The bulk of ill-fitting wool was in her damn way. Her fingers blindly fumbled for his brass buttons, and she heard his breath hitch in his throat when he realized what she was doing. She managed to get the buttons loose without too much trouble and stepped back to pull the coat from his shoulders.

"What if someone means to use this room?" Henry said in a ragged whisper. He made no move to turn around, and Cate seized upon the opportunity to pull down his suspenders and release the buttons of his shirt as well.

"Then we'll skedaddle."

"What if they see you?"

"That's what the lock is for." Cate pushed him up against the door again for emphasis, taking hold of his shirt collar and squeezing it over his shoulders, letting it hang at his waist as her hands indulged in dragging over his bare skin.

God, but he was such a well-formed man. His shoulders were broad and his waist tapered, his back a delicious topography of muscles and bone under smooth, lightly freckled skin. He let her roughly turn him round, pressing his back against the door and pressing her mouth hungrily to his. His hands twisted in her sack coat, seeking her own buttons, but she wasn't about to let herself get distracted from her study of his bare skin.

She pushed fingers through the blonde hair that dusted over his chest, dragged them over his ribs, slipped them into the edge of his waistband. She tore her mouth away from his and began kissing down his neck and chest, tasting sweat on his skin and feeling his chest heave with breath. He smelled so good—not in the traditional sense, because God knew they were both ripe again from drilling in the pleasantly warm Kentucky weather—but in the Henry sense. He smelled so well, like himself, that full, round, masculine scent of sweat and wool and earth. From an objective perspective, his smell couldn't possibly be interpreted as ideal, or even good, but she breathed it in nonetheless like a man just saved from drowning.

"God, yes," Henry said as Cate palmed his growing erection through his trousers. His hips jerked into her hands.

"I want to kiss every damn inch of you," she murmured into his sternum as she pulled at the buttons of his trousers. She wanted him muttering and shuddering and begging for her. Then she wanted him to throw her back and fuck her through the bed. She distantly understood that these things were potentially at odds, but she didn't give a damn because his cock sprang free as she shoved his trousers down to his ankles. She was struck by the urge to taste it. What would he look like if she got on her knees, used her mouth to pleasure him? Would he like that? She could hardly imagine he wouldn't, although she feared he might never look at her the same way again. It was certainly not something a good girl would do.

Cate looked up at Henry, her chin set in his navel, and wibbled.

"What?" he asked breathlessly. His chest was flushed and sweat was forming in the hollow at the center of his chest.

"I want to taste you," she whispered, watching his face desperately. Would he think her disgusting for such a thing? *Please say yes*, she thought. *Please want me.*

His eyes were round and his breath hitched in his throat. He managed a stilted nod, and Cate felt her overly eager desire waver for a moment. She wasn't a good girl by any means, but neither was she a Cyprian, and she hadn't strictly done this before. She became aware that there was probably a wrong way to do this, and she didn't know precisely what it was. She realized she was still staring at him, holding relentless eye contact as his rapidly hardening prick poked at her breast.

Cate bundled her doubts away and applied herself to the relatively easier task of kissing her way down to her knees, breathing in the smell of him that became sharper as she settled herself between his legs. She kissed the hollows where hip and thigh met and listened to Henry's ragged breath as he hung against the door, frozen and waiting. She imagined he was veritably dying of anticipation, and she smiled to herself as she let her lips brush down the length of his shaft. His skin was so soft, so velvety smooth and hot to the touch. She wrapped her fingers around the base, pulling his foreskin back as she pressed her lips to the tip. There was a bead of moisture there, and when her tongue flicked to taste it, she was surprised to find a pleasant salty sweetness.

"God, Charley, you beauty," Henry muttered and pushed his fingers through her short hair. Would he rather be looking down at a woman elegantly dressed like Miss Lucy, with long hair he could unpin to adorn her sloping shoulders? She shoved that thought well away before it could shake her and wrapped her lips round his cock, earning a desperate gasp. "Yes, please, Charley. *Charley.*"

God, but she loved how he said her name. The name he gave her. That she'd taken for herself. Damn Cate Stowell Ellis. Damn to hell Richard's useless name. Damn her father's name too. Even her given name. Cate was never good enough. Cate was too much, too loud, too opinionated, too tall, too burdensome. Fuck Cate.

Charley pulled back from him, suddenly realizing that throughout this entire endeavor, she had forgotten to breathe, and pulled in a shuddering breath. Henry looked drunk, eyes half-lidded and mouth hanging open. She probably didn't look much different.

"Come here," Henry ground out and pulled her up by her collar. Charley stared at him and he stared right back, breathing heavy, then yanked her in and kissed her. She could hardly believe it. She wondered if he could taste himself on her tongue. Shouldn't someone want to avoid such a thing? Shouldn't one probably not want to put one's mouth down there in the first place?

"This needs to come off," he muttered, pulling at her coat buttons with clumsy fingers. "I want to see you."

He gave up on the buttons quickly and pulled her sack coat over her head. Then she let him grapple with her shirt buttons for a minute before she intervened and finished them off. "Don't pull my buttons off."

"You have too many buttons," he replied, shoving her shirt open over her clavicle and shoving her suspenders down. He regarded her trousers mournfully. "Entirely too many buttons."

Charley rolled her eyes and shucked her trousers off herself. Henry took the opportunity to step out of his as well, toeing his boots off. His eyes were on her and she became painfully aware of how her shirt exposed her down to her navel, no stays or chemise or other modesty garment to hide her. The shirt was her last frontier; she'd never been seen by a man in less. Richard hadn't really bothered with any part of her apart from where he breached, proceeding with the most utilitarian of touches. It hadn't been careless, though it had felt rather impersonal. Charley always suspected wanting her too much would violate his propriety, and she hadn't thought much of it, given she'd scarcely wanted him at all.

But she wanted Henry. She wanted him badly, and the thought of standing in front of him fully exposed made her throat clench with worry. She bent and busied herself with unlacing her boots. She didn't look like Miss Lucy. She hardly looked like a woman at all, which had been a boon these months she'd been passing as a soldier. But surely Henry would miss the gentle curves and hilly breasts, the soft, feminine submission a man should expect from a woman worth wooing. She toed her boots off and reluctantly straightened.

Henry watched her with keen, blue eyes. He'd shucked his shirt and stood before her in a glorious display of masculine form, like a classical statue on a traveling display from Europe. He was all smooth skin and strapping planes, though she supposed the Greeks wouldn't be particularly taken with his chest hair or freckles in their pursuit of the ideal human form in marble. Perhaps they wouldn't have been keen to carve that furious erection, either, all the more pity. Charley didn't look anything like that either, as masculine as her features tended. She was angular and skinny, with small breasts and no visible musculature. Something in between, not either ideal.

"Go on," Henry whispered. "I want to see you."

Charley let out a high squeak of a laugh. "You know, I've never ... um." For the love of God's green earth, do *not* talk about Richard. "I find myself quite bashful, all of a sudden."

Her cheeks flamed, and she looked at the floor. She hated how vulnerable this felt. She wanted the heat back, the desperate lust. Despite how she'd longed to see him bare, to study his naked body at her leisure, at this point, she would rather he rip her shirt off her and get on with it. She frowned at her shirttails then glanced up at him. Henry saw her looking and squirmed a bit under her gaze.

"I suppose I can see what you mean," he said, shifting his weight somewhat awkwardly. Charley smirked. "You don't have to if you don't want to. I want to see you, but not if you don't want to be seen."

"No... it just feels strange," she said, watching him as she picked at the hem of her shirt. He was going to see her naked—she wanted that. They were both just going to have to face the fact that unlike him, she wasn't anything near to a Greek sculpture. "But I'm not convinced, at least not in present company, that that's such a bad thing."

———

XIV

Lebanon, Kentucky
Sunday, December 15, 1861

CHARLEY ACTUALLY BLUSHED. HENRY thought he had better save that coy, unsure expression in his memory forever, because it did things to him—delicious, pulsing things. A strip of pale flesh down to her navel taunted him between the parted buttons of her shirt. It was long enough on her that she didn't have to shuck it over her head; she could just shimmy her shoulders out and let it drop. Henry licked his lips, and his painful awareness of his own nakedness subsided as Charley evened the odds. Her large, dark eyes watched him carefully as she shrugged the shirt onto the floor.

She was perfect. Henry knew he must have looked like some sort of half-crazed lunatic with a gaping maw and a raging horn, but he really didn't care because she was unlike anyone he had ever seen.

Her small breasts were dominated by dark nipples that were already tight and hard, like they were beckoning him. Her belly was firm and flat, her waist not much narrower than her ribs or her hips, which flowed gently out to her thick, strong thighs. She could still pass for Smith, if it weren't for teacup breasts and her glaring lack of a cock. He smiled, a little ferally, and stepped toward her.

"Don't," Charley folded her arms over her chest.

Henry froze. That was certainly not the desired response. "What?"

"I know I'm not the Venus of Lebanon by any stretch of the imagination, but I don't need you to mock me for it."

"Did I mock you?"

"You can just wipe that snide little smirk off your face."

"That's what you thought that meant? I was smiling because I—"

"—Oh, this is gonna be rich—"

"*Because*," he repeated a little more forcefully, "I think you're exquisite, and I can't wait to fuck you."

Her mouth dropped open, and Henry felt a furious flush of embarrassment rush into his cheeks at how lewd he sounded. How did she get away with saying such filthy things while he sounded like some horrific villain in a novel? Her eyes softened as they flicked down to his cock, which seemed to have no qualms about saying such things and was continuing to point at her as though she were due north. It did nothing to help his embarrassment, that was for certain. He searched her expression for any sign of reticence.

"I'm sorry, that was—"

"No," she interrupted emphatically. "Say it again."

Henry hesitated. "I can't wait to f—"

"No." Her brows crumpled together. "The other part."

Henry blinked. It felt like something slid neatly into place. "You're exquisite."

He'd never seen such a raw expression on her face before, not even when he'd had her up over a barrel gasping for him to fuck her. She was naked in every sense, and he moved toward her cautiously. Cupping her face gently with both hands, he looked her squarely in the eyes.

"You are beautiful," he stated firmly and with feeling. "I love every inch of you."

Her eyes were wide and deep, and her breath shook as she exhaled. Then her hands were pulling his neck and her mouth crashed into his with a quiet whimper. The feeling of her hot, bare skin pressed broadly against his was a relief of unspeakable magnitude; he hadn't realized he could miss something he'd never had, but once he had her flush against him, he knew it was this he'd been longing for since he knew how to. She was soft, hard, warm, silken, and his hands skimmed over her sharp shoulders, smooth sides, pulled her hips in hard by the soft flesh of her buttocks. His cock was trapped between their bellies and the pressure was at once both superlative and not nearly enough.

Charley wrapped her arms around him in equal force, lips hungry and refusing to part even for a moment as she yanked him down over her onto the bed. Its ropes creaked as he caught himself on his elbows over her. He tried to pull back to grin at her, but she craned up. Her kisses were sloppy as she chased his mouth and wrapped her strong thighs around his waist. She ground her hips against him. He felt a scorching hot wetness at the base of his cock that made him gasp. Made him remember the fleeting feeling of sheathing himself inside her back in Pittsburgh. Her hands clutched at his shoulders, at his waist. She moaned loudly. Her cunt slid up and down his cock and reduced him to gasps and the mounting fear that he might come.

He pulled back more forcibly this time, earning him a frustrated growl.

"Where's the French..." he gasped and found himself grasping for the word. "...thing. Letter."

She regarded him with a predatory grin, then squirmed out from under him and rolled to her feet, comically graceful. Henry collapsed onto his back on the bed and tried to catch his breath, squeezing his thumb and forefinger around the base of his cock and pressing against his balls. He feared it would only be a matter of a few thrusts for him before he came, which seemed like a waste of this whole production with the French letter, but he wasn't about to yank back on the reins now.

Every time they'd been together this way, she'd talked about how much she wanted him to fuck her. In the novel Elias had bid him to read back in Faribault, the maidens had all cried at the pain of it. The fellow had struggled to even get it in at all and when he had, it was all rended flesh and searing pain. Henry had always imagined his first time would be with a girl similarly inexperienced. He'd assumed as a matter of course that it would be painful for his partner, something he could only mitigate but not prevent. But when they'd coupled in Pittsburgh, Charley had been slick and yielding. She'd made all manner of sounds, some he hadn't been sure were encouraging or plaintive. He'd hardly lasted long enough to find out. She'd squeezed around him like a vice—it seemed inevitable that it had hurt, at least a little. He didn't want to hurt her. He wanted to please her, to push her to that sweet revelation, to watch what it did to her with the light of the oil lamp illuminating her bare skin. He did not, under any circumstance, want to waste himself too quickly or watch Charley merely endure it.

It was with these thoughts spinning through his head that Charley clambered back onto the bed with a triumphant expression, bearing the paper packet with the French letter. His nerves dissipated as she climbed onto his thighs and pressed her warm folds against his balls.

"Is that how you did it that night in the barracks," she purred.

"What?"

She nodded to his hand around his prick. He flushed.

"No, I was just, um—"

"Trying to keep things going?"

He cleared his throat awkwardly. "The opposite, actually. Trying to pull myself back from the brink."

She bit her lip and smiled down at him like the most licentious libertine as she ripped open the packet. Removing the rubber sheath from its wrapper, she regarded it with scrutiny for a moment before pulling his foreskin back and putting it resolutely on over his hard length. Then, grasping him with one hand, she shifted over him and pressed his head into her soft, yielding entrance.

Henry let out a shuddering breath. The sheath muted the sensation, which was a relief since he'd been fearful of spending too quickly. She sank onto him slowly, bobbing her hips to work him in and out, each time a little deeper. Her expression was far away, her lips trembling as she exhaled. Henry watched her carefully for any signs of discomfort even as he was slowly enveloped in tight, hot ecstasy. How? How could this not hurt when she was stretched so tightly around him?

But Charley sighed as her hand fell away and let gravity bring him full hilt inside her. Henry's eyes flickered, and he groaned at the sweet bliss of it.

"Yes," she hissed, and he knew she felt what he did. She slid her hips up and down, forward and back, her thighs working as she fucked herself before his eyes. He could only heave for breath, his hips rising to meet hers on instinct.

Henry couldn't look away from her. Her jaw was slack, her mouth open and wanton, and her head thrown back as she placed her hands on his chest and rode him. Her firm breasts scarcely shook with the motion, flushed tips tight and his attention was seized. He reached up and brushed his thumb over one. Charley whimpered. It was a sound he was determined to earn again.

He pressed his hand over her, her breasts a satisfying palmful, and flicked his thumb over her nipple, back and forth. Her chin trembled, and she squeezed her eyes shut, her expression tight and twisted and desperate as she swallowed a moan. She wrapped one hand around his and coaxed his fingers to roll her nipple between thumb and forefinger. He eagerly seized upon this new information and carried on as her hand dropped. Then, he felt her squeeze around his cock and goddammit, how was that even possible?

She was so responsive, so lithe and sure, taking what she wanted and unafraid to demand it. She was a vision, riding him with grace, her nipple in his fingers and her curling lips gasping pleasure. As he felt his rapture coil tighter in his belly, his chest felt tight too. Sensations that he had only previously experienced around his cock reverberated through his entire body.

"Charley," he murmured without thinking. "My Charley." His other hand gripped her waist like a lifeline and his hips rocked up into her, trying to match her rhythm.

"Henry, I want you..." she gasped. He watched her dazedly, dark hair tumbled over her brow as she struggled to catch her breath. "I want you on top of me."

He could distantly sense that he might be overly eager as he seized her hips and pushed deep inside her as he rolled her onto her back. She gasped and wrapped her legs around his waist. She yanked on his shoulders and he fell onto his elbows over her, driving into her with abandon. He didn't know what he was doing, his body just took over, and he hoped he was doing it right—it certainly seemed like he was, if her expression was any indication.

Her lower lip was trembling, and her eyes regarded him as through a haze. Her muscles seized around him, her breath and hands shaking, and she blinked her eyes shut in a grimace. A cry ripped out of her throat, something raw and deep and carnal. She was coming, she was coming around him—he could feel every spasm and pulse tight around his cock. Just when he thought it was over, she carried on over again, keening as though struck by the pleasure of her climax in relentless waves.

He let go, let himself close his eyes and sink into sensation. It was so intense it almost hurt, his muscles aching and sweat slicking his back, but in the most exquisite way. He rode through it, losing all sense of his surroundings until nothing else existed but Charley. Her hands gripping his shoulders. Her thighs around his waist. The slick slide of their sweaty bellies together. Her mouth and her smell and her eyes—her goddamned incredible eyes, deep and dark and captivating and beautiful. His hips lost the rhythm. His muscles shuddered and his release wracked through him. He pumped into her, his thighs shaking with the effort. When it was over, he let himself sprawl over her, boneless.

Charley's breath tickled his ear. Her scent was in his nose, her hair stuck to his sweaty forehead. Henry distantly realized he was probably crushing her. He started to rise, but her hands held him fast.

"Not yet," she murmured, her fingers curling through his hair. Her lips pressed a kiss to his jaw. Henry tentatively let his weight back down on her, and she hummed, a sound halfway between pleasure and distress. "I've, um ... I've never..."

"What?" Henry said, startled, shifting so he could regard her with incredulity.

She snorted at his confusion. "I don't have an explanation for it. But before you, I've never ... uh, finished? If that makes sense?"

Henry frowned at her as he rolled off, making sure the French letter came with him. "I've made you finish before, surely?"

She nodded and flushed. "Just so. With fingers, of course. But I didn't think it was possible without fingers. This is ... new." She exhaled and looked at him significantly. With her cheeks flushed like that, her lips red and swollen from kisses, she looked in every way the wanton Venus she'd denied she was. He felt that tight feeling in his chest again, the one that drew him so inextricably toward her.

He kissed her sweetly. She buried her hands in his hair, arching into him.

"I could go again," she whispered, her lips brushing against his.

"I could ... not," he replied, chuckling incredulously. She couldn't be serious, could she?

Apparently she was, because she drew his hand down between her thighs and urged him to help finish her again.

———

XV

Lebanon, Kentucky
Sunday, December 15, 1861

CHARLEY FELT LIKE HER limbs might just melt right off the edge of the bed. She had anticipated a singularly enjoyable time with Henry, of course. Her only previous experience having been with Richard, she'd expected at least an elevated level of enjoyment by virtue of the fact that Henry was a man she was actually very much attracted to. She'd thought Pittsburgh had been an anomaly, a desperate, forbidden encounter, intense with its taboo. But it wasn't. It was him. It was Henry who turned her inside out.

She was tucked into Henry's shoulder, still catching her breath and playing idly with the sweep of hair on his chest.

"Well, how was it?" she asked, her tone more nonchalant than she strictly felt. "In a bed, I mean?"

Henry turned his face toward her. He was so earnest when he said, "It was ... incredible is insufficient. I always assumed it would be awkward and painful. At least, painful for you. Which would then ruin it for me. I can't understand how a fellow would be so swept away with it all to not care for his partner in discomfort."

Charley snorted. "You may be more singular than you know. It has never been more than passing uncomfortable for me. It can pinch a bit if you go deep too fast. I don't understand why everyone whispers about how much it has to hurt. Honestly, I think the parents are trying to put all the young people off."

"And rightly so. If everyone knew it could be like that, everyone would run off to get married immediately."

"You know," she said, putting herself up on an elbow to drink in his naked form more efficiently, "if more people knew about—and I suppose had access to—French letters, perhaps they would be running to the altar. There's a strong appeal to fucking when one removes the threat of children."

Henry smiled, looking at her with those warm, open eyes. He reached out and touched her cheek, his smile turning wistful. "I wish..."

Charley flinched. "Don't."

His hand fell to her shoulder, his eyes skimming over her breasts before meeting her eyes again. "You're so beautiful."

Charley rolled her eyes. "Don't start that again."

He gave a long suffering sigh. "Oh, so I can't wish and I can't admire you. What would you have me do, then, sir?"

"Your mouth has many other talents."

He shook his head but grinned, then hauled her up on top of his lap. He leaned up and kissed her clavicle, winding a trail down her pale skin. She smiled. "That's better."

"*Du bist wunderschön,*" he murmured, "*und erstaunlich.*"

"What the hell are you saying?" she complained distractedly. "You had better not be admiring me in German."

He cupped her breast in his palm. "*Deine Brüste sind perfekt.*" He kissed the soft curve of flesh in emphasis.

Charley shivered in spite of herself. "Perfect in any language is not a term I identify with."

"*Ich liebe es, wie stark du bist.*" His hands skimmed over her shoulders, and he looked at her earnestly. She had no idea what he was saying, but it sounded so good. "*Und eigensinnig.*"

"You're going to need to stop that," she warned ineffectually. Worse than her body responding, her heart skittered in her chest, and she felt quite nauseous with affection.

Henry ignored her and propped himself up on his elbows thoughtfully. "How did you get so strong anyway?"

"Strong?" Was that what he'd been saying? It was certainly not a sentiment she'd ever thought a man would whisper to a woman over the pillows. Maybe it was a German thing. "I took in laundry for years. Scrubbing and wringing all day is hard work, I suppose."

He ran a hand up and down her arms. "That's right."

"I thought I might earn enough to support myself, but then my father got sick. We needed the extra funds while he was out of work so then I ended up ... stuck. And he wanted me out of his house so..." she shrugged. "Richard took me on."

"You make it sound like he gave you a job."

Charley cringed. "I guess he did, in a way, as his housekeeper and mother of his children."

Henry choked.

"No no no, I don't have any children, don't panic!"

He breathed again.

"The wedding was in the spring. It hasn't even been a year, and I've spent most of that time enlisted."

"Still. Any amount of time spent like that sounds awful."

"Well, he didn't hurt me or anything, so it could have been worse."

"That's a pretty low bar." He watched her with some concern. "I didn't realize people still ended up in arranged marriages like that. At least not folks of our class. It seems rather transactional to me."

Charley nodded and shrugged. She hadn't felt terribly self-conscious in her nakedness since they'd come to bed, but she suddenly realized she had crossed her arms over her chest protectively.

"Dare I ask what your father got out of the arrangement?" Henry sat up so both his hands could caress her arms with care.

"Got rid of me," she said. "Which was what he wanted all along."

He was watching her with something that felt like pity. "I'm sorry that happened to you."

She rolled her eyes dismissively. "It didn't happen to me. No one forced me to the altar at gunpoint or anything."

"They didn't need to. It's not like you had the means to do anything else. Just because you technically could walk away doesn't mean it's a real alternative."

"I did walk away eventually," she shrugged, avoiding his gaze. "Although if I could do it again, I would have walked away earlier. Preferably before it became legally binding."

Henry's hands pulled her gently down, holding her tight to his chest for a moment. There was a tightness in her own chest, a vague nausea, and a horrifying urge to cry riding up in her throat. If she didn't do anything, she felt like she might crawl out of her skin. Her hand snaked between them and she grasped his chin, turning his face toward her so she could apply a pitifully desperate kiss.

"You're well away from all that now," Henry assured absently as he kissed her back. He smoothed his thumb over her temple and kissed her so tenderly that she thought it might rend her in two. "And you will stay that way, if I have anything to say about it."

Charley flinched away from him. As she guardedly studied his face, the doorknob clattered in its mortise lock.

"Hello? Lucy? Who's in there?"

Charley's heart ricocheted in her chest. She scrambled off the far side of the bed, snatching clothes off the floor with no regard for whether they were hers or Henry's.

Henry sat bolt upright and stared at the door like a mule deer. Charley ducked behind the bed and shoved her legs into trousers.

Inarticulate muttering could be heard on the other side of the door. Then, the scrape of metal and a clatter as a key was inserted from the other side of the door, pushing the key that had rested in the hole to the floor of the room. The bolt turned just as Charley managed to yank a shirt over her head. She could scarcely breathe.

"Lucy?" The brunette Miss Sterling ducked her head into the room. "Oh!"

What a scene they must have made. Henry curled up naked on the bed, Charley ducking fearfully in the corner, trying to get her clumsy fingers to fasten the buttons of a shirt that was most definitely not hers.

Miss Sterling blinked at them and licked her perfect bow lips before she spoke. "Well, gentlemen. We're closed up now and your friends have gone."

Charley wasn't sure her face could be any redder. There was a distant sense of relief that the woman had addressed them both as gentlemen, but that was hardly a consolation. In fact, this might be even worse in terms of court-martial. Henry curled his knees up to his chest, but made no move to get up.

Charley snatched the rest of their clothes up off the floor and looked Miss Sterling defiantly in the eye. "Apologies, Madam. How much for the room?"

Miss Sterling raised a brow, her eyes darting between them. "This room is not available for the night."

"No, uh, we are headed back to camp," Charley said awkwardly, trying to keep her voice low and even. "I mean for the time that we occupied it. We didn't mean to put you out."

"Five dollars." Miss Sterling looked unamused and unsympathetic that she'd just asked for the equivalent of two weeks pay.

Henry balked, but Charley just reached into the pocket of her trousers and found the fold of greenbacks she'd placed there in anticipation for the evening's events.

"I'm sorry Madam, but I only have three," she said, wincing in spite of herself.

Miss Sterling looked more disciplined school marm than madam of a brothel.

Henry cleared his throat. "I have some too." He shuffled awkwardly off the bed, trying futilely to keep his prick shielded from view with his hands. He seized his clothes from Charley and stuffed himself into his trousers before digging in his pocket. He came up with a dollar in coins.

"Leave it on the dresser, and I'll put the rest on your tab," the madam directed. Charley and Henry exchanged glances and did as they were bid. "I will list you in the books as Johnny Soldier."

Miss Sterling looked entirely nonplussed, her face fixed in neutral, business-like efficiency. Charley pulled her boots on with as much dignity as she could muster. Henry pulled on the rest of his clothes too. Her shirt stretched endearingly over his chest.

"Next time," Miss Sterling said smoothly, "let us know in advance, and we'll make arrangements for you. You'll find the fee more reasonable if you plan ahead."

Charley looked sharply up at her, but said nothing. That sounded too good to be true. Running a brothel was one thing, but a molly house was quite another. Did she see through Charley's disguise? Had she noticed? It was certainly possible she did and was pretending not to know. Charley shrugged into her sack coat as the madam led the two of them out the door.

Miss Sterling stood in the doorway and watched them as they went, Charley's shoulders hunching under her gaze.

Charley and Henry tramped quietly down the steps and past the doorman into the night. The two of them turned down Water Street and made their way toward camp in a tense silence.

After a few moments, Henry did something completely unexpected. He laughed.

"It's really not funny, Schaefer," she groaned.

"Oh, come on," he chortled, "it was a little funny."

"We either have to deal with that madam assuming we're both men and knowing we're together, or that she knows I'm a woman. Either way, we're one morally-bereft woman away from a court-martial."

"We're together, hm?" Henry grinned. Charley shot him an impatient glare and shook her head. "Come on, Charley. We'll be gone from here in a week or two. If we return and pay her for the room, or even pay for use of a room again, I expect she'll be happy to keep our secret."

"You are insatiable."

"No, that would be you."

"You also have a naive assessment of the kindness of strangers."

"You have an overly cynical assessment of strangers."

"Honed through years of having my more generous assumptions thrown in my face."

Henry didn't say anything but he bumped his shoulder into hers. He grabbed her hand and for a few minutes, under the twinkling stars and the setting moon, they were able to walk simply hand in hand.

————

XVI

Lebanon, Kentucky
Monday, December 16, 1861

CHARLEY STARED UP AT the gray canvas of the tent. She could hear Henry's deep, sleepy breath in her ear, but she couldn't bring herself to look at him. She shifted slightly, the memory of their activities the night before imprinted on her skin. Henry had convinced her. He'd made her believe that she was the kind of person he could want. Perhaps she was being foolish. Maybe she was wrong. But hell—she'd rather be a fool and believe in something good than be disappointed and right.

She spared a glance over at Henry. His mouth was slack with sleep, hair tousled over his brow, the intensity of passion wiped clear to peaceful neutral. Looking at him like that, in the dim pre-dawn light, Charley understood that as much as she resisted naming it, she was in much deeper with this sweet man than she had ever intended to be. She found that she trusted him. She believed it when he said he missed her, that he wanted her, that he loved every inch of her. She knew what she looked like. She knew how difficult she was. And yet ... he was still here. Still trying. Still wanting her.

It was enough to rend her heart in two.

The bugle sounded Reveille. The squad stirred and groaned groggily. Henry opened his eyes and met hers. He smiled. The way it made her feel, the way it clenched around her chest and exposed her heart, couldn't be mistaken. She wouldn't name it. But she knew. And unlike him, she knew how much it would hurt. So she flinched.

"Do you all know where Elias has gone?" Robinson asked, frowning down at the place where Hower usually slept. "His blankets are still folded. Did he come back last night?"

Charley seized on the opportunity to sit up and inspect Hower's effects from across the tent. Anything to preoccupy her mind from the most inconvenient feelings. "Perhaps he just rose early and put everything away again before we woke?" she suggested.

Robinson shook his head and peered at the pile. "That seems unlike him. Henry, didn't you all go to Sterling House last night?"

Henry opened his eyes too wide and frowned. He was the picture of guilt. "No..."

"Oh, come on, no one's going to snitch on you," Robinson said with a roll of his eyes. Webster and Krüger exchanged glances as if to suggest Robinson should speak for himself. "If Elias was there with you, I guarantee he would not have gotten up early to go ... I don't even know what. I don't think he slept here last night."

It wasn't until they all lined up at the kitchen tent that they learned what happened.

"There was a group of fellows arrested for drunkenness," someone from Company H confided from in front of them in line. "They snuck out to town and came back a belligerent heap. Captain Bishop came upon them and brought them up on charges."

Charley exchanged a glance with Henry. Robinson regarded them sidelong. He let Webster continue to interrogate the Company H fellow as he pulled the two of them aside.

"There's something you're not telling me," Robinson muttered under his breath. "How come you two didn't manage to get caught?"

Henry looked like a gasping fish out of water, so Charley did her best to seize control. "They left before we did. We, uh..." She glanced at Henry and blurted out the first lie that came to her mind. "We ended up visiting Miss Sterling's chamber..."

Not a lie. But also leaving space for Robinson to make assumptions. Which he did, if his gaping mouth was anything to go by. Henry looked horrified.

"Together?!" Robinson might have an apoplexy.

Charley rolled her eyes. "Christ, Robinson, not simultaneously. We ..." She frowned, the words going sour in her mouth. She gestured uselessly.

Henry and Robinson seemed in competition for who might hyperventilate first. Charley shrank, disgusted with herself at the implication of two men taking turns on a public woman like they were splitting the cost of dinner or something. But the camp was so full of bawdy talk. It wasn't so outrageous? Was it? Oh hell and damnation. She hadn't really thought the excuse through before she implied it and now suggesting such a thing to her comrade made her feel rather ashamed. She could feel her cheeks heat, and she tried her best to keep her expression firm.

"It's really none of your business," she snapped. "Suffice to say, we returned after Hower and the others did."

Robinson looked at the two of them, his eyes darting back and forth. He blinked. "I think you two need to stop spending so much time together."

Then he turned and rejoined the line, which had significantly advanced without them.

"Charley..." Henry began.

She scrunched her nose up and scrubbed her face with her hands. "I know, I know, that was too close."

"That was *horrible*. I think you took ten years off his life for the shock. Maybe mine too. I was going to say we were playing billiards and the rest got so drunk, they forgot about us and left."

"That would have been a much better excuse," she groaned into her hands.

"It's too late now, I guess."

Charley glanced up at him through her fingers. Henry was looking after Robinson with a wistful twist of his mouth. A jumble of feelings bubbled up for her, affection and desire and a heaping helping of fear. His connection to her was tenable at best. She needed to rein herself in before she said something so stupid, she was no longer worth the effort.

"That wouldn't have worked anyway," she said, grasping to cover her own stupid mistake. "As soon as Hower got out of lockup, he'd tell them he looked for us in the billiards or something and we'd be caught out."

"Providing he remembers leaving at all. Then only if he *did* remember would we trot out this yarn about ... Miss Sterling ..." He grimaced then glanced over at her. His head tilted as he frowned. "Don't look so upset. *Smith* wouldn't care. He'd be nonchalant about the whole thing. Your reputation is only going to be even more notorious, that's all. Come on, let's get some food."

Charley nodded slowly and followed Henry back to the line.

"You know," Henry said conversationally, but keeping his voice low so that others in the line would not overhear. "My uncle said that lots of men find comfort in all sorts of ways in the army."

"I'm sure they do," Charley replied glibly, glowering at the camp writ large as they waited their turn.

"He, uh, he said some fellows find comfort with each other and that it's more common than one would think."

Charley whipped her head around to glare at him. "What did you tell him?"

Henry startled. "Nothing, I didn't say anything. I swear."

Charley continued to glare, compelling him to come clean through sheer force of will.

"He thinks I'm, uh, doing that with you—" Henry whispered awkwardly under his breath. Charley snarled. "—but he doesn't suspect anything amiss with you. He just thinks I, um, like other fellows."

Charley frowned. Fellows were nigh on insatiable if this was the kind of nonsense they got up to when ladies were scarce. Not that she had any legs to stand on in the matter, given what she'd risked last night for a little "comfort."

"It's not so unusual. The Greeks did it, after all."

"The Greeks?"

"Had, you know, love, between men."

Charley blinked. Love? This had … not occurred to her.

"Love?" Charley was grasping. "Like, two men, in love?" How could that possibly work? She supposed the romantic tragedy was that it couldn't.

"Yes. Some of them thought it was a love more pure than between a woman and a man—well, mostly because they had some pretty awful notions about women's intelligence and personhood, but they did nonetheless."

"And your uncle thinks that you're … in love … with me?"

"Well, yes." Henry blinked. "I am."

Oh fuck. Charley wanted to crawl into the ground, but she couldn't take her eyes off of Henry. He looked at her with such nonchalance. Such naive confidence, while meanwhile, her fear threatened to consume her. Her chest felt so tight that her breath came shallow.

Henry studied her face, and his brows started to gather together. "Aren't you?"

Charley's eyes were pricking. She had to look away. She couldn't bear to see him look at her like that, and yet she couldn't find a way to say the thing she knew he wanted her to say. If she told the truth, what then? What would she owe him? What would he owe her? What would that mean for her secret, for her position in the ranks, for her entire life in the regiment? He couldn't marry her—for a multitude of reasons—but he had a great deal of power over her just as it was, by virtue of knowing her secret. If she admitted she loved him, if they were two people in love together, what would that entitle him to? And if she didn't return the sentiment, if she denied it or said nothing, would she break his heart? Would he put an end to things? And what if they made a go of it and he found he could no longer bear what an insufferable ass she was? Would he expose her in revenge? Goddamnit, Henry! Why? Why did he have to say that?

Charley gritted her teeth and glanced significantly at the people surrounding them. "We'll talk about this later," she ground out, but looked into his eyes for assent. He nodded curtly, and she turned away, fumbling in her haversack for her tin plate. Her fingers trembled as she held out her cup for coffee.

XVII

Lebanon, Kentucky
Thursday, December 19, 1861

IT WAS WARM AND pleasant. While Kentucky left much to be desired in a whole host of categories, the weather was most welcome. Henry was delighted to see Hower and the others back in ranks during forenoon drills. They had served several days in isolation as a penalty for sneaking out. Captain Bishop seemed to have decided to make an example of them. They were now saddled with extra guard duty until Christmas, which they bore in addition to drills.

What was worse was that Lieutenant Thomas had ordered Hower demoted from corporal to private, and had quietly promoted Webster to the position instead. The Hastings squad had suffered similarly, with Corporal Harris demoted to private, and some poor moralizing fool from First Sergeant Nelson's squad assigned to be their new NCO. Meanwhile, the rumor about Henry and Charley's misadventure with one of the Miss Sterlings spread like wildfire, although in the retelling, Henry rather faded from the story, while Charley became the swaggering libertine who single handedly seduced the girl out from under Hower. Henry was not sure how to feel about this, but had to admit he wasn't surprised. He tried to clarify that it was not the Miss Sterling that Hower had had his eye on (and technically, the Miss Sterling who had caught them out was indeed not the red-haired sister but the brown-haired one). But as the story circulated, the fact that there were multiple Miss Sterlings got lost in the mill and it became the tale of how Webster cuckolded

Hower out of his rank while Charley cuckolded him out of his girl. Hower was miserable. Henry felt awful about all of it.

What's more, Charley was being strange again, no doubt because anything resembling feelings made her snappish and mean. Henry knew why. He hadn't rightly meant to tell her he loved her so casually, but it was too late to take it back, and he didn't want to anyway. It was true. He felt confident that her feelings were similarly attached, so he didn't understand why she was so tied up in knots about it. It was one thing to have feelings that ran unreturned. But why hesitate when they clearly both liked each other, depended on one another, and enjoyed being together? It seemed a whole lot of pain for nothing, in Henry's estimation.

Henry tried to find Karl Thursday morning in an effort to quell the increasingly persistent tightness in his chest as he tried and increasingly failed to take Charley's standoffishness with good humor. It wasn't as bad as the last time she'd pushed him away, but it felt like the beginning of that, and Henry really didn't think he could bear for her to do that to him again. It was one thing if it had been a courtship that wasn't working out. But they were in the same squad. They had to go to battle with one another, have each other's back. So Henry really wanted to figure out how to come to a mutually-agreeable arrangement. Which he'd probably royally messed up anyway by being overly eager—or perhaps he'd been too flippant? He had no idea what he was doing.

Karl was nowhere to be found, and the time ran away before Henry could ask around as to his whereabouts, so he ended up having to double back for drills empty-handed. They were practicing regimental maneuvers. While Henry was sure it was very helpful for companies of nearly one hundred men to be able to turn and charge and pivot as one, his attention was focused elsewhere. Namely, a foot in front of him, where her soft nape peeked out from between her collar and hair. Torture. If he was ever captured by the Rebs, all they'd have to do was dangle Charley Smith as bait to get him to talk.

About halfway through the maneuver, Henry made up his mind. He wasn't sure what he was supposed to do, but he did know he couldn't continue lurking and wondering what Charley felt. He was pretty confident that she shared his tender feelings. Whether she would admit to it, however, that was the tough part. He resolved to find a place where they could speak privately and just ask her point-blank how she felt. He was also resolved to accept whatever her feelings were (or were not) with dignity and not descend into a self-loathing mass. The way her mouth went soft and vulnerable when he paid her compliments—he was *sure* she felt the same.

Yes. He would talk to her. He would expound upon the long list of things he liked about her, catch her unawares, and then confess his love again, in a more sincere way. If he could manage a little privacy, he was sure she would reply in kind.

Henry didn't manage to catch up with Charley until after dinner, when he found her sidled up outside the mule pen of all places. Several of the teamsters were practicing driving the mules, and a crowd of soldiers had gathered to watch. Certainly not the private environment he'd been hoping for. As he joined, Williamson leaned over, eagerly informing him, "They say that no man ever broke a team of six green army mules without breaking his Christian character, so the chaplain has offered a reward of one hundred dollars for any man who can drive a team for thirty days without using profanity."

Henry snorted and sidled up to the fence to join the fun. The teamster presently at practice was attempting to get his team of mules to do a relatively simple command—drive the wagon out of the opening at the south end of the pen. It was proving enormously difficult.

Charley was laughing full-bellied, and the sight of her smile made the fine weather feel even finer. "Look at this blowhard, he can't even get them out the pen! Hey, bear left, man! LEFT!"

The teamster glowered at the row of soldiers mocking him, but pressed his lips together determinedly. Henry supposed the ranks of men shouting were probably not helping the poor fellow.

"As hilarious as I'm sure this is," came a voice that Henry, turning his head, found belonged to Osborn, "it is high time we get to the parade ground for Battalion drill."

The fellows grumbled and begrudgingly followed Osborn, at least the fellows from their squad did. Others still remained heckling the poor teamster, whose reddening face suggested he was becoming increasingly frustrated.

"Damn! I was sure he was going to cuss," Charley said, glancing over her shoulder to look at the man again. "He seemed so close, but he just wants that hundred dollars!"

"He's got a long way to go," Williamson said. "He can't have been driving that team for more than ten days. He's still got twenty more to go."

"Seems like they stacked the deck, with all those fellows heckling him," Henry put in. Charley glanced up at him, her expression somewhat abashed. It did nothing for his anxiety to see her look at him that way.

"Well, my father is a teamster, and I can tell you, that fellow didn't know what he was about," she grumbled with a nod, as if convincing herself.

Henry thought about pointing out that they scarcely knew what they were about either, but he held himself back. No need to rain on everyone's parade just because Charley was driving him to madness avoiding him. *We'll talk about this later, indeed...*

When they were gathered on the wide field with the rest of the companies, the captains gathered them together into ranks on horseback. When Captain Noah had Company K together, he called out an announcement from the head of the ranks.

"Men, we are anticipating forward movement soon. We have received assignments for our brigade, and are officially members of the Third Brigade of the First Division of the Army of the Ohio, along with the Ninth Ohio and the Eighteenth U.S. Regulars. Our brigade is under the command of Colonel McCook, formerly of the Ninth Ohio. The Thirty-Fifth Ohio will also join up with us, but they are now at Somerset."

The men stirred and looked among each other with excited anticipation. A hum of speculation arose, and Captain Noah raised his hand, commanding their attention upon him once more.

"We understand Zollicoffer has advanced his rebels on General Schoepf, who is also fortified at Somerset. At present, they are simply watching his movements. Prepare yourselves, for we march as soon as the orders arrive from General Thomas. The paymaster is anticipated before departure."

In hindsight, perhaps it may have been wiser for the captains to provide this information at the end of the drills, as the entire battalion was distracted for the rest of the afternoon, speculating about the prospect of battle drawing near. Osborn shushed them almost every five minutes as they (Hower and Robinson mainly) whispered eagerly about how this maneuver might be used in battle, or what it might take to get orders in the morning. Webster started fretting about writing to his wife and wondering where she should address her correspondence once they were on the move. Krüger looked like a half-crazed fiend when the captains ordered them to fix bayonets and charge, as if he could see in his mind's eye the enemy, and he was eager to slice him from navel to nose.

Henry's fists gripped his rifle with frustration. If they were to march on, they'd be in tents or sleeping under the stars or on guard duty. He'd have no chance to catch Charley alone. Not to confess his finer feelings, not to touch her or embrace her or otherwise enjoy the fact that they belonged to one another. It would be like Lebanon Junction all over again. Complete and utter lack of privacy. Dammit. Karl Joseph said that it was not uncommon for men to find comfort among one another in an army camp. But how? They certainly weren't making it known, which meant they must have found a way to get some goddamned privacy. And once they were on the march, any semblance of that would be gone.

Henry approached Charley as soon as they were dismissed for supper and jogged to catch up with her.

"Can we speak?" he asked and realized too late that he sounded about as snappish as he felt.

Charley turned to regard him. "About what?"

"About Sterling House and the—"

Charley's chin dipped and the corners of her mouth twitched in a knowing smile. "Ah, yes. It would be fine to have a return visit."

"I...uh, yes it would," Henry said, flustered by the appeal of the prospect, then quickly added before she turned away, "But I want to talk to you just very quickly about the other matter."

Charley raised one brow and her mouth went flat. "Can't we talk about that later? I'm half-starved and there's turkey for supper."

Henry bit the inside of his cheek.

"Of course. Yeah. Let's eat."

———

XVIII

Lebanon, Kentucky
Sunday, December 29, 1861

IT WAS STRANGE HOW fast time went, and yet how slowly it seemed to go, when awaiting marching orders. Truly, the worst part about being in the army was the waiting. Every day that orders didn't come felt like torture and the hours of drill and meals and more drill and guard duties rolled out before Charley in a tedious rote of endless anticipation.

Every day they'd wake to the sound of Reveille wondering if they were going to strike their tents and be gone before the day was out, but each day ended with them back in their tents, exhausted yet unable to sleep for anticipation of what might come the next day. The paymaster came and settled their wages, and the Christmas dinner was full of revels, but Christmas cheer swiftly gave way to more earnest preparations to march. With every day that passed, the impending marching orders became an increasingly foregone conclusion, until the day after Christmas, when news of the orders spread like wildfire across the camp. Prepare to march upon the order to intercept rebel troops. Stand in readiness. Zollicoffer was lurking across the river and the top brass had finally decided to put a stop to it. Charley experienced a rush of anxious excitement, pushing herself hard to every task they were set and dogging after Osborn with questions and ideas for ways they could increase their efficiency. Every idea seemed imperative. *Lives were at stake*, she kept insisting to her direct officer.

Between her courses and the preparations for Christmas and marching out, Charley was scarcely able to snatch a moment or two with Henry before new duties were foisted upon them both. Extra cooking, extra guard duty, loading wagons with provisions. Suffice to say, by the time they got back to the tent each night, she and Henry were so exhausted they scarcely brushed their fingers together before they fell into a deep and dreamless sleep. It was torture to have known him so intimately that night at Sterling House then be denied again, but it was also a kind of relief, because it allowed Charley to avoid the conversation he clearly wanted to have about his feelings. Their feelings. The thought of it all made her itch with discomfort. Made her want to load up ten more wagons instead of lingering on what she might say to him.

That is, until Sunday, when Henry nudged her shoulder at breakfast and whispered that he'd borrowed some extra money from Williamson and was planning a visit to Sterling House after the Sunday service. The utter disregard for the holy day of rest in the manner he delivered this information struck Charley right between her thighs, and she could only glance up at him from beneath her eyelashes like a schoolgirl and murmur yes. After all, if they could receive marching orders any time, she was veritably obligated to seize the day.

They made a point to go to town separately after the service was done, staggering their departure for maximum discretion. Given that, it was somewhat of a surprise when Charley entered the second-floor room Henry had engaged at the Sterling House and was greeted with a curt: "What took you so long?"

He sat on the edge of the bed with his coat and boots discarded, his shoulders tense and his eyes intent upon her from under his heavy brow.

"I'm not late," she replied indignantly, a little flustered by his intensity.

"Fine, I'm not about to argue. There's no time to lose," he declared and yanked her toward the bed.

Charley rode Henry again, sweat soaking through her shirt as she drove herself increasingly harder and more raggedly on his rubber-sheathed cock. She had her eyes squeezed shut because whenever she opened them, she saw Henry looking up at her with a curling smile and pleasure-spent eyes. It was easy to believe he loved her when he looked at her like that, but the reminder made her feel all sorts of things she was terrified to name, so eyes shut it was. She could feel tension building between her legs, squeezing in opposition to the cock that stretched her, filled her, drove every thought from her mind until it was just her and him and the insatiable need they shared.

Henry's arm swooped round her waist and it took her by surprise because she didn't see it coming. Her eyes flew open as he sat up and held her tightly, his cock pressing so deep it nudged the end of her. Her fingers curled around his shoulders as he flipped her onto her back. He pulled out a bit, not all the way, as he sat back on his haunches. He gave her a crooked grin before he gripped one of her thighs and drove into her, his rhythm steadier and his angle deeper. His other hand shoved her shirt up to her neck, baring her, then settled between her legs and stroked her in time with his thrusts. Charley tipped her head back and keened, her hands grappling above her head for purchase as she felt her edge draw near. She couldn't get enough of him, even though she was getting all of him. She didn't think there could ever be enough of this, with him. She wrapped her thighs around his waist like a vice and gripped the bed sheets tight in her hands. Her climax barreled toward her and all her muscles seized tight to brace for impact.

Henry's mouth was tight again, almost mean, his nostrils flaring as he watched her hungrily. "God, I love you like this," he grunted. "Please, Charley, come on. Come for me."

How could she refuse? It was rather a forgone conclusion. Her voice caught as bliss crashed through her, cracking her open like dry earth and rending her bare. He rode her out but didn't slow, kept pushing her as she became entirely too sensitive. She was reduced to a gasping, whimpering mess as he leaned down over her, elbows on either side of her head.

"Yes, Charley," he growled into her ear, pumping ceaselessly. "More. God, I love you. I love you so damn much."

Charley very much wished that those words would take her out of it. But they didn't. Much the opposite, in fact. They wrapped around her heart and squeezed it like a vice as he drove relentlessly into her, pressed his weight over her. It was entirely unfair that the combination of these things pushed her overly-sensitive body to shake again with pleasure, wringing sobs from her throat so feral and desperate she entertained a distant worry that it might cause the proprietors some concern. Heaven knew she was being loud enough for them to hear her. Mortifying. She could scarcely bring herself to care, though, as she shook with the tremors of her second climax.

Henry's thrusts grew heedless and harried as he shook and came inside her. How she wished she could feel that heat fill her up, but the India rubber shielded her from that particular guilty pleasure. Which was good. She understood that distantly. Safety and rationality didn't often feel very important when one was ragged and stupid with lust. God, Henry looked so good when he came. Deliciously desperate, shaking with effort, his nipples tight and his chest flushed and slick with sweat. Shoulders straining. Damn. It made Charley want to lick him.

He nigh collapsed on top of her, breath rushing past her ear and his heart thrumming against her chest. Charley blinked and felt her blood pulse through her cunt with such heat it made her go cross-eyed. Henry shifted on his elbows and pressed his lips to hers. Charley's hands held him there by the back of his head, fingers threaded in his wheat gold hair. He tipped his chin down and held her eyes. "I love you, Charley."

It was lucid and sincere and it made her stomach curdle with panic. Why did he keep saying it? Was he trying to get her to say it back? Of course he was. She pressed her lips hard against his, kissing him fiercely so that he might know her feelings too, even though she couldn't bring herself to say them. As much as they'd become friends in the past months, she didn't know what he might expect from someone he loved. She was already too far in his thrall. He might expect all the fool things she had once thought she wanted—a marriage, a home, a family, with their endless cycle of mindless drudgery and isolation. And she was so stupid for him, she might compromise herself to give them to him. Thank heavens marriage was securely off the table.

Henry kissed her back eagerly, pressing their bodies together, letting her revel in the bliss of his weight crushing her into the mattress. But then he broke the kiss again and looked at her with doleful blue eyes.

"Charley..." His lips twitched, like he was uncertain. Charley's heart slammed in her chest. His brows slanted like a hurt dog, and Charley braced herself when the knock came to the door.

"Come on, Privates," the muffled voice on the opposite side of the door called. "You're not the only ones looking for clandestine meeting locations on the Sabbath and I need to turn over the room."

Henry looked at the door, then back down at Charley. She let a lazy smile creep over her lips.

"Time sure flies when you're having fun," she quipped. The smile she'd been hoping for her reward didn't come. Rather, Henry tucked his chin sheepishly and grunted in agreement as he pushed himself up and off her, rolling to sit on the edge of the bed. His bare thigh was right next to her head, so she curled to one side and pressed her lips to his skin, flaxen hair coarse on her lips. He had to know how she adored him, right? She couldn't give the promise she knew he wanted, but she could show him, with her touch and her kisses and her constancy. Couldn't she?

"We'll be just a moment," Henry called to Miss Sterling on the opposite side of the door as he bent to retrieve his blue wool trousers. Charley rolled to her knees and perched beside him on the edge of the bed as he gingerly removed the French letter.

"Here, let me," Charley said, taking it from him and kicking the chamber pot from under the bed. She was wholly disturbed by her own thoughts as she disposed of the French letter's contents in the pot, wondering how it might feel dripping down her leg or how it might taste on her tongue. She was utterly addled. Lust had gone and rendered her a feral galoot.

She padded across the room to the pitcher and basin on the dresser that faced the foot of the bed, rinsing the rubber in the water as thoroughly as she could manage before she tucked the wholly too-expensive item in her breast pocket. As far as she could tell from the packaging and the very limited advice the pharmacist would offer, French letters were not expressly meant to be reused. But after disposing of the first, she'd determined to take a more economical tack. Especially considering how damn much the Sterlings were charging for the use of this room.

Henry was fully uniformed when she turned back, albeit rumpled. He tossed her trousers to her and then pushed his hair back as he screwed on his forage cap. His eyes danced away from hers, which caused her some dismay as she pulled her suspenders over her shoulders and yanked her arms into her sack coat.

They ambled out of the room together, tight-lipped and guilty-faced. Miss Sterling stood by with her arms crossed over her austere gown, watching as Henry started down the stairs. Charley was about to descend when Miss Sterling's hand shot out and pulled her back.

"I assume you're being careful," she murmured under her breath, "but if you run into any trouble, you will find friends here."

Charley froze. She stared at Miss Sterling. Miss Sterling met her gaze squarely, her chin arch with a quiet confidence, and Charley realized she knew. She *knew*.

Miss Sterling's large brown eyes blinked twice with a shrewd-ness that seemed strange on such a placid face. "Your secret is safe with me."

Charley couldn't make her legs carry her away after hearing that. "Um..." she stammered.

"Think nothing of it," Miss Sterling said, a little louder. "I hope we see you two again before you march on."

Charley's legs were unsteady as Miss Sterling herded her down the stairs. She tried to press hard against the urge to panic. This had to be the easiest money the Sterling sisters ever made. All they had to do was keep quiet, and they could charge literally any sum they wanted. And Charley would pay it. Because they had her up a creek, but also because she was completely besot-ted. What was the point in resisting saying it aloud? She was already too tied up in knots over Henry to think clearly about her future. Who was she kidding? She really hadn't allowed herself to think of what might come when the war ended. Who she might become then. Because there was no good answer, so why bother worrying?

When they were alone together in the muddy courtyard behind the hotel, Charley found herself reaching out and snatching Henry's sleeve. He turned and regarded her with a tired expression.

"I'm sorry," Charley blurted before she could think better of it. "I know what you want me to say and I want to—please understand that I want to—but I just ... I have never known a man who didn't think he knew better than his wife or mother or daughter—"

"—I'm not laying claim to you," Henry hissed, moving closer so their conversation could not be overheard by an errant passerby. "I don't want to control you. I want to love you."

"I know, I understand that. It's just never been my experience."

"Why do you assume I'm going to be like everyone else you've ever met?" His hurt dog expression was back. "We've spent months and months together, but as soon as I confess I have tender feelings for you, I'm a threat? Am I no different than Richard, or your father? What have I *done* to make you think that I mean to possess you?" His voice caught and his lips pressed firmly together. Charley felt a flood of guilt rise up in her gut and before she could even realize what was happening, she felt a tear fall down her cheek.

"Henry, I—"

"If you want to say it, then just say it. But I'm beginning to wonder if you really do."

"I'm telling you I do!"

"Why spend all these words talking around it, then?" He sighed. "You either love me or you don't. Maybe that could change, I don't know. But just tell me the goddamned truth."

There were several more tears gathering. Charley tried desperately not to blink so they wouldn't fall as well. Her throat closed, but she swallowed through it. "How I feel. I feel ... I feel like I ... can't imagine what I've done to deserve your affection. I am truly ... just ... thrown for a loop."

"That's how you feel about how I feel, Charley. What do *you* feel about *me*?"

Charley looked up at him desperately and hoped to God no one could see her face right now, because it was surely unmistakably broken. "Dammit, Henry, I don't just love you. I *adore* you. I have wanted you since the moment I saw your stupid perfect teeth and you tried to give me the big-brother treatment before the enlistment inspection."

Henry blinked. "My *teeth*?"

"Do you understand how many men with nice faces have terrible breath and missing teeth?"

"Since the *inspections*? The day we met?"

"Yes? I used to, uh, loiter in my bunk at the Fort to watch you get dressed." His brows flew up. "I'm not proud. When you mentioned reading Frederick Douglass, and I realized you weren't just an empty-headed pretty boy, I was—I was done for. I've probably loved you since you put that stupid piece of sweetgrass in my mouth." She scrubbed her eyes with her sleeve cuff before any further emotional evidence could spill out over her face. While she was temporarily blinded, Henry reached out and grasped her by her shoulders, pulling her into an embrace. It was so horrifically unfair. How dare he treat her with tenderness when she was already battling her extremely untoward response to having emotions?

"There, was that so hard?" he murmured into her hair.

"Yes," she grumbled into his shoulder, even as she clutched the wool of his sack coat in her fists. "Get off me, what will people say?"

"Fellows can embrace. We'll just tell them you got news of a beloved uncle's passing," Henry replied, giving her a squeeze. "I'm comforting you."

Charley screwed her eyes shut and scrunched up her nose, inhaling deeply. She looked up at Henry and stepped back, away from his arms. "I know you know this, but it must be said. These feelings don't entitle you to make decisions for me."

"I know."

"Seriously. I mean it. You have me over a barrel with the things you know about me. And I feel like I'm slipping. I'm fairly certain Miss Sterling knows. The pharmacist too."

"The pharmacist?"

"And now Jacob thinks we're flagrant libertines together. I need to stop gaining any further notoriety."

"I wholeheartedly agree." Henry's lips turned up and his eyes sparkled.

"It's *not* funny. And while I own that I certainly haven't been disputing any of these rumors, it's not all my own fault. I just ... I would rather die than be sent home."

"I know," He reached out affectionately and brushed his fingers down her arm. "If you need to walk the straight and narrow, now's a good time to do it. We won't have much if any chance to be together once we're on the march anyway."

———

XIX

Campbellsville, Kentucky
Friday, January 3, 1862

"MY FEET ARE LIABLE to fall off," Jacob moaned, collapsing next to Henry by the campfire and digging in his haversack for his rations. On the morning of January 1st, the whole brigade had folded up the tents, loaded the baggage train, and, with bands playing and colors displayed, marched out on the Columbia Pike. They had marched that day fourteen miles south and the next, twelve miles, encamping near Campbellsville. Thirteen wagons had been allotted for the tents and baggage of each regiment, and they were loaded to their canvas covers. Thankfully, the roads were hard and smooth, so the wagons came up in good season and it was easy to set up a comfortable camp that evening. What was neither comfortable nor easy was how unaccustomed the soldiers were to marching such distances. Henry's legs tingled and his feet groaned as he sprawled them out on the ground, using his blanket roll as a seat.

"Where's your blanket?" Henry asked, twitching a brow at Jacob as he gnawed on salted pork from his own haversack. Each man was expected to carry his rifle and accoutrements. With forty rounds of ball cartridges on his belt, a knapsack with all his personal property, overcoat, blanket, canteen, haversack with three days' rations—it was a load of nearly fifty pounds.

Jacob sighed as he ripped a hunk of bread off the heel he'd pulled from his haversack. "It was too damn hot and heavy. A bunch of the others were abandoning their loads too."

"What if the weather turns?" Webster asked.

"We're in the South," Jacob dismissed. "We don't need to haul supplies for a New England winter below the Mason-Dixon line."

"Did anyone else end up with the rivets in your knapsack straps digging right into your collarbone?" Williamson asked, shrugging the straps of his knapsack off and rubbing at his clavicle.

"Yeah, now that you mention it," Henry said.

"Me too," Krüger added.

"How does that make sense?" Williamson cried. "Tall, short, big, or small, the rivets find their way to every man's collarbone?"

"Why do you think I'm dumping everything I can?" Jacob said. "We need to travel light and spry."

A hulking shadow cast over them, and Henry looked up, squinting against the setting sun. It took him a moment to register that it was Smith, her frown ominous and her form dissonantly large. Henry blinked in confusion for a moment before he realized she had slung multiple blankets over her shoulders. Henry could detect at least three.

"Where'd you get all that?" Henry asked.

"Robinson's loss is my gain," Smith growled, looping one of her new blankets over her head, unknotting it, and spreading it over the grass. "Plan to make a bit of pocket change when the weather inevitably turns and all these idiots realize they want their blankets back."

Jacob rolled his eyes. "Sorry to break it to you, Smith, but you're wasting your effort. Not only is it warmer here, but we make our own heat when we're on the march. I was sweating bullets all day, and I had to refill my canteen twice. Do you know how many times I had to stop for relief?" He paused for effect. "None, boys. None. I *sweated* it all out."

"So that's why you smell like that," Smith muttered as she sat next to Henry. The boys laughed. Jacob frowned and pulled out his collar to sniff himself.

"Well, I'm no spring daisy, that's for sure," he grinned.

"My trouble wasn't the knapsack," Elias said, joining them on the grass. "It was the rifle. Dear lord, those things are heavy.

I mean, I knew they were heavy, but holding it on the same shoulder for mile upon mile. I don't think I'll regain feeling in my right arm for a week."

"Lieber ein Ende mit Schmerzen als Schmerzen ohne Ende," Krüger said.

Henry gave a wry smirk. "You said it." Charley raised her brows at him, so he translated. "'Better an end with pain than pain without end.'"

"I dunno, Schaefer," Elias said. "We're marching for the foreseeable future. This might be a pain without end."

"I'm sure we'll get used to it," Williamson said uneasily, as though he needed convincing himself. "Like my father always says, folks can get used to just about anything."

Jacob snorted. "Easier said than done."

Williamson shrugged. "He's seen enough hard winters to earn the right to say that."

"Who's your father again?" Elias asked. "I mean, not his name, we know you have the same name. But I swear it sounds familiar."

"It should. You're from Faribault, right?" Williamson grinned. "He's your state senator."

Elias frowned. "Really?"

"Oh yeah!" Jacob cried. "I voted for him."

Elias's frown deepened. "I voted with you. I don't remember voting for him."

"That's because you didn't," Jacob said. "You voted for the Republican."

"Why do you remember who I voted for?"

"Why *don't* you remember who you voted for?"

"Your father's a Democrat?" Smith said, her sharp eyes honing in on Williamson.

Williamson didn't pick up on it. "Yeah, he's essentially Henry Sibley's right hand man."

"Oh, is he the fur trader fellow with the dogs?" Webster asked. "The one who stole the bill so they couldn't move the state capital to St. Peter?"

Williamson grinned. "Yeah!"

"Good," Webster said. "St. Peter was too high in the in-step about that. It made no sense to move the capital on the sole basis of physical geography."

"You'd be singing another tune if it had been Faribault inheriting the capital," Jacob pointed out.

"Of course I would," Webster sniffed. "Faribault is perfectly equipped for state business."

"Even though it's nowhere near the middle of the state," Williamson rolled his eyes.

"If your father's a Democrat, why did you enlist?" Charley asked abruptly.

"What?" Williamson seemed startled.

Webster was ruffled on his behalf. "If all Democrats were anti-Union, the army would be a sorry state of affairs indeed."

"What's that supposed to mean?" Charley snapped.

Henry tried not to sigh audibly.

Webster didn't know better. "That there are plenty of Democrats and non-partisan folks joining this fight. We're not all Lincoln loyalists."

Henry had the self-awareness to feel embarrassed. It had only been a month or two ago that he'd cornered the squad with his half-baked theory that Charley was a Democrat spy in league with the likes of Henry Sibley and other Democratic state leaders. It was an outrageous notion, upon reflection. It was difficult to afford all the competing political factions with the benefit of the doubt, however, in the midst of civil war.

"State politics is a different animal entirely from national politics," Williamson said affably. "From what I can tell, there's barely any difference between Minnesota Democrats and Republicans."

"I should think not," Charley retorted. "In St. Cloud, their Democratic mayor enslaves people illegally in his household."

"That's a rumor—"

"I lived in St. Anthony, Webster, and Southern Democrats brought their slaves there for vacation all the time. Local Democratic sympathizers were more than happy to let them do it, too, until Eliza Winston sued for her freedom and the Southerners all ran away." Charley crossed her arms. "Slavery isn't some distant moral quandary on some other men's shoulders. We in the North are complacent too."

Williamson's brow was furrowed. "Lots of the Democrats in the Minnesota government have kinship ties to the Indians. The Republicans hardly remember that the Indians even exist, much less honor their treaties."

Charley opened her mouth. Henry glanced up and saw Sergeant Osborn behind her with his arms crossed.

"The army is no place for politics," Osborn said. "We're all Union men. Aren't we?"

Webster looked around at the other fellows for a long moment with expectant brows before he said, almost promptingly, "Yessir."

"Yessir," a few of the others chorused haphazardly.

Charley tucked her chin into her chest. Henry tried to catch her eye, but she wouldn't look at him. Williamson was looking at her with a grim line to his mouth. He didn't look angry. More disappointed, really.

"What's the latest, Sarg?" Elias asked, leaning back on his knapsack and crossing his ankles.

"We're laying over here for the next couple of days," Osborn said, lowering himself to the grass with a sigh. "The wagons are overburdened, so they're sending them back to Lebanon to divest of unnecessary supplies and bring back more commissary stores."

Charley made a short, exasperated noise and got to her feet. She slung all her scavenged blankets over her shoulders and stalked off toward the Sibley tents all staked out in neat rows. Henry started to get to his feet himself.

"Don't bother with him, Schaef," Elias drawled with a roll of his eyes.

Osborn turned his head to watch Charley stalk away and then gave a long sigh. "Happy for the messenger to not be shot, for once."

"Sending the wagons back *is* a tremendous waste of time," Henry pointed out. His legs didn't want him to stand, and his feet protested bearing his weight.

"Of course it is," Elias said. "It's the army, what do you expect?"

Henry frowned. "It doesn't have to be this way."

The boys laughed.

Henry rolled his eyes and forced his legs to take him across the grass to the lines of Sibley tents.

He found Charley in their tent, stacking her knapsack and other sundry items in her usual spot. She looked up when he stepped into the tent and shoved her hands over her face and into her hair.

"I don't know why you let it get to you so easy," Henry said. As soon as it was out of his mouth, he worried he was too provoking, but she just tipped her head back and let out a frustrated groan.

"I know, but it's *so infuriatingly inefficient*," she grated out. "We spent over a week packing those wagons to the gills with orders from the captains. What changed between then and now?"

"I suppose some of those commanding officers experienced the march for the first time, along with the rest of us." Henry set all of his kit down next to Charley's and his shoulders sang with gratitude.

"Don't those stupid manuals they all carry around have information about how much commissary stores they need for a regiment? Honestly, this is absurd."

Henry shrugged and wondered whether it was rude to sit down on the stamped-down grass floor of the tent mid-conversation. His ankles felt like brittle twigs.

"For heaven's sake, just sit down," Charley said, then collapsed in a huff on the blankets she'd scavenged, legs sprawling out in front of her. "I asked Osborn why we were packing the wagons with so many nonessentials. He said we had to listen to the fellows who knew what was what, and look at us now? Just because we're not captains doesn't mean we're too ignorant to have suggestions."

Henry followed suit, laying back on his knapsack and plucking a blade of sweet grass to chew between his teeth.

"You know," he mused, "maybe you should pursue a promotion."

"What? Come on."

"No, really, hear me out. You have plenty of ideas, you feel strongly enough about them that you're willing to argue for them, and you don't care a fig about telling other fellows what to do. You'd be a good officer."

"I'm not sure being bossy makes one a good officer."

"Being indecisive sure doesn't. We've got a fair number of those."

Charley twisted her mouth to one side of her face. "I don't think so. I think we've mostly got a bunch of high-falutin' blockheads blowing smoke up each other's asses."

"All the more reason to put your hat in the ring for a promotion."

"I don't blow smoke for anyone," Charley said, then glanced over at him. "Not even you." She reached over and yanked the grass out of his mouth.

"Hey!"

"Oh, I'm sorry, did ol' Bessie not get enough to graze today?"

"I think it makes my breath smell nice."

"Let me be the judge of that." Charley leaned over him. He could feel the soft huff of her breath on his lips, and for a brief moment, Henry was also incensed that they had to layover for days in the middle of nowhere. They could have spent this time in Lebanon prepping the wagons right the first time, a stone's throw away from the Sterling House and a private room for rent.

"Your breath smells normal," Charley concluded.

"But not bad, right?"

He thrilled that she wasn't moving away from him. "No, your breath is never bad."

"Do I taste sweet?"

Charley's lips curled into a smile. "Nice try, but those dopes will be back any minute."

"I'm not trying anything. I just need an objective second opinion."

"I'm objective, am I?"

"Of course. I can always trust you to tell me the truth," Henry grinned. "That's why you'd make a good NCO."

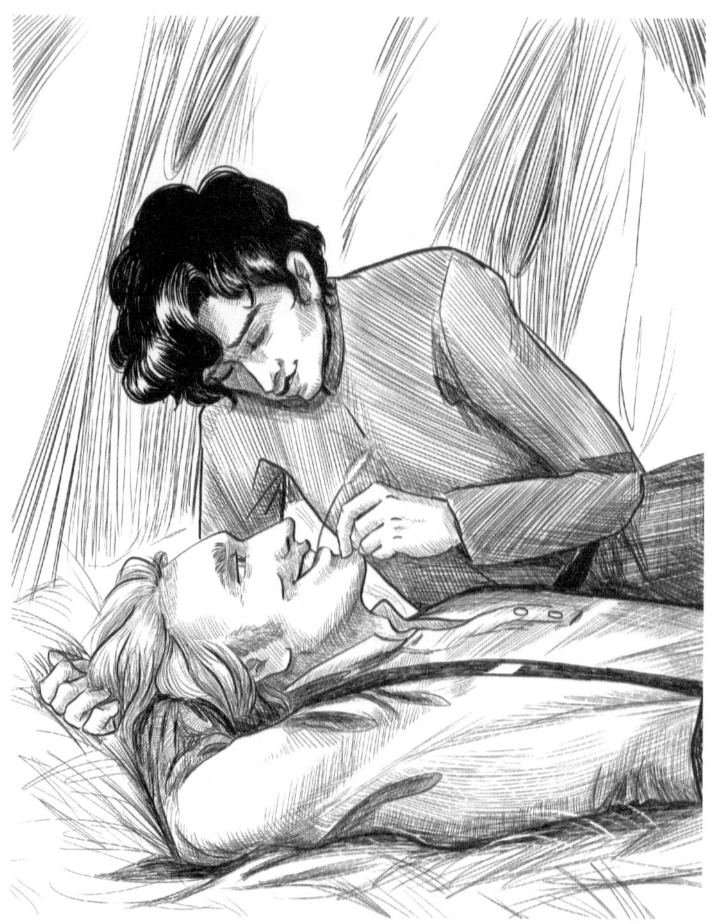

Charley's eyes narrowed and she swatted at his shoulder. "How dare you talk to me like that?"

Henry grinned and wrestled her by the shoulders into the grass, so that he was propped up over her now. Her dark curls framed her square face that was making a futile half-effort to suppress a smile. He leaned in and he was almost sure she was going to kiss him when they heard the heavy tread of tired footsteps and the bray of Elias announcing his latest gossip. Henry rolled off her and back onto his own knapsack with a sigh. What he would have given for a few more days with an accessible bedroom.

———

XX

Columbia, Kentucky
Wednesday, January 8, 1862

"My nose is cold," Charley grunted as she strained under the log she and her squad lifted.

"Your nose is always cold," Henry replied, shoving his shoulder against the end of the log and slotting the tenon into the rough mortise.

Charley sniffed. "Irrelevant—just because my nose is always cold doesn't make it any less distressing."

"My nose is the least of my worries," Hower put in as the squad stepped back from the bridge scaffold. "What I'd really like is a remedy to this damp."

"I'm sure this weather will clear soon," Robinson insisted. He'd been saying that since yesterday, when the temperatures dropped along with the clouds and a relentless drizzle soaked the chill into their bones. Charley had three dollars tucked away in her knapsack, her profit after selling blankets back to the fair-weather fellows who'd dropped them on the pike. Robinson had been sore to part with a dollar, but he'd eventually become more uncomfortable than he was stubborn. That, and no one else in the squad wanted to bunk down with him without a blanket to contribute.

"Wishful thinking only makes the truth more painful," Charley replied.

"That's grim," Williamson chimed in.

"By your logic, then, you should accept your cold nose and dispense with this complaining," Webster moralized.

They were walking back to the campfire now, where a pot of coffee was percolating for the bridge builders. After turning off the Columbia Pike yesterday, the damp had rendered the dirt road into a mud slick, and they'd come upon a rushing river too deep for the wagons to ford. Command had ordered Companies F and K to build a bridge. So here they were, damp and mud-caked, felling trees, hewing logs, and erecting a temporary bridge. Charley would have been annoyed at the delay, but the wagons were already lagging behind because of the muddy road conditions, so they might as well build a bridge while they waited.

"Is there mud in my hair?" Henry asked her as the others hunkered down around the fire.

Charly couldn't help but smile. "You have mud everywhere."

Henry's cheeks were pink—from cold or from Charley's smile, she could not tell—and he gave her shoulder a little nudge with his.

Charley took her tin cup from her haversack and held it out for Webster to fill with coffee.

"Drink up," he said. "You don't want to end up in the hospital tent with Captain Noah."

Webster was taking his promotion to corporal very seriously on the road—except the part that required his reading of the tactics manual. It appeared that in the absence of letters from his wife and children on the march, he'd decided to apply his considerable fatherly energy to his squad instead.

"Those Kentucky boys are dropping like flies, I heard," Hower said of the unorganized companies of Kentuckians for the Union that marched with them. "They're not used to being exposed to the elements like this."

"Well, that's one good thing about miserable Minnesota winters, I guess," Charley shrugged.

"You can get a cold nose without dropping dead?" Henry laughed.

"That remains to be seen," Charley grumbled into her tin cup. The coffee was too hot to drink yet, but the steam felt good on her face.

Henry snorted. "Come on, Smith, you're tougher than that."

"Yeah. It'll take a lot more than a little rain to whip us," Williamson grinned.

"How do you do it, Williamson?" Charley frowned at him.

"What?"

"Be so damn cheerful all the time?"

He shrugged. "I dunno. I'm drinking warm coffee with my friends on a grand adventure. If my nose is cold, that's hardly worth worrying about, is it?"

"I suppose not."

Charley didn't really understand how Williamson managed to be so easygoing. It was his secret strength, though, and Charley was surprised to find that she envied him. Charley couldn't help but see all the deficits and inefficiencies everywhere. They'd camped in Campbellsville the better part of a week waiting for the wagons to get back from Lebanon. It was painfully frustrating to watch the army scramble when it was so clear what needed to be done.

After the coffee was finished, the squad headed back to the clearing where the Hastings boys were stripping bark from pine logs felled by another squad. As they walked, Henry leaned in to Charley and said, "Osborn's lagging. Might be a good time to talk to him."

Charley's stomach clenched. She didn't have a retort, then nor now, except that the mere idea of approaching Osborn to make her case made her physically ill. She'd caused so much trouble—how could she presume to ask for advancement? Regardless, Henry didn't think that mattered. She so wanted to be who he thought she was. What could it hurt to try?

"Ngg," she groaned, pressing her forehead to his shoulder miserably. "Now?"

"If not now," Henry said, "when?"

"You're mean."

"I have other redeeming qualities."

Charley shoved him with her shoulder and hung back to walk side by side with Sergeant Osborn.

"Sir," she said with her chin tucked down. "Are you still angling for a promotion to first sergeant?"

Osborn looked at her with a brow raised for a moment. They were of a similar height.

"Yes," Osborn answered slowly. "Why do you ask?"

Charley steeled herself. She'd jumped into cold creeks in the spring as a child. She could do this. "Because, sir. I think perhaps I could help you."

"Help me? Why? You trying to get rid of me?" Osborn asked with a wry twist of his mustache.

"Criminy, no! That's not what I meant," Charley scrambled. "I mean, I think I'd like to take on more responsibilities too." She took a deep breath and made herself say it. "I work fast and I can get a lot organized efficiently." God, she sounded like a proud Mary.

"That's true enough," Osborn said. "You made quick work of those wagons back in Lebanon."

Charley had to physically bite her tongue to stop herself from griping about how little good that had done after they brought half the provisions back. She cleared her throat. "I'd like to apply those skills more broadly, sir."

Osborn cracked a smile. "You don't have to call me 'sir.' You don't usually anyway."

Charley winced.

"I think you've got good potential, Smith. You're smart, you're driven, and like you said, you do first rate work fast. But I don't think I'm saying anything surprising when I say that if you want to rise in rank, you'll have to get a hold of your temper."

"I know, sir," Charley said. "I have maybe ... been speaking more freely than I should since joining up. It was ... well, a big relief being on my own." Understatement. "I'm able to be more diplomatic. I have been before."

Osborn nodded. "Good. It would be a shame to see your potential wasted."

Charley frowned. The comment made her mouth sour in a familiar way. "I aim to do better, sir."

Osborn smiled at her. "Good. I think you'd do well with more responsibility."

"I do too, sir," Charley agreed. "I think I'd be less frustrated too."

Osborn winced. "I don't know about that."

Charley found herself laughing. "I suppose. Maybe being less frustrated is more of a long game."

"Maybe. There's only one way to find out."

———

They had roast goose for supper. In Campbellsville, the Ninth Ohio had defied orders and set fire to a haystack where a local farmer had hid apples from potential foragers. Afterwards, the Big Bugs had seemingly loosened the reins a bit and let the soldiers forage for "wild" fowl. The birds as well as a few chickens and a hog had been mustered into service with alacrity and for the last four days or so, the brigade was eating quite well indeed.

"I'm going to visit my uncle after supper," Henry told Charley. He had a sheen of goose fat running down his chin. "Do you want to come?"

"Hm?" Charley's attention snapped up to his eyes.

"To the Ninth's camp. To see my uncle."

"Oh. Sure, yes."

Henry's mouth melted into that half crooked smile. "Great."

There was a wooded track between where the Second Minnesota and the Ninth Ohio had made camp. Henry and Charley picked their way through the soggy leaves and brambles as the sun set below the rolling hills.

Henry checked the sky through the bare branches. "That's a lovely sunset."

Charley looked over her shoulder. "Yeah, nice."

"How'd it go with Osborn?"

"Oh, fine," Charley replied. "He told me I need to work on my temper if I want a promotion."

Henry frowned. "Really? Lieutenant Woodbury has an awful temper, and he seems to be doing fine for himself, especially now that Captain Noah's sick."

Charley kicked a rock off the deer trail they were following. "That's different. He only applies his temper to the privates, not the Big Bugs. And he never got caught at a brothel out of hours."

"You didn't either," Henry pointed out.

"Yeah, but everyone knows anyway after I started that awful rumor."

"Officers went to Sterling House. Remember, we saw Lieutenant Thomas in the billiards room."

"Somehow, I think it matters less once you already have the rank."

"What do you hope for?" Henry asked.

Charley had to pause and think. She was deep in critique and it was hard to pivot. She still couldn't imagine even a rise to corporal, much less anything higher. First sergeant seemed nigh impossible, much less lieutenant or captain. And who knew how long it would take for positions to open up at each level to work her way up? "I don't know. I haven't even thought of trying for a promotion since Hower got corporal."

"Well, it doesn't hurt to think about it and dream."

"Yes it does. Dream too much and then you feel extra stupid when things inevitably don't work out."

"I guess you know what you're doing," Henry shrugged his hands into his pockets. Charley glared at him, frowned, then gave up trying to ignore how damned provoking he was.

"Of course I know what I'm doing," she snapped. "I'm not naive—I know this is a long shot. What confuses me is why you don't."

"See, that. That's the kind of confidence that we need leading the company."

"Are you trying to pay me compliments again, because if you are—"

Henry dissolved into laughter. "You're not fooling anyone but yourself."

"How dare you?" She smiled. "I fool everyone every day."

"No, you don't, Charley." Henry shook his head wistfully. "You're probably more honest now than you've ever been."

Charley stilled.

He couldn't know that. He'd never known Cate Ellis. But still, the words seized her heart in a way that stole her breath and pricked her eyes. She sniffed as quietly as she could.

"Oh no, Charley," Henry turned toward her and grabbed her shoulders. "I'm sorry, I was just assuming—"

His touch, his concern, snapped whatever thread of control she had left, and she felt water well in her eyes. "No, you're right. I've, um. I've never felt more like myself." She sniffed it all back, grappling for control. "Wearing a uniform doesn't make me any easier to get along with, but here, I feel ... alive. I feel pure and right and I ... I like myself more than I ever have."

Henry smiled and brushed his fingers over her forehead, her cheeks, her jaw. "Good. You should. You're the fiercest, bravest person I've ever met." He brushed his lips against her cheek. "I love you."

"Ugh," Charley groaned and shoved her face into the damp wool of Henry's shoulder.

"What was that?"

"I love you too, you jackanape," Charley hiccoughed, throat tight.

Henry pushed his hand into the hair at the back of her neck and guided her mouth to his. Charley kissed him back, her lips savoring the slip of soft lips, the bite of his perfect teeth, the feel of his skin as she released his lapels and gripped his jaw in her palms. She tipped her chin down, breaking them apart for a moment, and whispered, "I really do love you, Henry. I don't know what I did to deserve you."

"There are greater rewards for courage than a third son of a failed German revolutionary with no land to speak of," Henry chuckled.

"I can't think of any," Charley retorted and kissed him so hard, he staggered back against a nearby tree trunk. She let his scent fill her nose, his warmth heat her skin, and his taste incite her to craving. God had made no other person so perfectly suited to her. The way he'd missed enlisting in the First Minnesota, the forces that brought them to meet on the parade ground that first day, that brought him to call for her to join his squad—it was nothing short of serendipity. He very well could be her reward for seizing her fate in her own hands. Her spoils of war.

Her hand wedged between them now.

"Charley, it's not even dark yet," Henry hissed weakly as she squeezed his half-hard cock through his trousers. It swelled under her touch.

"You asked what I hope for," she exhaled. "Well, it's everything. I can't help myself. I want everything all the time and sometimes I think the longing will kill me, but I never stop wanting. Wanting more choices, more justice, a better society, better systems. Recognition and accolades. Wanting adoration and love and you, God, Henry, *all* of you. I love you so bad I want to crawl inside your skin—dammit, that sounds horrific, but I don't know how else to explain it. I took a chance to enlist, but I haven't ever been brave without you. I don't know if I'd even want to."

"Oh, Charley."

His hands pulled her in so tight she knew he understood. Her hand was trapped between them, and she wanted to fuck him, fiercely, with the same longing she always felt pounding in her blood. But it was also different. He was hers, she was his. They belonged to each other. She wanted him inside her in the same way she wanted to inhale his exhale, and curl into the shell of his arms each night when they slept. To melt into him, share his heat until she didn't know where she ended and he began. She wanted to be a part of him the same way she wanted to set fire to the entire Confederacy. More, even, because this was a love that multiplied, not a fury that divided. She had the French letter in her pocket. It was a distant reminder in the rush of her ardor, but it was there all the same. It was so tedious to stop and get it out and fuss with it, when all she really wanted was to feel him skin to skin inside her—

That pulled her up short. The fervor with which she wanted him muted her better sense. She wouldn't put herself through that fear and uncertainty again. Her fists, curled in his coat, shook as she forced herself to put an inch or two between them. It might as well have been a canyon for how wrong it felt to part from him.

"Charley." He was breathless and flush, lips full and pink from kissing. His chest rose with each breath. It was hypnotic. "My Charley. I don't know if I've ever wanted anything the way I want you."

Charley melted back into him. How could she hold her distance when he looked at her like that, spoke to her like that?

"I gave up everything to fight in this war," she confessed into his ear, "but damn, I could give it all up if it meant getting some goddamned privacy with you."

Henry groaned. "My country for a bed."

"What if we went west?" Charley blurted, pressing kisses and mindless wantings into his neck. "After the war, I mean. Somewhere no one knew us. I could be me and we could be together. Two war buddies sowing fields, living the dream we fought to preserve."

"That sounds perfect," Henry murmured into that tender spot below her ear. "You would want that?"

"I already told you, Henry. I want everything. Which includes homesteading, I suppose. As long as you're naked in my bed, and I don't have to wash the damn dishes."

"I will wash every dish for you," Henry crooned. "Every spoon. I'll learn to cook for you."

"That is the most arousing thing I've ever heard."

"We're not going to make it to the Ninth's camp, are we?"

"Not at this rate," Charley said, chasing his mouth with hers. She glanced around the wood, assessing. "These pine branches are pretty low."

"You're wishful thinking."

"But there's no pickets here, and it's almost dark."

"Don't tease me like this."

"I'm not teasing. I've got the French letter in my pocket, and we have at least half an hour before taps."

"It's raining," Henry swallowed weakly. "And muddy..."

"You've already got mud in your hair. What's a little more?"

Henry leveraged his weight against the tree and yanked her in by the coat, smashing their mouths together.

"Ow—"

"Shh." His lips curled against hers, and she licked his teeth and she didn't care, she didn't care, it was *him*. He opened his mouth and she found bliss in the heat of his mouth, relief groaning out of her as she tasted him, at once familiar and fresh.

"Do you always clean your teeth after supper?"

"Yes, don't you?"

"No—is this why your teeth are so nice?"

"I guess. Why don't you clean your teeth after you eat?"

"I clean them before bed, what do you want?"

Henry's hands wedged under the waistband of her trousers. "These, open."

Charley shuddered and reached down to unfasten the first few buttons on her trousers. "Happy?"

"Very."

His hands were icy on her belly. He made quick work of her shirt, worming beneath it without trouble and pushing his fingers into the springy hair over her mound.

"Christ, yes," she hummed as his finger slid between her folds, tracing a trail of cold over her hot flesh. She grappled with his trouser buttons, but his fingers sliding over her, up and down, slicking with each pass, made her stupid. She made sounds into his mouth, soft desperate ones, and her hands yanked at his waistband.

"You feel so good," he murmured, even as he reached with his other hand to help her with his buttons.

"No, that's you," she replied with a sigh as her hand plunged beneath his shirttail and took hold of his rigid cock. "Oh, this is a great way to warm up."

"We should tell the whole squad," he panted against her mouth as she gave him a firm yank. "Ah—soon they'll all be doing it."

Charley let out a short, half-hysterical laugh as his fingers pressed inside her. It had to be two at once. She gripped the back of his neck with her other hand and sank onto them. He bit at her bottom lip as she smeared her palm with his wetness, then pumped him slow and steady. His fingers were deep in her, the heel of his palm solid against the place she most wanted pressure, and she rode his hand for a moment both brief and timeless.

"Oh, Henry," she murmured. "You've got to stop or I'll come before we even get to the French letter."

"That's fine," he replied. "I'll just make you come again."

God, this damned man. She stopped trying to hold back and let sensation drive her hips, his fingers and palm her saddle, and her mind flooded with all manner of things she wanted to do to him, many of which were now set in the austere room of a frontier log cabin of all ridiculous things. The notion that she shouldn't be so easy, that she should require time and attention and elaborate seduction, made her come faster than she could ever recall. Undone, with all her clothes on against a tree, reckless and unplanned, where anyone could find them. She pressed her face into Henry's chest to muffle the almighty groan her climax shoved out of her.

"Ah, wait," Henry panted and his other hand slowed her wrist, still pumping—though significantly more slick now. "Gimme a second."

Charley's legs were shaking, but she nodded and pulled her hand out of his trousers to fumble for the French letter in her pocket. "Oh, look at the mess you made of my hand."

Her palm was shiny in the twilight.

Henry bit his lip with those perfect teeth and smiled his crooked smile. "You think that's messy?"

He held up his fingers. Charley could imagine, in the farthest reaches of her mind, some sense that this should be disgusting. Perverted. Strange. But in her conscious estimation, it was goddamned erotic and the faster they got themselves to Hell, the better it was going to feel.

"Taste it," she heard herself say. Christ, she was possessed.

Henry's lips parted, and he pushed his glistening fingers into his mouth. His eyes never strayed from hers. He moaned.

"What are you thinking?" Charley pressed. *Say you love it. Say you want more.*

"I'm..." he murmured around his fingers. He trailed off, sucking his fingers down and making Charley deliriously wish she had a cock just so she could see those lips around it. "I'm thinking I want to taste you."

Charley moved in closer. She had the French letter in her hand. "You are tasting me."

His flushed cheeks. His kiss-plump lips. His stubbly cheeks. She was drunk with him.

"I mean, you know... direct."

She breathed hot on his mouth, felt his breath back, inhaled his exhale and was dizzy with the notion of his mouth between her thighs. "Henry, dear God, I need you to fuck me right now."

He gripped her lapel in assent, and she shoved the French letter over him. They fumbled for a moment.

"Dammit. Damn trousers," she muttered.

"Turn around," he growled and seized her greatcoat, moving it out of the way and pressing her up against the tree trunk. Bark bit into her cheek, and her hands pressed against it. Henry released her suspenders and pushed her trousers down her buttocks. She whimpered. She could feel the cold air kiss the wetness between her legs. Henry gripped her hips and then she felt heat, pressure, against her cunt.

"Oh my God, Henry," she babbled. He pressed into her, and she stretched around him. She could not help the sounds she was making, and she panted into the tree bark, hands scrabbling for purchase. Oh, it felt so different this way. Intense. Animal. Henry's fingers dug into her hips, and he pushed into her, shallowly at first to get the French letter slick, but then deep, deeper than she had ever experienced before.

She babbled nonsense—formless, desperate sounds. She felt tears well in her eyes. Her entire body was on fire, overwhelmed by the sheer presence of him inside her, at this angle. God, it was everything. It was *everything*. She squirmed against the tree, and a second climax scrambled through her belly, through her blood, through her bones. She shouted. She couldn't have stopped herself if she'd tried. She would have blinded herself if she'd managed to experience this silently.

Henry was pounding into her now, his mouth panting against the back of her neck. She shook and clung helplessly to the tree trunk, lest her legs give out entirely. God, even the aftershocks with him like this were like nothing she'd ever felt before. Her voice would not stop keening with every stroke.

"Charley, I love you. I love everything about you. Your smell, your hair, this spot on the back of your neck." He was rambling, his words slurred like he was half drunk. "I look at it every time we're in ranks. Even before I knew about you, I couldn't stop thinking about your neck." His hands gripped her buttocks, pulled them apart so he could press in deeper. Charley let out a sob. He strained. She could feel him surge inside her, felt the heat through the French letter. A part of her wished it was in her, filling her up till it spilled out. A part she didn't care to hear from, but she was already in oblivion and her defenses against errant, animal thoughts were completely demolished.

Henry stilled. They stood that way for a long moment, joined together in the dark silence, their breath slowly catching up with them. Birds fluttered through the trees, and pine needles sprinkled down as a squirrel skittered somewhere above them. He breathed against her neck, and she could feel him going soft inside her and for that moment, she didn't want anymore. She had everything she needed.

———

XXI

Outside Columbia, Kentucky
Friday, January 10, 1862

THE NEXT DAY, THE sick were sent back to Lebanon in the wagons. They laid over for two days, taking some much deserved rest after building the bridge, but it was cramped and damp because the rain kept coming. By Friday, the cold had cut to Henry's bones, and he drank extra coffee trying to banish it. It was no wonder so many fellows were getting sick.

"It's the measles," Jacob was saying as he and Henry trudged across the camp to fetch rations for the rest of the squad. "Steer clear of that hospital tent. The fellows in the Kentucky regiment are falling like flies."

"We've worked so hard for so long to see battle. I'll be damned if I get sick and miss it."

"Tell that to Captain Noah," Jacob agreed. "He's in that wagon train heading back to Lebanon."

"Is he on leave, then?" Henry turned toward Jacob in interest.

"Yeah, either Lieutenant Woodbury or Thomas is gonna get promoted to captain."

Henry's eyes lit up. "Do you think Osborn will get picked up for first sergeant, if Nelson is promoted to lieutenant?"

"I know he's been angling for it. I guess we'll find out."

"I keep telling Charley to go for Corporal," Henry said. He steeled himself to be cautious with his pronouns and added, "This might be his chance."

Jacob gave him a sideways glance.

"What?"

"Nothing."

"No, you gave me a look. What?"

"Oh, I dunno, Schaefer. Do you really think Smith would make a good corporal? Seems like he'd be a tyrant, if you ask me."

Henry frowned. "I don't think so."

"Well, you wouldn't, being his bosom friend and all."

Henry felt his face get hot. "I don't think he'd play favorites."

"No, he wouldn't play favorites. He'd push us all to the brink, except you."

"I really think you're being dramatic."

Jacob rolled his eyes. Then, he huffed a laugh. "It would be funny, though, to see Smith try to keep us all on a tight leash under Webster, who just wants to tuck us all into bed and tell us a bedtime story."

Henry laughed too. "That would drive him nuts. Wait—if Osborn is promoted, does Webster decide who gets corporal?"

"I suppose he would."

"Hm. I'd better remind Charley to make his case to Webster, then, too."

"Oh, I see how it is."

"What? No you don't."

"I do. You're encouraging him. What's your game, Schaef? Looking for privileges?"

"No," Henry retorted reflexively. He already had all the privileges he could ever want when it came to Charley. Except privacy. "I just think he'd be good at it, is all." Jacob gave him a sour look. "I'm serious! Smith doesn't lose his temper unless the top brass is already doing something profoundly stupid. Wouldn't you like to have someone with a thimbleful of common sense moving up the ranks? Someone who doesn't just sit quietly and fawn over the fellows in charge?"

"Men like that never get promoted," Jacob sniffed.

"They do if the men listen to them," Henry insisted. "If Charley is given the chance, I think we'd better support him. A little goes a long way with him."

"What does that mean?"

Henry blinked. "I just mean that … if you give him one measly compliment, he'll fight to the death for you. It doesn't take much to earn his loyalty, and he fights hard for people."

Jacob gave him a flat look. "I think that might just be you, Schaef. We haven't seen battle yet, but I'd bet fifty dollars that that boy will take a bullet for you. I wouldn't make the same bet for any of the rest of us."

Henry stilled. He couldn't think about that. No, he couldn't consider that scenario at all, so he grabbed at his indignation like a life preserver. Jacob was several paces ahead of him by the time he got hold of it. "You're wrong. Smith would do that for all of us. You're just sore because you had to buy your blanket back from him."

"Should I not be?"

"You dropped it in the ditch! If it weren't for Smith, you would have no blanket at all and probably be on the sick wagon back to Lebanon."

Jacob frowned. Henry seized his advantage. "Smith isn't nurturing like Webster, I'll give you that. But he takes care of people. He'd make a damn good corporal, or any other rank they'd be smart enough to give him."

Jacob sighed. "Damn, Schaef. You got it bad."

Henry blanched. "I don't know what you're talking about."

"It's fine. Everyone knows. You follow Smith around like a puppy dog." Jacob didn't appear at all concerned. "It's okay. Lots of young men love their best friends. It's how we learn how to love, isn't it?"

Henry's mouth dropped open.

"I don't know what you're all embarrassed about. I loved Hower for a time, before you ever came to the farm back in Faribault." Jacob shrugged. Henry suspected that the way he had loved Hower was not at all comparable to the way he loved Charley. But Karl had said something similar, so perhaps Henry was simply naive.

Regardless, he was grateful when they arrived at the commissary tent and he had a moment of distraction to wrangle a parcel of rations in his arms and think.

"I can carry it, if you want," Jacob offered reflexively.

"No, I got it," Henry replied. Their squad was issued but the one parcel, so unless they wanted to carry it between them, it was one or the other. "It's really not that heavy."

They started back toward the tent.

"You know, maybe I am letting my own resentment color my opinion of Smith," Jacob said idly as they walked. "I suppose when it comes down to his actions, he's an honorable sort of fellow. He's just such a blowhard, it's hard to see past it."

"I know," Henry replied. "He's all bark, though." And sometimes bite. But only in the best way. "I, um. I guess you're right. I do love him." God, it felt so good to say. He'd been wanting to shout it from the rooftops, but he'd been terrified of compromising Charley. He thought he'd have to keep his distance. But if he could speak of love with Jacob, even if it was presumed platonic, well ... it was a comfort. "I never expected to."

"I know. You thought he was a spy."

"Shut up."

Jacob laughed. "Turns out you're just a glutton for punishment."

"I am not. I was just wrong. Very wrong. He's smart and passionate and entirely uncompromising. I admire him so much."

"Aw," Jacob said, chuffing him in the shoulder. "I knew you had it bad."

Henry swam in the comfort of being seen.

"I just think," Jacob began slowly, "that you ought to be careful."

"I know, it's unseemly. Krüger already looks like he wants to rain hellfire down on us whenever he sees us."

"Not that," Jacob rolled his eyes, as if Krüger's propriety was as inconsequential as worrying about French-Russo relations. "I mean, make sure Smith is above board. He's very determined in his thinking. I'm sure it's easy to get swept along. But he's not morally consistent."

"What do you mean?"

"I mean that damned Sterling House affair! I know we're at war, Schaef, and fellows have needs, but whores are the quickest path to syphilitic insanity. That bunk can ruin your whole life."

Henry paused. It was a tell and he knew it, but he was already doing it before he could think to stop.

"Unless he was lying..." Jacob said, looking back at Henry under a raised eyebrow.

Henry winced. Jacob's other eyebrow went up to.

"*Oh*," he said. A slight blush crept over his cheeks too. "I suppose kisses are not outside the affection of bosom friends," he added quickly, not meeting Henry's eyes. "I'm sure it's none of my business if you wanted a little privacy."

Henry's mouth dropped open, and then an embarrassingly high laugh came out of his throat unbidden. "Did you do that with Hower, then?"

Jacob looked scandalized. "Of course not! Not that he didn't try. He was all, 'Come on, Jacob. I'll teach you how.' But he had nasty breath back then. I guess his mother never taught him to brush his teeth, which is really no excuse because I didn't have one to begin with and I still have all *my* teeth. I loved him, but not *that* much. It was all bluster anyway. He was just angling for practice for himself. I really don't think that lunkhead can back up any of his boasts."

"He loves yellow-jacket novels," Henry agreed.

"Yeah, I think he fancies himself some sort of gothic rake." Henry snorted.

"It was short-lived anyway. I was on my own for the first time, and I was so damn lonely, I just attached to the first person who noticed me. Soon as I got the attention of girls, I didn't need him so much anymore. That's usually the way of it."

Henry stayed silent. Maybe that was what Charley was so afraid of. That Henry would meet a girl and forget about her. But that was the thing. Charley was both the bosom friend *and* the enigmatic girl. She was more than an infatuation or a youthful loneliness displaced. She was everything Henry had never even known he wanted.

"I suppose it'll be a long time before any of us are able to meet any girls, though," Jacob said, more like thinking out loud than anything else.

"Do you miss her? Your wife, I mean?"

"I knew it was going to be torture," Jacob replied, kicking at the ground. "But it's so much worse than I imagined. There's no letters, Henry. I write her every day, and I never get anything back. I keep telling myself it's the mail, it's delayed or held up somewhere outside of Louisville, but what if she's forgotten about me? What if she met someone else, someone who is actually there. I did her a nasty turn, marrying her then marching out."

"No you didn't," Henry replied, shifting the parcel to one hip. "You gave her everything you could, given what you'd already promised to Lincoln."

"Do you ever wish you didn't enlist? No, don't answer that. Of course you don't. You've got your bosom friend in your arms every night. Sometimes I wish she could have followed the camp or ... or dressed up in trousers so she could be with me. I know, it's crazy. She never would have anyway. She's too correct to follow an army camp or do laundry for the troops. And it wouldn't have worked anyway because they sent all the camp followers away in Lebanon. I don't know, I'm rambling."

"You just miss her," Henry said, using the arm he'd freed up to squeeze Jacob's shoulder and ignoring the way his heart was racing. "You should miss her. You love her. I mean, it'd be a bad sign if you didn't."

"I know. It's just unbearable." Jacob wrinkled his nose, then laughed. "Maybe I can attach myself to you and Smith. Just snuggle up on the other side, make a little Smith sandwich."

Henry glowered.

"Oh my God! Look at you, so jealous." Jacob slapped his knee. "Never mind. I wouldn't dare get between you and your Confederate spy."

"Don't say that! What if someone heard!"

"That's right, your boy wants a promotion. Apologies," Jacob teased. "Don't let him aim too high, though. He gets promoted enough times, you won't see him anymore."

———

After the midday meal, Company K was called together on the makeshift parade ground. The rain had turned to sleet in the cold and the ground was more a swamp, the boys' boots all sinking into the cloying mud as they turned their attention to Lieutenant Woodbury.

"Soldiers, attention!" Woodbury shouted. Henry noticed that the men seemed to stand taller for him than they had for Captain Noah, though he suspected that was because Woodbury had done much of their beginning drills at Fort Snelling and had no compunction using a cane to correct them. "Captain Noah is still ill, but despite what you may have heard, he is still here with us in camp and has not been sent back to Lebanon on sick furlough. He is on the mend and will be back in ranks with us again soon."

Henry could see Charley's shoulders slump slightly in front of him.

"This afternoon, you'll receive orders to prepare the wagons for an early departure in the morning. See your sergeants for further instructions. Sergeant Osborn's squad, see Lieutenant Thomas. The rest of you, fall out!"

Henry exchanged a curious glance with Robinson as Williamson asked, "Are we in trouble?"

Osborn's mustache curled up at the corners. "I don't think so. Come on!"

Charley fell in by Henry's side as they trudged through the mud to Lieutenant Thomas.

"So much for a power shift," she muttered, shoving a palm across her nose.

"Yeah, I guess Captain Noah's eager to keep hold of his position," Henry replied. "Is your nose cold again?"

"Yes, dammit."

"Do you want me to warm it up?"

Charley cast him an alarmed look. "No. Don't touch my nose."

They scrambled into the best ranks they could muster given the terrain as Sergeant Osborn gave a salute and said, "Squad Seven, sir, reporting for duty."

"Sergeant Osborn, soldiers," Lieutenant Thomas greeted with his hands behind his back. He seemed more poised than Henry was used to seeing. Usually, Thomas was in a constant snit trying to get the privates to make him look good in front of Captain Noah and the Colonel. "You've been selected to conduct an advance guard this afternoon."

"Sir!" Sergeant Osborn responded. Henry couldn't see his face, but he could tell he was fighting a grin.

"Looks like Sarg's brownnosing paid off," Robinson said to Henry out the side of his mouth.

"Shh!"

"You'll pair your squad off and go out about 20 rods in advance of the company, which should be about 80 rods in advance of the regiment. Your mission is to scout the route ahead and determine the location of any enemy forces in our path in season to prevent a surprise. Do not engage the enemy. Do not fire unless fired upon. If you are fired upon, retreat to the regiment and inform command immediately. Do you understand your orders?"

"Yes sir," Sergeant Osborn confirmed, then glanced back at the squad. Webster took the invitation.

"Sir, are we to understand the enemy is within 20 rods?" he asked.

Lieutenant Thomas's countenance was usually exasperated, but this time, it was more guarded somehow. "Perhaps. That's what we need you to find out."

Henry looked at Robinson with some alarm.

"Reports place them within ten miles, so it's unlikely they're that close, but we need to check and find out. Sergeant Osborn, your squad has been dependable on the march. I look forward to your report."

"Sir, yes sir," Osborn confirmed and the whole squad saluted with him.

They walked tall back to the tent to gather their knapsacks and materials.

"Make sure to bring everything, boys," Sergeant Osborn said. "If we are engaged, we might not have a chance to return before the camp is struck and we march on."

Henry could feel the tent hum with excitement. Hower could barely hold in a grin, and Charley had this expression on her face that was both grim and eager. It was rather chilling. Henry shoved his things into his knapsack and checked his haversack to make sure it was filled with rations.

"Does everyone have a full complement of ammo?" Charley asked, checking her own cartridge box.

Henry looked in his box and said, "Yup."

A chorus of confirmations rang around the tent as the others checked theirs as well. Henry smiled at Charley, then glanced at Osborn who was looking at Charley consideringly. Webster didn't appear to have noticed anything at all—he was too busy checking his cartridge box as directed.

The squad emerged from the tent and headed south and east toward the Cumberland River. The rain misted over their faces, the clouds gloaming the light and making it feel almost like it was dusk, especially under the cover of trees. When they reached the edge of the picket line, Osborn turned and paired them off.

"I have selected these pairs intentionally, and they're not your bunkies, so no complaints, you understand?" the Sergeant preempted. Henry exchanged a glance with Charley, whose expression darkened. Her eyes sort of smoldered as her mouth tightened into a line, and Henry felt his stomach flip to be regarded so possessively. "I'll have Robinson and Williamson, Hower and Krüger, Webster and Smith, and Schaefer, you'll be with me."

Henry frowned. Why pair Charley with Webster? Unless he was letting the Corporal take stock of Charley's skills. "Oh, okay."

He wasn't sure why he felt so discomfited as he watched Charley and Webster lope off to the north east, heading into the cover of a pine grove.

"Come on, Schaefer, let's go," Osborn said. Henry followed him due east, down a grassy hill snaked with a split-rail fence.

Henry and his sergeant travelled silently for a while. The mud was less troubling in grassy areas, but it slopped anywhere the ground was bare. Henry's feet were already damp, and it took less than an hour for his boots to become saturated. The wetter the weather, the colder it felt.

Osborn led the way around trees. They moved as quietly as they could, staying behind cover and peering around trees when they reached open areas to survey for enemy scouts. Henry was wound tight at first, imagining greybacks lurking around every shrub. Imagining Charley off in the woods with Webster, who was a lovely man in many respects, but without the fighting spirit that Charley had. He couldn't help but fear that if they met hostiles, Charley would defend them both and Henry couldn't bear the risk that posed. He quickly squashed these imaginings, filling his mind instead with a Heine poem he'd memorized at Turner Hall. "Die Lorelai" just made him think of Charley, though.

After an hour, Henry adjusted to the rhythm of their scouting. Moving methodically, looking carefully for any movement or disruption. The mud was thick and would have shown footprints readily, so it was heartening in a way to be taken by surprise when stepping on a misleading mud slick. He couldn't help but wonder if the other fellows were having a better time, chatting together quietly as they surveyed their assigned tract. He supposed Osborn was right to split him and Charley apart. Henry was pretty confident that he would not be as attentive were she there to distract him.

Around three o'clock in the afternoon, Osborn gestured for Henry to join him under the canopy of a pine tree and break for water. Henry took a swig out of his canteen, looking around the wood.

"I understand Smith is looking for a promotion," Osborn said.

Henry glanced over at him. "Yeah. I think he'd be good for it."

"I do too," Osborn agreed. "I put him with Webster in hopes he can win him over. If he can manage some diplomacy, it'll go a long way."

"Do you think there will be a shift in command soon?" Henry asked. "What with Captain Noah being sick and all?"

"There's lots of rumors," Osborn said. "I don't know what will happen. Getting this assignment is a good sign, though, for me and for anyone else looking for advancement."

Henry nodded and thought for a moment.

"Sir, do you think Charley could move up?"

"What, do you mean higher than an NCO?"

"Yeah."

Osborn tilted his head consideringly. "I suppose he could, if he could make the right impression. Why, are you worried about getting left behind?"

Henry pursed his lips and gave a reluctant nod. "Yeah, I guess so. I think he'd be great, but I was talking to Robinson about it this morning, and I didn't really think about that."

"It certainly would be a big change," Osborn agreed. "I myself am nervous about what a promotion beyond first sergeant would mean for Webster."

"Sir?"

"We're old friends, you know, and Webster has such a hard time being away from his family. I worry if we aren't able to bunk up together, he's going to be lonely."

Henry considered Osborn for a moment. "It would be lonely if Charley ended up in an officer's tent."

"An officer's tent has its perks, and lots of fellows promote their friends behind them. I wouldn't worry too much, Schaefer," Osborn smiled. "That's a long way off, anyway, and he'd need to get past first sergeant to make it out of the squad. That's a challenging jump to make, given there's almost ten fellows to choose from among the sergeants."

"You're making a good go of it, though."

"Thanks." Osborn gave a small, private smile. It made his face seem younger, somehow. "I'm really heartened that we got this assignment."

"Yeah," Henry replied. "Here's hoping we don't mess it up."

———

Henry and the rest of the squad returned to camp for supper having found no enemy worse than the mud through which they had to plod their way. The camp was buzzing with grumbles.

"What's going on?" Charley asked Corbett from the Hastings Squad, Henry close on her heels.

"We've run out of firewood," Corbett replied. "After two days camping here and building a damn bridge, turns out we can't find any more to forage."

"Couldn't we fell a few trees?" Henry asked.

"Sure, but it'd be green wood and it would smoke to high heaven, giving away our position," Corbett replied. "Fellows have been eyeing that split rail fence over yonder, but the damn Big Bugs are fussing that it's private property."

"Not this again," Charley glowered, crossing her arms. "This is such bunk. Why do we hand them this power? Freezing our soldiers will help no one, especially as close as we are to catching up with Zollicoffer."

"Oh yeah, did you see anything on the advance guard?" Corbett asked, grinning.

"No, nothing but mud," Henry replied.

"That's too bad. Would have been nice to finally shoot a Reb instead of treating his property like a goddamned church."

"This is nonsense," Charley said, throwing up her hands. "Come on Henry, let's go talk to Lieutenant Thomas."

"What?"

Charley grabbed his sleeve and dragged him down the row of tents. "I gotta practice my diplomacy, after all."

Lieutenant Thomas was hiding in the Company K officer's tent. It was a large A-frame tent, big enough to stand in. From what Henry had heard, it fit two trundle beds and a table that they lugged from camp to camp in the wagon.

"Oh, how civilized," Charley sneered as they approached.

"You think Captain Noah's in there?"

"No, I doubt it. Not if he's got the measles like everyone says. They've got them all quarantined up that hill." Charley kicked her chin in that direction as she reached out for the tent flap poised to knock. She looked at her hand for a moment, shook her head, and called out, "Lieutenant Thomas? Do you have a moment, sir?"

Lieutenant Thomas peeked his head out between the tent flaps. "If you're here about the firewood—"

"—I know, sir," Charley cut in. "I'm sure you're freezing too—"

Henry doubted that given the smoke puffing out of the tent's stovepipe.

"—but the men are cold and tired and this rain just won't stop," Charley finished graciously. Henry shook his head and looked at her more carefully. He could imagine her asking for church donations. Sort of. She was still in trousers, mind, but he could see that righteousness in her countenance.

"Don't you think I know that, Private?" Lieutenant Thomas tilted his chin up to give them a lowering look. "Top brass won't budge on it. Says it's a matter of propriety."

"Sir, all due respect, but to hell with propriety," Charley replied with the relish Henry was more accustomed to hearing. "No one ever won a war for respecting their enemy's propriety."

Thomas's eyes did a movement that suggested he was trying to keep from rolling them. "I'm with you, Private, I am. But my hands are tied."

"That's too bad," Charley said. "Everyone's rooting for you to get captain if Noah gets furloughed. Woodbury's a hard case and no one likes him. It'd be better for us all if we had a captain we wanted to fight for."

Thomas stared at her a moment. "That's very flattering. I'll see what I can do. You're dismissed." He disappeared and swished the tent flaps closed.

Charley frowned and turned back toward their tent.

"Is that true about the captaincy?" Henry asked as he caught up to her.

"No," she replied. "I haven't heard anyone say two nice words together about Lieutenant Thomas."

"He could be worse, I suppose."

"Right. He could be Woodbury. But lots of fellows like being bossed around. Makes 'em feel wistful for their mothers or something."

Henry shot her an incredulous look. "Seems like we don't have much in the way of good options if ol' Noah has to go on leave."

"What's new?" Charley shrugged. "They've all got their heads up their asses about something or another."

"That's a fine thing to say to get a promotion." Robinson had caught up with them at the head of their tent row. "Any news on the firewood situation?"

"None. Thomas said he'd see what he could do."

"Criminy. We'll be froze half to death by the time he gets all his i's dotted and t's crossed," Robinson said with a shiver. "Come on, get inside and dry off. We're so close to battle I can taste it. This is no time to get sick."

Inside the tent, no one worried about anything except sharing blankets and getting warm. Henry sat with Charley between his legs, leaning back on his chest with both their blankets over them as they all complained about the cold and the officers. Despite the fact that he couldn't hardly feel his fingers or toes, he felt positively serene. He thought a lot about the word comfort and its relative meaning. Was there any condition in which a man must be utterly miserable? At Fort Snelling, they'd complained up and down about the fare when they'd been eating like kings compared to what they had now. The men were over the moon for a scrap of fresh meat, no matter its origin. Perhaps it was man's nature to be fickle, to long for more when life was abundant, and to thank one's good fortune when pickings were slim. Hardship sure was exceptional at forcing people to get their priorities straight.

It was nearly taps by the time word finally got around that they were clear to harvest firewood from the split-rail fence.

"Orders are top rail only, fellas," Osborn directed as the whole squad hightailed it down the hill.

Other squads were on their heels and it was a free-for-all along the fence, squads pulling rails off the top all the way down the line.

"How are we supposed to know which rail was the top?" Webster asked as they approached the fence.

Henry and Charley already had the rail half-off the fence before they paused. Henry looked down the line. The rails were stacked the same way a log cabin wall would be, zig-zagging across the landscape so that it was held vertical by plodding angles instead of nails or pilings.

"What do you mean? That rail's the top one," Williamson said.

"That's right!" Charley agreed. "Only the top rail, and this one's on top." She shoved it toward Henry and he grinned, lifting it off.

Robinson and Hower were bent over laughing while Charley and Henry carried the rail back toward their camp. They'd only gone a few paces when Osborn's voice rose above the din.

"Hower, come now, we *know* that one's not a top rail!"

Hower's voice was gleeful when he replied, "It is now!"

Henry glanced over his shoulder and saw Hower and Robinson squealing with mischief as they followed, another rail supported between them. Osborn was throwing his hands up while Webster just shrugged. Henry hoped they would just lift a third rail and be done with arbitrary appearances. He knew better though. Besides, just as Osborn was starting after Hower and Robinson, Krüger and Williamson lifted the third rail and scampered off the long way round.

Back at the tent, roll call accounted for, Henry lounged back on his bedroll with a merry fire warming his toes.

"See, I told you that you had the makings of an officer," Henry murmured to Charley, who was curled up next to him.

"You know, some men see danger and they fight, others flee, but I forgot how effective fawning can be," Charley replied, voice quiet in his ear. "I guess there's still a bit of use for my feminine wiles."

"Don't talk to me about your wiles," Henry intoned. The squad was hunkering down for sleep, and Charley and Henry weren't the only ones snuggling up together. Robinson was kicking Hower for hogging their blankets, while Krüger had Williamson tucked under his chin like a child with a doll. Webster was reading a few lines aloud from his Bible with Osborn curled on his chest. Henry had his arm around Charley and the fellows were all still awake. No one batted an eye. Henry supposed he wouldn't have either, if he hadn't had Charley. He wasn't sure whether it was her sex or whether he was in love with her that made him self-conscious of any outward appearance of intimacy, but it was clear neither would be revealed if they shared their bedroll. God, a man could get used to this kind of freedom.

"It was a long day," Henry yawned.

"A long couple of days," Charley replied, catching the yawn too. "We built a bridge."

"A temporary bridge."

"A *real* bridge. With trusses."

"Next time, we'll add turrets."

"We'll make a whole drawbridge."

Henry smiled, but it felt a little hard to get his whole face behind it. Battle was bearing down on them. In a matter of days, they'd gain their enemy. The faceless enemy who had been dogging his dreams for months. Perhaps all of this jockeying for power and position was fruitless in the face of what inevitably was to come. Maybe this time next week, he'd look back on himself with shame for his naivete, his privilege. Perhaps these conditions they were under now, which were the most austere they'd experienced, would seem like luxury in the face of what was yet to come. He couldn't worry about that now. Battle would change him, that was sure. He longed for it, in a strange duplicity of excitement to finally do something of consequence and a dread that made him just want to get it over with already.

He looked down at Charley. She was curled into his side, her cheek nestled in the dip between his shoulder and chest. Her hair was tumbled over her brow and her eyes were closed, dark lashes sweeping her cheeks. God, but he loved her. He felt such relief knowing that, almost as much as he felt knowing that Robinson and the others weren't batting an eye every time he touched Charley. That perhaps they had greater liberty than they realized. In many ways, despite the cold and the sparse rations and the mud, he didn't want this march to end.

———

XXII

Outside Columbia, Kentucky
Sunday, January 12, 1862

"You know what I have a newfound gratitude for?"

Charley looked up and caught a faceful of cold rain. "Ugh, what?"

"Roads," Henry replied with a huff of effort. "Paved roads. With cobblestones, or pea gravel. Flagstones, even if they have a little moss growing between them."

"I suppose I never expected to wax poetical about road surfaces," Charley replied, tucking her face down again so that the brim of her forage cap caught the blowing sheets of rain. "But I must admit I'm enamored with the notion."

Robinson gave a shrill laugh.

"Bricks," Henry continued. "Strong, well-baked bricks, tightly packed." His voice tightened as he started to slide in the mud, and he reached out for Charley's shoulder to steady himself. She put a hand on his waist and guided him upright with a fistful of his greatcoat.

"Wood block pavement," Henry intoned, and his voice was positively erotic.

"Stop, I can't bear the longing," Charley replied, and it was true, both in terms of the paved roads and in terms of what she wanted to do to him when he used that voice.

They'd been marching all morning, through the relentlessly terrible weather. They'd only managed nine miles the day before, and ended up waiting for hours in the elements for the wagons to come up, pitching tents and cooking supper long after dark. Even after loitering in the freezing rain for hours, no one complained because they could have ended up gnawing hardtack under the shelter of their cannons with the artillery-men, whose wagons never arrived at all. Charley's mind spun for those hours spent waiting, trying to figure out a better solution to the wagon problem. Supplies were imperative to a healthy army. Given the number of men falling to disease—measles was still running rampant, especially among the Kentucky regiment that had been battalioned with them—the present system was inherently flawed. The enemy could cut them off easily from behind. It seemed to Charley that the only solution was to carry a greater burden of the supplies with the men.

That, or march a shorter distance so they didn't leave the wagons too far behind.

"Goddamn this damned cursed creek!" It was Hower's voice ahead of them. Charley looked up and caught another faceful of rain. Henry's shoulders fell despondently.

"Again? We just crossed it not thirty minutes ago," Robinson whined.

"I don't think I've ever seen a creek that winds so much," Williamson added. "And I've been up the Rum River all the way to Mille Lacs."

"Ah, come on," Henry said. "My boots just stopped sopping from the last time."

"That can't possibly be true," Charley replied, even as she took up his elbow to raise both his shoulders and his spirits. "Maybe our boots are so packed with mud now, it'll serve like a sort of waterproofing."

"Or, the creek will wash the mud away," Henry countered. "Which, now that I think about it, doesn't really serve any great purpose, but I hate this mud more than I've ever hated anything in my whole life and it would give me satisfaction to see it dashed on the rocks."

"We must take our solace where we can." Charley squeezed his arm with deeper affection than she'd previously dared. The nasty weather, the slog of the march, and the uncertainty of battle lurking over every hillock made previous fears seem frivo-lous in comparison. Besides, as Henry had pointed out astutely yesterday, the men writ large paid utterly no notice to scarcely any of the affection they increasingly dared to express. In fact, they seemed to expect it. At one point over coffee the previous day, Robinson had made a jibe at them about being an old married couple, and the squad had laughed. Only Krüger had rolled his eyes, and he'd been doing that for months now with no consequences.

It was all too good to be true. Charley watched water drip down the end of Henry's nose and couldn't help but imagine it as blood. The closer they got to battle, the more intrusive these thoughts became. He was so good, so captivating and pure, and he loved her. It was only a matter of time before he was snatched away. They were at war for God's sake. If battle didn't take him, he'd eventually tire of her and find a woman more suited to the roles of wife and mother. Besides, she couldn't ever have the assurances of marriage with him. No matter how much time passed, that would still hover over her.

She let the icy water of the creek shock these thoughts from her mind as they trod across it for the umpteenth time. The wagons were going to struggle with this crossing. It was rocky and uneven, and the swell of the creek after days of rain had eroded the banks to a sharp drop almost a foot deep. She allowed her thoughts to spin strategy of how the teamsters might remedy this most efficiently, not because it would do any good at all, but because it was preferable to worrying about the future.

It was dinner time when the ranks slowed to a stop. Charley could tell not because of the position of the sun in the sky, which was entirely unknowable behind the heavy, low clouds spitting rain upon them, but from the grumble of her belly.

"How far have we gone?" Charley asked Hower as the ranks oozed out of the woods and into a clearing, the mud slopping less as the men covered a wider ground and the grass tamped down in a layer of protection.

"I'd reckon about eight miles," Hower said, squinting up at the sky like it could tell him anything about how long they'd been marching. "Not as far as yesterday."

"Hm." Charley sloughed rain from her face with her hands as the squad fell into ranks on the latest makeshift parade ground.

From behind her, a hand snaked around and pinched her nose. She reeled and smacked the hand away, spinning on her heels. "What the Sam Hill—"

Henry blinked at her placidly. "Your nose looked cold." He was barely holding in a crooked grin.

Charley's mouth pinched and she refused—she positively refused—to let anyone see the affection purring in her chest. "That's not any of your—"

"—*Is* your nose cold?"

"Shut up, Schaefer, you're not—"

"—Is it?"

She scowled. "Yes, but—"

Henry reached out and put his fingers over her nose. It was a gentle gesture, but she shook her head sharply away. His hand chased her and after a moment, she found herself grappling his arms as he laughed and she dodged and the boys all howled with laughter.

"Why won't you let me—oof—help you?" Henry laughed as Charley twisted away from him. He held onto her with both arms.

"I don't need your help!" Charley insisted and tried to hold the laugh out of her voice.

"Your nose is going to fall off," Henry said and pulled her back into his chest with his damnable *gymnasticks* strength.

"It is not, you're being ridiculous. Stop this at once." Charley's voice went tinny as Henry's cold wet hand went over her nose again. His other hand held her by the waist, and she stopped bothering to struggle against him. Her voice was honky when she said, "There. Are you happy now?"

"Incandescently," Henry murmured into her ear. His hand was cold. Objectively, it should have helped not at all. But his closeness, his dearness, raised the flush in her cheeks and it did warm her, from her toes to her nose. Of all the damned silly things to do...

"In ranks, soldiers," Osborn reminded, but he was grinning too. They were all laughing at Charley's expense, except it didn't feel like that at all. It felt comfortable, almost familial. Like how Charley imagined a fine party full of friends would be, laughing and ribbing each other in casual affection. It was something she'd only ever observed from outside before. Nothing she'd ever felt included in. Perhaps Henry's embrace wasn't the only thing warming her from the inside.

"Yeah, Schaefer, in ranks," Charley said, shrugging him off and trying not to smile.

Lieutenant Thomas called the ranks to attention, and the whole squad straightened up and assumed the position of the soldier.

"Soldiers, we will stop here for the day and wait for the wagons to come up," Lieutenant Thomas announced. "There are a few structures on this clearing, but as you well know, Command will not stand for the disturbance of private property. We're here to fight a war for honor and fidelity and respect. We're not looters. As such, Captain Bishop has ordered his company to stand guard on all the outbuildings."

Charley's lip curled slightly as her eyebrow rose. Sure. She glanced at her comrades. Hower was leaning around Osborn and mouthing something at her with waggling brows. Charley frowned and shrugged. She couldn't understand what he was trying to convey. It didn't matter anyway, because Osborn quickly noticed him and reached over to pinch him in the arm. Hower yelped back into position and stayed that way until they were instructed to fall out.

When they were dismissed, most squads made for the scant cover of the trees that lined the clearing. Charley's squad huddled together under some pine boughs, which brought more reprieve than most of the desolate winter branches. All except Osborn, who was called away by Lieutenant Thomas for some mundane task he was more than happy to perform if it meant more recognition in anticipation of a promotion. Hower was positively shaking with news as soon as they all made it under the boughs.

"It's a still," Hower gasped when he had their attention. "The private property. An applejack still, and it's *loaded* with barrels of the final product."

Eyes rounded across the squad.

"But Command has instructed us not to disrupt private property," Webster reminded.

"Command also told us to only take the top rail," Charley couldn't help but reply, "and we saw how well that turned out."

"Well, we knew what they meant, didn't we?" Webster said, exasperated.

"We did, but it wasn't enough," Charley retorted. "Men who are well-provided for don't have any need to loot."

"I'm not sure that's true—" Webster started.

"Regardless, we certainly haven't had an easy time of it. We're not complaining—you don't see any of us complaining—"

"I think I see you complaining right now."

"I'm not complaining. I'm arguing."

"Ah, so that's why this feels so exhausting."

"Webster, that's not the point I'm trying to make."

"Yeah," Hower put in. "The point he's trying to make is that we've worked damn hard and put up with a whole lot and if anyone deserves a goddamned drink, it's us."

Webster threw up his hands. "What if the enemy bears down upon us, and we're all sodden beyond comprehension?!"

"We're already sodden," Charley muttered. The boys all laughed. Webster glared at her. "Sorry, but we're expected to take a whole lot, sir, without complaint. We're not good soldiers if we fuss, but Command can carry on making slapdash decisions and blaming the weather for their incompetence, then calling us selfish and weak for wanting basic creature comfort like wood for our fire. Fellows are catching the ague left, right, and center, and it's *preventable*. We don't have to go on living like animals and calling it living like *men*. But heaven forbid anyone point that out. If they wanted praise, they could show us what it looks like."

The boys all nodded. Webster sighed. Hower gave her an approving pat on the shoulder.

"I for one walked through ice water six times today," Hower declared. "And I guarantee you the Hastings boys are already tapping one of those barrels. If I can't warm myself by a fire under an actual shelter, I'm damn well going to warm myself with applejack."

Hower turned on his heel and made for the clearing. It didn't take the boys much time at all to decide which corporal to follow. Charley looked up at Webster for a moment and shrugged. She might have wrecked all the goodwill she'd built with him while on advance guard, but she knew that he knew she was right. If he was so petty as to pass up good sense for loyalty, then he was just as bad as the rest of the big bugs.

"Charley, you coming?" Henry was hovering outside of the pine boughs.

"Yeah," Charley said. "Webster, how about you?"

Webster sighed so hard he slumped back against the tree trunk. "I don't know why I even try to hold the line with you all."

"It was a very valiant attempt," Charley comforted. "So valiant, in fact, that you deserve a drink."

Webster's faced cracked a smile.

"See, doesn't it feel good to have your effort recognized?"

Webster rolled his eyes and straightened, following Charley and Henry out into the clearing. "Criminy, Smith, do you ever just let anything go?"

"I've been asking that question for months now," Henry laughed.

Charley grinned. "No. Never."

———

XXIII

HOWER WAS RIGHT ABOUT one thing—the Hastings boys had made first rate work of that still. Perhaps that was giving them too much credit. The only reason the other soldiers were at liberty to molest it was because the Big Bugs were on reconnaissance. In the absence of Captain Bishop, who was officer of the day, the guards of Company A had taken first pick and were now so sauced they could not do their duty. Other squads rolled barrels out of the building with abandon, the rain and muck forgotten in the joy of striking gold. The applejack was flowing deeply before any of the commanding officers could manage any counteraction. Perhaps they didn't have the heart to, after all. The colonel and their captain were both back with the wagons, so Lieutenants Thomas and Woodbury were in charge. Woodbury was incensed, but Thomas knew better than to waste his energy. After the haystack the Ninth Ohio had burned down, and the rails, it was clear that the men knew their strength in numbers. If they all decided to loot an abandoned applejack still, then that was what they were going to do, commanding officers be damned. Besides, in light of Captain Noah's sickness, which seemed less and less likely to improve the longer it went on, the Lieutenants were competing for a promotion. It certainly didn't hurt to have the men's goodwill on that count, for men who respected their leader, who trusted them, were worth their weight in gold.

Or in this case, applejack.

"God, this stuff's vile," Charley said, taking another glug from her tin cup to confirm.

"Not at all," Webster argued. "This is finer than any we had back home. Right, Ned?"

Osborn was with them now, begrudgingly holding a cup of applejack he'd barely sipped at all. He looked up at Webster sharply and said, "It's certainly stronger."

"That's how you know it's good," Hower replied. "If it tasted good, there'd hardly be any alcohol in it."

The afternoon whiled away with no sign of the wagons. The applejack flowed from the still's storehouse, barrel after barrel rolling steadily away into the woods where the soldiers took cover from the endless rain.

"What the hell is on your head, Smith?" Robinson slurred hours later. They sat around a smoking wet fire, the flow of applejack slowed as their senses were slowed by it. Williamson was already snoring against Krüger's promontory shoulder.

"It's my gum blanket," Charley sniffed. "It's waterproof. It's keeping my head dry. Tha's how you prevent colds, you know."

"Keeping your head dry?"

"Naturally."

"Keeping your head dry, and your mouth wet," Hower shouted, swilling a mouthful of applejack. The boys roared laughing even though the wordplay was terrible.

Charley couldn't help it. Her eyes swivelled over to Henry. She thought about the other night in the woods. About fingers and mouths and God, she was lusty when she'd been drinking. Either that, or the sinking ache in her belly the previous night had in fact been a sign of her impending courses rather than hunger. Counting the days, it was expected soon. Battle or marches aside, her infuriating womb waited for no one. God, that didn't bear thinking about. Lusty inspiration was much preferred.

"I'm sick of sitting in the mud," she declared. "I'm gonna go take the measure of this place." She got to her feet and found they were fairly inept at finding solid purchase with the ground.

"I thought you wanted to keep dry?" Robinson asked. He sure was dim when he was drunk.

"My gum blanket can go with me everywhere," Charley replied, flapping its edges like wings. "Come on, Henry."

"What?"

"We're taking a ramble," Charley repeated, rounding the smoking wet fire they'd barely managed to light and standing in front of him. "Keep up."

"You don't have to go with him, Schaef," Robinson said with a roll of his eyes. "Just because he's fool enough to go bandying around camp in the rain. What d'you think you're gonna find, Smith? Another storehouse, but full of cake?"

Charley ignored Robinson and held Henry's gaze instead. His smile was even more crooked when he'd been drinking. His blue eyes searched hers for a moment. Christ, if they could find a merely empty storehouse, Charley would be delighted. A shack—anything, really. It had been four days since the woods, and Charley could not hardly close her eyes without seeing the memory of Henry with his fingers in his mouth. Somehow, even though they had increasing liberty to touch and show their fondness in small ways around camp, it had become even harder to deny her desires. She wanted him all the time, now that she knew the scope of what she was missing.

"Sure," Henry said and took Charley's hand to pull himself up. He glanced over at Robinson and grinned. "I gotta walk off this applejack if I wanna drink more."

Hower snorted. "Lightweight."

Charley was willing to bet that Henry could hold his liquor a mite better than their fool ex-corporal, but she had better things to do than challenge him. She didn't drop Henry's hand once he was on his feet, but rather swung it a bit as they walked off into the clearing.

"I never dreamed joining the army would be the path to walking hand in hand with a lover on a fine spring day," Charley mused as they proceeded out of earshot from the boys.

Henry snorted. "Fine spring day? Is this what you call spring?"

"It's very like April in Minnesota. Don't you think?"

"I s'pose." His fingers squeezed hers. They walked apace, heading toward the outbuildings across the clearing where the still was humming with soldiers. "I don't know how you do it."

"Do what?"

"Argue with officers like that."

Charley wrinkled her nose and twisted her mouth. "I s'pose I was out of order, earlier, wasn't I?"

"Maybe, but it worked. I wish you could do that with the Top Brass."

"I don't think they'd listen to me. They'd probably demote me or discharge me." Charley smirked wryly. "Throw me in the guardhouse. That's been a popular one so far."

Henry snorted. "Sure, but not since we marched out. Anyway, I could never do it."

"Why not?"

"'Cause... I dunno. I just couldn't." Henry sighed. "I've only ever followed orders. I don't even think to challenge them."

"A product of a Turner upbringing?"

Henry laughed. "Not hardly. Questioning authority is our central principle."

"And you question clerical authority very well," Charley said. She squeezed his hand in hers. "I think you might be more defiant than you think."

Henry shook his head, but he also didn't argue with her.

"So what are we looking for on this ramble?" Henry asked.

Charley's smile grew into a grin, and she craned to whisper in his ear. "A dry, private spot with a roof to fuck you in."

"Charley!" He shoved his shoulder into hers, but he was grinning too. Charley was so off kilter from the applejack, she stumbled, and he had to steady her with their joined hands.

"Where there are products, there are storage buildings," Charley declared as though she hadn't missed a step.

There were storage buildings. There was the still itself, set near the winding creek they'd had to ford over and over again, and the out-building where all the casks had been stored—a very busy and decidedly not private area. A rod or two off was a vacant pigpen whose residents had already been mustered into service. There was a privy, as well, farther off still, but also in heavy use by the soldiers.

Charley frowned. The area was a veritable marketplace of sodden soldiers. "Hmph. Let's walk down the apple orchard. Maybe there's something on the far end."

She pulled on Henry's hand. Her feet and legs groaned at the prospect of extra exertion, but she ignored them. Just as she ignored the several braying soldiers who bellowed out, "What's that—a nun? Come to drink with us?"

They could only be referring to her gum blanket. Charley glowered and charged on.

"You've got a fine-looking soldier, there, Mother Superior! Gone to convert him?"

Henry was laughing. Charley couldn't manage to join him. The feminine connotations rankled, made her feel exposed and vulnerable, and she didn't like it one bit. The sooner they could find some privacy, the better.

They turned down the first avenue between bare apple trees, dwarf-size in comparison with the towering oaks, maples, and hickories of the woods proper. Goddamn it—nothing about this property afforded any cover.

"Who do you suppose owned this place?" Henry wondered aloud as he ambled along the deadened grass path.

"Probably some Reb who's gone and joined up with Zollicoffer's army," Charley replied, kicking at the ground. It was sloppy in places, squelching beneath her boot.

"I s'pose," Henry acknowledged quickly, then pointed. "Say, what's that down there?"

Charley glanced down the line of trees and spotted what Henry had with a jolt of excitement. "Is that a shed?"

"Only one way to find out."

They hoofed it to the end of the orchard, where a ramshackle little shed stood soggily with a tin roof and weathered clapboards. The door was ajar, so Charley swung it open. Inside was a wheelbarrow, pruning shears, and other sundry items she assumed were tools of the trade for apple farming, all covered in a delicate layer of dust. Without thinking at all, she seized the handles of the wheelbarrow and began to haul it out.

"What do you want with a wheelbarrow?" Henry laughed. He was swaying a bit on his feet, cheeks pink with applejack.

"I want it out of our damn way," Charley said, dumping the thing up against the side of the shack so that the rain slid over the bottom of the barrow. "Come on."

She hauled Henry inside the shed by his collar and shut the door as firmly as she could.

"It doesn't latch from the inside," Henry noted.

"That's fine," Charley said, pulling Henry in by the waist of his trousers. "There's no reason anyone will come over here when there's alcohol over there."

"Unless someone else is looking for a place to slip away."

"Who on earth would do that?" Charley pressed herself against the wall to one side, dust kicking up and making her sneeze.

"I dunno," Henry said, bracing himself on the wall over her and sending a shiver up her spine. "Other bunkies similarly enamored with one another."

"Do you really think there are other bunkies that have made a surrogate of one another? I know your uncle had some wild notions, but really—"

"I think he has those notions from experience," Henry said. He pressed his mouth against hers and for a moment, her mind went blank in the bliss of homecoming. But good as her reputation, she didn't let it go.

"Experience? With whom?"

"Kloepfer, I'd wager."

"But he's his NCO!"

"You'd be mine if you get promoted to corporal." His expression darkened. "You wouldn't let that get in the way of this, would you?"

"No, don't be a lunkhead," Charley waved away. "Now I see why Krüger kept cautioning me from you."

"Did he? What did he say?"

"Oh, you know, that Turners are all deviants. He implied you'd take advantage of my boyish innocence or something. I can't remember." Charley said as she worked free the buttons of his greatcoat and sack coat.

Henry snorted and took up her greatcoat buttons as well. "When was this?"

"Way back at Robinson's wedding."

"Robinson too, now that you mention it," Henry said. "He said he'd been in love with Hower when he first met him."

"*WHAT*? No. That cannot be. I refuse to believe that."

"It was unrequited, but it's not uncommon among young men."

Charley blinked for a moment. Then, her lips curled up at the edges. "So what you mean to say is that I'm perfectly capable of loving you and being a man at the same time?"

"It seems that way," Henry said with a sly smile.

"Wonderful," Charley replied with gusto.

They kissed, decadently at first, then with thickening urgency. Charley had her hands behind Henry's neck, under his collar, tracing down his suspenders.

"No waistcoat?"

"It's filthy. I need to find someone to wash it." Henry gave her a twinkling, winning, devastatingly crooked smile.

"I heard that teamster, Griffith, is taking in laundry," Charley said flatly, then yanked him in for another kiss. His hands finished working her sack coat buttons free, then started at her waistcoat.

"Too many damn buttons," he muttered, then dove down to press his hot mouth over the slope of her scant breasts still swathed in her flannel shirt. She gasped and arched against him, uncomprehending the reason why it felt almost more erotic for him to mouth at her through her shirt than it would to push it aside in favor of bare skin. She'd have to test the latter for an accurate comparison. Her fingers curled in his hair as he pulled on her trouser buttons.

Next thing she knew, his hands were under her shirt, pressing into her belly and tracing lines of shivering awareness across her skin. Oh, that was incomparable, but also, not the same as his mouth. She pressed his head down with her hands, but he didn't stoop to push her shirt up and expose her bare skin to the chill air. On the contrary, he dropped to his knees without a second's hesitation and pressed his mouth to her bare belly.

"Oh," she managed as his searing blue eyes glanced up, filled with mischief. He unfastened her suspenders and pushed her trousers down to her knees, nudging her legs apart with his thumbs pressing into the insides of her thighs. "*Oh.*"

"I want to taste you," Henry whispered, his eyes entreating. She must have nodded or blinked twice or something, because with a twitch of his crooked smile, he pushed his nose into her curls and pressed his tongue in between her folds. She made a very unmasculine sound as she gripped his hair with both hands.

"You're so soft," Henry breathed, his voice almost reverent.

"Dear God, Henry, don't *tell* me about it," Charley gasped as his breath tickled her wet skin.

"Like satin," he murmured and buried his face between her legs. The sensations she felt then made her wonder quite hysterically what on earth he could possibly be doing. There was hot, wet pressure, then slick sliding, then suction, *good God*. Her hands grappled at his hair—his cap was on the floor somewhere—and she let out an ungodly moan. He was working the spot at the front of her cunt, where she swelled and pulsed when she used her own fingers. She must have been swelling and pulsing now, underneath his mouth. She wondered if he could feel it, feel the difference, when he travelled lower and breached her with his tongue.

She held back a shout, just barely, seizing his hair and pulling him closer, even though there was nowhere left for him to go. She threw her head back against the wall. Her thighs shivered, and she gave the wall her weight. She felt her edge, but only danced upon it even as he worked her with his tongue. Christ, it was maddening. Exquisitely maddening.

She yanked at his hair. He seemed to understand her rudimentary language, because he moved his attention back to her swollen nub, though not before licking around the circumference of her entrance. She shuddered along that edge, like a train on a tight-turning track. Her thighs tightened around his head as he worked her, pressing firm with his tongue or sucking or something—whatever it was, it felt *marvelous*. She felt herself slide over that edge, exquisitely, bountifully, and it was like a train crash, cargo spilling everywhere, car after car. Her muscles seized in waves of it, shaking with effort. He gripped her thighs and pressed his mouth open over her, intent, as though it gave him great pleasure to feel her pulsing. To taste her. She shuddered, then the door to the shed shuddered too.

"Oh, there you both are—CHRIST ALMIGHTY!"

Charley screamed. Henry reeled backwards and fell in a dusty pile against the opposite wall. Charley's heart wailed in her chest, and she yanked at the tails of her shirt down instinctually as she faced the intruder. It was Jacob Robinson, pink-cheeked and bleary-eyed with drink, clutching his collar like a lady with pearls and stumbling over his own fool feet in the doorway.

"Smith!" Robinson slurred. "What—what happened to your *cock!?*"

Fuck.

Charley scrambled to pull up her trousers, tucking her shirt between her slick thighs and cursing every goddamned ancestor Robinson ever had for bringing him into the world. She had to do something. She had to act, *now*, before he left and ran his big damn mouth to Osborn, or worse, Hower, and she ended up on the first wagon back to Lebanon.

"Shuddup, Robinson, come in here," Charley hissed.

"I will *not!*" Robinson squawked. His shoulders and hands twitched with an anxiety that his voice did not. Charley glanced over at Henry and saw him rising to his feet.

"Henry, get him in here and shut the door," Charley said.

Henry, bless him, did just that, yanking Robinson into the shed and shutting the flimsy damn door that didn't lock as best he could. It was so tight in there, they were all nose to nose. Robinson's breath reeked of applejack.

"Listen up," Charley whispered, "and be quiet about it. You didn't see nothing. You hear me? *Nothing.*"

"I damn well did," Robinson said obstinately. "I knew you two were up to no good, but I didn't ever imagine he'd snuck a damn *woman* into the army."

"He didn't *sneak* me in," Charley exclaimed, affronted. "I enlisted myself. Keep him out of it."

"So you don't deny it?"

"How could I, you son of a bitch? You caught me in fla-grante."

Henry's fist tightened in Robinson's collar and yanked him hard enough that his head snapped about.

"Listen up, Jacob," Henry said low. The rumble of his voice sent entirely unwanted shivers down Charley's spine. "We have two choices. Either, you conspire with us to keep Charley's secret, or—"

"—Or what?" Robinson scoffed.

"Or I hurt you so bad you won't be able to tell anyone anything."

Charley turned her head slowly to look at Henry. Dear God, he looked like he meant it. He could too, his strapping shoulders square and imposing. He looked huge in this tiny shed. Robinson looked up at him, his upper lip quivering slightly.

"Come on, Henry, we're friends..."

"There's only one thing a friend would do in this situation," Henry retorted.

Robinson's eyes flicked between the two of them. He licked his lips tentatively. "I wasn't gonna say anything. I never was. I was just gonna—"

"—Shut up and swear," Charley said low. "Swear to God, swear on your honor, swear on your *mother's grave* that you won't tell a soul. I've given up everything to fight and I won't lose it now, not when we're so close to finally seeing battle—"

"Right, okay, fine," Robinson blathered. "I swear. I swear on my mother's grave. I won't tell anyone, not a soul. Wait—does that include Mary?"

"*Yes!*" Charley and Henry said over one another.

"You can't *write* anything down!" Charley exclaimed. "Forget this ever happened. Forget you even know."

Robinson's chin quivered. "Yeah. Know what? Heh heh. It's easy enough. You're not much of a—"

"—Don't. Finish. That. Sentence."

"How do you do it?"

Charley gave a deep glower.

"I just—why? Why give up so much?"

"Why give up your wife?" Charley shot back. "I'm here for the same reasons you are. I want to fight for the Union. I want to fight against slavery. I can't stand on the sidelines and wait for all of you idiots to take care of it."

"Was I this tedious when I found out?" Henry asked.

Charley let out a frustrated growl. "Yes, dammit."

"Oh, when did you find out, Schaef?"

"After we were in the guardhouse together," Henry replied.

Robinson snorted. "Which time?"

"We're not doing this. Not right now. Not ever," Charley cut in. "Because you're not going to remember this happened, right, Robinson?"

"Right."

"Because you were way out of line spying on us."

"I wasn't spying! I was just trying to find you."

"Oh really? For what?"

"The wagons arrived," Robinson said. "Oh yeah, the wagons arrived. We need to go and help unload and set up the tent."

"Oh," Charley said. She looked over at Henry. "You can let him go, I guess."

Henry frowned, but he released Robinson's collar. Robinson looked between the two of them, almost obediently.

"What are you waiting for?" Charley asked after a moment of unnerving eye contact.

"Permission to fall out, I guess," Robinson said, as though he surprised himself with his answer.

"Oh," Charley said. "Well, repeat back to me who you're gonna tell."

"Just—oh! Wait a minute," Robinson smiled tentatively. "That's a trick question. No one. Not a soul. It never happened."

"Right."

"Great." Robinson turned and pushed the door open, taking a step outside. Then he spun back. "Wait—what if I have questions?"

"Give up on them," Charley replied with her arms crossed over her chest.

"All of them?" Robinson frowned. "Come on, if we're all alone, can't we talk about it?"

"No! What part of 'forget it ever happened' don't you understand!?"

Robinson smiled sheepishly and rubbed his shoulder. After a moment's thought, he pushed himself back inside the shed and shut the door. "Sorry. Just a couple questions."

"No!"

"How long you been married?"

Charley flinched. "I'm—I'm not."

"What?"

"I'm not married. Not anymore."

"What? No, I mean, you and Schaefer gotta be…"

Charley winced. Henry was looking anywhere but at either of them, which was a feat considering how small the shed was.

"But… but if you're not married, how come you're…"

Henry grew silent. Charley's eyebrow raised high on her forehead. "Folks don't have to be married, Robinson. Come now, you know that."

Robinson frowned, a curl to his lip. "Why not? Are you just here as a bed-warmer then?"

Charley saw red for a moment. "How *dare* you!"

"Jacob, that's out of line," Henry added with a growl.

"Well, I don't know! You're not married, but it's not a practical arrangement—what *is* it, then?"

Charley didn't have any kind of answer for that. Neither, apparently, did Henry. But that didn't matter, because Jacob Robinson wasn't owed anything of the kind. "None of your business, Robinson. Now forget it. Let's go."

Robinson glowered but he went, thank God, and Charley and Henry followed him out the door and into the rain.

———

XXIV

Outside Columbia, Kentucky
Wednesday, January 15, 1862

TWO DAYS LATER, CHARLEY'S hands were still shaking. It was really frustrating, because it had made her fumble the iron tent pole and canvas as they packed up the camp that morning. She'd like to say it was because of the cold—they'd had some light snow in the morning as they were loading the wagons. But she knew better. She could ignore it for one day. But two? She'd eaten some rations before marching out, she'd had a good, long swig from her canteen—there was no reason her hands should continue to shake like this.

There was no good reason, but she did have a notion as to why. She'd been careless, and now she was so full of regret, her hands were shaking. She ran the situation in circles around and around in her head as they trudged through the muddy slop, rain spitting down upon them. Charley shouldn't have been so reckless as to let her desire for Henry overshadow the fact that she was always—*always*—in a precarious position in this squad. No matter how comfortable she was with them, no matter how tolerant they were of her and Henry's particular friendship, she could never, ever let her guard down. She was walking around in a primed cannon of a body—it could blow up her life at any time, just by virtue of existing. It was a goddamned trap, is what it was. From the inherent risk it posed by being female, to its monthly courses and insatiable desires—it felt like all of its functions, apart from eating, posed a risk. Just because she'd gotten used to some of its challenges didn't mean she could let her guard down.

Jacob Robinson had kept his mouth shut so far, thank God. At least, as far as Charley knew. Every time she lost sight of him, her heart skipped a beat, until she found him again, lagging behind on the march or emerging from the soldier sinks. Goddammit, she shouldn't have drank so much applejack. She'd impaired her judgment and now she had a massive liability on her hands.

"I think you're unsettling Jacob," Henry hissed in her ear. "You've been watching him like a hawk for two days straight now."

"Good," Charley growled.

"He's as good as his word," Henry said, grasping her elbow as she teetered on a particularly slippery patch of mud. "He would never break a vow on his mother's grave."

Charley frowned but didn't reply. She didn't want to argue about her perfectly rational fears. It was nice of Henry to try and reassure her, but her fear served a purpose. It kept her vigilant.

They marched through the afternoon and stopped somewhere outside of Columbia to wait for the wagons. Rain was coming down steadily. Lots more fellows were using their gum blankets as a hood now. They took cover under a small wood of oak and maple. There wasn't much shelter to be had under their bare branches.

"Let's make a fire," Webster said.

"Oh, a fire," Williamson sighed, like he was dreaming of a sweetheart back home.

"Everything is soaked through," Hower pointed out. His teeth were chattering. "And all the axes are back in the wagons, which are probably stalled a half mile from where we struck camp this morning."

Krüger grunted. He'd borne most of the march thus far in stoic silence. "To hell with that. We are men. We make fire."

Maybe Charley's shaking hands were just from the cold. All she knew was that she couldn't bear sitting and waiting. She had to be doing something. "That's right." Her eyes snapped to

Robinson, but he didn't even flinch. "There's got to be something we can do to get the tinder to light."

The boys scattered, scavenging branch and bramble wherever they could find it. They worked fast—other squads were doing the same, and soon the forest floor was picked over.

"Looks like the Hastings squad beat us to this area," Charley said. She'd ended up with Krüger, and she surveyed the barren ground with her arms crossed over her chest.

"Look. That branch is dead," Krüger said, pointing up above. Charley followed his gaze. The silver maple tree did indeed have a branch a little ways up that had no bark, with a brittle crack down its length.

"Yeah, but we got no axes," Charley murmured, thinking.

"Climb on my shoulders," Krüger said. "Climb up there and kick it down."

Charley regarded him warily. She didn't want him handling her liability at all.

"I will not drop you," Krüger said flatly. "What do you weigh? A half stone?"

Before she could put him off, Krüger seized her by the waist and lifted her. She reeled in the air for a moment, then grappled for the first sizable branch of the tree. It was slick with rain, and she faltered, slipped, and fell backwards into Krüger's barrel chest. Her heart was slamming, somewhere up in her throat.

"I need to get higher," she choked out. Her fear could keep her vigilant, but it would not own her. "Grab my leg, give me a boost that way."

Mercy, but necessity was the mother of invention. Krüger crouched and gripped Charley by the muddy boot, boosting her higher this time. She managed to cling to the first branch, and Krüger shoved her leg up enough that she could leverage herself onto the branch.

"Ah, there!" Charley was astonished. "I'm up."

"Go higher," Krüger pointed.

She looked up. She could see her path easily. A handhold, then a foothold. Her body was light enough to haul up to the dead branch without much effort at all. Perhaps it wasn't entirely a liability. When she got her hand around the dead branch, she gave it a firm yank.

"It's on there good," she reported.

"Go higher," Krüger called up. "Kick it."

Charley frowned. She wasn't going to have the balance to just kick it while perched on a tree branch. She climbed higher anyway. The dead branch stuck out from where the main trunk of the tree bisected into two main branches, orphaned. It was a strange place for a tree branch to die and made Charley wonder for the longevity of the tree in general. She braced herself against one of the large branches, wrapping her arms around behind her, and wedged the heel of her boot against the dead branch. She pushed her weight against it in sharp bursts, a little at first to test its strength, then harder as it held.

"Antauchen!" Krüger called up. His face was intent, the same way it was when he was gambling. "Give it a swift kick!"

Charley sighed. "I dunno. Maybe you should come up here. You're stronger."

Krüger let out a jolly laugh. *"Nein, nein.* You can do it."

Charley winced at the encouragement, then frowned at the branch. Carefully, she got both her feet braced against the dead branch, her arms holding onto the living tree for dear life, and shoved as hard as she could. The branch splintered with an ear-splitting crack, startling her back to solid footing.

"There it is!" Krüger crowed.

Charley grunted. "Not quite." She positioned her feet again and shoved the branch again. It broke through this time, swinging down and hanging on by a splinter. Charley climbed down a bit, then reached out and yanked the branch. It came free and she let it drop to the ground.

Krüger bent and picked it up like it was the sword of his enemy. Charley couldn't help but cheer him on. It was deeply satisfying.

"Nun." Krüger put the branch down against the tree, then reached up toward Charley. "Jump down."

Charley regarded him for a moment. "No, I got it." She slid her feet down and found herself sort of dangling out of the tree. It was still a ways down to the ground. Well, there was nothing for it. She let herself drop, then felt Krüger's paddle-sized hands on her waist, catching her.

"Ah, Krüger, get off," she snapped, twisting out of his arms and stumbling onto her own two feet. He looked at her with his distant, Krüger-esque amusement, but he didn't say anything. She scowled at him, her fiercest one. Her shoulders were tight and so was her chest. She didn't want to consider the possibility that these utilitarian touches could have revealed anything to him, but the notion was already making her hands tremble again. For Chrissakes.

She snatched up the branch and charged farther into the woods, picking up anything that looked remotely flammable. Krüger followed, but he didn't speak. His English wasn't great, so his stoicism was understandable, but Charley hated what her mind filled into those silences. God, she was a wreck. She'd passed for months and months. Robinson's rude interruption just had her spooked.

Back at camp, which was nothing more than a regiment of men loitering in the woods without the wagons, the squad pooled their forage. Webster was crouched on the ground over a small, carefully constructed pile of tinder with his matches, but match after match was wasted on the sodden tinder.

"Ugh, it's no use," Webster grumbled after a few minutes.

"Let me try," Hower said. He spent another few minutes doing the same thing to the same results. "Nah, it's too wet. I told you all it was too wet."

"Give me the matches," Robinson said. Charley rolled her eyes. Were they all going to take turns doing the same damn thing? This was nonsense. They needed something dry, maybe a scrap of cotton or linen cut from their shirts or ...

Charley's eyes alighted on the branch she'd kicked down from the tree earlier. It was wet, too, but it was thick enough, unlike their other tinder, that it might be dry in the middle. Charley grabbed it and held it between her knees.

"Anyone got a sharp knife?" she asked.

Krüger handed her a rusty jackknife. She took it, frowned, and started whittling away at the branch, scraping off curls of wet wood.

"These are still wet," Hower said, picking one of the curls up off the ground.

"Yeah, but maybe it's dry at the center still," Charley replied, not pausing at all in her efforts.

Henry walked over and held his gum blanket out to shelter the wood. When she got to the heart's wood of the branch, she crouched down and made a little pile of the driest shavings. Someone put the matches into her hand and she struck one. It still wasn't catching.

"Henry, stay still," she said and unbuttoned his coat. "I'm just going to take a scrap of dry linen from your shirt."

Henry gave her a look of supreme consternation but he didn't say anything. Under layers of wool, his shirt was dry, or at least, much drier than it was at the collars or cuffs. Charley used Krüger's knife to cut away the bottom of his button placket, no more than an inch square over his sternum. It was sewn on over the shirt, so it wouldn't leave him with a big hole or anything. Just a raw edge at the bottom of the placket that would need repair at some point.

Charley took the scrap of fabric as Henry furtively buttoned his sack coat and great coat again. She glanced up and saw the rest of the squad huddled around them, watching intently. She picked at the square of fabric until she got the threads unraveling. Dry linen would foster the spark, which would hopefully get a flame going long enough to light the dry wood shavings, which would then gain strength enough to light the other, wetter tinder and fuel.

"What are you doing?" Hower was skeptical.

"Patience," Charley murmured as she rubbed the threads she'd unraveled between her palms. The ball of linen fluff was placed on the tiny bed of wood shavings. Charley reserved the driest shavings. "Here, someone hold these. Keep them dry."

Someone did—she didn't look up to see who. Charley struck the match again and held it to the linen. It caught.

"Here, more shavings. Quickly," she said, and took them from the proffered palms of Robinson. She fed them to the tiny flame until it was happily licking a half foot high, feeding greedily on the dry tinder. "Quick, more tinder. The driest we've got."

The squad scattered while Charley stayed crouched under the cover of the gum blanket Henry held steady above her. She blew on the sparks and took twigs and leaves, carefully building up the fire. Meanwhile, several of the other fellows took up larger branches and started scraping the wet outer layers off those too. The flame dried the smaller tinder with its growing heat, gaining strength until it could handle the larger branches. Before she knew it, they had a merry little fire going.

"Oof, it's hot," Henry said, gingerly still holding his gum blanket over it.

"I think it's alright now," Charley said. The rain was spitting more than pouring. The fire was hot enough that she was pretty sure it wouldn't make a difference.

Henry took a step back, and the whole squad crouched around the fire, holding their hands out and warming themselves.

"Commendations, Smith," Webster said after a long moment.

"Good things come to those who wait," Hower said. "I thought we were never gonna get it."

"The thread was a good idea," Robinson said.

Charley cringed at the attention. "Necessity is the mother of invention."

"I hope you'll be fixing my shirt," Henry said with a nudge to Charley's shoulder.

"No," Charley replied glibly. "I'll be needing a lot more where that came from if this rain keeps up."

"Hey!"

The other boys laughed.

"Schaef will be our walking, talking tinder box," Hower declared. After the long day, the relentless hardship, it felt good to laugh.

Long after dark, when it became clear the wagons weren't coming, Williamson had the bright idea that they use their gum blankets to make a shelter. Everyone agreed it was preferable to huddling under their own alone, so they worked together to drape their gum blankets over a low branch. The shelter was only large enough for three, maybe four of them, so they moved the fire close and took turns catching some sleep in the shelter, while the others fed the fire carefully with the cape of their greatcoats flipped up over their heads. It was a boon to Robinson in particular, because he'd tossed his gum blanket too when the weather had been good at the start of the march. Charley could see how humbled he was when they insisted he get some sleep in the shelter somewhere in the wee hours of the morning.

Despite the horrid weather, Charley felt warmer than she had in days. It felt wonderful to work as a team, to make decisions together and take care of one another. She'd never known this sort of reciprocity before, not even in her own family. Maybe this was what family was supposed to feel like. Around dawn, she noticed her hands had stopped shaking. Must have been the cold after all.

———

The rain stopped around noon the next day. The wagons were still nowhere to be found. In Captain Noah's absence, Lieutenant Woodbury ordered a contingent of men to go catch up with them and help them along. With nothing to eat but the dwindling hardtack in their haversacks, Charley rounded up a few fellows from the Hastings squad and went a-foraging. Henry stayed behind, tending their smoky fire and a nasty headache that set in after they missed their morning coffee.

"Is that...sun?" Jacob said as he approached, squinting up at the sky.

"Couldn't say," Henry replied. "I can't remember what it looks like."

Henry had his boots off and propped up near the fire to to dry out. He had a hole in one of his mud-stained stockings.

"It's hard to say behind those clouds, but I could swear I see it," Jacob said, then looked down. "Can I sit?"

Henry nodded and scooted over on the mud-smeared gum blanket he was sitting on. He wasn't sure which one was his anymore. Jacob sat next to him, shoulder to shoulder, and pulled something out of his knapsack.

"It's been too wet to write," Jacob said as he unwrapped a small notebook from a layer of waxed canvas. He took out a pencil and started scratching on the page.

Henry looked into the fire. They hadn't had mail since they left Lebanon. No newspapers either. Nothing to indicate what was happening anywhere outside of the muddy hills they were mired in.

"You writing to the Missus?" Henry asked.

"Yeah," Jacob replied. He wrote a line or two more, then looked up. "The mail's so bad, I can't tell if she's forgot me or not, but on the off chance she hasn't, I'll keep sending letters every chance I get."

"She hasn't forgotten you," Henry chided.

Jacob sighed. "I can't help but envy you," he said in a low voice. "You've got your sweetheart right here with you."

Henry knew this was going to come up as soon as Jacob sat down. He pushed his face into his hands. "We shouldn't talk about that."

"No one else is around," Jacob replied. "They're all off chasing geese."

"Well, I'm not answering any questions, if that's what you're angling for. If you want to satisfy your curiosity, you can ask Charley." Except he'd really rather Jacob didn't. He didn't want Charley to have any other confidants other than him.

"And get my head bit off? No thanks." Jacob tapped his pencil on his paper. "But I do have a question."

"No," Henry replied, and reached back to grab another half-whittled branch to put on the fire. He couldn't answer any questions, because he couldn't breach Charley's trust, but also because he didn't have any answers. They weren't married, and they didn't have a practical arrangement. Henry couldn't articulate answers to Jacob's questions, and it was humiliating because if they were in love, shouldn't he? So much about their relationship was impossible or untenable. He didn't want Jacob poking around in it and finding all sorts of holes, especially be-ing married and settled himself. He knew things Henry didn't. These things were, by and large, things Henry didn't want to know. If he didn't know what a blissful marriage was like, he couldn't miss it.

"Come on, it's not about Smith," Jacob wheedled. "I just wanna know how you found out."

"I told you. When we were in the guardhouse."

"Right, but *how?*"

Henry turned and glowered at him. "Smith just told me."

Jacob's head twitched in surprise. "Really? Why?"

"Because I'd accused him of being a spy. He traded the truth for me to back off."

"Oh," Jacob looked up thoughtfully. "I thought it'd be a better story than that."

"You're incorrigible," Henry grumbled. "What are you writing about to Mary?"

Jacob shrugged. "I dunno. It all feels so trivial when I write it down, but I want her to know what I'm doing and that all I do is think about her. But when we're entrenched in the rain with no food or coffee—"

"—Ugh, coffee...don't remind me—"

"—it feels like such a waste to be here and not with her." Jacob sneaked a glance up at Henry. "You're so lucky."

Henry poked the fire. "Maybe not. What if we see battle tomorrow and one of us dies?"

"You can't think about that."

"I do though. I can't stop thinking about it."

"The same goes for me. Mary could get measles or some other damned thing and be gone before I ever know she was sick. It's a fragile world, Henry. There's nothing to be done about that."

"I suppose you're right."

"Though, if I might make a suggestion—"

"—Something tells me it won't matter if I agree or not."

"Very true. I don't know why you ain't married, but you should do, and fast."

Henry paused. "We can't. She's not—Smith's not... able to."

"If you don't, and then you die, she'll be up a creek without a paddle."

"Just say 'he,' Jacob." Henry looked around. There were fellows from other squads milling around, but they were well out of earshot. "He wouldn't be. He'd stay and fight as before. If I die, Smith'll have a proper vendetta to carry out."

"But if you die and you're married, then Smith could get your soldier's pension." Jacob frowned. "That's my greatest comfort. If I die, then at least I know Mary is provided for."

Henry frowned. "Smith provides for himself. He'll have his own pension, if he survives the war."

Jacob raised his eyebrow. "You really think so? You think he'll make it through without ever getting caught?"

Henry didn't say anything.

"Even if you believe he would, it's still a possibility. Reckless as he is, I'd say it's a probability. If you go, and he gets caught, that pension would be a mighty fine safety net."

"There's nothing to be done about it now. There's no point. We'll see the enemy any day now. There's no one and nowhere we could go to get married anyway. And it wouldn't be a legal marriage." Henry buried his face in his hands. "It'd be bigamy."

Henry was glad he couldn't see Jacob. He didn't want to see the pity in his face.

"Does that bother you?" he said after a long moment.

"I'd be lying if I said no," Henry moaned into his hands. He really shouldn't be talking about this. "But there's nothing to be done about it. If she could get a divorce, she'd have done it, but there weren't any grounds. So she left him. And I believe her, that she'd rather die than go back to him. But it still leaves me without anything to hold onto."

"What if she used a different name?" Jacob asked.

"That wouldn't hold up legally either."

"Then what is the law, really, but a bunch of words we all agreed to? If you have a marriage license and a pension and she has the name, what's the problem? I don't see why anyone would look into it."

"Until the same person is collecting two pensions," Henry replied.

"No, no, in this scenario, there'd have been a dishonorable discharge. The pension is only for that case." Jacob made a wry expression. "Which, I think we can both agree, is pretty likely."

"Only if chin-waggers like you don't keep your damn mouth shut." Henry tightened his fists. "Seriously, Jacob. I've made my peace with this. And it's none of your damn business what we do or don't do. Just because you've got a wife you miss, doesn't mean I need to have one too."

Jacob wrinkled his nose, but he didn't say anything more. He looked down to his paper and started scratching away again.

"Nothing in writing," Henry reminded.

"I know, I know. I've been as good as my word and more, give me a break."

Henry stared at the fire for a long while, listening to the soft sounds of Jacob's pencil moving across the paper.

"What, do you just save the letters until you have the chance to send them?"

"Yeah."

"You must have a big stack by now."

"Nah, I sent what I had with Captain Noah when he went back to Lebanon. He took a whole bunch of fellows' letters."

"Oh. That was nice of him."

"He really didn't look good, Schaef."

Henry sighed and wrapped his arms around his knees. "Between disease, starvation, and exposure, the Rebs won't have much left to fight."

"You *are* melancholy."

"It's just because I haven't had any coffee."

"Buck up. Wagons will be here soon. Rain's stopped. Sun's coming out soon, I can feel it."

"I hope you're right."

———

Charley got back with the others clutching a veritable gaggle of geese by the neck. The relief Henry felt upon seeing her windswept face, grinning and proud, was palpable. They cooked their goose up over the open flame, Henry seated shoulder to shoulder with Charley and taking what little comfort he could from that slight contact. Jacob was right. He was melancholy. It was a blanket of malaise he didn't want to look under, because beneath he knew he'd find fear, uncertainty, and panic about the impending battle. Rumors were abound that they were within ten miles of the enemy, and they were sleep-deprived, half-starved, and freezing. Even with months of training, Henry didn't like their chances for success.

The sun didn't come out from behind the clouds, and the wagons didn't arrive until after dark, but as soon as they did, kettles were brewing coffee over every fire. They toasted to Sergeant Osborn, who'd got wind from the brand new Captain Woodbury that he'd be back-filling the position of First, now that Sergeant Nelson was promoted to Second Lieutenant. Henry couldn't remember tasting a better cup of coffee. Then, they raised the Sibley tents.

Inside, as the squad settled in for a much-needed night's sleep, Henry found relief in holding Charley close, underneath their two musty blankets.

"Do you think my coat will dry by morning?" Charley asked, glancing up at where she'd hung her greatcoat from the tent-pole.

Henry glanced up and shrugged, pulling her in closer. She smelled like sweat and rain and everything that was good. "Dry enough."

"I've never been more grateful for this damned Sibley tent," she muttered into his neck. "Or for the ability to lay out flat to sleep."

"That was a brutal night," Henry replied. "You did some quick thinking."

"Thanks. Wasn't anything anyone else wouldn't do."

"Yeah, but you did, and I'm proud of you."

"Ugh," Charley replied. "You can't say that kind of thing to someone's face." But she snuggled close to him anyway, and he smiled into her hair.

———

XXV

Eight miles outside of Somerset, Kentucky
Friday, January 17, 1862

"Are you sure we shouldn't just carry it with us?" Jacob fretted. He held the kettle, hovering over the opening of the back of the wagon. The teamster rolled his eyes. "Don't look at me like that, Griffith! We were desolate. You could never understand!"

"Put it in the wagon, Robinson," said Webster long-sufferingly. He was presumed sergeant now, though not yet officially. Osborn was running ragged across the camp making sure everything was being struck smoothly.

"Rain's stopped, Jacob," Henry said. "It won't be so bad today."

"We might be in battle before we get a next time," Charley muttered.

"Don't tell him that," Henry replied out the side of his mouth as they turned back to pick up the next load. "I barely survived that long without coffee."

"I was surprisingly fine," Charley mused.

"That is surprising. I had a headache like the dickens."

"I did too. Made me a ruthless goose killer, though."

"Maybe it's not a bad tactic to prepare us for battle. I'd do a lot of desperate things for a cup of coffee."

The wagons were loaded within the hour. The boys were loathe to march ahead of them again, but orders didn't care about that, so off they went. The sun came out from behind the clouds and though their clothes were still pretty damp at the outset of the march, they dried in the pleasant heat of the sun. After a few hours of marching, it got warm enough to take off their greatcoats and unbutton the sack coats, letting the breeze sail through.

"When do you think you'll find out about corporal?" Henry asked as they walked.

Charley's mouth twisted. "Who knows. Soon, I hope?"

"It's up to Webster, I suppose."

They both glanced up the ranks at the man in question. He'd been presumptive sergeant for five hours now and his shoulders were already sagging.

"I feel like I have a pretty clear idea of what his wife's like, seeing him like this," Charley mused.

"Oh, yeah. She's definitely the disciplinarian, don't you think?"

"Definitely."

The roads improved somewhat as the day warmed. They marched ten or eleven miles, till they were just outside of Somerset. Rumors abounded about the proximity of the enemy, with word from the head of the column sighting the Cumberland River proper. They were set loose in an orchard near a pleasant running stream to start preparing camp while they waited for the wagons. With the sun shining and the temperature mild, Henry was sure it was the most pleasant camping ground they'd had since they arrived in Kentucky.

"The enemy is all dug in," Elias reported back after his requisite tour to gather the camp gossip. Henry was helping the others find dry tinder while Charley started another fire with some lint from everyone's pockets. "They've got works on the shore of the Cumberland at Beech Grove. They may not deign to stand a battle at all, and we might have to shell them out first, then take them by storm."

Charley's face twisted as she looked up from her tinder. "What? The cowards!"

"We're close though, right?" Williamson asked.

"We're within eight miles of the enemy works," Elias replied. "This is it boys. Any day now."

"We've been saying that for months," Jacob said. "I'm tired of saying it, to be entirely honest."

"Yes, but this time it's true," Elias said.

"Care to make a wager?" Jacob shot back. "I'll bet you we won't have seen battle by the end of the Sabbath."

"I'll take that bet," Elias replied. "Your next month's pay."

"Not a chance," Jacob said. "Five dollars, that's it."

"Must not be so sure, then. You have a deal." Elias grinned at the other fellows listening. "Any of you want in on this? Henry?"

"No thanks."

"Aw come on. Krüger? I know you like to gamble."

"*Nien.* I don't gamble without knowing my odds."

After a measly dinner of hardtack and salt pork rations, Henry walked up and down the orchard rows with Charley, sunlight brindling the ground with a criss-cross of branches.

"Wish they had a storehouse stashed with apples," Henry said, looking up at the hibernating branches.

"What would be the odds of a third apple-related windfall?" Charley said. "Surely that would be some sort of sign from God—or whomever—that we were favored."

"I'd be happy to receive it as such."

They walked on apace, until they had left the bounds of their camp and climbed up a small hill. They could see for a mile or two in either direction, and as far as they could see in both directions were Union soldiers, tents, wagons, and fires.

"Look at us all," Charley said.

Henry pointed to the southeast. "I think that's the Ninth Ohio, over there."

"Very nice," Charley replied. "Shall we go over and visit your uncle?"

"Will we actually get there this time?"

Charley tried to hide a blush. Henry grinned. They started off in that direction.

"I talked to Jacob yesterday."

Charley got quiet. "Oh? What'd he have to say?"

"Just wanted to ask questions. Don't worry, I held him off." Mostly. "Say ... do you have a plan for if you get caught?"

Charley stopped and glared at him. "What?"

"Just in case, I mean. Not that you'd plan to, but if something happened. Like, if say Krüger had walked in on us instead of Jacob."

"I don't want to talk about that."

"I understand, but..." What did he get himself into? "But if that were to happen, it would affect me too. I want to be united in our response."

"What's there to do?" Charley muttered, kicking at the clods of winter grass as she walked. "If I'm caught, then I have to go. You have to stay, so that's that."

"That is not that. Charley. Are you serious?" Henry grimaced. "That is *not* that!"

"Well, what do you want me to say? 'Desert the army and abscond with me into the night?' I can't ask that of you."

"I know you won't, regardless of whether or not you think you deserve to. Charley, if you're caught, I'm implicated. I could be discharged too, for indecent conduct."

"Well, I'll do my best to protect you—"

"—I don't *want* you to protect me!" Henry threw his hands in the air. "I don't want to be here if you're gone."

The gravity of his words echoed off the tree trunks. Even the birds seemed to hush. Charley was staring at him with those round, brown eyes, dark and guarded. He'd looked into those eyes so many times, wondering what secrets she was hiding. She gave away so little, and he'd just given away everything, without even meaning to.

"I know your first priority is soldiering," Henry said. "I know that. You've made it abundantly clear. But I don't think mine is. If it comes down to a choice between my duty to the army and my duty to you, dammit Charley, I'll choose you."

Charley blinked.

Henry barrelled on. "Jacob said he thought I should propose to you, so if I die in battle and you got caught before your three years are up, you'd have my pension. And I know it's not possible, and it's not what you want, but that's the kind of thing I want to do for you. I want to ... to provide for you." Her eyes widened. "Not in a patronizing way. In the way people love each other, the way people belong to one another. It's not owed, it's not obligated. It's freely given, joyfully given." Henry shook his head, tried to find the thread of what he was actually trying to say. "So I want to have a plan, together, for if you get caught. Maybe we'll never need it. But I'd feel a lot better if we had one."

Charley's jaw worked. Her arms were wrapped around herself, and she looked about as uncomfortable as he could have expected going into a conversation that touched on tender feelings. "I... I thought, if I were to be discharged on the march, I'd travel back to Lebanon. Miss Sterling, I think she saw through me. She said I'd find friends there."

Henry experienced a clutch in his chest, a strange, jolting rage entirely unexpected. "No," he gritted. "No way in hell." He stepped forward and took Charley by her shoulders. "Promise me, if I'm not there to go with you—"

"—You can't just go with me, you're a soldier, you're the property of the Union—"

"—*Promise me* you won't do that."

Charley looked at him like he'd just grown horns. "What? Oh—*that?* Henry, did you think I meant to whore myself in consolation of a dishonorable discharge? Dear God—no, I meant I'd go there to regroup. I have no intention of divesting of my masculine clothes, or taking up the oldest profession, for that matter. I like swiving but not that much." She reached up and touched his face. He realized his jaw had been set like an anvil. "I don't know what I'll do if I'm caught. I don't know where I'll be or who will be with me. I don't want to think about it. If I think about it too much, it feels like I might make it happen."

"If I'm there," Henry gritted out. He stopped to swallow around the prospect of his own death, then carried on, "If I'm there, I will go with you."

"You can't."

"Army be damned. I will go with you."

"Lots of couples have had to separate for the Union. We'll find each other after—"

"You're not hearing me. I. Will. Go. With. You."

Charley looked up at him. For a long, breathless moment, Henry feared he had disappointed her. After all, he knew how much she cared about this fight. Would she think him a coward? To abandon his duty for her? Even if it was in some hypothetical story about a possible future they both had no intention of allowing?

"We'd sneak away in the night," Charley whispered. "We'd find disguises, travel behind enemy lines."

"What?"

"We'd sabotage Confederate works from the inside," Charley said, a smile forming on her lips. "We wouldn't have any orders to follow. We'd be a force to be reckoned with."

Henry's face split and a laugh came out. "Alright, yes, we could do that."

"We could pull up rail ties," Charley went on, laughing now too. "Set fires to storehouses."

"You are a demon."

"I am a valkyrie," she replied. "Like you said. And if the army won't take me, I'll find some other way to fight."

"Charley, I love you."

Henry didn't need to look around before he pressed his lips to hers. They were on the ridge, under the cover of trees and shadows. The pickets were still a handful of rods beyond where they stood. He could kiss her here. Hell, he would kiss her here. Damn the consequences.

"Are you sure you don't want to just abscond now?" Henry murmured against the comfort of her mouth.

"And do what?"

"Like you said." He held her head in the cradle of his hands. "Sabotage. Behind enemy lines. Together."

"We'd still have to sneak around." Her eyes were sad. "I think we might always have to."

"Always?"

"I don't know, Henry." She looked down. "I just ... I can't marry you. And regardless of whether we get to have a future after the war or not, I'm not sure I can stomach walking the world as a woman again." She winced. "When I put a dress on, I disappear. I'm not me anymore. Does that make any sense?"

Henry took a deep breath. "I'd be lying if I said I hadn't imagined a future with you after the war. Hell, leaving the army sounded pretty damn good as recently as yesterday. And it brought me comfort to imagine what we'd do, where we'd go. If we were free to do anything. And I think I do understand, because any fantasy of domestic bliss felt ... I dunno, wrong, I suppose. False. Hollow." He ducked his head and laughed. "And it's strange, because isn't that what I'm supposed to want? Father, mother, children—family—in a house, with some productive enterprise to sustain it all? Isn't it our nature to want that comfort, the kind we grew up in? But I can't ... because I still can't imagine you in a damn dress!" He threw his hands up and laughed some more at the absurdity of it all. "That's not a future I can see you in. And I can't see any kind of future for me without you in it."

Charley bit her lip. Then she reached out and pulled his face toward her, her face crumpling as she kissed him. "Goddamn you," she whispered tightly. "I love you so damn much, I can't ... I don't ... *Hell*."

Her cheeks were wet but she kissed him harder. Henry wrapped his arms around her and held her tight. He'd never let her go. Not ever. Maybe his life would be upended, maybe it would be nothing like he'd ever imagined it. But he wanted whatever that uncertainty might hold, as long as it was with Charley.

———

XXVI

Henry Schaefer was going to die.

Charley was sitting next to him at the fire in the Ninth Ohio's camp, pretending to listen to the admittedly very gracious translation Kloepfer was providing for Henry's uncle's amusing anecdote. Henry's vibrance, his smile, his joy—it was all further evidence of his doom. There was no possible way God would let Charley keep him.

"Rosencrans was going through all the troops with a kind word and a quip. Sometimes clever, sometimes not, but always apt to the unit at hand, you see." Kloepfer was explaining in her ear. She glanced over at him in an approximation of listening. "When he got to our unit, he said, in English of course, 'Company B stings, I hope!'" Kloepfer stole a glance at Henry's uncle. "Well, Sergeant Schaefer was still fiercely and stubbornly struggling with English, and he was locked in mortal combat with the difference between *g* and *k* in pronunciation. He couldn't understand why the general, with a straight face, was hurling such an insult at the company."

Kloepfer looked at her expectantly. Charley tried to catch up.

"What?" she said dumbly.

"'Company B *stings*,'" Kloepfer repeated. When she didn't respond, he glowered. "He mixed up the *g* and the *k* sounds…"

Charley blinked. "Company B stinks?"

Kloepfer grinned, but it didn't last long. "You're supposed to laugh."

"Oh. Sorry." Charley looked down at her hands.

"Amerikaner haben keinen Humor," Kloepfer muttered.

"Sorry," Charley said again, "I'm just in a brown study."

"Concerned about the impending battle?"

"Yes."

Kloepfer raised a brow at her, then glanced over her shoulder at Henry and his uncle. "It's not so bad."

Charley frowned. "Kill or be killed is 'not so bad'? Sorry, I'm confused."

Kloepfer shrugged. "The idea of it is harder than the action. When you're fighting, that's all you know. You can't even remember half of it afterward."

"If there is an afterward," Charley muttered.

"Afterward feels exhilarating. You'll never be more grateful to be alive."

"Until you find out who you lost."

"Until then. Yes." Kloepfer finally looked at her. "You're determined."

Charley swallowed hard over a tight throat. "I am determined. But no amount of determination can save lives. I can't be everywhere at once."

"You're not here to save lives. You're here to take them."

Charley winced. "I am. I thought I was." She glanced at Henry, then back at Kloepfer. She pitched her voice low. Most of these fellows couldn't speak much English anyway, but she was feeling particularly cautious. "How do you stand it?"

He leaned into her conspiracy. "What?"

She sure hoped Henry was right about Kloepfer and his uncle. "The risk of losing him? Every time?"

Kloepfer blinked. Not blankly. Just slowly, consideringly. He took a deep breath and sort of shrugged as he exhaled. "I'm not sure. I just … do, I suppose." He looked at her again, so squarely, so matter-of-factly. "You can't save him, or you'll die trying. You just have to fight and hope and trust that you'll get through together."

"But you won't," Charley insisted. "It is guaranteed someone will die."

Kloepfer snorted. "Boy, none of us leave this earth alive."

Charley grimaced. Was this what passed for comfort among the areligious?

Kloepfer shrugged and gave an easy grin. "Now, do you want to hear about the time we had nothing to forage for supper but snakes?"

"Dear God, no." Charley buried her exasperated face in her hands.

———

By the time Charley and Henry returned to the Second Minnesota camp, the wagons had arrived and the Sibley tents had been pitched.

"Good of you to return from the Castle of Indolence," Robinson complained as they arrived. "Lolly-gaggers."

"I don't know why we had to put tents up in the first place," Williamson said. "This weather is so fine, I might sleep out under the stars!"

"Speak for yourself, Williamson," Hower put in. "After last night, you'll have to pry these tent poles out of my cold, dead hands."

Twilight was falling, limning all the tree branches with pink and gold, when Sergeant Osborn returned to their campfire. He looked drawn and tired, but happy.

"There's some forage at the kitchen tent," he said. "Hogs."

Hower sprang to his feet and dug into his haversack. "I've never met more first-rate Union soldiers than these Kentucky hogs."

Robinson laughed. "They muster in faster than a shot off a shovel. They can't wait to go for a soldier."

Charley followed them all on apace to the kitchen tent and got her portion of ham.

"You look like you've got a cudgel to your brain," Osborn observed as they walked back to the fire.

"Hm? No, I'm fine." Liar.

"You know, I never thought I'd be so grateful for a scrap of overcooked ham," Osborn mused.

Charley knew she was being a terrible conversation partner, but she couldn't manage more than a shrug in reply. Fact was, she agreed. She just couldn't muster a thought for anything that could pierce through the thrumming refrain in her brain chanting, *You're going to lose him.*

"Well, come on, Smith," Osborn said as they approached the campfire. "Your time has come."

Charley looked up. The rest of the squad was watching her as she entered the circle around the fire. Robinson was wresting a cork out of a bottle, and Webster was grinning.

"We had some news while you were gone," Webster said.

"Yup, he's Sergeant Webster now," Williamson reported with a grin.

"Officially?" Henry asked. "Congratulations!"

"Yes, thank you," Webster smiled as Henry shook his hand. "And we had a little vote too."

"A vote? On what?" Charley didn't like how everyone was looking at her.

"On corporal," Webster replied.

"I thought you were choosing."

"I thought we're here to defend a democracy, and perhaps we'd better act like it," Webster replied.

"That sounds like something Smith would say," Williamson laughed.

Robinson poured some golden liquid from the bottle into his tin cup and held it out to Charley. "Congratulations, Corporal."

"Oh." She took the cup. It smelled like applejack. "Oh!" She looked up. They were smiling at her, expectantly. She was going to lose them. Maybe all of them. "Thank you."

"Anything the matter, Smith?" Osborn asked, putting a hand on her shoulder. "I thought you were eager for a promotion?"

"I am," she said woodenly. She pushed the corners of her mouth into a smile. "I'm just surprised. Thank you."

Henry laughed. "He's just terrible at taking a compliment. Look, watch. Charley, you're going to do a great job as corporal. You're smart and decisive and you have the best ideas."

Williamson cackled. "Ah, look at 'im blush!"

She was blushing. She also felt like she was choking on something. She hadn't taken a single bite of supper yet. She took a sip of the applejack to force whatever it was down.

"Ha! I thought you were gonna crow night and day for weeks," Hower said, slapping a hand on her other shoulder. "Looks like you might have an ounce of humility after all."

Charley shoved him with the shoulder. "I do not. Take it back."

"Hower, how come you weren't putting yourself up for it?" Henry asked.

"Ack, Captain Bishop said I can't," Hower said. "Unless..." he looked at Osborn.

"No," Osborn said. "I just got promoted, I'm not tangling with Captain Bishop. Besides, you already voted for Smith."

"I did, at that," Hower agreed and poured a slug from the bottle Robinson passed him.

Charley took another drink. "Where'd you get this, Robinson?"

"Found it slipped away in one of the wagons," Robinson replied with waggling eyebrows. The bottle was making its way around the circle. "Don't tell the Hastings boys."

"There won't be any left for the Hastings boys," Henry said, swirling the bottle. "There's already hardly any left and Krüger ain't even got any yet."

"Hey," Krüger boomed. "Who is taking my share?"

Hower laughed weakly and poured a little from his cup into Krüger's.

"A toast," Sergeant Webster said, "to some right honorable soldiers."

"Here here!"

"Cheers!"

———

XXVII

Eight miles outside of Somerset, Kentucky
Sunday, January 19, 1862

ROBINSON LOST THE BET. Saturday it rained again, all day, and the state treasury officer came with the allotment rolls for all to sign. Troops arrived, company upon company, all along the Mill Springs Road, Generals Thomas and Schoepf along with them. In all, they had seven regiments, two battalions, and two batteries. Company A was sent out on picket that night. By morning, Charley woke to the relentless long roll of the drummers and men shouting.

"They're making a feint!" Hower called as the squad scrambled to secure their kit and fall in. "They're feinting on that road while they come in force on ours."

"Which road is ours?" Williamson gasped as he buckled his knapsack on his back.

"The Mill Springs Road." Hower was whipped up like a preacher on Sunday as he confirmed his bayonet was secured in its scabbard. "That's our road. They've gone and attacked the Tenth Indiana. There, yonder." He pointed.

There was nothing to see. Dawn was caught in the mist made by the rain and the undulating hills were mostly woods and dense brush, obscuring any view at a distance. Charley's heart slammed in her chest. Her hands were moving on their own, buckling her gear with deceptive efficiency. She was Corporal now. She didn't even have her stripes yet, that was how new she was, and now they were going into battle. She had to be responsible for her squad, keep them together. Keep them calm and united under orders. Dear God, how was she going to do that?

A pair of hands gripped her shoulders. She spun around and looked up into Henry's eyes.

"This is it," he said. His blue eyes were intent, his lips curled in a way where it wasn't clear whether he was happy or determined. Maybe both. Dear God, please give her a chance to look into those beloved blue eyes again when the day was through. To hell with it. She grabbed his cheeks and kissed his mouth. It was just a quick kiss, perfunctory even, like a child might kiss his mother. Even so, Hower immediately hollered.

"Hoo boy, you can't do that, you're corporal now!"

"No favorites!" Robinson added, laughing, though to Charley's ear it was a little tight.

"—If you're gonna kiss one of us, you gotta kiss us all!" Hower laughed.

"A kiss with a fist is all you're getting, Hower," Charley growled. Her cheeks were hot. The squad erupted. Henry was laughing hardest of all. Every ounce of joy felt like a conviction.

"Come on, you dogs," Charley said.

"Fall in!" Webster called.

There was no time for dramatic speeches to fire up the troops. In truth, they didn't need it. The Second Minnesota was surging down the Mill Springs Road, marching in formation tighter than when they'd paraded the streets of Saint Paul for their families and friends as they departed for the front. Charley was swept along with the fervor, her rifle tucked to her side solidly, the comfortable presence of Henry at her back. It would be alright. Surely, it would be alright.

None of us leave this earth alive.

The terrain worsened as they neared the boom of the cannons. Sounds of gunfire and shouts ricocheted off the tree trunks until they reached a clearing. Charley's boots were soaked through with mud. They sucked and squelched as they marched. Sleet cut through the misty air, raising the hair on the back of her neck and freezing her fingers around the trigger guard of her musket rifle. Her heart hammered in her chest, and her nerves and vessels all sang with prickling energy, every tiny hair on her skin alerted to the action. Her thoughts became strangely distant and lucid. They marched to battle. It was too late to stop it, now. Too late to go back. They'd been waiting for this, preparing for going on six months. The chance to make a difference. And now, as her feet carried her rote forward, shoulders jostling her squad members on either side, she couldn't fathom what kind of difference she would make. She would set her musket rifle to her shoulder, fire bullets into the thick mist. If she was lucky, kill a faceless Rebel or two. Gain some ground for the Union.

Charley swallowed against any fear or doubt. It would matter. It was the part of a hundred thousand men. They each did their bit and together, it turned the tide. There was no divine justice. It was people, pushing together in the same direction as one. If she thought she were so important to turn the world to justice all on her own, she was dreaming. She was part of it. Something bigger than herself. She had a role to play, though miniscule, as corporal, and if Webster fell or failed in his leadership, she'd fill his role too. For as she put one mud-slick boot in front of the other, she felt her teeth set determinedly. She would do this. Didn't matter if she was ready or not—there was only one path forward.

They reached the edge of an open field just northeast of the road, shrouded in morning mist mixed with acrid gun smoke. Union soldiers were just visible dug in behind a split rail fence. Sparks of gunfire flashed in the mist from a ravine directly before them, obscured almost completely in the underbrush. Captain Woodbury's order to halt ricocheted down the regiment from sergeant to sergeant. Charley's senses jangled with the wild screams of men and guns and horses, the clatter of guns and bayonets a harsh reminder of how insignificant and fragile she was. They all were.

The battery was behind them somewhere and as they waited for orders, shells soared over them and exploded in the dirt not thirty feet off, tearing the winter field in great gashes and sending shrapnel into the ravine. Men across the regiment shouted and ducked, but Charley's eyes just followed the shells. Though her breath caught, she did not flinch. She glanced to her left.

Jacob Robinson's mouth was a thin line, his eyes wide and his knuckles white. She was grateful Henry was behind her. She remembered that morning at Fort Snelling, when he'd stood in her place for the demonstration for the St. Anthony mayor, hiding her from view as best he could. She'd been terrified that morning, petrified that Richard would recognize her and drag her off in shame. Strangely, walking into battle felt less frightening than that had been.

Orders to advance to the front line rang across the companies. The Second Minnesota Regiment flowed to fill the gaps along the fence as sections of the other regiments fell back. Charley had no idea which they were. The only other regiment whose position she knew was the Ninth Ohio, who marched on the heels of the 2nd, driving them on with their German battle cries. Their blood-lust was chilling and awe-inspiring. She didn't hear them now. They must have been directed to a different position.

Charley approached the fence rail. Her ears rang with the cracks of gunfire as the lieutenants shouted for them to load in nine.

"They're dug into that ditch," Hower cried, pointing to the ravine.

Charley's fingers were strangely nimble for being so numb with cold. She loaded her weapon smoothly, the months of practice driving her muscles through the familiar movements. She found great satisfaction in the ungodly crack as their squad fired as one into the misty ravine, toward the shifting shadows and explosive flashes that betrayed their enemy's position. Her blood surged in her ears and she grinned as she ripped through the paper on her next charge.

Out of the corner of her eye, she could sense Robinson's movements synchronizing with her own. It was like a dance, more graceful than any she could remember. Entrancing. Her arms and hands kept the rhythm tapped out by the drummer boys, graceful and lithe, loading charge after charge, firing with conviction into the smoke as cannons produced staccato crashes like symbols, their explosive fire perceptible now on the far left of the field.

She could perceive movement in the misty ravine where they aimed their fire. The thought that she had finally turned her weapon on another human being stuck in her chest, but only for a moment before a bullet splintered the fence rail not two feet from where she stood. It was kill or be killed. There was nothing more.

It wasn't long before Charley's ammunition ran out. She fell back, and Henry assumed her place. His hands were shaking as he began to load in nine himself. Her heart caught in her throat. *Don't be afraid. He knows these dance steps. He's the strongest person you know.* He fired his rifle into the mist, then reloaded, faster than she'd ever seen him. She was frozen, watching his profile as he fired again. Any moment now, it would happen. Any moment now he'd be snatched away, his bloody end smeared on her memory like a triptych to her hubris.

Behind her, Sergeant Webster knocked her shoulder.

"Here, more ammunition," he shouted at her. She shook herself from watching Henry and looked at him. "Make sure everyone's reloaded."

Charley accepted the armful of cartridge boxes. The bullets. The things that would stop the enemy. God, what was she doing? She shook her head for focus and swept into action.

When Henry fell back to refill his cartridge box, Charley moved to take his position and fired once again. His hand lingered on her shoulder as she loaded in, his touch feeding a heady sense of power that pumped through every vessel, angry and audacious and bottomless. It felt like sex, in that way. Through the din, she thought she heard his voice.

Her neck swiveled as she packed gunpowder into the barrel of her rifle. "What?" she shouted.

"They have terrible aim, I said."

He was right. They did. Charley laughed, big and full. Then she turned, cocked her weapon, and squeezed her trigger. The crack of the rifle sang in her ears. She almost felt drunk. Their aim was terrible. Or the Rebs were firing on the regiment to her company's left, that had taken heavy fire before they arrived. But the flashes in the mist were not nearly as frequent as their own regiment's blasts. Charley sucked in a breath like a prowling wildcat. Fucking fools.

Down the line, she saw someone climb up on the fence. Wondering if they were to advance over the rail, her movements slowed as she tracked his movement. It was an officer, but not one she recognized from the Second Minnesota. The man waved his saber wildly in the air and bellowed into the mist.

"Stand and fight like men, you bastards!"

A roar of voices exploded from the officer's men. Charley and the rest of the Second took up the cry as well. A bellow of hundreds of voices answered them from the ravine and lines of grayback soldiers began charging out of the smoke with muskets brandished, some with bayonets, others without. Charley straightened and scrambled for her own bayonet in its scabbard as the captains hollered the order to fix bayonets. The blade locked on the end of her rifle, and she finished cocking and capping her loaded weapon as the Secesh barreled upon them.

"Charley!"

Henry was shouting in her ear, his hand on her shoulder. He wasn't holding her back, though, and his voice carried a thread of encouragement that bolstered her, made her brace one boot on the lower rail of the fence as she drove the butt of her weapon into her shoulder and fired at a Rebel swiftly sharpening into focus as he ran toward her.

There was a kickback to her shoulder, the brace of Henry behind her, and the fall of the enemy under the feet of his fellows. One Reb stooped over him, but quickly gave him up for dead. And Charley wasn't sure if it had been her bullet or Robinson's or Hower's, but it didn't matter because the man went down and she crowed, even as another greyback filled in the line and crashed his weapon down on the fence before her.

Blades flashed and crashed together. Fire sparked and combustion rang in her ears so that she couldn't tell what was the sound and what was the echo. Henry fired rounds over Charley's shoulder as she slapped bayonets away with her own, pushing herself up on the rail of the fence and driving the enemy down in hand-to-hand combat no less dramatic than the demonstration Sergeant Schmöckel had made at Fort Snelling two months and a lifetime ago.

She drove her blade through one fellow's hat and cut another's neck where it connected with his shoulder. It was a haphazard fight. None of the men were particularly skilled in hand-to-hand combat, and the grappling was sloppy and awkward and deadly. The enemy brandished their guns like clubs and spears, not bothering to load them. Many of them had flint-lock muskets, which explained why they hadn't been firing fully. The rain must've drowned their powder pans.

A fellow barreled down on Charley, using superior height to swing his musket like a bat toward her head.

Henry's rifle intercepted, and she found herself squeezed out of the frontline as he struggled against the strength of the enemy's blow.

Charley dropped the butt of her rifle and loaded in faster than she had ever done in her life. Lifting the barrel, she pointed the bayonet at the enemy's face and squeezed the trigger. Blood sprayed and her eyes somehow managed not to perceive the way the man's face rended as he crumpled to the ground.

Another Reb was visible behind him, and Charley shoved her weapon forward, driving the bayonet into him with a soft squish. She shoved a ball of nausea down—strange, that—and struggled to pull her bayonet back out of the body that had draped over the fence rail, trapping her blade at an awkward angle. She squeezed back into the frontline as she struggled and managed to retrieve the blade with a sickening fleshy sound as Henry wiped blood from his pale face with a shaky arm.

XXVIII

IT COULD HAVE BEEN five minutes or five hours. Henry lost time in the rote of battle. Gunpowder smoke stung his nostrils and his breath came fast and short, whether from fear or effort he wasn't sure. Both, most likely. There was no time to think, no time to consider the best way forward. There was nothing but desperate movement, because if he slipped, if he missed, if he didn't see an imminent threat coming, it would be the end of him. Or worse, of Charley. He had only a vague sense of his comrades but they moved together like one, united in purpose. The only thing that seemed able to stick in his mind was a desperate gratitude to his father and the Turners. He was strong and fast, faster than he'd ever thought possible. His body reacted, and he felt like he was constantly trying to catch up to his hands, to comprehend the bloody work that his body applied itself to with such familiar expediency.

The fence was at once a monstrous annoyance and a blessed barrier. Bayonets clashed over its top rail, stuck through the rails halfway down. Hower was crouched in one of its zigzag corners, thrusting his bowie knife through a gap and slicing at the knees of the Rebels on the other side. It was not the honorable clash boys fantasized about, of glory and dignity and righteousness. It was dirty, desperate, and fumbling. When Henry ended a life with his own hands, he sort of watched it happen with detached bewilderment, his bowels clenched in panic and his voice a ragged, wild thing he didn't recognize. He'd spent a year longing for this chance to prove himself, but now that he was here, he didn't feel like a man. He felt like a feral animal.

Somewhere off to their right, an unholy roar of voices shook him. In his periphery, he saw a huge mob of men in Union blue charging full tilt at the far end of the enemy troops, barreling without hesitation into the field with bayonets fixed. The Rebel's left flank scattered like leaves before the force of the furious charge.

"Is that the Ninth?" Charley shouted in Henry's direction.

He felt chilled, but he couldn't determine whether it was from fear or awe. "Yeah."

"Damned Dutch indeed," she gritted as she took a Rebel's bayonet blow with her own. Henry sliced the man's neck below the ear with his own bayonet, and he slumped over another still warm body on the rail. Charley shoved them both off. No time to assess, no time for moralizing. Even if the coffee roiling in his stomach seemed desperate to evacuate. He swallowed and loaded in nine, firing over Charley's shoulder as she engaged their attention with her bayonet.

After the Ninth's charge, the enemy troops thinned considerably. Shouts that sounded like "fall back" ricocheted from the mist and smoke. Some rebel companies retreated together, others just scattered back into the woods. Sergeant Webster stood on the rail a few feet to Charley's left and relayed orders to mount the fence and charge. His face was sweaty and mud-smeared and the man who had always seemed so soft, so caring, had his face twisted in disgust, in battle-charged fury. He turned to face the remaining enemy soldiers, pointing his rifle, and shouted, "Surrender, you dogs."

A Secesh officer was trained under Webster's aim. His men had gone, or died. *Shoot*, Henry thought. *Shoot now*. The Reb straightened, the flat planes of his face stark in disgust as he stared Webster down. He made no reply.

Charley saw the revolver before Henry did. She scrambled over the fence and dashed toward the Reb. Henry vaulted the fence after her. His heart was choking him as the Rebel took deliberate aim. Charley barreled forward and the Reb fired. Henry's ears were full of cotton. So was his throat. Charley stumbled and fell. Webster made an animal noise and fired on the Rebel. The greyback took his bullet with honor and proceeded to die.

The Second Minnesota surged over the fence and pounded down the hill in pursuit of the remaining Rebels scattering into the woods. Henry shouldered against the surge and stood over Charley, a pillar parting a rushing tide of men with a thirst for blood and vengeance.

"Charley, what the hell were you thinking!?" His ears were ringing. He was shouting at her, probably. "You had a gun! Why didn't you shoot him?"

"It wasn't loaded," Charley croaked. She pushed herself up on unsteady feet, and Henry caught her round the waist. "Ah, get off."

"Smith! Are you alright?" It was Jacob, running and skidding to a stop next to them. Elias, Williamson, and Krüger were at his side. "Osborn is down. What happened?"

"Osborn?" Henry asked, looking up. Charley managed to flinch out of his arms.

Elias looked back toward the rail. "Yeah, I think that's what got Webster on that fence. He's with him now."

"Is he dead?" Charley asked, drawn.

"I don't know." Jacob was breathless. He gave Charley a glance. "What about you?"

"I'm fine." She sort of tipped into Henry's shoulder. He caught her again, her hair in his face a most familiar and comforting scent. In the strange calm of smoke and mist, the sounds of battle ebbing, Henry looked down and saw they were standing in a graveyard. A surge of panic broke through.

"Charley, you're hurt," he sputtered, his hands patting over her uniform, trying to discern whether any of the blood on it was hers.

"No, I'm not," she snapped and tried to step away again. She swayed on her feet and put her fingertips to her forehead. "I'm just drunk on ... battle."

"*Schlachtwut...*" Krüger was saying. Henry's eyes saw it then. A rip in her sack coat, under her left arm. He snatched her arms and pulled at her buttons.

"Stop, stop it!" Charley bellowed at him, batting at his hands. They didn't look like his own. They were smudged with soot and blood and his knuckles were scraped all to hell, though he couldn't say when that had happened, or how. But those hands managed her brass buttons fine, and he swore when he saw her shirt dyed bright crimson at the armpit.

"You're hurt," Henry said again, stupidly. He looked up, swinging his head around to determine what to do.

"We have to fall back, go to the hospital tent," Jacob said. "Come on, we have to find Webster. He's already taking Osborn, I'm sure of it."

"No, we can't!"

Henry looked up at Charley. Her countenance was a fierce grimace, cheeks smudged with soot and blood. She was gripping her coat together in one hand and looking at each man of their squad like a threat.

"I will *not* be sent back now. Never. I'd rather die."

Henry's stomach dropped to his feet. What had he done? He hadn't revealed her to everyone. He hadn't secured her doom. Had he? He looked to Krüger. At Elias, and Williamson. Jacob had his teeth gritted. But none of them appeared to be shocked or appalled.

"No one's sending you anywhere," Elias placated. "I'm sure it's just a flesh wound."

"If you need stitches, I know how to sew," Williamson offered.

"I'll carry you," Krüger added.

Charley looked at Krüger with particular incredulity. "I'm fine. I'll walk."

"No, please Charley. Let us carry you," Henry heard himself say gently. "Not because you can't walk, but because it will help if you don't have to."

Charley stared at Henry. Her jaw was set so tight it trembled. He took her hand.

"Please, Charley," he whispered. "No matter what happens, I'm with you. Remember?"

Her fingers curled around his. Then, like an avalanche, she fell into him. She pressed her face into his shoulder. "Henry, I thought you were going to die."

Henry shook his head, bewildered. He put his hands on her shoulders. "What?"

"In the battle. I thought you were a goner."

Henry looked up at the others. Robinson was sheepish, Williamson amused. Elias laughed. "I told you. The Turner spends too much time learning fancy tricks. Can't do an honest day's work to save his life."

His ribbing cut through, and the other boys laughed, though not so uproariously as they normally did. Henry scooped

Charley up in his arms and lifted her over the fence rails as the rest of the boys climbed over.

On the other side of the rails, at the edge of the woods, they found Webster. He had Osborn draped over his back, half carrying and half dragging him off the battlefield. The First Sergeant hung like a dead weight.

"Blessed Mother of God, is he dead?" Jacob exclaimed. He and Elias ran over to Webster, Krüger on their heels.

Webster turned and saw them. All of a sudden, his drawn expression cracked and he began to cry.

Henry hurried over as quickly as he could with Charley in his arms as Jacob and Elias pulled Osborn's body off Webster's back. Webster stumbled, but stayed on his feet and choked on a sob.

"He's not dead, he's not dead," he gasped. "He needs help."

Krüger didn't hesitate. He pulled Osborn's arms around his neck and hoisted the man onto his back like his weight was nothing at all. Elias and Jacob helped Henry situate Charley similarly, as it was a mile and half back to camp, while Williamson held Webster up while he caught his breath. The whole squad trudged back toward the camp with their wounded in arms.

———

XXIX

Henry hung back when they reached camp, and Webster and Krüger made a beeline for the hospital tent. He let Charley slide off his back, but she didn't seem steady without his support. Jacob came up next to him.

"Schaef, you gotta do it," he said under his breath. "Look at her."

Henry looked down at Charley slouched in the crook of his arm. Her eyes were squeezed shut, her brow furrowed, her breath short and staccato.

"Charley, I'm going to take you to the hospital tent now."

"No," she grit out. "Don't. Please."

"Why doesn't he want to go to the hospital tent?" Williamson asked.

Jacob let out a frustrated sound and dropped the butt of his rifle to the ground in exasperation.

"Does he not want anyone to see his body?" Williamson asked.

Henry looked at him sharply. His eyes narrowed. "Yeah…"

"That's okay," Williamson said. "I understand. I can sew. Maybe we take a look at the wound in our tent first?"

Henry was not sure Williamson did understand, but he followed the boy back to their Sibley tent. Jacob trailed behind. Elias spluttered for a moment, but then followed.

"Why not just take him to the hospital tent?" Elias demanded.

"I'm fine," Charley said weakly.

"You're not fine," Henry replied. He thought fast, then addressed Elias. "He might have to wait, though, especially if it's not serious. It's better to tend to the wound quickly."

Williamson held the flap of the Sibley tent open. Henry scooped Charley up into his arms and ducked in. When he set Charley on her feet inside, she teetered.

"Elias, get your gum blanket out, would you," Henry directed.

"Aw, come on, he's gonna get it all covered in blood."

"Better his than yours. Come on."

Henry helped Charley lie on the gum blanket. She looked so fragile that for a moment, panic shot through him. Had the bullet pierced her lung? Her guts? Had she already spilled too much blood? Then she glared at him and the moment passed.

"Don't you dare, Henry Schaefer," she said. Her eyes were wide, her lips pinched in pain, or fear, or rage at him.

"Dare what?" Elias scoffed. "Save your life?"

"Hower," Williamson said, voice bright as ever. "Go get some yarrow."

"What?"

"I seen some, out in the woods, over where we were gathering firewood yesterday."

"For what?"

"To stop the bleeding, of course," Williamson said. He smiled a little, like he wasn't sure whether Elias was teasing him.

Elias blinked for a moment then nodded, and ducked out of the tent.

"Some plant's going to stop the bleeding?" Jacob asked incredulously.

"My mother used to always put it on skinned knees and elbows," Williamson replied. "Didn't yours?"

Henry and Jacob exchanged looks. "No."

Williamson gave them a confused frown, then crouched down next to Charley. "It's great medicine. I used it for my stomach when we drank that bad water, and it helped Smith get over his cold back in Lebanon Junction."

"Sounds too good to be true," Jacob muttered.

Henry crouched down beside Williamson. Charley was glaring at him like he was a snake looking to bite her.

"Why don't I just rip his shirt up the side?" Henry said tentatively. "I think the wound is under his arm."

"Good idea."

Henry flipped the sack coat out of the way. On her back, her breasts weren't as obvious, but anyone looking would notice. He left the sack coat covering her right side as best he could. He pulled Charley's shirt gently out of her waistband. She watched him with eyes hard and painful. He pulled on the edge of the shirt at the side seam, but it didn't budge.

"Here," Jacob said. Henry looked up and accepted his jackknife. He made a small cut into the fabric.

"Your knife is dull, Jake."

"I know. Rusty too, come to think of it."

"Maybe we shouldn't use it near an open wound," Williamson pointed out.

Henry nodded. He had been hoping to carefully slice the shirt open, so as not to reveal anything, but there was nothing for it. He gripped the shirt in his hands and yanked the seam open, snapping threads all the way up. He was pretty confident he didn't reveal anything, especially since Williamson and Jacob were both on Charley's right side, but he couldn't be sure.

Henry choked on his inhale. It was a mess of blood under her arm.

"Here, put your arm over your head," Henry managed to say, gently guiding Charley's arm up. Charley gasped.

"I think I mighta broke a rib," she winced. Henry gingerly released her arm, then carefully folded the fabric aside, just enough so that they could see the wound.

Williamson got up on his knees and poured his water canteen over the wound. Charley gritted her teeth, her breath fast. Congealing blood cleared enough that they could see the deep cut running along Charley's rib.

"I think it grazed him," Williamson said. "It doesn't look like the bullet's in there anywhere. Does it feel like it is?"

Charley growled. "How should I know? It hurts like hell. Does that help?"

"Yeah, you did probably break a rib," Williamson said thoughtfully.

The tent flap opened again, and Elias said, "Williamson, what the hell does yarrow look like?"

Williamson looked up at him with a curl to his mouth Henry had never seen before, like he thought Elias was saying something extraordinarily stupid and couldn't understand why. He gave an exasperated sigh and got to his feet.

"Come on, I'll show you." Then he looked over his shoulder. "Schaefer, grab a clean shirt and hold it firm over the wound until I get back. He's still bleeding."

The tent closed again. Henry scrambled to get his pack off his back.

"Can't you use his shirt? It's already ruined," Jacob said.

"No, a clean one. I don't want to risk any infection," Henry replied. He didn't know much about wounds, but he knew that much. He pulled his clean shirt from the bottom of his knapsack and used Jacob's jackknife again to hack one sleeve off at the elbow. He bundled it up and pressed it on Charley's wound.

"Ouch!" she cried.

"Here, put your arm down, hold it there."

"Shut up, Robinson, you damned piece of horseshit."

"What did I do?"

"Did you tell Williamson?"

"No! I ... how dare you? I didn't tell a soul! I swore on my mother's grave, how could you even think—"

"Leave off it! He's got a full view of my chest, and he hasn't said nothing. He's the dimmest boy in the entire world. If he didn't already know, there's no way he wouldn't be surprised to learn it now."

"Clearly not that dim, since he's the only one who knows about yarrow." Henry lifted his eyebrows and pressed his mouth into a thin line.

"Yarrow, that's nonsense," Jacob flapped his hand. "You're taking your life in your hands, Smith, and you need to know I think it's damn foolish."

"Oh, thank you very much for your concern. WHAT MAKES YOU THINK I CARE WHAT YOU THINK?!"

"Don't shout, Charley, come on. You're hurt." It looked like it hurt to shout like that too.

"Henry, just you wait, I've got words for you too—"

Henry bristled. "You're wounded! Stop this. Just let us help you!"

"I don't want your help."

"Yeah, yeah, you'd rather die. I know." Henry growled. "Over my dead body."

"Can you two stop acting like Romeo and Juliet for two minutes please?"

Henry and Charley both turned and snapped, "Shut up, Jacob!"

"We're back!" Williamson sailed into the tent with Elias on his heels. His hands were clutching handfuls of a wilted, weedy-looking plant, its leaves a little yellowed but still bushy with fronds. He looked between Henry, Jacob, and Charley and lifted his brows. "Excuse me."

Henry and Jacob moved aside.

"Nice bandage, Schaefer," Williamson said. "Here, Smith, open up." He proffered a few fronds at her mouth.

"I'm sorry, what?" Charley snapped.

"Chew the leaves up."

"Why?"

"So I can put them on your wound."

"I'm hurt, you do it."

"That's precisely why you have to do it." Williamson waited, but she didn't open her mouth. He gave a long sigh. "You don't want to get an infection. But you can't infect yourself, can you? Whatever's inside you is already there."

Charley glowered for a moment longer. Then she opened her mouth. Williamson merrily stuffed her mouth full of delicate fronds. They looked remarkably like dill, to Henry's untrained eye.

She chewed and glowered and chewed some more.

"That's good," Williamson smiled and put his hand out for her to spit the masticated leaves out.

"Ugh, disgusting," Elias said.

Williamson gestured for Henry to lift his makeshift bandage, which he did. Charley put her arm gingerly up over her head again, and used the other to clutch the opposite edge of her sack coat tightly over her chest. Williamson patted the leaves down over her wound in an old-fashioned poultice.

"There," he said, sitting back on his heels. He looked at Henry expectantly.

"What now?" Henry asked, feeling rather stupid.

"Oh," Williamson said with a start. "Right, sorry." He stood up. "Come on, fellows, let's go."

"What?" Jacob said.

"Why?" Elias added on top of him.

"So Schaefer can bind his wound," Williamson said, again with that exasperated tone as though it were obvious. "He'll want some privacy, I should think, since it'll need to go around his whole chest.

Elias' eyes sharpened at that, looking right at Charley's chest.

"Jacob," Henry hissed.

"Yeah, yeah, I'll take care of it." Jacob flapped a hand and hauled Elias out of the tent. Williamson hovered at the entrance.

"You do know how to bind a wound, don't you?" he asked.

Henry threw his shoulders back. "No, I don't. But you're right, Charley won't want you here."

"He can help," Charley said. Henry looked over at her with such relief he could hardly stand it. He didn't realize how afraid he was to hurt her until she conceded to help. "As long as he keeps in line."

"I don't have to touch you at all," Williamson said with his hands up. "I'll just tell Schaefer what to do."

"With your eyes closed."

"Sure, of course."

———

If Charley laid perfectly still, the pain dulled to a throb. A steady thrum of ache consistent with the rhythm of her heartbeat. She had to focus on breathing shallowly; if she forgot and took a deep breath, she'd disrupt her ribs, which would spark her wound, and set off the entire cycle of pain and fear all over again. The only thing she could do was focus on breathing shallowly, carefully observe that dull thrum of pain, and *not* think about how everything was falling apart.

Snippets of battle skated across her mind, along with half-formed worries and blunt facts. Henry was alive. She'd killed three men with her bayonet. She'd managed to avoid the hospital tent. Williamson knew her secret now. Hower too. Henry's hand was stroking her hair.

"Where are the others?" she whispered. It didn't hurt to speak anymore. Thank heavens for small miracles.

"Outside," Henry replied. His voice was also quiet. The squad must be nearby if he was being so quiet. Every sound carried through the canvas of the tent, even the sound of footsteps approaching. Charley's eyes swivelled to the tent flap.

"Oh, you're all here."

She could hear the voice clear as day through the walls of the tent. It was Webster and his tired voice was somewhat surprised. He must have finally returned from the hospital tent.

"Are we supposed to be elsewhere?" Hower inquired.

"Most of the regiment is chasing Rebs over hill and dale," Webster replied. "I'm a little surprised to find you all here."

"You needed help getting Osborn back," Hower said. Charley could hear the shrug in his voice.

"I did, though I'm not sure I needed all six of you."

"Smith's wounded too," Williamson said.

Inside the tent, Charley squirmed. She felt Henry sit up straighter to listen too.

"What?" Webster, bless him, sounded so concerned. "Is he alright?"

"Yeah," Williamson replied. "He's just in there."

A moment later, the tent flaps flung open. Webster and his drooping side-whiskers leaned in. "Corporal? Are you alright?"

Charley tried to sit up. "Yessir." She winced, then winced again for giving her pain away.

"What happened? Did that mangy Reb actually manage to shoot you?"

Charley gave a weak gesture that referenced a shrug, but she couldn't manage a real one because it hurt too much. "Seems that way."

Webster's face fell into a grimace. After a moment of his chin working, he stomped into the tent. "What the hell are you doing in here, then? Get to the hospital tent!"

Charley wasn't sure she'd ever heard Webster swear. Williamson, Robinson, and Hower were cramming in behind him, and Krüger's face loomed between the tent flaps. The tent got very crowded very quickly.

"It's just a flesh wound," Charley said, attempting to sit up properly without wincing, to prove her ease. "Williamson cleaned me up. I didn't even need any stitches."

Webster spluttered. "Who would be giving you stitches? Nevermind, don't answer that."

"How's the Sarg?" Williamson asked.

Webster's face, already pale and drawn, sagged. "Not well, but he's with the surgeon now. As you should be, Smith, if you value your own well-being."

Charley attempted a smile. "I don't need to worry the surgeon over something so little."

"Little? *Little?* Smith, you took a bullet for me, the twin of one that has Ned in a fit of fever!" Webster shouted. His voice was hoarse and wavering. "I will not have your life on my conscience as well. Get to the hospital tent now. That's an order."

Charley's throat felt tight, like someone had their boot to her neck. Henry's hands gripped her shoulders. He was still sitting behind her. "Webster," Henry said, "it's really not necessary."

Webster stared at Henry for a moment with a truly exasperated expression. He threw his hands up. "Have I died and gone to some level of purgatory where my endless punishment is to have you lot refuse to listen to me?"

He looked back at the other fellows at his shoulders. Robinson avoided his eyes, and Williamson shrugged.

"Why on God's great, green earth would you not want to have the surgeon see to a wound?" Webster spluttered.

Hower snorted.

Charley's heart was slamming in her chest now.

Webster spun to look at Hower. "What? What is going on here?"

Hower threw his own hands up as he looked around. "Come on, really?" He turned back to Webster with an exasperated expression. "He doesn't want to go to the hospital tent because he doesn't want anyone finding out he's a girl."

"Elias!" Jacob shouted and smacked him in the chest.

A din of voices went up inside the tent. Charley wasn't following it all, wasn't hearing much of anything except the roar of blood in her own ears. Her chest seized until it hurt, like her own body had her by the windpipe, and it was so much worse to breathe so shallowly with a broken rib. Fuck. *Fuck.*

"A woman?" Krüger boomed, then set off in German. Charley couldn't understand anything he was saying, but it incited Henry enough that he shot up from behind her and charged at him. Williamson caught him by one of his arms before he could land a fist in Krüger's eye—

"ENOUGH!" Webster shouted.

The din stopped short. Charley was curled in on herself, just watching it all happen. Watching it slip away into nothing, all the months she'd spent hiding in plain sight, everything she worked for, everything they'd been to her. It felt almost satisfying, to see it all go up in smoke like this. Well, not satisfying, but inevitable, at least. Next, they'd look at her the way her father did, the way Richard did, with that exasperated frustration. She'd been a fool to dream this. She'd been mad to try. She'd gotten a lot farther than she'd ever imagined, though she'd wished for so much more. She looked at Henry, held by Williamson with an arm around his chest, his face angry and pained. He met her gaze with a furiously helpless expression.

"Enough," Webster repeated. He looked down at Charley, his mouth a grim line. Something about his face resolved, because Charley felt her fate seal.

"Smith, you're being a damned careless fool, as usual," he said. "But if you weren't, I'd be carrying that bullet wound instead of you." Webster blinked hard. "You saved my life. And for that I'm grateful."

"Webster, you're not just gonna—"

"Hower. Shut up." Webster had a commanding voice when he needed it. "We've seen a whole lot of things today we'd never thought possible."

Hower was taken aback, but he didn't say anything. His eyes glanced at Charley, then skidded away, abashed.

"Sir, we cannot stand by while such..." Krüger said, English failing him as he flapped his hand between Charley and Henry.

Webster regarded the connection that gesture implied. His eyes tracked up to Krüger's face and the grimace he settled on him was fierce indeed. "We fought for our lives today. We survived, in no small part because of the duty and courage of your corporal. I for one will not hear a word against him." Webster turned to Hower. "You hear me? After what we've seen today, I should think you were ready to set aside baseless gossip. One of our number is on death's door. A friend, a comrade. And *this* is what you concern yourself with? You should be ashamed of yourselves. As far as I can tell, every one of us in this tent fought today like men. I don't need to know anything else. Neither should you."

Webster gave Charley a hard look. "If you say you don't need the surgeon, then I believe you. I apologize for interfering."

Webster pushed his way through the other men and out of the tent. Robinson's mouth was hanging open. Hower looked like he wanted to crawl into the ground. Williamson had released Henry and was rubbing his forehead with his hand.

Krüger glowered at her and shook his head. "This is unacceptable."

"They're married!" Robinson blurted.

Krüger was taken aback for a moment. His lip curled incredulously as he looked between Henry and Charley again. "What?"

"You heard me," Robinson said more firmly. "And you heard the Sarg." He looked over at Charley. "We'd better let Smith get some well-deserved and much-needed rest."

"Yeah," Williamson added. "He's got a lot of healing yet to do, and we'll be on the march again as soon as the regiment gets back."

Robinson ducked through the tent flap, pulling Krüger along with him. Williamson followed. Hower dithered at the exit.

"Smith, uh," he said. "I didn't mean—Well, yeah. Sorry."

Charley could not bear to dignify that with a response. She aimed her fury down at the packed earth floor until she heard the tent flaps close behind him.

Henry exhaled all at once, like he'd been holding his breath the whole time. "Jesus fucking Christ." The next moment, he was kneeling in front of her. "Charley. Oh, Charley."

Charley opened her mouth and gasped in a big clutch of air. It *hurt* and her voice hitched, and then she was in Henry's arms, weeping through a cycle of relief and shame and pain with every inhale.

"It'll be alright," Henry murmured into her hair. "I'm with you, no matter what happens. It'll be alright."

———

XXX

8 miles outside of Somerset, Kentucky
Monday, January 20, 1862

CHARLEY WOKE FROM A fitful sleep to the painful reminder that she was still wounded. Still wounded, and her secret still ruthlessly exposed. In spite of Webster's orders, that wound felt even more tender than the one the bullet had rent in her side.

"Oh, good." Williamson's face swam into her vision. "Time to change your dressing."

Charley winced. "You just put it on."

"That was yesterday. It's Monday, Smith, and guess what?"

"What? Where's Henry?"

"He's sleeping just there," Williamson nodded to her side. Henry was curled up, his mouth soft with exhaustion. "We have only twelve dead and twenty four wounded. Well, twenty five, including you."

"Oh," Charley thought about that for a moment. "Wait, is that all? In the whole Union army?"

"Well, no, just in our regiment. I think I heard something like thirty killed and maybe two hundred wounded?"

"Well, still." Charly was astonished. "There must have been at least five hundred rebels lying on that battlefield. That has to be a Union best."

"It's the greatest victory the Union has ever seen!" Williamson smiled, and he didn't look silly or vapid or dim. He looked kind. Charley blinked. Had she been misreading kindness for foolishness her entire life? Dear God. That couldn't be.

"I have some more yarrow for you to chew up," Williamson said, holding up the leaves.

"Oh, goody." Charley turned her head to see who else was in the tent. She was careful not to move too much but still, oh, it hurt like the dickens.

"Don't worry, they're all gone."

"Where'd they go?"

"Hospital tent," Williamson said. His smile fell. "Sergeant Osborn isn't doing so well. He was shot through the body, straight through. The bullet didn't lodge, so that's good, but it's still a damn painful wound, and he's got a terrible fever."

"Oh no," Charley said. "Did you check on him?"

"Oh, yes, I already brought him some yarrow yesterday," Williamson said. "Got some extra bandages from the surgeon, too. Here, let's just change out yours."

Charley frowned. "Do I have to?" Changing the bandage meant sitting up, and moving at all sounded like a terrible idea.

"I'm afraid so," Williamson said. "Come on."

Charley steeled herself and sat up. She tried focusing all her attention on chewing the slightly bitter yarrow, breathing heavily through the pain. Henry woke up and helped wrap her new bandage after Williamson packed her wound with fresh yarrow. The whole routine highlighted in sharp relief how very exposed her secret was.

"Well, you're all set," Williamson said, standing and dusting his hands. "I'm gonna go make some coffee."

"Thanks, Williamson," Henry smiled wistfully. "You're the hero of the Battle of Mill Springs."

"Ha ha, that's Smith," Williamson said and made for the exit.

"Williamson," Charley said before she realized she was speaking.

"Hm?"

"Thank you," she finished. She didn't know how to qualify it, or whether she even could.

"Of course," Williamson grinned. He tipped his forage cap and tied the tent flap behind him.

Henry helped Charley as she laid back down on the gum blanket. He regarded her with serious, earnest eyes in a way that made her feel flayed. "Charley, it's risky to stay. You're wounded, and we'll be back on the march as soon as the regiment gets back."

"Are they still gone? Did they catch up to the Rebs?"

"No, they got away."

"Damned sons of bitches."

"It's not all a loss—the Colonel of the Fourth Kentucky shot General Zollicoffer dead on the road before the battle had scarcely started."

"What?"

"They were both on the Mill Springs Road, maneuvering their troops. It was so foggy and they were wearing rain ponchos, they didn't realize they were facing the enemy. They drew revolvers when they figured it out, and our man shot Zollicoffer straight through the heart."

Charley stared at him. "That is ... extraordinarily stupid."

Henry smiled crookedly. "I thought you'd like that."

"Well, I won't begrudge the rebels for having incompetent leaders. In fact, they could use a lot more of them in my estimation."

Henry nodded. Charley let her eyes fall closed for a moment. Rain was pattering on the tent canvas again.

"Henry," Charley said after a moment. "Do you think I have a chance to stay?"

"What do you mean?"

"If the whole squad knows, how can I go on?"

Henry sighed. "I don't think anyone's going to report you. Webster made his orders clear. Hower and Krüger both seem abashed, or at least assuaged."

"As long as I belong to someone, my presence here can be excused?"

Henry shrugged. "I dunno. I guess. At least for now." He wrapped his arms around his knees. "I think you could manage a furlough for your wound."

"But what about you?"

"I'll go with you."

"You can't. They won't let you."

"They can go to hell."

"But then, when I'm well again, you can't come back with me."

Henry searched her eyes for a moment. "You want to come back?"

"Yes," Charley said. "Yes, of course."

He blinked at her. "Why?"

"Why? Why? *Why* does everyone keep asking me that? Aren't you all here too, enlisted to fight in the single-most important war our country has ever seen? Don't you have a duty to the Union? Don't you *care*?"

Henry's brows knitted together. "I do care. But I care about you more. And I think, after yesterday, after seeing what glorious battle actually looks like... I'm not sure it's worth the lives being spent."

"So you'd just let the rebels have their slave country?"

"No, of course not."

"You'd let other men fight and die for you?"

"No. No! Of course not!"

Charley scowled. "If I wasn't here, would you keep on fighting?"

"Yes, of course."

"Then why do you think we need to stop now?"

Henry spluttered. "Charley, you're *wounded*—"

"So is Sergeant Osborn. Do you see Webster at his sick bed imploring him to desert, to go back home and let someone else fight?"

Henry's mouth hung open. He didn't say anything.

Charley hissed. "I don't need you to protect me." She held her chin tight against its trembling. "I can fight. I can take a hit. I can win. I thought you believed that too."

"I do, Charley, I do," Henry said. "I just ... dammit, Charley, you could have *died*. I was terrified. I can't lose you."

"You can't control that," she shot back. She sounded like Kloepfer. Perhaps his was a wisdom one could only earn with cannonfire. "This is what I want. This is where I belong. I'm going to stay until they force me out. If you think the boys will keep it secret, then I'm going to see it through."

Henry looked like she was causing him pain.

"Henry, please."

He seized her hand with both of his. He pressed his lips to her knuckles.

"I'm going to have to march no matter what," Charley said. "Whether I'm sick or well. A furlough would take me away from you, which you don't want. So I'll just have to get better."

Henry looked up at her. His blue eyes were round.

Charley steeled herself. "Go on. Tell me the truth—how bad is the wound?"

"It's stopped bleeding." His voice sounded tired and scratchy. "It'll leave a scar, but it doesn't need stitching. At least, that's what Williamson thinks."

Charley nodded. "I haven't been feverish either."

"That's really good."

"It's just going to hurt for the first few days."

That looked like it hurt Henry. Charley reached out and touched his cheek. "It'll be alright, Henry. I'll be alright."

His face was still pinched. "You'll tell me when you get tired."

Charley tried not to roll her eyes.

"No, Charley, I'm serious. Don't push yourself too hard. You're not alone, not anymore. You're in a squad, and the only way through is to work together. Surely we've learned that by now. If you would just let us help you the way you help us, then I think I can believe that it'll be alright. But if you refuse help and suffer silently, I won't be able to trust you when you say you're fine."

Charley's lip curled. She didn't like that. She didn't like that because ... because ... well, what if she took too much?

"You have that look on your face."

"What look?"

"The one that breaks my heart and I don't know why." He reached out and touched her face. "I will help. We all will. You can depend on it."

"I cannot."

"No, you have not, because you haven't been able to depend on it in the past. Take a leap of faith, Charley. It's paid off so far."

Charley swallowed that and made a face. It didn't go down easy. She reached out and held onto him by his lapels.

"I love you, Charley."

"Ugh, why do you have to be like this?" she said into his chest.

Henry laughed. "What, loving you?"

"Yes." Charley twisted his coat in her hands. "You invite all sorts of misfortune."

"I do not."

She looked up at him. "I got a bullet wound that says otherwise."

Henry shook his head. "Shut up. I'm going to kiss you now."

"If you must." Her words were cut off by his lips, pressing down onto hers. God, this would never get old. If she lived for a hundred years, the warm application of his lips would never stop feeling like a homecoming.

"Coffee's ready!" Williamson's voice called from outside the tent.

Henry pulled back. "Do you want to try getting up?"

"Do you think I should?"

"I dunno..."

"Hey, Williamson!" Charley shouted. "Can I get up?"

"Sure! Give it a shot!"

Henry was wincing. "Well, you can't be that bad off if you can shout that loud."

Charley laughed and let Henry help her to her feet. It felt nice, once she shucked off the fear that he was a finite resource. Well, it also hurt like hell, but the pain wasn't so bad either, if she didn't believe it was an infinite well.

Henry helped her through the tent flaps and out to the campfire. It felt good to move her body, stiff from lying on the ground. Hower, Robinson, and Krüger were out there, tin cups at the ready as Williamson served from the percolator. Charley's heart beat double quick time, not sure what they would do.

"Hey, he's up and walking!" Robinson cheered.

Charley gave a weak smile. "It's just a broken rib. The bullet only grazed me."

"Only grazed him, ha," Robinson said. "If you hadn't gone after that reb, Smith, Webster would have taken that bullet."

Krüger said something in German around his cup of coffee. Charley looked to Henry expectantly.

Henry grinned.

"What? What'd he say?"

"You're not gonna like it."

Charley glowered. "Tell me."

"He said, 'That makes you a hero.'" Henry's crooked smile crinkled his cheeks. "By definition, in fact."

"Schaefer told me you'd take a bullet for any of us," Robinson said. "And I didn't believe him, but look at that, he was right."

"Glad we elected you corporal," Hower said as he sidled up, digging his cup out of his haversack. "I don't think I could have done it."

"You wouldn't have even thought to do it," Robinson corrected.

"I'm not taking bullets for all of you, if that's what you're thinking," Charley said as she sat gingerly on a log with Henry's arm to steady her. Williamson filled her cup with coffee.

"How about we don't take anymore bullets at all?" he suggested, setting the kettle to the side of the fire to keep warm.

"I'll drink to that!"

"Here here!"

Charley held her cup out with her right hand. Her ribs hurt like the dickens, but the bitter, watery coffee was satisfying. There was something about coffee that made everything feel more surmountable.

"Where have you been?" Henry asked Hower as Williamson filled his cup. Charley's eyes swiveled to look at Hower sideways. Out of all the fellows, he was the least reliable with her secret, proven already during the confrontation with Webster that still made Charley feel like she was going to puke just thinking about it.

Hower looked down into his cup sheepishly. "I was over talking to Griffiths. He said if Smith needs a break from the march tomorrow—or whenever we head out on the road again—he can ride with him and the other teamsters."

Charley couldn't help but squint in confusion. "Why?"

Hower rolled his eyes. "Because your rib is broke and marching for 20 miles with 45 pounds on your back is probably not the wisest path to recovery."

"No, I mean why did you arrange it for me?"

Hower opened his mouth, but didn't say anything right away. "I, uh . . . yeah, I guess I owed you one. After last night . . ."

Charley blinked at him. She really hadn't expected anything from Hower, except perhaps for him to double down and maintain he'd done nothing wrong. But apparently, he was compunctious enough to make arrangements for her.

"What exactly did you tell Griffiths?" Henry asked delicately. Christ, of course. Charley's lungs seized a bit while she waited for Hower's response.

Hower's eyes went wide and innocent. His mouth flapped aghast. "I refuse to acknowledge what you're implying, Henry Schaefer. I simply informed Griffiths that Smith had sustained an injury that, while not immediately serious, would make marching exceedingly uncomfortable."

"He didn't wonder why I wouldn't travel with the surgeon and the other wounded men?" Charley was fairly impressed with how even she was able to assert that inquiry, given that she felt almost lightheaded with dread.

Hower shrugged. "I think he just thought if you were that hurt, you'd be with them, and if you're not, you're probably just fine and looking for an excuse to skirt the tedium of the march."

"I'm surprised he'd take anyone on," Henry said. "After all those nights waiting for the wagons, I imagine the teamsters have to beat fellows back with sticks from trying to tag along with them."

"It's too bad it's so wet in these parts," Williamson mused. "If it were colder, they could convert all the wagons to sleds and it would probably be easier going."

"Maybe we'd have more reliable access to supplies, but we'd still have to march in the snow," Hower argued.

"It's already cold enough for me, thanks," Robinson added.

Charley sipped her cup of coffee and watched as the banter bounced casually around the campfire like it always did, like nothing whatever at all had changed. It hadn't, mostly, except it had in an extraordinary way. But it seemed the squad had no interest in discussing Charley's sex any further, and it wasn't just because Webster had ordered them not to. It seemed quite possible—probable, in fact—that the fellows were operating not under orders, but under their own sense of duty.

The realization of this felt more like wishful thinking than anything, but Charley sucked it in and held it close. When she'd stolen trousers and signed her name to the enlistment roll, she'd expected to struggle, to work hard, to fight and get hurt and face death square in the face. She hadn't anticipated fellowship. Love. Belonging.

Hell. She stared hard into her coffee cup until the prickling behind her eyes subsided.

———

Epilogue

Faribault, Minnesota
September 28, 1873

HANNAH SCHAEFER STEPPED OFF the train at the Faribault station alone. There had been plenty of people onboard, but it seemed no one else was especially interested in disembarking at Faribault, not when the train was bound for St. Paul. The sun was bright in her eyes and she adjusted her flat straw hat with one hand, the other clinging to the handles of her bag that contained all she had ever owned in her eleven years of life.

Hannah's heart began to race. She didn't see her uncle anywhere outside. If he wasn't here, she wasn't sure what she would do. Wait, she supposed. What more could she do? She walked across the dry gravel and stepped up onto the boardwalk that lined the front of the station. Behind the train loading passengers departing Faribault was only rolling prairie. There didn't seem to be a town.

Hannah entered the train station. It was just a small room, with a few benches and a booth for the conductor. The conductor wasn't there, though. Her uncle wasn't there either. In fact, no one was inside the station but Hannah. She started to sweat.

She crossed the station and exited the other side. There were railroad tracks on this side as well, and, blessedly, a view of the sprawling town dotted with houses among many shady trees. There was a river beyond. The tall bluff on the other side was the only landform that was anything but flat. The breeze stirred her calico dress and made her braids dance over her shoulders.

"Hannah!"

She looked over her shoulder, northward toward a road that passed over the railroad tracks. Her uncle was striding through the grass toward her, waving his arm and grinning as he held his hat against the wind with his other hand. Hannah's relief swept through her, so much so that she felt her eyes water. Everything, it seemed, made that happen now. If her prevailing feeling wasn't fear, tears were never far from her reach.

"Uncle Henry!" Hannah cried in return, waving her arm back as she started toward him. She almost lost her hat as the breeze picked up, the ties behind her head sliding off. Her braids kept it in place, but half running, burdened by her heavy carpetbag, she ended up abandoning her wave to adjust her hat as she trundled along.

Uncle Henry cantered up to her and picked up her bag like it was nothing. "You're here!" he exclaimed. "I'm so glad."

He looked at Hannah for a long moment. He had very straight teeth and a very crooked smile. Hannah couldn't help but smile a bit in reply. It had been a long time since she'd seen him. Christmas, perhaps? He always came calling in New Ulm that time of year with a sackful of oranges, if the weather permitted. She felt like she should embrace him now. It would be the normal thing for family to do, especially in these circumstances, but they hadn't yet, so it felt strange to do it now.

"Thank you," Hannah said politely, though she wasn't sure what for. For taking her bag? Meeting her here? Taking her in when the only person in the whole world who cared about her had gone?

The tears pricked again. Hannah tried to smile, to push them away.

Uncle Henry was tall. He crouched down a bit so his face was even with hers.

"Don't worry," he said, a bracing hand on her shoulder. "You're here now. Come on, Charley's over there with the wagon. Let's get you home."

Hannah blinked back her tears and nodded. She wouldn't be pitied. There were many children who didn't have a kind relation at all to take them in under circumstances like these.

The pastor at the church had reminded her as much as they interred her mother. He'd told her about orphans in the eastern cities loaded up on trains to be adopted by complete strangers out west. How lucky she was, that she had family to look after her. She counted her blessings and followed Uncle Henry to the road, where a wagon waited.

Seated on the bench was a wiry man, with dark hair and heavy brows. He had a sort of romantic look to him, serious and clean-shaven, with hands gracefully holding the reins.

"Hannah, you remember my buddy, Charles Smith?" Uncle Henry said.

Hannah did. She'd met him a handful of times. He was quiet and Hannah hadn't the faintest idea about him, other than he worked the farm with Uncle Henry and they'd fought together in the war. "How do you do, Mr. Smith?"

Mr. Smith nodded at her. He only glanced at her before he turned his eyes back to the reins, his chin working around the piece of sweet grass he had between his teeth. Hannah could tell he didn't like her much.

Uncle Henry helped her climb up onto the bench, where she sat between him and Mr. Smith. The wagon lurched forward and trundled west, out into the rolling prairie.

———

"Hannah, are you ready? Come on, you're gonna be late!"

Hannah scampered down the steep steps from the attic chamber she'd made her bedroom in. It was nothing more than a narrow bed, a chest of drawers, and a window, but she'd made it her own with some wildflowers and the quilt her mother had made her.

"Yes, sorry," Hannah called as she reached the bottom of the stairs and snatched her hat off the peg on the wall. The room might be called a foyer, but it was rustic enough that the name didn't suit it well.

Mr. Smith came through the door from the kitchen with a basket. "You'll bring your lunch. You won't have time to walk back."

"Yes, sir," Hannah said, accepting the basket with both hands. Mr. Smith hadn't warmed much to her in the week she'd been in his house. His cold, serious manner made her uncomfortable addressing him with anything but honorifics, which felt both respectful and alienating in a house that was supposed to be her new home.

Mr. Smith was looking at her with narrowed eyes. Hannah shrank a bit under his study. "Sir?"

His mouth twitched for a moment. "Your braids are crooked," he finally said.

"Oh." Hannah wilted. She wasn't used to braiding her own hair yet—her mother had always done that—and she didn't have a mirror in her room. She didn't want to complain, or be pitiful, so she said nothing and blinked the pricking in her eyes away.

Mr. Smith sighed. "Come, sit." He gestured into the kitchen. "Quickly now."

It took a moment for Hannah to comply. "I thought we were already late?"

"Better to be a little late and make a good impression than to be on time and slovenly," Mr. Smith said. Hannah bowed her head. He winced slightly.

In the kitchen, Uncle Henry looked up from the percolator on the hob. "Charley?"

"It'll take just a minute," Mr. Smith said as Hannah sat in the chair at the work table. "Can I fix your braids?"

Hannah couldn't help but regard him dubiously. "Yes?"

Mr. Smith pulled the ribbons off the ends of her braids and pulled his elegant fingers through to release her hair. Uncle Henry was looking between her and his farmhand with some skepticism, but said nothing.

"Sorry, Uncle Henry," Hannah felt compelled to say. "I ... I'm not very good at braiding my own hair."

"Don't apologize for anything that isn't your fault," Mr. Smith said crisply as he parted her hair cleanly. "You did as well as you could have given we haven't even got a mirror."

Hannah nodded and choked down the urge to apologize for apologizing. It hadn't been long since she arrived, but she couldn't stop thinking about the orphan trains. She didn't want to impose upon Uncle Henry or Mr. Smith, and she was sure two bachelor farmers had no interest in the trials and tribulations of a little girl. They'd only taken her in out of duty. But she wanted to stay, and she intended to make herself as useful and unobtrusive as possible. Except, well, she had already failed.

Mr. Smith was surprisingly deft. He braided each side so tight Hannah's eyebrows were pulled halfway to her crown.

"There," he said, letting Hannah tie the ends off with ribbon herself. "That's better."

"Very sharp," Uncle Henry agreed, absently holding out a tin cup of fresh cup of coffee to Mr. Smith as he regarded Hannah. "You'll make a fine impression."

Hannah ran her fingers lightly over her braids. Mr. Smith had braided them the French way and the braids went all the way up over her temples. She looked at him. "How did you know how to do that?"

Mr. Smith looked down into his cup of coffee and shrugged. "Sisters."

––––––

The waning sun set the fall colors alight in orange and pink and violet. The hill across the Straight River was ablaze as the cold breeze undulated across the woods, with the School for the Deaf perched atop like a royal fortress. The view squeezed Hannah's heart, reminding her of the oaks and maples that had framed the drive to her mother's house in New Ulm.

Faribault was aflutter with harvest activities, wagons hauling in grain to the elevator from the fields and farmhands, tired out from long hours in the field, drinking their fill at the saloons on Main Street. Hannah bumped along the road on the wagon seat, shoulder knocking against Uncle Henry's as they slowly made their way down Fourth Street. Hannah's bones were tired too. It had been a hard day in the sweltering kitchen, canning with her uncle and Mr. Smith, but it could have been worse. It wasn't near as hard as flailing wheat or shocking corn.

"This'll be a good break," Henry said, pulling the horses up in front of Hower Hotel. "Their cook does an excellent roast."

A dinner prepared by a professional cook. Hannah had never imagined she'd be eating a meal like that. Serving it, perhaps, but dining as a guest at a fancy hotel? She supposed it was the kind of class-mixing that only happened when fellows had served in the same regiment. She reached down and pulled at the cuffs of her sleeves. She had her Sunday best on, but it was a little small. Mr. Smith thought she was hitting her growth spurt. It was a lonely feeling, growing into womanhood all on her own. It made her miss her mother all anew.

Uncle Henry handed the horses' reins to the hostler of the hotel, puffing his chest out and making some joke that made the young hostler's cheeks crack with a laugh. Her uncle was dressed in his best wool suit, with a fine felt hat and his beard freshly trimmed.

Mr. Smith was turned out nicely too. He was always closely shaved, but he'd combed his dark hair back and spent the previous evening brushing his suit coat while Uncle Henry read aloud by the hearth. It seemed that even though the owner of the hotel was an old war buddy, they didn't get invited to dine all that often. Hannah was determined to make a good impression.

Uncle Henry led the way into the front doors of the hotel, striding right up to the innkeeper's desk. Hannah supposed at a place this nice, he probably wasn't called an innkeeper, but she didn't rightly know what to call him, so she kept her mouth shut.

"We're Mr. Hower's guests this evening," Uncle Henry said. "Mr. Henry Schaefer and Miss Hannah, and Mr. Charles Smith."

Hannah stood between her two new guardians as the innkeeper, for lack of a better title, led them back through the hotel to a small private dining room with windows that looked out over Main Street. There was a group of people standing around the table, grouped up into smaller conversation groups. They all turned when they arrived.

"Schaef!" cried a man with sandy blond hair and a mustache that curved round his mouth and connected with his sideburns. "Smith! So glad you could make it. And this must be your new ward."

Hannah smiled politely at the fellow. He was dressed in a fine wool suit with a silk vest and a gold watch chain.

"Yes, this is Miss Hannah Schaefer," Henry introduced with a fond expression that soothed some of the tension in Hannah's shoulders.

"Your brother's girl?" asked a lovely blonde woman with a kind, heart-shaped face. She wore a sumptuous violet gown with a large bustle trimmed out in exquisite, box-pleated ribbon. Hannah tried not to gape as the woman grasped her hand. "I'm so sorry to hear about your mother. My deepest condolences, my dear. We're so glad you can be here with us tonight."

The woman's eyes were a sparkling blue and when Hannah looked up into them, she was surprised to find that the woman was deeply sincere.

"Oh, but where are my manners?" the woman laughed. "I'm Mrs. Hower. It's so nice to meet you. But of course, you don't want to spend the evening with us boring old folks. Come, let me introduce you to the others."

Mrs. Hower delivered Hannah directly across the room, to where a girl and a boy stood together. The girl was younger than Hannah, but the boy appeared around Hannah's same age, but it was hard to tell.

"Miss Hannah Schaefer, please meet Miss Mary Robinson," Mrs. Hower introduced. "And this is her brother, James Robinson."

"How do you do?" Hannah said with a little bob. Immaculate manners felt like a matter of course with Mrs. Hower in that gown, but the Robinson children's regard made her wonder if it was a bit overly formal.

"Good evening," James Robinson said, reaching out to clasp Hannah's hand. His sister, Mary, snatched Hannah's hand first.

"Oh, I know you from school!" Mary exclaimed. "You're not in my form, but I remember seeing you."

"Yes, of course," Hannah said, blushing a little. She did recognize them both from the schoolhouse, but she hadn't had the courage to say much to anyone at school yet even though she'd been there for almost a month now. "I'm glad to see you again."

"Hannah just started last week," Mary informed her brother in a superior tone as Mrs. Hower melted back into the group of fellows that had formed around Uncle Henry and Mr. Smith, collecting firm handshakes and hearty smacks on the back. "She's just moved here from New Ulm because her mother died."

"Mary!" James admonished. "I'm so sorry to hear that, Miss Schaefer. That must have been a real blow."

Hannah swallowed hard. "Thank you very much. My uncle and Mr. Smith were kind enough to take me in."

"How do you like Faribault?" Mary asked. She looked at Hannah intently. She had spritely eyes and a mouth that curled with mischief.

Hannah shifted under the girl's intense gaze. "It's fine. I grew up in New Ulm so it's not all that different."

"Oh, is that the German town?" James asked. "I went there with my father once, and everyone spoke German. It was like going to another country."

"Do you speak German, Hannah?" Mary asked eagerly.

"Yes, I do," Hannah replied, her cheeks hot under all the attention.

"Oh, speak some to us!" Mary cried, clapping her hands.

"I don't know—" Hannah started to demure, but then she was blessedly interrupted by the sharp ding of a spoon against a crystal glass.

"Thank you all for joining us this evening," Mrs. Hower announced as the din in the room settled and the guests all turned to regard her and Mr. Hower at the head of the dining table.

"It's my honor to host this annual gathering of our squad from the Second Minnesota," Mr. Hower put in. "It's been eight years since the war ended, and eight years that we've gathered thus. While we remember the comrades we lost, we also celebrate our victory and the beautiful families we are so lucky to have now that the war is done. So come, share our table and eat your fill in celebration of another harvest and another year on this blessed earth."

The guests all moved toward the table and took their seats. Hannah noticed there were little cards on each plate with their names. Golly, she felt like the queen of England.

"Come on, you're next to me," Mary whispered, taking Hannah's arm.

They were toward the foot of the table, on the far side from the windows. James was across from them, and at the foot of the table sat another little girl about six years old. She had shining gold hair in careful sausage curls framing her face.

"This is little Miss Minnie Hower," Mary said.

"Good evening, Miss Minnie," Hannah said. "I'm Hannah Schaefer. Thank you for having us."

"How do you do." The little girl nodded imperiously at Hannah.

"Do you know what's for dinner, Minnie?" James asked conspiratorially.

"There is a big apple strudel for dessert," Minnie replied. "I don't know what else. That's all I smelled."

Mary laughed. Minnie glowered.

"Do you know everyone here?" Mary asked Hannah, ignoring Minnie and the menu both as two servers came and set bowls of pea soup in front of each guest.

"Oh, no, I've never met anyone here before," Hannah replied distractedly as she tried to figure out which spoon to use. "Except you and James, of course. And my uncle and Mr. Smith."

"What's it like living with Mr. Smith?" Mary asked, her eyes wide.

"Oh, Mary, don't start," James sighed.

"I'm not!"

"Mary has a little crush on Mr. Smith," James intoned.

"I do not! I just think he's very interesting," Mary pouted.

"Yes, yes, very *interesting*," James teased.

"Hush you," Mary snapped.

"I don't think there's anything all that interesting about him," Hannah hedged. "He sort of keeps to himself." She didn't add that she was still quite sure he was none too pleased about Hannah coming to live with them.

"That *is* interesting!" Mary exclaimed. "Have you ever seen him do anything funny?"

Hannah frowned. "What do you mean?"

"I don't know," Mary shrugged. "I just think it's a little funny, you know, how clean shaven he is. Most fellows these days have beards, but Mr. Smith doesn't."

"I've never seen him with a beard in my whole life," James conceded.

"What do you mean?" Hannah asked, confused.

"It's just funny, how Mr. Schaefer never married. How they live together in the same house. Do they have separate bedrooms?"

Hannah frowned. "Of course they do. Well, at least they did before I arrived. There's only one bedroom in the house, though, apart from the attic, which is where I sleep." It was no wonder Mr. Smith was annoyed to have Hannah. He'd had to give up his room to her. "What are you getting at?"

James shook his head and pressed his face into his hands.

"I heard this story from out east, where a woman wrote a book about how she dressed up as a man and fought in the war—" Mary said eagerly, but James cut her off.

"And that's quite the sensational story, but we live in Faribault, Minnesota and nothing half so exciting has ever happened here," James said. "And even if that wild notion was true, why would Mr. Smith continue to dress as a man after the war?"

"I dunno, maybe he likes it?" Mary argued.

"Or maybe Mr. Smith is just one of those fellows who can't grow a proper beard," James replied, rolling his eyes. "Really, Mary. What must Hannah think of us?"

Mary glowered but didn't say anything more.

Hannah shifted uncomfortably and tried to come up with a different topic of conversation. "It's alright. Um, do you all live on a farm? Or here in town?" Hannah asked.

"On a farm," James replied. "We've got a homestead across the river, just south and east of town."

"Our father is a wonderful farmer," Mary said haughtily. "We grow wheat so fine they ship it up to Minneapolis for milling."

Hannah didn't think it would be polite to mention that most farmers in the area sold their wheat to the growing mills in Minneapolis.

Just then, a short, dark-haired woman stooped over Minnie ."Angel, are you eating your soup?"

"I don't like it," Minnie sniffed.

"Of course you do. You tried it last month and you were surprised how much you liked it. Remember?"

"No."

Hannah tried not to laugh. The woman studied Minnie carefully for a moment, and as she did, Hannah studied her. She had a severe low bun and an austere, black gown, though still finely made and fashionably bustled.

"That's Minnie's widowed aunt, Miss Sterling," Mary whispered in Hannah's ear. "She lost her husband in the war. She's like the queen of England, in mourning forever. So she lives here with her sister, Mrs. Hower, and helps run the hotel."

"Oh," Hannah said. "She's Mrs. Hower's sister?"

"I know," Mary squealed excitedly. "They look nothing alike!"

"Who is everyone else?"

"Right," Mary nodded. "Well, there's Mr. Osborn, the one with the mustache. He was their captain in the war. He's got some sort of medal for bravery. Charged some Rebels on a hill in Tennessee somewhere. Anyway. Mr. Williamson doesn't live here anymore, since his family went to Nebraska after the outbreak, but he comes back for this dinner every year. It's easier now that there's a train. Sometimes he brings his wife. She's the Indian lady sitting next to him. And that's my father, of course, and my mother. She grew up in St. Paul. We go back sometimes. The dress shops are *so* much nicer there."

Hannah pulled sheepishly at her too-short sleeves and tried to smile.

"And Mr. Kreuger—he's the big man by your uncle—he was in the regiment too."

Hannah could hear Mr. Kreuger talking animatedly to Uncle Henry. "Oh! He's Bavarian!"

"Huh?" Mary asked.

"From Bavaria. It's one of the German kingdoms. I can tell because he speaks German like my mother does. Did." Hannah frowned.

Mary reached out and squeezed her hand.

"It's alright," Mary whispered. "It's alright to be sad. You should be. If I had a daughter, I sure would feel bad if she didn't miss me when I was gone."

Hannah squeezed her hand back. "Thanks."

———

"Um, I was wondering..." Hannah started one morning over breakfast after autumn had faded into the stark cold of winter. "Do you think it might be alright if I went with Mary Robinson when her mother takes her to St. Paul?"

Mr. Smith was just resuming his seat, having topped off his coffee. It was dim in the kitchen, the single window framing the snowy prairie under perpetually low, leaden clouds. Uncle Henry looked up from his plate of fried eggs. "What for?"

"My Sunday dress needs replacing. I thought..." Hannah squirmed under his gaze. "I just ... well. Mary says the dress shops there ... they have more choices..."

Uncle Henry furrowed his brow. "There's nothing wrong with your Sunday dress. It looks very smart. Are those Robinson kids giving you guff?"

"Oh, no! Not at all. They're very kind," Hannah hurried to correct. "It's just... the sleeves on my dress are getting short, so I thought—"

"Is that all?" Uncle Henry grinned and leaned back in his chair. "That's an easy fix. We have some scrap linen somewhere. We'll just add some cuffs. That'll smarten up the whole get-up in a jiffy."

Hannah squinted as she tried to imagine Uncle Henry, with his big, blunt hands, sewing. She supposed he did. Neither of her guardians had a wife, after all, to do their mending. Mary was right. It was a bit odd.

"You can travel with the Robinsons, though, if they invite you," Uncle Henry added with an apologetic grin. "Get some ribbons or some other frippery, if you'd like."

Mr. Smith gave a cough.

Uncle Henry's eyes flicked to him immediately. "What?"

Mr. Smith looked up at him. "I don't see why she can't have a new dress."

Uncle Henry's brows knitted. "I thought we were drawing the purse strings after the bank panic?"

Mr. Smith pressed his lips together. "Yes. I know. But she's growing so fast. Pretty soon she'll be a young lady."

Uncle Henry blinked blankly. "And that warrants a new dress?"

"Yes," Hannah said, and was surprised when Mr. Smith said the same thing in chorus. She exchanged a glance with him, an awkward acknowledgement of fellow feeling.

"Yes," Mr. Smith said again. "At least get some new fabric. We can make it at home—"

"—We can?" Hannah blurted. Fellows sewing was one thing, but it was impossible to imagine they knew how to pattern a dress.

Mr. Smith shrugged. "I seen patterns in that magazine Henry was reading from the other night."

Hannah tilted her head to peer at him, quite at a loss.

"Jiminy, you don't know how to make a dress, do you?" Uncle Henry laughed. Mr. Smith hunched down into his chair and glowered. "How much does a girl's dress go for these days, anyway?"

Mr. Smith cast him a sidelong look and shrugged. "These days? Have you ever known how much a girl's dress goes for?"

Uncle Henry chuckled. "I suppose not."

"Who knows, now that gold is the only standard to be had..." Mr. Smith sighed. Hannah had heard many adults in the past year talking about gold and silver and coinage, but she hadn't the faintest idea what any of it meant. "If you wouldn't mind something secondhand, Hannah, I'm sure we can manage a new dress for you."

Hannah deflated a little. It was selfish of her to wish for a brand new dress, but she had allowed herself to hope, in the excitement of Mary's encouragement. "Of course, sir," she said, looking down into her toast.

"If your heart is set on new, we can try to make one," Mr. Smith offered, flickering an annoyed glance at how Uncle Henry snickered at him. "Honestly. I've sewn shirts before. It's a dress.

It's just a bunch of square panels gathered around a shirt, how hard can it be?"

Uncle Henry laughed, a warm booming sound that tempered the room. "I admire your optimism, Charley."

Mr. Smith glowered at him from beneath dark brows as leaden as the sky. Hannah giggled. He glanced at her and crossed his arms. "We'll make do."

Uncle Henry nodded and argued no further.

"Thank you, Uncle Henry," Hannah said, then quickly added, "Mr. Smith. Sir." She cleared her throat and glanced down at her empty plate. "May I be excused?"

"Of course," Uncle Henry said.

"Say, Hannah?"

Hannah froze from standing at her chair and looked up at Mr. Smith.

"You don't have to call me 'sir,'" Mr. Smith said. "Charley will do just fine."

Hannah blinked. She'd not expected that.

"Oh," she said. "Alright. Mr... Charley."

It felt so strange to say. Mr. Smith's shoulders tensed, like he felt it too. Uncle Henry glanced between the two of them, then laughed.

"What's funny?" Mr. Smith snapped at him.

"Nothing, nothing," Uncle Henry said with a lopsided grin.

"I have to get to school," Hannah said, turning to the foyer. She didn't have time to figure out how to deal with her uncle's surly roommate who was also her guardian too, in a way, but not really.

———

The winter persisted with bitter cold winds. After Christmas, there was a week where it was so cold, no one could go anywhere at all. Uncle Henry had fretted over Mr. Smith's scarf when he went out to make sure the cow's water didn't freeze over inside the barn. Apparently it was so cold, just a short trip to the barn could have given Mr. Smith frostbite.

After the holidays and the cold snap, Hannah visited St. Paul with Mary and her mother. She brought twenty dollars for a new dress and found that the amount did not get her far. Mrs.

Robinson was generous, though, and provided her with the difference to buy a bonafide poplin from the Montgomery Ward catalog, displayed near her size at one of the dress shops. It had some fading from being in the window, which garnered a small discount. When she brought the dress home, Mr. Smith insisted on fitting it to her properly. It was a bit long, so they added a few tucks to the skirt with the Singer machine. Mr. Smith was surprisingly deft with it.

School was back in earnest after the cold snap. By early February, the cold seemed like a given. By that point, the adults didn't seem to care if the wind burned the children's cheeks on the way to school.

One day at lunch, Mary turned to Hannah and without any preamble, asked, "Did Mr. Smith grow a beard yet?"

"Hm?" Hannah's mouth was full. There weren't many other children around, thank goodness. She and the Robinsons usually had the schoolhouse much to themselves, as most other children lived in town and walked home for lunch.

"It's been so cold, and I was wondering if Mr. Smith has grown a beard yet?"

Hannah swallowed. "I think you were right. I don't think he can."

Mary's eyebrows went up, just as James let out a long sigh.

"Mary, let it go," he groaned.

"I *cannot* let it go, James!" Mary cried. "I have a hunch and it's been months and there's still no evidence that conclusively proves I'm wrong."

"I think you have to prove you're right," James pointed out. "It's innocent until proven guilty. Not the other way around."

"But I'm not putting him on *trial*," Mary complained. "I only suppose that there's something about him that's *interesting*, and I want to know what it is."

"Do you?" James asked. "Or do you just want to keep believing in your cockamamie story that he's a woman in disguise?"

"Wouldn't that be so romantic, though?" Mary exclaimed. "Sarah Emma Edmonds did it! She was never caught, neither. She deserted so they wouldn't catch her when she got sick, but she got the government to give her an honorable discharge after all. I think it's perfectly possible that other women did that and just never got caught."

"It's ridiculous."

"I just told you it's not!" Mary stuck her tongue out at James.

Hannah sat back and thought seriously about it. She'd never seen Mr. Smith shave. But she'd also never seen him dress or cut his hair or even trim his fingernails. She knew he brushed his teeth, but she'd also never expressly seen him do that either. He was a private man and did private things privately. There was nothing strange about that.

"I don't think there's any basis for it," Hannah said finally. "If Mr. Smith were actually a woman, that would... well, what would that make him to my uncle? They were friends in the war and now they're business partners."

"Maybe they're secretly married!" Mary whispered loudly, with wild eyes.

Hannah stared at her for a moment. "No. That's nonsense."

———

That evening, Hannah sat near the fireplace in the kitchen while Uncle Henry read aloud and Mr. Smith sat back in his chair and listened with his eyes closed.

"'Now hear me, both of you,'" Henry read. It was a story from some serial journal. He liked to do theatrical voices for all the characters. According to Mr. Smith, he'd done that for years before Hannah had ever arrived. "'You have betrayed my confidence in the most shameful manner by endeavoring to elope with my daughter.'"

Hannah was working on the hem of her new dress, but the light from the fire was poor.

"'I won't be snubbed so. I am old enough to love—' cried Emily. Her father raised his hand to her. 'You are but a child, and this man, a villain for stealing your heart!'"

Hannah sighed and set the work down so she could stand and throw another log onto the fire.

Uncle Henry paused from reading as she did so. "I suppose that means you'd like to hear another chapter?"

Hannah shrugged. "I suppose so."

"I didn't think you cared much for this one."

Hannah sighed. "I don't. I just don't think it seems very reasonable. It's all flights of fancy and melodrama. Real life isn't like that."

Uncle Henry ticked an eyebrow up at her. "Isn't it? I saw some pretty dramatic affairs during the war, I'll tell you that much."

"Yeah, but that's war. That's different."

"Sometimes, I think a boring life is the best thing we can hope for," Mr. Smith piped up.

Hannah couldn't help but let out a snicker as she remembered Mary's crackpot theory. "My friend Mary would disagree with you. She loves to tell tall tales."

"A sign of a peaceful youth," Uncle Henry grinned.

"She told a really funny one about you today," Hannah said with a grin to Mr. Smith.

"Oh really?" Mr. Smith said. "What did she say?"

Hannah opened her mouth to reply, then stopped. She wasn't sure if Mr. Smith would be insulted to be supposed a woman in disguise. "Oh, well..."

Mr. Smith held her gaze. "I'm sure it isn't anything I haven't heard before."

Hannah dithered. She tried to catch Uncle Henry's eye, but he was looking at Mr. Smith quite hard. "Oh, well. It's so silly, you'll laugh. She just read a book about this woman, you see, who dressed as a man to fight in the war, and she caught this fancy that you had done the same thing..."

Hannah cringed and looked down at her sewing. When she looked up again, Mr. Smith had his lips pressed into a thin line, and Uncle Henry had reached over to grip his hand. "I'm sorry. It's such a stupid notion. Insulting too, probably. I apologize for repeating it."

"No," Mr. Smith said slowly, giving Uncle Henry a long glance. "I'm glad you told us."

"What? Why?"

"Well," Mr. Smith played his fingers over Henry's. "Because, frankly, it's true."

Hannah gaped. "*What?*"

"We didn't know how to tell you, Hannah," Uncle Henry rushed in. "We wanted to, but as you can imagine, it's in Charley's best interest to keep that information quite close—"

"—But when we agreed to bring you here," Mr. Smith continued, "we knew we wanted to tell you. You'd be a member of our household and we didn't want to pretend that the pair of us are something we're not—"

"Something you're not?" Hannah whispered. She suddenly saw their enfolded hands in an entirely new light. "So you *are* secretly married? What? *What?*"

"Hannah, I know it's a lot to take in—" They'd been sharing a room right under her nose this entire time! Had Mr. Smith ever actually had a room in the attic in the first place?

"—Mary is going to be *overjoyed!*" Hannah exclaimed. "James is never going to live this down!"

"Hannah, Hannah, calm down," Uncle Henry said, and Hannah realized she'd stood from her chair. "We didn't want to tell you like this, but we do need you to understand that this information isn't to be shared."

"Oh," Hannah said. She could feel her heart thrilling in her chest. She made herself sit down. "Right. Of course."

Mr. Smith's face was quite serious. Of course, he was always serious. But he was especially so now. "For all intents and purposes, I live my life as a man. I want to continue to do that. It's easier if people assume it to be so."

"Of course," Hannah said, nodding. Her throat squeezed. "Of course you can count on me. I owe you everything. I would never betray your trust." She looked up at them both imploringly. "Please. I'm sorry I got overly excited. Please believe me. I promise I'll keep your secret."

Uncle Henry leaned forward and squeezed her hand in his. Now all three of them were linked. "I believe you."

"I do too," Mr. Smith said. "I think it's best if we can all be true to ourselves, at least in the privacy of our own home."

Hannah blinked hard, just once. It felt good to be included in that *our*, in that *home*, and to feel it was true, not just for Mr. Smith, but for Hannah as well.

"So..." Hannah said at length. "This is why you know how to braid my hair? And sew a dress?"

Mr. Smith gave a sheepish smile. "Yes."

"Huh." Hannah took that in. "But, wait. You did this to enlist? How did you manage it?"

Mr. Smith glanced at Henry and smiled. "Well, it's a long story."

Hannah shrugged. "I did just put another log on the fire."

ALSO BY JANE HADLEY

Telling stories is inherently vulnerable. Publishing novels doubly so! If you saw something true in this work, something that sparked a connection, I hope you'll pass the story on. Write a post, leave a review, tell your book club, buy a copy for your sister-in-law as a gift—whatever makes sense for you. Word of mouth is still the best marketing tool around!

I hope that if you found this book satisfying, you'll check out some of my other titles too. I write across time periods, but I always ground my stories in Minnesota. What can I say, I like sweaters.

————

Mrs. Milner Gets a Kitchen
A divorced mother contracts the installation of a new electric kitchen and falls for her contractor under the nose of their conformist 1950s immigrant community.
Free to newsletter subscribers on janehadleywrites.com

————

A Fine Looking Soldier
A woman dresses as a man to enlist in the Union Army only to fall in infuriating infatuation with her strapping bunkmate.
Secret Soldier: Volume 1. Out now.

————

Oh! You Pretty Things
A closeted genderfluid university student joins a 1970 proto-glam rock band and gets drawn into a messy love triangle that pushes him to find and claim his own identity.
Out now.

————

Mr. Milner Gets Divorced
An upstanding husband, father, and city official reignites an old high school friendship at the 1954 Winter Carnival and proceeds to blow up his life.
Prequel to Mrs. Milner Gets a Kitchen. *Coming 2026.*

———

A Rogue's Gallery□
An aimless flapper contrives a fake relationship with the queen of the St. Paul gangsters to shake off a persistent ex-boyfriend, only to find herself longing for it to be real.
Coming 2026-27-ish.

FOOTNOTES

You have just read what happens when an author sacrifices plot on the altar of historical accuracy. There's probably a lot of mistakes still in this volume, because historical research is never done, but I had such a wonderful time reading diaries, letters, and accounts of the Second Minnesota Regiment's trials and travails. I was only able to tip my historical fiction cap to so many of those stories, and of course all errors are entirely my own.

If you subscribed to *Hadley's Romance Book* and read this story issue by issue, you will have had in-line footnotes, but in an effort to be less distracting, I have pared it down to my favorite tidbits here.

Regiments

I used accounts from William Bircher, JW Bishop, DB Griffin, and Thomas Fitch frequently to put together the experiences of the Second Minnesota on the march. Thomas Fitch was my favorite, because his account was a diary he carried with him on the field and he always led with the weather. Griffin's letters make clear how common the slang "first rate" was, for everything. (It was like the 1860s version of "cool" or "awesome.") I also had an 1858 copy of Roget's Thesaurus with a slang section that I am still unironically obsessed with. Constantin Greubner's *We Were the Ninth,* an account of the Ninth Ohio's experiences translated from German, was a much-referred to volume while writing. German Turners fascinate me (the anti-clerical *gymnasticks* of it all!) and realizing that the people I had already written into Henry's backstory had formed an all-German unit that fought alongside the Second Minnesota made me feel like fate was asking me to write this stupid book. Please refer to Kloepfer's campfire stories in Chapter 26 for some accounts pulled straight from *We Were the Ninth*.

Gender

One of the reasons why I wanted to write this story was I wanted to understand how female and AFAB soldiers navigated menstruation and other necessaries while on the march. In imagining a relationship between two soldiers, one of them with a uterus, it became evident that contraception was also of deep interest. When I encountered sources about abortifacient pills readily available to women who needed to "regulate their period," I was floored. I think there's this assumption that people in the present are so much more liberal and open-minded than Victorians, and in many ways that is true, but when it comes to mid-19th century Americans and abortifacients, it most certainly is not. In fact, there are many ways women's bodies are more highly regulated in our modern society than in the past. Judith Giesburg's *Sex and the Civil War* revolves around the thesis that the Civil War and efforts to regulate soldiers' morality gave way to the anti-abortion movement as we know it today.

In this volume, Charley makes the conscious decision to stop using her birth-name, Cate. This marks a turning point in the narrative for Charley, because she doesn't ever again present herself as female. I choose to continue using she/her pronouns for her character throughout the narrative for a couple of reasons. First, for continuity. Second, because there isn't historical evidence of nonbinary pronouns used in this period. There is, however, a lot of evidence of transgender and genderfluid people. *Redressing America's Frontier Past* by Peter Boag was a fascinating account of trans experiences in the mid-late 19th century. (One fascinating take-away was that trans-masc people were generally regarded as romantic or sympathetic in newpapers, while trans-femme people were treated with more hostility. The patriarchy strikes again!) Charley's aspiration to walk the world as a man coincides with multiple accounts drawn from Boag's book. While I claim no ownership of trans experiences, past or present, I hope that Charley's character rings true as one experience, one way a person who feels trapped by traditional binaries of gender might address that within the confines of the mid-19th century context.

Race and Racism

The Civil War was a violent conflict that rose out of enormous sectionalism and volatile identity politics. I think it is fair to say, though, that the Republicans and Democrats as they existed in the mid-19th century weren't fighting over issues of racism and anti-racism. Generally, they seemed to be on the same page about white supremacy. What they fought over was the lengths to which a racial social order should be allowed to go and who most deserved to be in its crosshairs. While the Republican party of Minnesota was solidly anti-slavery, they also aggressively pursued the dispossession of Native peoples in Minnesota. The Democratic party, on the other hand, was more free-soil when it came to slavery (states decide for themselves if they allow slavery to be legal in their state), but were also more likely to advocate for Native men to vote (just those who had adopted the ways of white settlers, mind). It's not a good guys and bad guys situation, is what I'm trying to say. White supremacy was insidious across the board. Even radical Republicans like Jane Grey Swisshelm advocated for actual genocide in response to the US-Dakota War of 1862.

I tried to get at some of this in the narrative of this book, but imagining the experiences of people of color, past or present, is a hubris I have no business indulging in. The characters of the pharmacist in Chapter 10 and Williamson's context as the mixed-race son of a prominent white Minnesota politician and a Dakota woman are both ways I try to point to the complexity of white supremacy and racism embedded in the Civil War within the narrative. The ways Charley in particular finds herself contending with her own assumptions and layers of supremacist culture also work to get at this complexity.

The Civil War was won, of course, by the Union, and there is great pride evidenced in the letters, narratives, and accounts left by Union soldiers in their opposition and ultimate abolition of slavery. The layers of white supremacy that they still carried, especially in the way they regarded Native people, went largely unexamined in my sources. It's unlikely that Charley, especially after the war, would be in a position to need to examine her own white privilege. Henry would certainly have to confront the role New Ulm Turners played in the US-Dakota War of 1862, being at the front with Williamson, who has Dakota ancestry. But that war is still a wound that hasn't healed in Minnesota, and I don't think writing fictional accounts of it would help it heal. I chose not to go there in this narrative, but rather rest on this footnote and my author's note at the head of the narrative to provide that context.

Romantic Friendship

The idea of romantic friendship was a light-bulb moment for me. Anthony Rotundo's article on the topic was enlightening on so many levels. It vindicated all those times I felt like historians were gas-lighting us by saying "they were roommates" and it also helped reduce the pressure to prove sexual intercourse in order to interpret queerness in the historical record.

Rotundo argues that romantic friendship was normalized among young men and women of any age in the 19th century. In Western societies where genders were often separated, it made sense that young people in particular would find deep emotional intimacy with their friends. Some of those relationships were physical.

Regardless, they defined themselves entirely differently in that period. Identities weren't formed around attraction, physical or emotional, because heterosexuality was assumed as a matter of course. Sex was defined by acts (the acceptable and the taboo) rather than proclivities or inclinations.

I don't mean to suggest that everyone was able to engage in same-sex relations, particularly physical, without any thought or consequence. It was certainly a time of conformity and propriety in many, many ways, and heteronormativity reigned. Romantic relations were private and sex was not polite conversation (though I will say, the stuff that got the Victorians fired up in erotic novels were very, very ... I shall use the Midwest term 'interesting'). But to read some of the letters Rotundo includes in his article, which were recorded without any evidence of shame or fear, is a refreshing way to remind ourselves that historical erasure says much more about historians than it does about the past.

———

Abbott, Karen. *Liar, Temptress, Soldier, Spy*. Harper Collins: New York, 2014.

Blanton, DeAnne and Lauren M. Cook. *They Fought Like Demons: Women Soldiers in the Civil War*. Louisiana State University Press: Baton Rouge, 2002.

Bircher, William. *A Drummer-boy's Diary: Comprising Four Years of Service with the Second Regiment Minnesota Veteran Volunteers, 1861 to 1865*. United States, St. Paul Book and Stationery Company, 1889.

Bishop, Judson Wade. *The Story of a Regiment: Being a Narrative of the Service of the Second Regiment, Minnesota Veteran Volunteer Infantry, in the Civil War of 1861-1865*. United States, Published for the Surviving Members of the Regiment, 1890.

Bishop, Judson Wade and Family Papers. Minnesota Historical Society, Manuscripts P1922 Box 1 vol. 1-2.

Edmonds, S. Emma E. *Nurse and Spy in the Union Army*. 1864, republished 2019 by Lakeside Press.

Thomas Fitch Diary. Minnesota Historical Society, Manuscripts, P961.

Giesberg, Judith. *Sex and the Civil War*. The University of North Carolina Press: Chapel Hill, 2017.

Goodman, Ruth. *How to Be a Victorian*. Liveright; Reprint edition. September 21, 2015.

Griffin, David Brainerd. *Letters Home to Minnesota: Second Minnesota Volunteers*. Minnesota Historical Society, Stacks E515.5 2nd.G75 1992.

Greubner, Constantin. *We Were the Ninth: A History of the Ninth Regiment, Ohio Volunteer Infantry April 17, 1861, to June 7, 1864*. Translated and edited by Frederic Trautmann. Kent State University Press, Ohio, 2009.

Lehman, Christopher P. *Slavery's Reach: Southern Slaveholders in the North Star State*. Saint Paul, Mn Minnesota Historical Society Press, 2019.

Lehman, Christopher P. *It Took Courage: Eliza Winston's Quest for Freedom*. Minnesota Historical Society Press, 6 Feb. 2024.

Lowry, Thomas P. *The Story the Soldiers Wouldn't Tell: Sex in the Civil War*. Stackpole Books: Mechanicsburg, 1994.

Olmanson, Bernt. *Letters of Bernt Olmanson, A Union Soldier in the Civil War 1861-1865*. Compiled and Translated from the Norwegian Language by his Son, Albert Olmanson.

Rotundo, Anthony. "Romantic Friendship: Male Intimacy and Middle-Class Youth in the Northern United States 1800-1900." *Journal of Social History*, Autumn, 1989, Vol. 23, No. 1. Pages 1-25.

Schmid, Bendict. *The Bendict Schmid Civil War Diary, Company G Second Minnesota Regiment*. Minnesota Historical Society Stacks E601.S35 A313 1976.

Wingerd, Mary Lethert. *North Country: The Making of Minnesota*. University of Minnesota Press, 2010.

Acknowledgements

A Fine Looking Soldier is the first full-fledged novel I've ever finished, and it sort of happened by accident. Charley Smith is a character dug up from the depths of my most stubborn inclinations, and she's absolutely impossible. I wrote all of *A Fine Looking Soldier* and over half of *A Right Honorable Soldier* before I realized that this was much too long to be one book and decided to cut Volume 1 to when they muster out. It almost felt like cheating, saying I had finished writing that book and calling it done, when I knew there was a second volume to finish. But it unlocked my ability to finish other stories, so when I came back to *A Right Honorable Soldier*, I was able to find the ending.

I could never have gotten this book across the finish line without the support of my indie authors-in-arms. To the Not Quite Write to Market group: I'm so grateful for your comradery and support and generosity every week. We truly all do better when we all do better.

To my kids, for being such energetic cheerleaders and putting "Only One Tent" stickers on your water bottles, even though you prefer adventure to romance.

An enormous amount of gratitude goes to my beta team. A huge thanks to Catie, who fact-checked everything and made sure my menswear was spot on (even when the suspenders logistically made a mess of things). To Katy, who I have never met but beta read both books because sometimes a love of historical romance is enough to bring people together. To Corinne, who copy-edited and gave me such moral support during the serialization of the book. And to my friend Louise Mayberry: thank you for your support and advice and vulnerability. Your careful attention and mentorship has made me a better writer, a better creative, and a better person all-around.

Finally, to my first and favorite reader, my spouse, who made Charley cut the bullshit and say the words "I love you" with no take-backs.

Thank you to everyone who read this book in its serial parts. It was my dream project to make *Hadley's Romance Book* and I'm so grateful I got to share it with you.

ABOUT THE AUTHOR

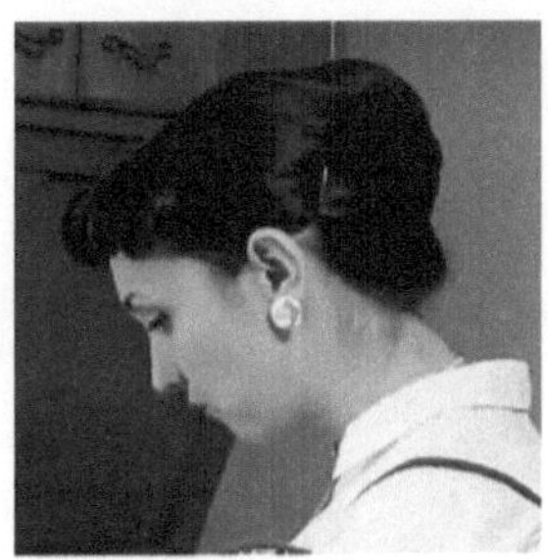

Jane Hadley writes historical romance teeming with footnotes and feels. She lives under seven layers of blankets where she can comfortably survey the cold tundra of Minnesota through wavy glass windows which she refuses to replace because old things are inherently valuable.

jane@janehadleywrites.com
On Instagram @janehadleywrites